WORLD THEATRE
AN ILLUSTRATED HISTORY

WORLD THEATRE

AN ILLUSTRATED HISTORY BY
BAMBER GASCOIGNE

EBURY PRESS · LONDON

© Bamber Gascoigne 1968

This book was designed and produced by George Rainbird Ltd
Marble Arch House, 44 Edgware Road, London, W.2.

House editor: Jocelyn Selson
Designer: George Sharp

Text Phototypeset in Erhardt by Oliver Burridge Filmsetting Ltd, Crawley
Printed and bound by Dai Nippon, Tokyo

For Christina

Author's Note

While researching for this book I have worked in some seventy museums and libraries in nine countries, and it is therefore impossible to express my thanks in detail. The museums whose material I have used are all credited in the notes, but I would like to record my particular gratitude to the following, and to their staff, for special and extended help: Karl Kup of the New York Public Library, Spencer Collection; A. Hyatt Mayor and John McKendrie of the Metropolitan Museum, Department of Prints and Drawings; Helen Willard of the Harvard Theatre Collection; Maria Teresa Muraro of the Fondazione Cini in Venice; Eric Alexander of the Theatre Museum in Amsterdam; Gunter Schöne of the Theatre Museum in Munich; André Veinstein of the Bibliothèque de l'Arsenal, Collection Rondel; Per Bjurström of the National Museum in Stockholm; and the staffs of the libraries and print rooms of the British Museum and the Victoria and Albert Museum, and John Freeman for supplying nearly all the monochrome photographs from these two collections.

There are also others outside the museums whose help has contributed greatly to the book: Ifan Kyrle Fletcher who has generously given me the benefit of his great knowledge of the subject, both by directing my attention to many sources of material and by even providing personal introductions to owners and curators; John Bury and his wife Elizabeth who, when I asked whether a drawing existed which I might use as my last illustration, promptly offered to create one for me; Granada Television, who have often deliberately modified their demands on my time to make this research possible; Jocelyn Selson and the Design Staff of George Rainbird, Ltd, who positively encouraged an author to poke his nose into every stage of the production of the book; and above all my wife who during our travels photographed several thousand prints and drawings, thus providing the practical basis of the whole subject.

B. G.

CONTENTS

INTRODUCTION

This is both an illustrated history of the theatre and a history of theatre illustrations. I have used the illustrations as my primary material and have tried to select for each period those that provide the most detailed and the most accurate picture of what a playgoer of the time would have seen, whether he kept his eyes firmly on the stage; or let them wander among his neighbours in the auditorium; or even allowed himself the indulgence of a visit behind the scenes to inspect at closer quarters the marvels of either the machinery or the actresses.

The book is concerned, therefore, with those practical and physical details in the theatre's history which illustrations are best able to reveal. It does not deal with plays as literature, nor even with individual playwrights or famous theatre companies – except in so far as their work coincides with important developments in production and scene design.

Having chosen my best possible gallery of some three hundred and twenty theatrical pictures, I have tried in the text to analyse what precisely they show and with how much accuracy they show it. The latter is particularly important since historians tend to welcome the stray surviving scraps of pictorial evidence with less critical suspicion than they extend to written source material – whereas in reality it is only in rare periods that artists and illustrators have been particularly concerned with precise accuracy. More often it has been the conventions of art which have dictated the details of their pictures.

Fig. 1 can stand as a good example of the whole process and its dangers. It is a woodcut which appeared on the programme of Robert Bolt's *A Man for All Seasons* as performed in 1965 by

Fig. 1 Theatrical woodcut, Gloucestershire, 1965

9

the Cotswold Players, an amateur group in Gloucestershire. If all evidence of theatre in the west of England should in the distant future be lost, with the exception of this one woodcut, it is a safe assumption that some scholar several centuries hence would present it as a fascinating survival of a much earlier and simpler style of staging. The outdoor setting, he would point out, with its flight of steps leading to an architectural *frons scaenae*, harks back to the very beginnings of Western theatre in Greece and Rome. Yet there are echoes too of the Elizabethan period, such as the inner stage which can be opened and closed by drawing a curtain, and the glimpse of the man blowing a trumpet on the right. He is probably summoning the country audience to the start of the play just as was done in Shakespeare's time.

The reality was rather different. The play was performed indoors on a proscenium stage at one end of a rectangular hall, making an adequate but entirely conventional little theatre. The woodcut, it turns out, has been used on the society's posters, programmes and writing paper ever since 1911, when it was designed by one of the two founders of the company. The reason, of course, why it contains traces of past theatre is that it was on precisely these familiar echoes that the designer drew when he wanted to create a generalised image not of any exact theatrical performance but of 'theatre' itself.

Usually one can test a picture's accuracy by comparing it with the facts established from written sources. If it meets the known facts, it becomes reasonable to regard it as valid evidence for other details which it may contain. But very often pictures themselves can be used even more convincingly to confirm or refute each other's evidence. For example Fig. 2, a painting by J. Hoffman of *Das Rheingold* during the first complete performance of *Der Ring der Nibelungen* at Bayreuth in 1876, looks at first sight a typically romantic and inaccurate fantasy on the theme of the Rhine maidens. Taken by itself, it would seem to offer the theatre historian very little reliable evidence of how the scene actually looked on that first night. However, when set beside another much more pedestrian view of the same scene on the same occasion (Fig. 3), the floating maidens and the high rock are suddenly explained in terms of theatrical carpentry and Hoffman's painting becomes established as an authentic image of what Wagner was trying to offer the audience.

In this way – treated with caution – paintings, prints and drawings can often yield more theatrical secrets than any other source.

Note

The footnotes are confined to giving sources which are referred to by number. For full details see the *Bibliography* (p. 317 ff.). Where several facts in one paragraph come from the same source, the reference is given only at the end of the paragraph.

The *Notes on the illustrations* (p. 301 ff.) are more detailed, and include references to the more important theatrical illustrations published in other modern works. The *Index* (p. 327 ff.) includes all the illustrations in this book and others referred to in the notes, thus constituting a quick guide to a very wide range of theatrical illustrations.

Fig. 2 *Das Rheingold*, Bayreuth, 1876

Fig. 3 The same, from backstage

1

THE BEGINNINGS

Primitive drama

Many different moments have been chosen by scholars as the true beginning of drama, including even that of a kitten playing with a ball of wool, stalking it, pouncing on it, endlessly casting it in the role of mouse or victim to the kitten's own hero.[1] The most primitive traces of human mime are certainly connected with similar hunting games or rituals, though men prefer to play the part of their quarry. The earliest reason for imitating an animal may have been as a direct means of communication: at a stage when language is very inadequate the returning hunter wants to describe what he has seen or done, and so acts out his adventures.[2] But the acting soon becomes part of the hunt itself. Hunters either imitate the animal they are pursuing in order to stalk closer unobserved – by dressing in seal skins and flopping along the ice, Eskimos can move much nearer to seals than they can without these props – or else they play the part of another animal whose skill is hunting, expecting that sympathetic magic will enable them to borrow this animal's talents. So the Cherokee Indians used to wear a wildcat mask (Fig. 4) when stalking turkeys. Clearly magic rather than camouflage was the intention, since they also approached their prey singing a song; and when close enough, as a Cherokee himself explained, they would 'shoot the animal, using the magic of the mask'. Suitable songs could be bought from the medicine man. One went:

> We are living in one cove.
> We are scratching, spreading leaves.
> *Sound of turkey call.*
> *Sound of turkey gobble.*[3]

So in sober fact the turkey was being stalked by a man disguised as a wildcat imitating a turkey.

Animal imitation of this sort has been recorded by anthropologists all over the world, but authentic drawings of it are naturally very rare. One of the most interesting is a Bushman cave painting, copied from an almost inaccessible mountain cave near the Orange river by G. W. Stow in the 1870s and never since revisited (Pl. I, p. 25). A Bushman, to whom Stow later showed it, recognised precisely what was going on and commented: 'Ostriches, three black males, two blue females. The 'nusa Bushmen, not the 'kham Bushmen, are said to hunt in ostrich skins.'[4] Again the disguise seems unlikely to deceive the ostriches, which understandably look very apprehensive, but the magic does also have a practical use in that a hunter who has observed his prey's habits will have a better chance of success.

The Cherokee Indians used their wildcat masks also for ceremonial dances in the camp both

Sources (*see* p. 317)   [1]271, 7;   [2]271, 18;   [3]324, 85–92;   [4]328, opp. Pl. 21

Fig. 4 Cherokee hunting mask

before and after the hunt,[1] and within the framework of such rituals there is room for a comic element to develop into something much more indisputably theatrical. Many tribes have hunting ceremonies in which an entire hunt is mimed, with one of the hunters playing the part of the animal, and among the Australian Aborigines this has led to a mock wallaby hunt which is performed purely for pleasure. An old man drives the younger actors, as wallabies, past another old man who sits waiting for them with a stick. This imitates the tribe's actual hunting method, but the joke here is that the old man with the stick fails to hit any of the wallabies and gets abused by everybody.[2]

Animal imitations are not necessarily limited to species that either hunt or are hunted. The chosen animal may be the tribe's totem, and therefore also magic. The most famous illustration of this type of early drama is a Greek vase of the sixth century BC (Fig. 5), showing a chorus of men mounted on man-horses and accompanied by the flute-player, who himself became a familiar figure in classical Greek drama. This chorus – possibly worshippers of Poseidon, for whom the horse was a sacred animal[3] – is over a hundred years earlier than Aristophanes, whose comedies are full of animal roles and who used just such a chorus of horses in *The Knights*.

Animal dances continued uninterruptedly in Europe until fairly recently. Ecclesiastical records of the fifth and sixth centuries contain repeated denunciations of revellers who dance with hobby-horses or who wear the skins and heads of beasts,[4] and a fourteenth-century manuscript in the Bodleian, probably Flemish in origin, shows just such dancers lined up in their masks (Fig. 6). By then they were performing their revels, of clearly heathen origin, within the Church's own festivals. Thomas Kirchmeyer, a sixteenth-century Puritan and poet, complained very strongly about what he regarded as a typical partnership of popery and paganism in the Shrovetide festivities:

> They counterfeit both Beares and Woolves, and Lions fierce in sight,
> And raging Bulles. Some play the Cranes with wings and stilts upright.
> Some like the filthie forme of Apes, and some like fooles are drest,
> Which best beseeme these Papistes all, that thus keepe Bacchus feast.[5]

In the same Bodleian manuscript is a man in a more complete animal disguise (Fig. 7); his head can just be seen appearing through the animal's chest. Like him, the Bushmen sometimes used sticks for forelegs when imitating animals. Another of their paintings (Fig. 8) shows this, and is particularly interesting in that it also shows the beginnings of an audience. The people standing around are joining in by clapping, but they are already very clearly spectators. At the most primitive level of dance ritual everyone is a performer.

The similarity of technique between the Bushmen and the fourteenth-century Flemish revellers is fascinating and yet is typical of nearly all aspects of primitive drama. Its details are both widespread and tenacious. Even the hobby-horse duly appears in India as a hobby-cow, which comes to 'sing the paddy and seeds into fertility'.[6]

As tribes progress from hunting to agriculture their rituals become more elaborate, evolving complicated myths based on the seasonal pattern of life, death and rebirth. Throughout Europe ceremonies survive, mainly clustered round the winter equinox or in the spring, which are

---

[1]324, 85;　[2]271, 192;　[3]105, 16;　[4]245, I, 258;　[5]294, 48;　[6]305, 29

Fig. 5 Greek dancers in animal costumes, *c*. 550 BC

Fig. 6 Animal dancers, fourteenth century

Fig. 7 Man in stag skin, fourteenth century

Fig. 8 Bushman cave-painting of animal dance
Fig. 9 Village mummers, sixteenth century. Woodcut after Brueghel

based on man's need to coax the new year into life. At their simplest these involve a terrifying demon who must be killed or tamed if winter is to be overcome. In the Austrian Alps, after Christmas, a creature called the *Perht* appears in the streets in a devil's mask and has to be chased and 'killed' by those brave enough to risk it.[1] The *Illustrated London News* printed a photograph in 1936 of villagers in Bavaria peering out of a window, awaiting the annual arrival of some rather alarming 'wild men' on skis,[2] and interestingly a very similar moment is recorded in a woodcut after Brueghel (Fig. 9), where in exactly the same way the villagers are sheltering cautiously behind their windows. Wisely the householder is slipping money into the collecting box, because part of the alarm caused by midwinter mummers was that they demanded much – kisses or more from the girls, food or money from everyone else. In Greece it was accepted until very recently that the mummers would steal chickens after their performance. And if the householder failed to offer them hospitality as well, there was a special song of ill omen ready to be sung on his behalf.[3]

The scene which Brueghel's peasants are watching is that of 'Valentine and his wild brother, Orson', and the quotation comes not from the woodcut itself but from Scrooge in *A Christmas Carol* when he remembers the Christmas delights of his youth; so the pair were still a familiar sight very much more recently than Brueghel's time. The story of Valentine and his powerful brother, whom he tamed, had become very popular in the fifteenth century. It derived partly from medieval romance, but the central character of wild Orson was very much older. His 'prototype . . . is the wood-spirit of popular belief. This creature, as modern folklore knows him, lives in the forest depths; has a hairy body, or green clothing; is frequently of great physical strength; sometimes carries an uprooted tree as a club; is sometimes reputed to attack the unwary passer, particularly the women and children; but sometimes, too, is captured, tamed, and taught to render useful service'.[4]

As such, under the name of the Wild Man (Pl. II, p. 25), he played an important part in European pageants and in particular in the Schembart pageant at Nuremberg in the fifteenth and sixteenth centuries. This was an annual pageant in which the butchers went dancing through the streets, jumping as high as they could – as do the Austrian mummers before the arrival of the *Perht*, and as primitive tribes do in the spring to set a good example to the corn.[5] Nuremberg believed that this festivity celebrated the loyalty of the butchers to the city council during a fourteenth-century rebellion, but it has all the marks of a much more primitive fertility ceremony. In Nuremberg the evil characters who had to be overcome were a pageant-cart full of fools and devils (Fig. 64), and the climax of the show came when all the dancers stormed the cart and set it on fire after a pitched battle with its inhabitants.[6] During the dance the Wild Man threatened the spectators a little with his tree and his wife sometimes threw one of her babies at women in the crowd and then pulled it back on a string, thus conferring the blessing of fertility.

Even in this late form the Wild Man can claim to be seen as a very important dramatic character indeed. A line has been suggested, convincingly, that goes all the way from Hercules (a leading character in Dorian mimes in pre-Athenian days) through Papposilenus (the main figure in later Greek farce) and so down to the devils in medieval mystery plays and the Wild Man in pageants, and finally to Harlequin.[7] They are linked in style: all are dangerous or tricky, and yet funny. And they have a very similar costume, in that all wear garments made up of

---

[1]42, 87; [2]reprod. 322, Fig. 1; [3]222, XVI, 1909–10, p. 237; [4]255, 114; [5]331, 88; [6]331, 139; [7]331, 100 ff.

shaggy pieces – Hercules of fur, Papposilenus of something like feathers (he appears in Fig. 18), the devils of fur (Figs 56 and 57), the Wild Man of grass or moss and Harlequin, in a final sophisticated form, of patchwork. The primitive origin of at least some of these costumes can still be seen in the few surviving English mummers' plays, where the actors are covered in strips of paper. The reason appears to be partly the fertility of grass and leaves, but also the magic of not being recognised; it used to be thought unlucky for a mummer if his papers left enough of his face bare for him to be identified.

Naturally, if these characters do have such a basic common origin, any awareness of it was very early lost. The comedian Hans Sachs was the first man, in 1548, to leave a description of the Schembart and he grievously underestimated the Wild Man by saying that he seemed to have caught a dwarf on his tree.[1] But the man on the tree gives the scale of the Wild Man. Like Hercules, he is a giant among men.

A beautifully concise example of this process, in which ritual lapses into comedy, Hercules becomes Harlequin, and the priest turns professional actor, comes from the Bismarck Archipelago. At each new moon a village used to be visited by a terrifying masked apparition, the Duk-Duk, which sailed in from the sea and could only be pacified by vast quantities of food which the villagers left out for it. Anyone who touched it was liable to die, and only the elders – who lived off the food – knew that a man, chosen by them, was inside it. Not very much later the custom had apparently lapsed, but the elders were the committee of a dramatic society which toured the district with a play in which two masked characters, Duk-Duk and his wife Tuburan, were the principle characters.[2]

Egypt

The earliest civilisation in which these primitive rituals developed into truly elaborate performances was the Egyptian, but in Egypt too the suppression of the forces of winter, death or night still played a very important part. It was believed that each night the sun god, Re, travelled through dark regions beneath the world where his ship faced destruction by a dragon named Apophis, and a papyrus in the British Museum recounts a ceremony based on this theme and dating from about 2300 BC. In it the priest playing the All-Lord demolishes Apophis in no uncertain terms, chanting:

> I have cut his vertebrae at his neck, severed with a knife which hacked up his flesh and pierced into his hide . . . I have made him non-existent; his name is not; his children are not; he is not and his family is not; he is not and his false-door is not; he is not and his heirs are not. His egg shall not last, nor shall his seed be knit together – and vice versa.[3]

The priests clearly enjoyed the violent aspects of the ceremonies. In the early days of the temple ritual at Edfu it was only thought necessary to stab twice the small hippopotamus, apparently made of cake, which represented the evil god Seth. Later the text of the ritual was lengthened to provide time for ten thrusts with a harpoon.[4]

Although Egyptian art survives in some quantity, direct illustrations of such rituals do not exist. Dancing and music, the secular entertainments of the pharaohs' courts, are well illustrated and there are several charming paintings, such as Fig. 10 from the tomb of Nebamun, of girls playing and performing at a banquet. But the rituals were religious, and the artists painted the

Fig. 10 Egyptian dancers and musicians, *c.* 1400 BC

Fig. 11 Horus and Ani, *c.* 1250 BC

myth itself rather than its enactment. Many of the paintings do seem to depict some type of performance, but the impression is misleading – largely because the convention of Egyptian art was to paint the gods as human figures with very practical-looking animal masks, usually with stabilising straps down over the shoulders. For example Fig. 11, from the Papyrus of Ani, shows on the left the god Horus in his falcon mask with the human scribe, Ani. He is about to bring him before the seated Osiris, and the scene is supposed to be taking place among the gods after Ani's death. But the priests, in their rituals, did wear masks to represent various gods,[5] and so such a painting can almost certainly be taken as a reliable image of the costume in which a priest would have performed Horus.

A very rare glimpse of a human being in such a costume can be found in an early relief, of about 3560 BC, from Gizah (Fig. 12). The inscription above it reads 'a dance by young people', and among the dancers is one central figure, certainly human, who is wearing the mask of a lion or of the god Bès. It is thought that the scene may be linked with ceremonies of puberty and circumcision at the time of the wine harvest.[6]

---

[1]331, 99;　[2]271, 197;　[3]302, 7;　[4]258, 143;　[5]254, 174;　[6]241, XXX, Part 1, p. 74

19

Fig. 12 Masked dance in ritual, *c*. 3560 BC

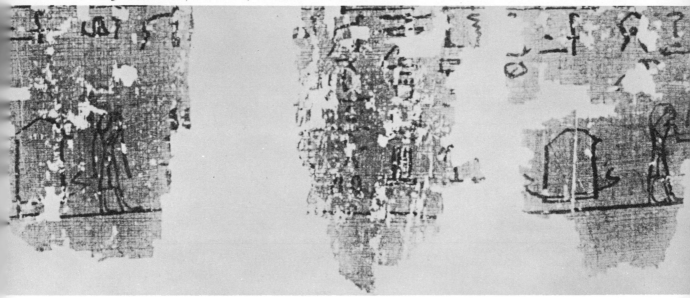

Fig. 13 Egyptian coronation ritual, *c*. 3300 BC
Fig. 14 The same, reconstructed

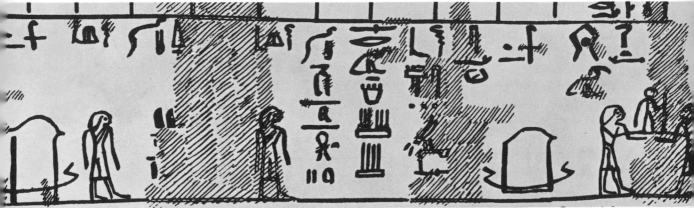

The most important Egyptian rituals followed the full fertility pattern of a fight, a death and a rebirth. They were based on the myth of Osiris, who was killed by his wicked brother Seth but was brought to life again by his son Horus. This theme provided both the coronation ceremony for a new king and the annual ceremony for the new year and it is the subject of an extraordinary document, the Ramesseum papyrus, which was discovered at Thebes in 1895. Part of it gave the text of a coronation ritual which its editor, Sethe, dated as deriving from about 3300 BC. This makes it the earliest written drama of any type, but – even more interesting – the papyrus was also illustrated with a strip of small pictures at the bottom of each column, representing the various scenes. Sethe judged it to be probably 'the earliest example of book illustration'.[1]

Sethe published photographs of the surviving scraps of the papyrus, together with a drawn reconstruction of the whole. Figs 13 and 14 show one strip of the illustrations, in the original and in the reconstruction. The condition of the original reveals how much speculation there inevitably is in interpreting such a text (even opening the roll of papyrus took twenty years of patient work), but it seems that on the left the new king has stepped from his ceremonial boat to distribute bread to the 'great ones' of Upper and Lower Egypt; in the centre he is brought sacred garments and objects; on the right the priests bring him a statue of his dead father, or Osiris.[2] This is all made slightly more theatrical than most pure rituals since when the king speaks his lines he speaks as the god Horus. The myth is enacted, not merely described.

The statue of a god, a more purely ritualistic detail, was present in many of these ceremonies. When Herodotus went to Egypt in about 450 BC he saw a ceremony, dramatising the battle against evil, in which priests carrying a statue had to fight their way through crowds representing the 'enemy' and bring the god safely to a sanctuary beyond. The battle was so violent, he said, that some people actually died. The central scenes of the rituals were usually performed in secret inside the temple. Herodotus was allowed to witness one of these on a vow of secrecy. Unfortunately he was true to his vow. He tantalisingly says that he saw the secrets but adds no more.[3]

These famous temple ceremonies were essentially liturgical drama, but there is evidence that there was also a thriving popular drama in Egypt. The popular plays were on the same religious subjects – the Egyptians, said Herodotus, were 'excessively pious, more so than any other people' – but the themes were treated more theatrically and more comically. A few details from various plays give a good idea of the difference: Horus is born as a baby but grows rapidly to an enormous size and develops a voracious appetite; his mother, Isis, chats with the audience; the dragon, Apophis, is tied up on stage and mingles threats, promises and tears in pleading for his release. There is a hint of simple theatrical machinery, and there is even a record of a wandering actor and of his hireling, who played the smaller roles.[4]

These plays occur in the later dynasties, and they represent the same development as the comic popularising of the Duk-Duk or the wood demon. Like their parent liturgical dramas, the plays treat mainly of the all-important seasonal pattern. And the god Thot, finding Horus dead from a scorpion sting and bringing him back to life, is the ancestor of the Doctor who until very recently in many European countries has always been on hand each midwinter to revive a fallen hero in the mummers' plays.

---

[1]318, 83 ff.; [2]318, 207 ff.; [3]259, 4–7; [4]259, 15 ff.

THE CLASSICAL ERA

Greece

Athens is unique in human history in having moved within not much more than two or three centuries from a primitive tribal existence to the highest state of civilisation. In the history of the theatre this meant that Aeschylus was able to write the *Oresteia*, consciously celebrating this very emergence of his people from primitive anarchy; that Aristotle could legitimately analyse the birth of theatre by looking back far less than the distance between ourselves and Shakespeare or even Racine; and that on Greek vases the most primitive rituals are recorded as almost contemporary reality at a period when vase painting itself is already a highly sophisticated art.

Pure disorganised dancing, done for sheer exhilaration, is probably older than any of the hunting rituals with which we began,[1] but I have so far made no mention of it because it has no dramatic content. It becomes interesting, though, in relation to Greece, since the revels of maenads and sileni can be shown to be close ancestors of Athenian theatre. The orgiastic dancing of these worshippers of Dionysus, at night and in the woods or hills, came from Thrace and spread towards Athens (Fig. 15). The women carried *thyrsoi* – rods with artichoke-shaped heads, which still appear two thousand years later in the hands of the Schembart dancers and of wild men in English pageants[2] – and they danced themselves into ecstasy until they tore at and devoured the raw flesh of a sacrificial animal. Their behaviour is best known through Euripides' *The Bacchae*, the great impact of which in fifth-century Athens suggests how near the cult still seemed, but it is their companions, the sileni or satyrs, who survive directly in Greek theatre in the satyr plays. The scene in Fig. 15 is pure disorganised revelry. In Fig. 16 a mood of performance and entertainment has arrived, combining acrobatics, farce and from one of the performers on the right a highly skilled sexual balancing act; and the central figure, wearing the costume of Hermes, is already distinguishable as the leader of the group.[3]

By the sixth century BC these followers of Dionysus had developed a definite form of choral performance, the dithyramb, in which they sang and danced the epic material of Homeric legend; and Greek tradition held that Thespis – himself a priest of Dionysus at some small temple in Attica – created tragedy when he introduced a new performer, the first Greek actor, who 'answered' the leader of the chorus and so made dialogue possible. A later tradition, first mentioned by Horace, added that Thespis and his companions set out in a cart and began travelling the country performing plays.[4] This may refer merely to the cart which is almost a practical necessity to any company of travelling players, but there could also be an echo in it of the ship cart which was closely associated with Dionysus, and which derived from the ship in which the god was supposed to visit Attica every spring. He is seen travelling in such a ship

---

Sources (*see* p. 317)   [1]271, 185;   [2]330, Pl. XXXII;   [3]105, 15;   [4]12, IX, 856

Fig. 15 Dionysiac revels, sileni and maenads

Fig. 16 Satyrs performing

cart, accompanied by two flute-playing satyrs, on a vase in the British Museum (Fig. 17). Later, when the great Athenian festivals were established, Dionysus in his ship cart was included in the processions and it is possible that this cart had played a part in the earliest organised revels of the satyrs.[1] If so Thespis, still essentially a follower of Dionysus, may well have taken such a vehicle with him on his travels.

By 534 BC Thespis had become established at Athens and in that year he won the first recorded competition in Greek tragedy, establishing the playing of tragedy as an official annual festival of Dionysus.[2] Tragedy was joined in the dramatic competitions by the satyr play, a burlesque and obscene offshoot from the same dithyrambic origin, in about 500 BC and by comedy in 486 BC. On the face of it, fifth-century Athens was the greatest playgoing community in history since a city of only some 30,000 male citizens needed a theatre which seated about 14,000 people. But the impression is a distorted one because an Athenian's playgoing was limited to seven days in the year: four consecutive days in the great spring festival, the City Dionysia, which was mainly devoted to tragedy; and three days in January during the Lenaia, chiefly for comedy.[3] These were times of public holiday and the plays were the central event in a festive atmosphere of procession and carnival.

The City Dionysia was an annual demonstration of the splendours of Athens, with many distinguished foreigners in the audience. Many months earlier the *archon*, a city official, had begun the preparations. He had chosen the poets who were to be allowed to compete; and for each poet he had chosen a *choregos*, a rich man who would organise the production, paying for it himself, and who would be competing for a separate impresario's prize.[4] The *choregos* under-took this in return for paying no taxes that year, but since the honour of winning was great and a winning chorus had to be very magnificently clothed, he was usually willing to provide much more than he would have paid in taxes – a method of subsidising the arts perhaps not sufficiently investigated since.

Each poet provided three tragedies and one satyr play, which in the fifth century BC were played consecutively to provide one whole day's entertainment, and since all the plays had to be new this single performance was the only occasion on which even the greatest plays were seen in Athens – until some seventy years after the death of Aeschylus, when his plays and those of Sophocles and Euripides began to be revived at the City Dionysia and soon drove out altogether the writing of new tragedies.[5]

In the fifth century a dramatist invariably directed his own plays and until Sophocles he was the leading actor as well,[6] but Greek art leaves us no convincing view of a tragedy being either rehearsed or performed. The characters of the plays appear often on vases; but, like the painters of Egyptian murals, the artists preferred to show the myth rather than a tragic performance of it, or in other words Orestes himself instead of an actor playing him. With the satyr plays the situation is a little better. A beautiful mosaic from Pompeii (Pl. III, pp. 26–7) shows a poet with some of the cast of a satyr play getting ready to perform. The two actors on the left, one with his bearded satyr's mask pushed back on his head, are wearing goatskin loincloths and are members of the chorus. On the right a dresser is pulling over the head of another actor the hairy costume of Papposilenus, the old silenus or satyr who leads the chorus. His mask is at the feet of the poet, who holds up the heroine's mask – to be worn, of course, by a man – and who has the hero's mask on the table behind him. In the middle is the all-important flute-player.

---

[1] 42, 39;   [2] 300, 73;   [3] 300, 56;   [4] 300, 84 ff.;   [5] 234, 120;   [6] 300, 93 ff.

Pl. I Hunter disguised as an ostrich: bushman cave painting
Pl. II Wild man and wife: from Nuremberg Schembartbuch, 1680
Pl. III Rehearsal for a satyr play: Hellenistic mosaic from Pompeii (*overleaf*)

164   Dieweil mein Mann ſich macht   Eines Wildenmannes geſtalt Ich   168
auf Straſſen, ſoll ich Ihm folgen   bey den Schönbart Luſt finden mich.
gleichermaßen.

This is a late mosaic, dating from c. 200 BC, but it has been suggested that the poet is intended to be Aeschylus himself since he was considered the greatest writer of satyr plays.[1]

A magnificent vase (Fig. 18), also in Naples and known as the Pronomos vase because it includes the flute-player Pronomos, provides an even more interesting glimpse of the cast of a satyr play a little nearer to the moment of performance. Many members of the chorus are again standing around, holding their masks, but this time there are also some individual performers in costume. The central couple on the couch, Dionysus and Ariadne, are drawn as part of the myth rather than as a scene from the play, but to either side of them there are indisputable actors: to the left there is one in a long decorated robe, holding the mask of an oriental king, and on the other side are standing Hercules with his club and Papposilenus – more visible this time in his shaggy suit made of bits of wool. All three are holding their masks and the two actors – as opposed to Papposilenus, who is the leader of the chorus – are wearing the soft calf-length boots used on the stage in the fifth century. The famous high-soled *cothurni*, so often associated with Greek theatre, are a late innovation of the second century, as are the huge masks with great foreheads. The classical Greek mask was a much more natural affair.[2]

Tragedies and satyr plays were performed by the same actors, and the costume of the two actors here shows no special link with the satyr theme of the chorus – so they may probably be taken as images of Greek tragic actors in full costume. As such they are unique. On the vases usually published as illustrations of classical tragedy, characters in costume are mingled at random with others who are naked. The artists were clearly thinking as much of the golden age of the myth as of any precise theatrical performance. But in the Pronomos vase the figures who seem purely mythical are kept in a distinct group in the centre – Dionysus, Ariadne and the tiny Eros above, and the figures beside the flute-player below. To either side all is reliably theatrical.

The most familiar surviving evidence of Greek theatre is, of course, the theatres themselves – but for the classical period they are highly misleading. All the complete Greek plays to have survived date from one brief period of a hundred years, from 490 to 390 BC, but the mighty Theatre of Dionysus which the tourists see at Athens consists of an auditorium from about 330 BC and a stage area, built under Nero and completed in AD 61. The only connection that this theatre has with the original performances of the plays of Aeschylus, Sophocles and Euripides is the actual hillside site and five surviving stones (Fig. 19) from the supporting wall of the earliest levelled dancing floor or *orchestra*.[3]

The reason why so little survives is that the fifth-century City Dionysia took place in a wooden theatre. Wooden seats or stands were put up for the spectators on the hillside, and for the earlier tragedies of Aeschylus the stage seems to have been just an open area on to which any large props such as tombs, rocks or statues would be carried. By the middle of the fifth century a temporary wooden *skene*, a low architectural façade containing three entrance doors, was being erected each year to provide a background to the acting. Painted canvasses could be fitted on this façade to show the location of the play, and this earliest scene-painting – introduced by Sophocles but adopted by Aeschylus for his later plays – must have been fairly elaborate since it is known to have involved the use of perspective.[4] The *skene* could also support some form of machinery, particularly the crane (*geranos*) or machine (*mekane*) for flying the gods – much used by Euripides, who found a *deus ex machina* a quick way of bringing the plot back to its traditional ending after his own free treatment of it.

---

[1]105, 20;   [2]109, 43 ff.;   [3]108, 5 ff.;   [4]105, 74–9

Pl. IV A lover visits his lady: Phlyax vase, fourth century BC

29

Fig. 17 Dionysus in his ship cart
Fig. 18 Performers of a satyr play

It was later developments over some six centuries which left the Theatre of Dionysus in its present form (Fig. 20). Under Lycurgus the auditorium and stage were for the first time built in stone, the work being finished around 330 BC.[1] The auditorium survived but the *orchestra* (the circular dancing floor) and the stage behind it were frequently rebuilt. Around 150 BC the stage was heightened, from the classical position where it had been almost level with the *orchestra*. Two centuries later, in the time of Nero, it was again greatly enlarged – this time encroaching on the *orchestra* and reducing it from the classical Greek circle to the Roman semi-circle. About AD 200 the famous reliefs on the front of the stage were added, and a century later the *orchestra* was made watertight so as to float gladiatorial sea-battles. From then on the theatre fell into disuse and decay. By the Middle Ages its site was not even known. It was rediscovered in 1765, but in the nineteenth century the Turks built a fortification wall across it, using many of the stones. Serious modern excavations began only in 1862.[2]

Such is the mongrel history of Europe's most famous theatre. However, one can see something a little closer to a classical Greek theatre in the remains at Epidaurus (Fig. 21). This was built by the architect Polycleitus in about 340 BC and was considered even in antiquity to be the

[1]108, 134–8;   [2]108, 247 ff.

Fig. 19 The entire remains of the theatre of Aeschylus, Sophocles and Euripides (*right*)

Fig. 20 Theatre of Dionysus, Athens

most harmonious of all theatres.[1] It originally had only the lower tier of seats, the higher level having been added in the second century BC, but it does still retain the original fully circular *orchestra* with a stone in the middle to support an altar. In these theatres the spectators entered through the gateways on ground level at either side, then walked round the edge of the *orchestra* and up one of the gangways. They had coin-like metal tickets which directed them to one of the twelve wedges,[2] and the tickets from Athens suggest that each wedge was occupied by a different tribe[3] – a fairly likely arrangement since another important part of the City Dionysia, quite separate from the tragedies, was a contest between all the tribes in performing the older choral form, the dithyramb.

Greek theatres do not appear in any Greek vases or reliefs, but there are two or three Roman coins which do show in miniature the Theatre of Dionysus at Athens. One in the British Museum (Fig. 22) shows the view looking upwards from the *orchestra*. The buildings of the Acropolis rise above the back wall, and the public road which ran across the auditorium and was only closed during performances can be clearly seen half way up.

The different types of drama were established in Athens in a reverse order to their actual age. Tragedy, the most recent offshoot of Athenian Dionysiac revels, arrived first; it was followed by the satyr play which had developed earlier from the same source; and last of all came comedy, which appears to have the earliest roots of all in the Dionysiac rites of other parts of Greece, particularly Sparta, Corinth and Megara. There, instead of the Athenian fur-clad satyrs, the early followers of Dionysus were seen as fat men, each with a huge paunch and a great hanging phallus. It was these figures who later became the actors in Athenian Old Comedy (a typical

[1]105, 71;   [2]105, 132–7;   [3]300, 278

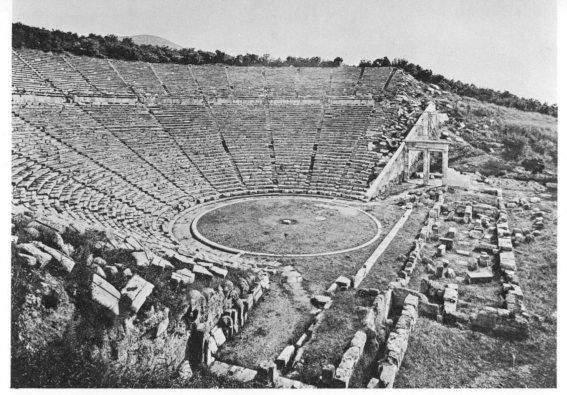

Fig. 21 The theatre at Epidaurus
Figs 22 *a & b* Theatre of Dionysus on Roman coin (*below left*)
Fig. 23 Dionysus and comic actor

Fig. 24 Greek comic actors

one is seen with Dionysus in Fig. 23), and this is the grotesquely padded costume which was worn in the performances of Aristophanes in fifth-century Athens.[1]

These splendidly bawdy and humorous figures were clearly very popular, since a great number of small terracotta statuettes of them survive. Most interesting of all is a group found together in a tomb in Athens (Fig. 24), which are thought to represent the complete casts of two separate plays.[2] These comic characters, all played by men, fell within certain well-defined categories and were quickly identifiable to the audience by their masks – though some of the minor distinctions may well have been too subtle for the majority of the spectators. Pollux, writing in the second century AD but probably basing his work on an Alexandrian source of the third century BC,[3] listed the various theatrical masks. His categories for Young Women alone ran to Garrulous, Curly-haired, Maiden, First False Maiden, Second False Maiden, Brindled, Concubine, Full-grown Hetaira, Little Youthful Hetaira, Golden Hetaira, Scarfed Hetaira, Little Torch, Shorn Maidservant and Little Maidservant.[4]

As well as the very common statuettes, the shape of the comic actor was also adapted to other uses. A jug from Gnathia (Fig. 25) makes good use of the actor's round shape for the body of the jug and of his bearded mask for the spout.

Apart from the official plays there were also some smaller scale private theatricals in Athens. Xenophon, in his *Symposium*, describes a show arranged in 421 BC by the father-in-law of Alcibiades to entertain his house guests, among them Socrates.[5] A travelling troupe of actors

34

Fig. 25 A comic actor as a jug

from Syracuse was employed. They put on a performance in which a young man and a girl played a love scene between Dionysus and Ariadne, and a similar occasion may perhaps be shown on a very interesting vase of much the same period (Fig. 26), where an actor is dancing Perseus in front of two spectators, possibly a rich man and his boy friend.[6] The dancer appears to be wearing no mask, and the only performers to play without masks were the mimes who came to Athens from Syracuse and who, unlike the Athenians, had actresses in their companies. This vase provides the only surviving Greek picture of a theatrical performance taking place with any sort of audience.

[1]32, 20–22; [2]105, 45–6; [3]340, 6; [4]340, 43; [5]238, 196; [6]105, 106

Fig. 26 A private performance, *c*. 420 BC
Fig. 27 Phlyax vase, Lipari (*left*)
Fig. 28 Phlyax vase, Leningrad

The simple wooden stage on which Perseus is dancing is very familiar from the many vases of Magna Graecia – the area of Sicily and southern Italy settled by the Greeks – which date mainly from the fourth century BC and which show the performances of the Phlyakes, or literally 'gossip' players of popular farce. This area was very important dramatically, and Syracuse was an early theatrical centre rivalled only by Athens. Aeschylus himself spent ten years there; a stone theatre was built in Syracuse in the mid-fifth century, a full hundred years before the first to appear anywhere in Greece; and it was through the Phlyax farces that the bawdy spirit of Athenian Old Comedy was to live on after it had passed away in Athens, replaced in the late fourth century by the more respectable middle-class comedies of Menander.

The theme of the Phlyax farce was invariably burlesque of the gods. A vase in Leningrad (Fig. 28) gives a good idea of the mood. Hercules, on the left, needs the help of Apollo who has climbed up to the roof of his temple to avoid him. Hercules is partly tempting and partly threatening Apollo, alternating the basket of fruit and cake in his left hand with the nailed club in his right in an attempt to get him to come down. Instead, Apollo will probably fall off the roof into a bowl of holy water below.[1] There is a similar knockabout spirit in the British Museum vase (Pl. IV, p. 28), where a lover is climbing up to a lady's window while a slave stands by with a torch and a bucket of wine. This suggests an upper window that could be used in the Phlyax stages, and this basic grouping of lover below and lady at a window above carries right through popular theatre to reappear as one of the favourite scenes of the Commedia dell'Arte.

As in all popular theatre, the Phlyax troupe had to be able to provide acrobatic entertainment as well. In the magnificent vase at Lipari (Fig. 27) the act includes a female tumbler, borrowed perhaps from their close cousins the mimes, who performs for the seated Dionysus while the two Phlyakes look on in typical comic amazement. It is only at a fairly sophisticated level of theatre that actors can afford not to be acrobats as well. At the private performance witnessed by Socrates in Athens, the girl performing Ariadne had just previously done some somersaults in and out of a circle of knives stuck point upwards in the floor.[2]

The Phlyakes put up their wooden stages in existing stone theatres and anywhere else where a play might be required. They moved slowly north in Italy, then in the district round Pompeii they merged with the rather similar players of the local farce known as the Atellana. Together they finally arrived in Rome around 300 BC, to become the first of the many links with Greece which make the history of Roman theatre little more than a rather lurid postscript to the theatrical splendours of the Athenian empire.[3]

Rome

The familiar image of Roman entertainment is exaggerated but not entirely inaccurate. The Romans did enjoy other forms of drama besides breakneck chariot races, gladiatorial fights to the death, and the hunting down by wild animals of prisoners, criminals or Christians, but plays tended to compete with these attractions on an unequal footing. It was the circus activities which were the first to be established. Under the Tarquins in the sixth century BC the *ludi romani* had begun to be held each September, when the harvest was in, between the Palatine and Aventine hills in the Circus Maximus, where wooden stands offered a good view of chariot

---

[1]105, 131;   [2]105, 106;   [3]105, 146–8

Fig. 29 Performers and animals in Roman amphitheatre

Fig. 30 *Frons scaenae* with actors, first century BC

Fig. 31 The amphitheatre, Pompeii (*below*)

races and boxing matches for a few select spectators while everyone else jostled on the ground as at any race course. A little later clowns began to appear casually at these harvest festivities, reciting obscene cross-talk acts which were only semi-dramatic and were known as 'Fescennine verses', but by 364 BC they had joined forces with flute-players from Etruria and had devised a musical performance with which they established themselves as an official part of the games under the title of *ludi scenici*.[1]

It was from this unpromising start, under the very wing of the circus, that Roman theatre grew. The players of the Atellana arrived about 300 BC to take part in the games, and the next two important events both derive from the First Punic War. In 264 BC, the first year of the war, gladiatorial combats were made part of the games, prisoners being allowed to hack each other to death for the amusement of the people instead of being executed. And – almost as if to balance this – the first year of peace, 240 BC, saw the arrival in the games of the first literary plays. The war against Carthage had been fought over areas settled by Greece, with the result that Greek influence seeped up to Rome with the returning soldiers, and these first plays were translations by Livius Andronicus of a Greek tragedy and comedy.[2] With this the pattern for Roman theatre was set. Greece was to be the source, so much so that not a single play survives with a plot invented by a Roman and the actors playing Plautus and Terence invariably wore Greek rather than Roman costume.

The players, at any rate during the early and most creative years, were to be in constant competition with the circus. The acrobat in the middle of the ivory relief (Fig. 29), who is balancing within inches of a bear's muzzle, is only undergoing in extreme form a predicament common also to his more serious fellow-performers. Terence's *Hecyra* is a good example. Its first production in 165 BC failed to attract attention because it was on at the same time as a rope-dancer and a boxing match. Its second performance, five years later, began well but the audience lost interest in the middle because word went round that the gladiators were about to start.[3]

All these spectacles were state-organised, and the official policy of bread and circuses increased with the years. In 240 BC the games lasted less than a week and included one day with plays.[4] By the first century AD there were sixty days of games at various times in the year, forty of them including *ludi scenici*. Three centuries later the figure had risen to one hundred and seventy-five days in the year, a hundred of them with *ludi scenici*,[5] and by then the games had moved from temporary to permanent buildings. The first stone amphitheatre to be built in Italy was the one at Pompeii in about 80 BC,[6] and it happens also to be the only amphitheatre or Roman auditorium of any kind to appear in a Roman painting, in one of the murals from Pompeii (Fig. 31). This shows particularly well the *velarium*, an awning which was drawn over the spectators to protect them from the sun and which was used also in theatres. It appears to show also, below the amphitheatre, a small refreshment booth. As in Greece, all official performances of any kind were a part of general festivities.

In keeping with their new lavish surroundings the shows by now offered even more extravagant horrors. Crocodiles, giraffes, bison, zebras, rhinoceroses, hippopotami, as well as the more familiar lions and tigers, were imported to fight each other or the gladiators. In AD 80 Titus dedicated the Colosseum in Rome with games lasting a hundred days, in which some five thousand wild animals and four thousand tame ones were killed in hunting scenes. The circus

---

[1]104, 10–11; [2]105, 148; [3]104, 163; [4]104, 152; [5]105, 227; [6]12, VIII, 319

Fig. 32 Tragic actors, Sabratha, *c.* AD 200

was now borrowing some of its more macabre thrills from the theatre. A criminal, dressed as Orpheus, was torn to pieces by bears among carefully constructed hills and groves. A bull thundered round the arena with a woman strapped to its back in the costume of Europa.[1]

The 'straight' theatre had by now detached itself from the circus. The first stone theatre in Rome was built by Pompey in 55 BC and was soon to be followed by two others,[2] but the change had come too late. The last recorded performance of a new Latin play is in 31 BC.[3] From then on theatre consisted of a few revivals, a great many productions of the debased forms of panto-mime and mime which I shall deal with later, and various spectacles not much different from the circus shows – as when under Nero a play was given, called *House on Fire*, in which a house was actually burnt and the actors were allowed to keep whichever of the rich furnishings they dared to bring out.[4] As with Greece, the creative period had been very short; all the plays of Plautus and Terence were written within eighty years of the first Roman play in 240 BC. And again as with Greece, the imposing stone theatres rose after the good plays had ceased to be written.

The stage on which both tragedies and comedies had been played at the time of Plautus and Terence was a temporary platform, not much more elaborate than that of the Phlyakes, with a plain wooden wall behind it containing three doors as entrances[5] – very similar, in fact, to the temporary *frons scaenae* put up behind the performances in fifth-century Athens. In a later and rather more detailed form the three doors can be seen in a terracotta relief (Fig. 30) which was on the funeral monument of P. Numitorius Hilarus and which shows a tragic scene, possibly one that had been performed at his funeral. Plays at funerals were not uncommon, and even gladiatorial contests were considered suitable for the occasion.[6]

The two actors on the right of this relief suggest well the mood of Roman tragic performance – more grotesque and exaggerated than its Greek original. In the second century BC tragedy had been very popular with an audience which wanted 'melodramatic effects, volleys of rhetoric, horrific plots and descriptions, flamboyant personalities, superhuman virtue, incredible vice.'[7]

Fig. 33 Theatre at Sabratha, *c.* AD 200

Instead of talking to each other the actors tended to come downstage and declaim to the audience. The flute-player would step forward to accompany each one in turn.

In keeping with this grandiose style, the figure of the actor grew larger. The two actors in Fig. 30 are wearing the high-soled *cothurni* introduced in the second century BC. A later relief, at Sabratha (Fig. 32), shows the process carried further. The actor's soles have grown so thick that he appears to be an inhuman figure on stilts, with his feet hidden under his robe. At the same time his mask has grown out of all proportion to a human head. Tragic actors looking like this were said to have so frightened the people of Seville that they fled from the theatre,[1] and a character in Lucian, translated into rich English in the seventeenth century, mocks such figures with the words:

> What a deformed, and frightfull sight it is to see a man raised to a prodigious length, stalking upon exalted buskins, his face disguised with a grimme vizard, widely gaping, as if he meant to devoure the Spectatours! I forbear to speake of his stuft Brests, and fore-Bellyes, which make an adventitious and artificiall complacency, least his unnaturall length should carry disproportion to his slendernesse.[9]

Nero is known to have declaimed the parts of Orestes the Matricide, Oedipus Blinded and Hercules Mad in public theatres, including even the Theatre of Dionysus in Athens, and it may well have been in a costume like this that he did so.[10] Recitation or declamation had become more fashionable than tragedy, and it was probably for this type of performance that Nero's tutor, Seneca, wrote his plays. Certainly they were never performed on a full scale in Roman times.

The stages too were becoming steadily more vast and ponderous. The contemporary story

[1]12, IX, 1520; [2]105, 281; [3]104, 233; [4]105, 247; [4]104, 180; [5]12, IX, 826 ff.; [6]104, 61; [7]105, 243; [8]285, 363; [9]104, 233 ff.

41

Fig. 35 Scene from comedy, marble relief

that Scaurus built a wooden theatre in Rome in the middle of the first century BC, which had three tiers and three hundred and sixty columns, was probably exaggerated;[1] but soon such a colossal architectural background, built in stone, was to become normal. Fig. 33 shows the stage at Sabratha, built around AD 200. It had two identical tiers above this one.

In some theatres the effect of this façade was occasionally lightened or varied by putting painted panels between the pillars. Wall paintings from the villa of P. Fannius Synistor at Boscoreale, dating from about 40 BC, have been shown to correspond roughly with the three types of stage scenery, tragic, comic and satyric, as described a few years later by Vitruvius. Fig. 34 shows the scene for comedy. If the artist, when painting the columns on either side of his composition, had in mind the actual pillars of the façade of a theatre, then the painting could well represent an entire panel of the type put up between the stage pillars, possibly even with a large practicable door in the middle of it. Certainly a similar type of architectual jumble, together with a large door, is seen in a marble relief from Naples (Fig. 35) which is clearly theatrical and shows a scene from comedy (the high-soled boots were worn only in tragedy). Small curtains, known as *siparia*, were used to conceal any painted panel which was not relevant to a particular scene, and one can be seen covering the panel in this relief. In the later Roman theatres there was also a gigantic curtain, the *aulaeum*, concealing the whole stage, which was lowered into a trench in front of the stage at the start of the play and not raised again till the end.[2]

Although no picture of the Greek originals survives, the painted panels between the pillars were another heritage from Greece. The later Greek theatres, built in the Hellenistic period

[1] 105, 168; [2] 105, 179–180

Fig. 34 Mural from Boscoreale

(*c.* 300–*c.* 100 BC), had included one row of pillars, and the stone pillars at Priene, dating from the early third century, still have the holes into which the painted panels were bolted.[1] The price of the panels at Delos survives from the same period – only 30 drachmas to make, but 100 drachmas to paint each panel, so the painting was clearly skilful.[2] Another Greek use for the pillars, also adopted by Rome, was that of setting an interior scene between two of the pillars; and a mosaic from Pompeii (Fig. 36) almost certainly shows such a scene. It is tempting to imagine, as has in fact been suggested,[3] that the strips to the left and above represent wings and borders of the type familiar on our own stages. But such strips were a contemporary convention in art to suggest a receding area, and so cannot be taken literally.[4]

In the great number of theatres which sprouted throughout the Roman Empire, but which arrived too late for tragedy and comedy, the main attractions were the pantomime and the mime. Contrary to our normal use of the words, the mime had dialogue and the pantomime had none. The pantomime, which became popular around 20 BC, was roughly speaking the successor to tragedy, but a chorus now sang the poet's words and narrated the plot while the actors, or more usually a solo performer, mimed or danced the action in a succession of masks. According to Lucian a pantomime at the time of Nero 'by himself danc'd the Adultery of Mars and Venus, the Sun betraying them, and Vulcan plotting, and catching them in a Wire Net; then every God, who was severally Spectator; then Venus blushing, and Mars beseeching'.[5] Love stories were the favourite plots, and exquisitely lascivious movements the chief source of delight.[6]

The mime had a far longer pedigree – we have come across his predecessors in Greece and Syracuse – and he would also survive long after the Roman pantomime was forgotten. At other periods the mimes were small troupes of simple performers, but under the Roman Empire they acquired a new dignity. An inscription of AD 169 honouring Eutyches, a leading mime, reveals that his company of actors numbered sixty – more than most modern national theatre companies. By the fifth century several mime actresses were exceedingly rich and were 'stars' of genuinely international fame.[7]

The productions must certainly have been more lavish with a company of sixty, but the material of the mimes remained much the same – a mixed entertainment of acrobatics, songs, and above all semi-improvised burlesque on the foibles of men and the antics of the gods, with a strong emphasis on the adulterous affairs of both. It was burlesque of the gods which was to hasten their downfall because, where Dionysus had presumably recognised that these were his true followers, the Christian Church proved less understanding. The new religion was an obvious target in the same old vein (baptism farces were particularly popular[8] and the comic potentiality of large quantities of water reminds one of the Phlyakes waiting for Apollo to fall into the holy water in Fig. 28), but the early fathers were not amused and did everything they could to eliminate the mimes. They also pointed out, in Tertullian's words, that it was they who had in their repertoire the last and greatest spectacle of all – 'then will the comedians turn and twist, rendered nimbler than ever by the sting of the fire that is not quenched'.[9] In the fifth century all performers of mime were excommunicated; in the sixth century Justinian closed the theatres;[10] and the end of theatrical entertainment was finally sealed with the arrival of the barbarians in 568.[11]

Yet even though they had no fixed or legitimate place to play, the mimes must somehow have contrived to carry on, because the Church fathers continued throughout the Dark Ages to issue

---

[1]105, 110;   [2]108, 187;   [3]105, 124;   [4]109, 25;   [5]285, 371;   [6]104, 234;   [7]32, 85 ff.;   [8]32, 121;   [9]245, I, 11;   [10]104, 240;   [11]105, 250

Fig. 36 Interior scene, mosaic

Fig. 37 A Roman mime, first century AD
Fig. 38 Pulcinella, 1643

new edicts against them.[1] They therefore constitute the only continuing link between the performers of ancient and modern Europe. It is first of all within the Church itself that theatre revives in the early Middle Ages, but soon there appear new traces of popular performers who will develop into the extraordinarily influential players of the Commedia dell'Arte. Even in appearance the link seems to suggest itself over the span of so many centuries. Fig. 37 is a terracotta statuette of a mime at the period of their greatest prosperity, the first century AD. Fig. 38 is a print dated 1643 of Pulcinella, ancestor of the English Punch. If anything his paunch, his mask and his tight, short trousers seem to bypass the mime and go back to the mime's close associates from Syracuse, the Phlyakes. But if so, let the mime claim Harlequin. For the mime, too, wore a 'motley dress of patchwork'.[2]

[1]32, 145–9; [2]105, 160

3

THE EAST

India

The darkest centuries of Western drama coincide almost exactly with the greatest period of theatre in the East. The first flowering came in India and it had at least a tenuous link with Greek theatre. By the second century BC, when Sanskrit drama was just beginning to develop, Greek influence had reached India in a series of invasions and several details of the early Indian theatre were borrowed from Greek New Comedy.[1]

Sanskrit drama was religious and aristocratic, the product of a highly developed minority culture in the palaces and temples, and the earliest surviving Sanskrit plays – which date from the first century AD and were only rediscovered as recently as 1911 – are also the earliest known examples of Indian literature of any kind.[2] The plays are romantic tales about the loves and adventures of gods and princes. They were performed by wandering companies of professionals whose stage – when they arrived to set it up in a palace – had to be very carefully consecrated, because, in spite of the flamboyant romanticism of the plots, these were religious performances. Each play had five acts, separated by interludes, and although such a form may sound typically Western the effect in performance was certainly very different. A major part of the actor's skill was his intricate repertoire of symbolic gestures and movements, each as carefully codified as anything in Western ballet. Significantly, there are no separate words in Sanskrit, nor indeed in modern Indian languages, to distinguish 'dance' from 'drama'.[3]

The best known author of these plays, Kalidasa, was born in the fourth century AD and the golden age of Sanskrit drama ran roughly from the third to the eighth centuries. It then began to lose its creative energy and from about the eleventh century until the eighteenth the only performances of any artistic importance in India were the various forms of classical dance. It appears that there is no surviving illustration of a Sanskrit play in performance; but dance is one of the most common themes of Indian sculpture and painting.

The oldest tradition of Indian dancing, the Bharata Nhatyam (Fig. 39), is also the most pure in that it has kept closest to the precepts of the ancient Indian tracts. It was danced in imitation of Krishna by temple priestesses, known as Devadasi, who were highly educated women with a very privileged position in society – they were officially married to the god, but were allowed to live with a succession of men of their choice and their children were considered legitimate. Every temple had several hundred Devadasi.[4]

The other most important style is Kathak. Whereas Bharata Nhatyam came from the south of India, was Hindu and was a religious performance connected with temples, Kathak was a northern dance which after the Mongol invasions developed largely as a secular entertainment at Moslem courts. The superb manuscripts illuminated with Persian-style miniatures, which

---

Sources (*see* p. 317)   [1]12, IX, 1251;   [2]276, 14;   [3]237, 9;   [4]12, IX, 1253

were produced for the Mongol rulers in the sixteenth and seventeenth centuries, provide many pictures of Kathak dancing girls entertaining the princes – in Pl. V (p. 61), the occasion is the birth in 1568 of Prince Salim, the future Emperor Jahangir.

Both Bharata Nhatyam with its emancipated priestesses and Kathak with its courtly dancing-girls contained inevitable seeds of degeneracy. Gradually – as dancers left the temples and courts, and began to travel the country on a freelance basis – dance became a much despised art, inseparable in the public's mind from prostitution. Fig. 40 is a charming picture of a Bharata Nhatyam dancer who has left her temple and is strolling with her personal band of three musicians or 'tickatoio men'. It was only in the early years of this century, with the new interest in India's cultural past, that dance was rescued as a serious and respectable art. Now there are again highly accomplished practitioners not only of Bharata Nhatyam and Kathak, but also of other ancient Indian dance styles – in particular a male dance, the Kathakali, which approaches nearer to the dance drama of China and Japan in the use of magnificently exaggerated costume and of make-up which turns the face into a grotesque mask.

Theatre returned to India with the British in the eighteenth century. The first permanent theatre, the Play House, was opened by the English for their own use in Calcutta in 1776 and began to be used by Indian companies in around 1800.[1] The modern Indian theatre, which has developed in Western-type theatre buildings, is naturally influenced by India's own theatrical past but does not derive directly from it. The only true surviving tradition of Indian theatre is that of the dance – which can justifiably be called theatrical since, like Western ballet, it almost invariably tells a story.

China

From as early as 700 BC there are records in China of mixed theatrical entertainments at religious festivals, combining pantomime, singing, dancing and acrobatics, but the serious Chinese theatre dates from the eighth century AD when the T'ang emperor Ming Huang set up a vast dramatic academy in the Pear Garden of the Imperial Park. In the early years of our own century actors were still referred to politely as 'Young Folk of the Pear Garden'.[2]

The plays performed for Ming Huang seem to have been fairly simple comedies, usually for just two actors,[3] and it was not until six hundred years later, in the fourteenth century, that Chinese drama began to acquire some level of real distinction, largely as an accidental result of the Mongols abolishing the old civil service. This had been the automatic career for the intelligentsia, who now found themselves officially reduced to a rank between prostitutes and beggars.[4] With nothing to lose they turned to the theatre, and their influence contributed to a rapid growth in its popularity. A hundred of their plays have survived in one collection, and one rather endearing characteristic of their work is that an abnormally high proportion of the heroes are civil servants.[5]

Chinese plays had always been performed in three separate environments; in palaces, in temples, and in the open air at fairs and public festivities. The actors originally used a similar type of temporary stage in each place, and it is the public ones which have been most illustrated. Fig. 41 is a small and very obviously temporary structure, standing on its exposed supports. As on the Japanese stage the musicians stand around the sides and at the back; a

---

[1]12, IX, 1262;   [2]110, xxiii;   [3]12, III, 74;   [4]276, 80;   [5]12, III, 774

Fig. 39 Temple dancers, Bharata Nhatyam, tenth century
Fig. 40 Bharata Nhatyam dancer, strolling, nineteenth century

Fig. 41 Chinese open-air theatre

carpet marks the acting area; some props are on the table behind, waiting to be used; and a dressing-room, with masks on a rack and a trunk of clothes, can be seen behind the stage and to the right. Fig. 42 is a more elaborate theatre, but it too could probably be dismantled and moved elsewhere. In this case actors can be seen making up in the small room to the left of the stage.

Naturally it soon became convenient to have permanent stages inside certain temples or palaces, but the shape remained that of the outdoor theatres with a roof over the stage and the audience on three sides. To accommodate more spectators, galleries were then built around the walls of the room; and the result, as has often been pointed out, was an auditorium remarkably similar to the Elizabethan pattern in England. The stage of the Empress Dowager's theatre, which still survives in the Summer Palace at Peking, even has 'three storeys with special devices which allowed evil spirits to appear on the stage from below and celestial beings from the second storey above'.[1] The balcony above the stage became usual in court and temple theatres, but seems not to have been used in the tea-houses where the outdoor theatres of the fairs were to find their permanent home. Originally the play was included in the price of the tea, like a modern cabaret or the beginnings of music-hall in the nineteenth century, but later there was a price for admission and an extra payment for tea.[2]

The style of traditional Chinese theatre, which is famous in the West as Peking opera but in

50

Fig. 42 Open-air theatre

China as *P'i Huang* or *Ching Psi*, emerged during the nineteenth century as a popular and spectacular version of the various earlier and more literary forms of Chinese drama.[3] Its techniques are typically Eastern but are more readily comprehensible to Western audiences than Indian or Japanese conventions – probably because, although the approach is stylised and symbolic, the ingredients of the symbolism are often realistic and therefore more recognisable. So, for example, to portray suicide by drowning, an actor will jump towards other actors holding banners painted with waves and fishes; they then quickly cover him with the banners and he moves off the stage concealed beneath them.[4] Similarly in Fig. 43, where Chieh Chih-t'ui is carrying his old mother into the hills, the hills are symbolised by two flats propped against chairs; but the two flats are themselves painted with hill scenery. It is this stylised combination of realism and symbolism, rather than the more pure abstractions of other Asian theatres, which has provided in our own century a strong Eastern influence on Western styles of production.

It would be misleading to suggest that all the symbolism of Peking opera is so easily accessible. Both in the costumes and the make-up there is a purely formal symbolism of colour; 'red, for example, generally denotes loyalty, sacredness or some other divine quality. Purple indicates loyalty to a lesser degree than red. Black indicates good but rather uncouth characters. Blue

[1]120, 4–6;   [2]118, 219;   [3]12, III, 799 ff.;   [4]120, 25

Fig. 43 Chieh Chih-t'ui carries his mother into the hills
Fig. 44 Hsiang Yü, a dignified villain

shows that the individual is of tiger-like ferocity, crafty, haughty, etc. Yellow shows all the qualities of blue, but to a lesser degree. Green indicates an unstable, unreliable character. Orange and pale-grey indicate old age'.[1] In the abstract swirls of Chinese make-up, by which the actor's face is turned into an unearthly mask, extraordinarily elaborate meanings can be concealed. Fig. 44, the make-up for Hsiang Yü, king of the Ch'u State from 233 to 200 BC, is comparatively simple; 'the oblique eyebrows represent him as a dignified villain . . . He is said to have had four nipples: and could hoist himself three feet off the ground by his own hair . . . The pale white face represents a villain of the deepest dye'.[2]

The actor's movement is both as precise and as flamboyant as his make-up. Pl. VII (p. 64), suggests well the rhythm and richness of a Chinese performance. Plays are divided not into categories of Tragedy or Comedy but into Military or Civil. This scene would certainly appear to be military, and nothing offers the Chinese performer such spectacular opportunity for showing his prowess as the famous dances representing battles. The scenery in this case is purely abstract, consisting only of tables, chairs and drapery without any realistic details. But the notice hanging on the chair shows that it is still, nevertheless, standing in for greater things. It reads: 'The village of the Taoist Magic-Makers'.

When the Communist regime came to power in China they encouraged Western-type drama (*houa-kiu* or 'spoken drama'), which had been introduced to China in 1906, had been very fashionable with the intelligentsia in the 1920s, and was clearly more adaptable to propagandist purposes. But the public resolutely preferred their familiar Peking opera, and official policy has been altered to support the traditional form with the result that it has recently been widely seen and much admired throughout the world. Admittedly even Peking opera can be forced to change with the times. Within China itself the old play *The King of the Monkeys turns the Celestial Palace upside down* was revised before China's break with Russia as *The Sputnik turns the Celestial Palace upside down*. Even so, the actor playing the Sputnik was costumed and made up in entirely traditional fashion, and in a theatre where the plot was never more than a pretext for a magnificent physical performance the violation is probably less extreme than it may sound.[1]

Japan

As in China, festivities in the Buddhist temples of Japan included simple forms of theatre from the very earliest times and after the eighth century AD several different styles of masked dance and pantomime can be identified, many of them imported directly from China. The two most important were the *dengaku* and the *sarugaku*, and by the fourteenth century these had evolved into such elaborate and sophisticated performances that they won for themselves the new titles of *dengaku-nō-nō* and *sarugaku-nō-nō* – the addition of *nō* apparently signifying 'art'.

From these, and in particular from the *sarugaku-nō-nō*, the famous *nō* theatre itself would develop. Amazingly, the entire creative achievement of *nō* can be credited to one enlightened despot, four members of a single family of actors and a span of only some eighty years. In the second half of the fourteenth century one of the wandering *sarugaku-nō-nō* companies was led by an actor called Kanami, who had radically altered *sarugaku* by introducing a new style of singing. A performance by this company in about 1375 so impressed the *shōgun* Ashikaga Yoshimitsu that he took Kanami and his twelve-year-old son Zeami into his service. Here they were free to develop without the pressures of a strolling life. Kanami continued to write plays, consolidating his new style which soon acquired the simple title of *nō*. Zeami proved himself a more distinguished though perhaps less original writer than his father, and his many plays refined and improved on Kanami's innovations. Zeami hoped that his own son, whom he described as 'an artist who had no equal in any time', would advance yet again the tradition; but he died tragically young with only a few plays to his credit and Zeami, by now very pessimistic about the future of *nō*, bequeathed the leadership of the company to his son-in-law, Zenchiku, who also wrote several of the surviving plays. Only a small fraction of the *nō* plays which have ever been performed were written after Zenchiku's death, so these three generations of one family created almost the entire *nō* repertoire.

They also fixed for ever the style of production. Zeami formulated his own and his father's ideas into a complete and confidential manual on the theory and practice of *nō*. Copies of his manuscript have been passed down ever since, among the five established families of *nō* actors, but the precious secrets were not published until 1909. It is the boast of the present day performers of *nō* that five centuries have enabled them to come even closer to Zeami's intentions than he was able to in his own day, though at a cost, apparently, of taking almost twice as long to perform each play.[4] Since the mid-fifteenth century, then, *nō* has been virtually a theatrical museum – but one of extraordinary beauty and power.

For most of its history *nō* has also been a minority taste, appealing to the nobility and the warrior classes, for whom it was the only type of theatre which they were officially allowed to patronise. Admittedly in its first two centuries, when there was little competition from other

[1] 110, 107; [2] 110, 108; [3] 276, 112; [4] 276, 137

Fig. 45 *Nō* play on *nō* stage, 1763
Fig. 46 Kyōgen on *nō* stage, 1763

forms, *nō* did reach a broader and more boisterous audience, but after the development in the seventeenth century of the much more popular *kabuki* and *joruri* most of the audience deserted *nō* and it became exclusively aristocratic.[1]

As a result, while *kabuki* and *joruri* are among the most common subjects of Japanese woodcuts, illustrations of the *nō* stage are extremely rare. However, a book of woodcuts by Harunabu, published in 1763 under the title *Ehon Shogei Nishiki* (Sketches Illustrating the Arts), does provide two very interesting views. Fig. 45 shows the *nō* stage from the front, and anyone who has seen a *nō* performance will immediately recognise that nothing has changed since 1763. At the back of the stage sits the orchestra and on the right hand side is the chorus. The character wearing a mask and dancing with a broom is the protagonist or *shite*, and beside him in similar costume is his assistant, the *shite-tsure*. The figure sitting by the pillar on the right is the second actor or *waki* (literally 'side man') with his two assistants; unlike the *shite*, the *waki* and his *waki-tsure* never wear masks.[2] Once the *shite* has entered, the *waki* retires to his pillar and by questioning the *shite* prompts him into some narrative dance or recital – which is being performed in this woodcut. As in all classical drama of the East, the plots are simple stories from legend in which magic transformations and the presence of devils and heroes provide opportunities for most magnificent costumes and masks.

The stage is made of polished cypress-wood, and the performers enter – often slowly and with most stately effect – along the passageway to the left, which always has three small fir-trees in front of it. The backing to the stage itself is invariably a painting of a very formalised pine-tree. The man sitting at the end of the passageway is the *kōken*: he will change or adjust the *shite's* clothing for him on stage, and he or his assistants will bring on any necessary props or extra pieces of scenery – free-standing and stylised structures, of which the small pine-tree in its frame on the stage is a more than usually naturalistic example.

Many modern descriptions of the *nō* stage show precisely these same details in diagrammatic form,[3] but it is most unusual to find them depicted not only during a performance but also in a woodcut from the past, and Harunabu's sketch holds true also for the three centuries before it was printed in 1763. Like the stage in Chinese tea-houses, the *nō* stage has kept the shape which it had as a temporary structure in temples and courts. The woodcut differs from the norm in only one respect: it lacks the three steps down from the front of the stage to the auditorium which are a regular feature of the *nō* stage. These steps have not been used for centuries, perhaps not even since the temple days, but typically they are still there.

Harunabu's other *nō* woodcut (Fig. 46) is less revealing, though it is interesting as showing a glimpse of the audience. The stage is seen this time from the side – the few spectators visible are in the corner between the left hand side of the stage and the passageway with its fir-trees – and the fact that there appear to be only two performers on the stage suggests that this may be a *kyōgen*, one of the short comic interludes which are performed, almost invariably by two actors, between each of the *nō* plays. The average modern programme consists of three *nō* plays and two *kyōgen*.[4]

Kyōgen, like *nō*, is an offshoot of the earlier *sarugaku* and in the seventeenth century this same popular tradition produced two more styles of theatre. One of them, *kabuki*, was later to become the mainstream of Japanese popular theatre but until the eighteenth century it was the other, *joruri*, which seemed likely to prove the more successful of the two.

---

[1]339, 39;   [2]12, V, 1234;   [3]e.g. 12, V, 1233;   [4]12, V, 1237

Fig. 47 *Joruri* theatre from backstage

Joruri was a theatre of puppets. There had been various types of puppet theatre in Japan since before the tenth century, but this particular style arose from a new alliance in the seventeenth century between the puppeteers and the ministrels, or singers of epic, who now sang the plot which the figures performed.[1] The manipulators worked in full view of the audience, though as a symbolic gesture to invisibility they usually wore black cloths over their heads (Fig. 47). A long masking strip across the stage represented the level at which the characters walked and lived; sometimes the strip was on the ground and the puppeteers sat down, sometimes it was at chest height and they stood. In Fig. 47 an assistant is about to push a curtain across to close the performance; a second puppeteer has just left the stage and is letting his puppet hang limp; on the table behind him are a pair of high blocks which were worn by the shorter manipulators to raise their puppets to the same height as the others; and on the right some property trees are stacked together, all on stands which lift them sufficiently high to be a background to the figures.

The puppets themselves were extremely elaborate mechanisms and some of the larger ones required three manipulators, with the leader working the head, the body and the right arm, while one assistant controlled the left arm and the other the legs. Fig. 48 shows an unclothed figure resting on its stand – this is the type that can be worked by one man – and beside it is another of the high soles for a short puppeteer to stand on.

---

[1]276, 144

56

Fig. 48 One-man puppet
Fig. 49 The *Kabuki* stage, *c.* 1800 (*overleaf*)

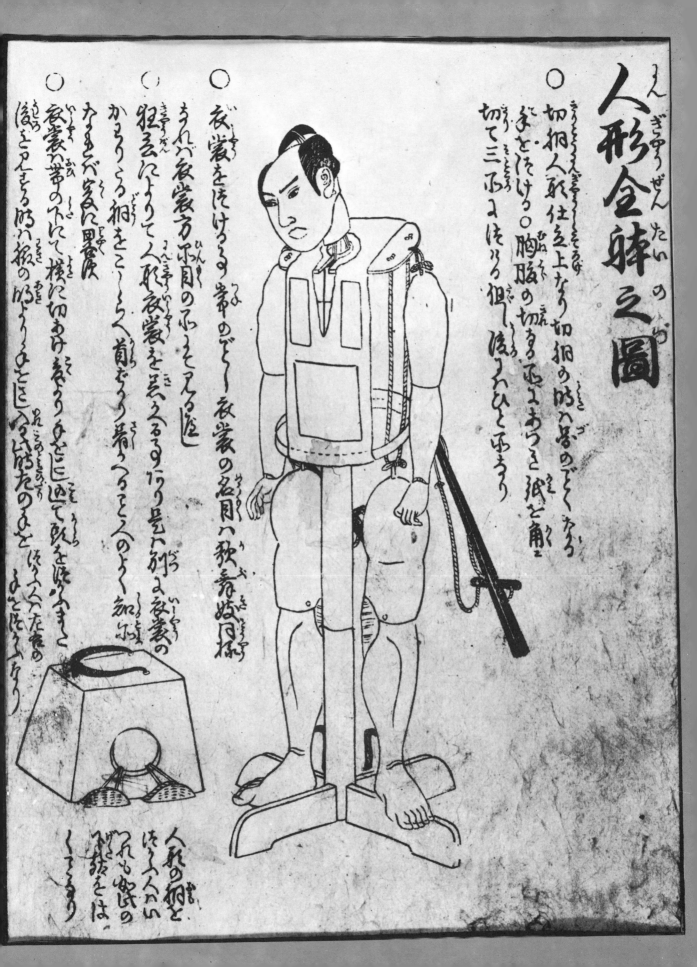

人形全躰之圖

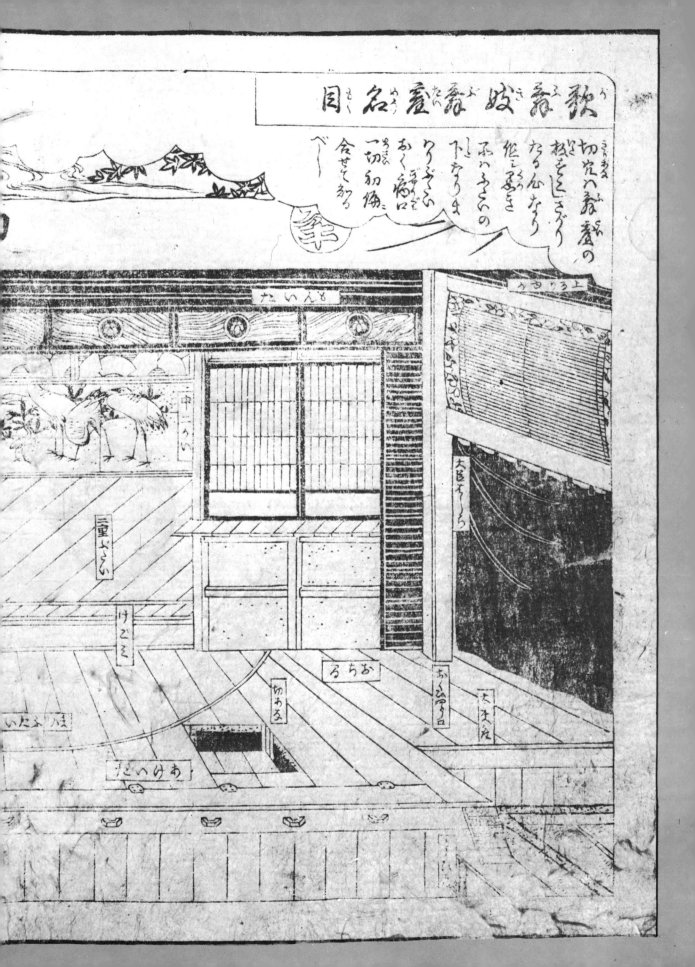

歌舞妓芝居名目

うらかた
切穴へ楽屋の
松をさぐり
たんねなり
伏やさくの
下へ
おります
ワりぐちは
おくへ入るで
おく楽口
一切初候
合せて初
べ一

たいへと

中へうい

三重べらい

けごミ

うちお

切わみ

いたふ　八五

ちへりあ

上るり口

大臣ぞち

ち久ちぼう日

大べう

The great importance of *joruri* in Japanese theatrical history derives from two facts; Chika-matsu Monzaemon, sometimes described as the Japanese Shakespeare, wrote his plays in the late seventeenth century for performance by the puppets;[1] and *joruri* had a great influence on *kabuki.* In the early seventeenth century the new *kabuki* theatre had a rapid success, due largely to the lascivious performances of the women and boys in the companies, but both were soon banned from acting and the male actors alone had to fight harder for an audience. To compete with the very successful *joruri* theatres, the actors began to perform the plays written for the puppets and borrowed many devices of stage machinery which had been developed for them, including trap-doors and a revolving stage;[2] they even, in their own performances, began to imitate the style and movements of animated figures.[3] The audience responded to the appeal of seeing its favourite plays writ large, and although *kabuki* has since gone through difficult patches, there are now many *kabuki* theatres in Japan but only one *joruri* theatre – sometimes also referred to as *bunraku* – to uphold the honour of the puppets.

At first *kabuki* used the *nō* stage, but being – unlike *nō* – a living theatrical tradition, the shape of the stage underwent continual modification; and by the late eighteenth century the two no longer bore any resemblance. A typical *kabuki* stage and auditorium of about 1800 can be seen in a triptych by Toyokuni (Pl. VI, pp. 62–3). The pillars of the *nō* stage have vanished and the roof has receded until it covers only an inner stage which is used for scenery. The passageway to the left, by which the *nō* actors entered, has been appropriated by the audience. The *kabuki* actors enter either from behind the small screen to the right, or else down the long gangway which slices at an angle through the auditorium: this is known as the *hana-michi* or 'path of flowers', and was introduced in the late seventeenth century. There are also two curtains which do not exist on the *nō* stage. One seals off the inner stage so that scenery can be changed behind it; the other, seen here furled up at the top left, conceals the whole stage area and much of the audience and is only used at the beginning and end of a performance.[4]

The auditorium itself is virtually a restaurant, and a waiter can be seen walking along the partition between the tables with a great plate of food. Unlike in China, the stages were not actually introduced into existing tea-houses; they had their own special buildings, around which tea-houses and food shops sprang up to supply the audience.

Another woodcut of much the same period shows more clearly the area of the stage itself (Fig. 49). The inner stage is visible, slightly raised from the main stage, with a painting of cranes as a blackcloth. In the stage itself a trap-door can be seen, as well as the outline of the revolve – though precisely how this works in relation to the inner stage seems rather vague in the artist's mind.

This particular period in the *kabuki* theatre is the most familiar, largely because the numerous woodcuts of theatre interiors nearly all date from the decades before and after 1800. But, unlike the *nō* stage, there was nothing final about the details. Away from their permanent theatres the *kabuki* actors seem to have been willing to perform in quite different conditions. A very unusual woodcut of the time (Fig. 50) appears to show some sort of performance in a more improvised theatre. Normally the dressing-rooms of both *nō* and *kabuki* are off the stage to one side, and the actor – in order to submerge himself in the role – gazes at himself in a full length mirror before stepping on to the stage. But here the dressing-room appears to be a wigwam on the stage, inside which an actor can be seen surrounded by his dressers, and taking a last look at himself in a

---

[1]276, 145;   [2]113, 53;   [3]12, V, 1244;   [4]12, V, 1245

Pl. V Kathak dancers at the court of Akbar: sixteenth-century Mughal miniature

Pl. VI Interior of *kabuki* theatre: woodcut triptych by Toyokuni, *c.* 1800 (*overleaf*)

Fig. 50 A minor *kabuki* stage and dressing-room, 1800

circular mirror as he begins to step out. The man already on the stage, holding two blocks of wood, is a musician. The woodcut also shows the various pieces of semi-symbolic scenery, in this case a small cloud and some fir branches, which are suspended above a *kabuki* stage in a manner as openly unrealistic as the upright rows of snow along the front of the stage in Pl. VI (pp. 62–3).

The *kabuki* stage has continued to change as radically since 1800 as before. Most of the present day *kabuki* theatres have an auditorium similar to any Western theatre or cinema, except that the 'path of flowers' still slices through it; and the stage itself has now retired behind a proscenium arch and become flattened across the whole front of the auditorium, presenting a view which is nearer to a wide cinema screen than to the square jutting promontory of its *nō* ancestor.

Numerically it is the Western style of theatre which dominates modern Japan, accounting for the major part of an amazingly thriving theatrical life.[1] In the 1950s Japan had about four thousand theatres[2] and some seven hundred professional companies.[3] But the traditional forms of *nō* and *kabuki*, though very much in the minority, are far from dying out. Even the uncompromising *nō* could boast, in the 1950s, as many as twenty-eight theatres.[4]

To end this brief section on the drama of the East, two more Japanese illustrations suggest well the elements common to nearly all Eastern performance. The first is one of the many thousands of Japanese woodcuts which depict actors Pl. VIII (p. 64). The magnificence of the actors' costumes – which makes them a subject so perfectly suited to the pure blocks of colour of the Japanese woodcut – and the superbly confident swirl of the movement as the warrior tosses his adversaries from him, are together two of the most important elements in a wide-

[1] 12, V, 1247; [2] 237, 321; [3] 113, 262; [4] 296, 9

Pl. VII Chinese theatrical scene: Cantonese painting on rice paper, *c.* 1860

Pl. VIII *Kabuki* actors: woodcut by Kunisada, *c.* 1830

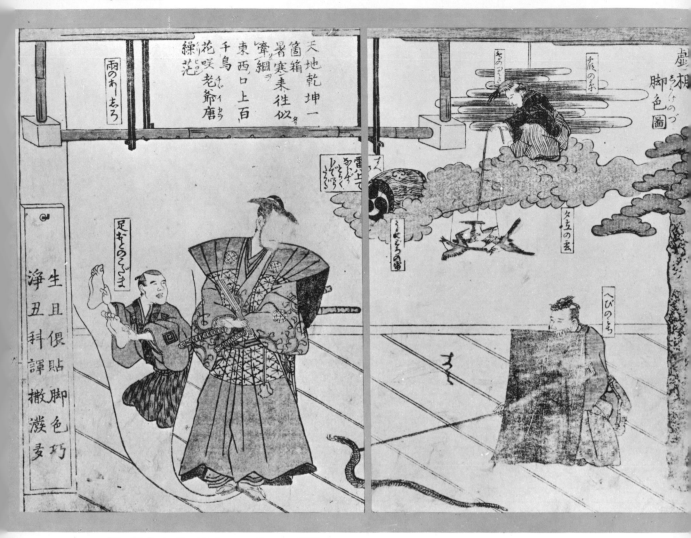

Fig. 51 Some theatrical conventions, *c*. 1800

ranging theatrical tradition, one of whose greatest glories is to dance the exploits of gods and devils and heroes – whether in the *kabuki* theatre or the Peking opera or the Kathakali dances of India.

The second is another woodcut by Toyokuni, showing various theatrical conventions (Fig. 51). The details here may not be entirely accurate, at any rate in conjunction, because the purpose of the woodcut was to illustrate a humorous book, but the various tricks being used sum up perfectly the theatricality of Eastern drama: whether in the 'invisible' stage hand manipulating the snake on the end of the pole; or his colleague aloft on the cloud, dangling a flock of birds; or the genie walking a pair of detached feet up a non-existent wall. This playfulness is the precise opposite of Europe's recent fondness for naturalism, and is certainly more central to the real nature and traditions of the theatre.

66

4

THE MIDDLE AGES

Liturgical drama

With the approach of the millenium the Christian Church seems to have been eager to make its liturgy more vivid. One interesting device developed in Italy between the tenth and twelfth centuries was that of the Exultet Roll, from which a priest chanted the text (Fig. 52), unrolling it over the back of the pulpit as he read his way through it. At intervals in the roll there were pictures illustrating the subject of his Latin words. To be the right way up for the congregation standing below, the pictures had to be upside down in the text; and towards the end of the roll the congregation even had the pleasure of seeing themselves being read to. Fig. 52 is an actual picture from an eleventh-century roll in the Vatican. The lettering above and below the picture can be seen to be upside down. But to the priest reading the roll, before it fell over the back of the pulpit, it was the picture which was upside down.

Of rather more lasting interest was the experiment, begun in either St Gall or Limoges in the early tenth century, of making the Easter liturgy more vivid by dramatising it. The first account that we have dates from about 970 when St Ethelwold, the bishop of Winchester, wrote that his order had decided to follow the custom of certain French monasteries so as to 'fortify the faith of the ignorant populace'.[1] On Good Friday the entombment of Christ was symbolised by laying a crucifix, wrapped in cloths, in a special recess in the high altar – which therefore stood for the holy sepulchre. Then, said Ethelwold, during Matins on Easter morning, a monk was to go and sit by the sepulchre. Soon three other monks were to join him. And the following description of this embryonic scene, from which the great religious theatre of the Middle Ages would later develop, is entirely Ethelwold's in the tenth century. Only the theatrical lay-out is mine.

Let these three be vested in copes, bearing in their hands thuribles with incense. And, stepping delicately as those who seek something, let them approach the sepulchre. These things are done in imitation of the angel sitting in the monument, and the women with spices coming to anoint the body of Jesus. When therefore he who sits there beholds the three approach him like folk lost and seeking something, let him begin in a dulcet voice of medium pitch to sing:

THE ANGEL: Quem Quaeritis? (Whom seek ye?)

And when he has sung it to the end, let the three reply in unison.

THE MARIES: Ihesu Nazarenum. (Jesus of Nazareth)

THE ANGEL: Non est hic, surrexit sicut praedixerat. Ite, nuntiate quia surrexit a mortuis.
(He is not here, he is risen as he foretold. Go, announce that he is risen from the dead.)

At the word of this bidding let those three turn to the choir and say:

THE MARIES: Alleluia! resurrexit Dominus. (Alleluia! The Lord is risen)[2]

Sources (*see* p. 317)   [1]246, 17;   [2]245, II, 14

SATAHN

LEVITA

CLERICVS

Then the angel was to take the three Maries to the sepulchre and show them the empty cloths in which the crucifix had been wrapped and buried on the Friday, and this would lead into the exultation of the *Te Deum* which ended the service of Matins. Fig. 53 shows the *Quem Quaeritis* trope from a manuscript of the eleventh or twelfth century. The script gives the text and its music, and the miniature duly shows the three Maries arriving with their censer, the angel by the tomb with the empty cloths, and below them – a slightly later addition – the sleeping guards. Soon, in imitation of this tiny Easter drama, an almost identical moment would be developed during Matins on Christmas Day. Some monks would enter as shepherds. Others, standing around a statue of Mary and the child, and representing midwives, would ask them; Quem quaeritis in praesepe, pastores? (Whom seek ye in the manger, shepherds?)

St Ethelwold had said that part of the altar was to be curtained round to represent the sepulchre,[1] and it is this feature which soon became enlarged into the first piece of scenery in the reviving European drama. As the Easter playlet became more elaborate, a separate structure was put up in the choir of the church to represent Christ's tomb, consisting of an open framework which could be closed by curtains and which was large enough for the characters to enter it; it could even contain a tomb in which there was room for the angel to sit, proving visibly that it was empty (Fig. 54). Such a structure was the direct ancestor of the separate *loca, mansions* or *houses* of the later mystery cycles. At the same time costume was becoming more ambitious. The garments were usually simple adaptations of ordinary clerical robes, but soon the angels were wearing wings – as they are in both these miniatures[2] (Figs 53 and 54).

More important, the scenes themselves began to proliferate. St John's gospel says that when Peter and John heard the news 'they both ran together: and the other disciple did outrun Peter and came first to the sepulchre'. The performance of this moment, introduced in Germany, became the first addition to the visit of the Maries; and two monks did actually race the length of the nave.[3] It is hard to believe that this could ever have been an entirely solemn moment and certainly by the sixteenth century a Puritan polemicist, Thomas Kirchmeyer, found this entire nucleus of the Church drama unseemly in its levity:

> The Maries three doe meete, the sepulchre to see,
> And John with Peter swiftly runnes, before him there to bee.
> These things are done with iesture such, and with so pleasaunt game,
> That even the gravest men that live, woulde laugh to see the same.[4]

Actual 'pleasaunt game' was improbable in the eleventh century, but one of the very next additions – the first purely secular and invented character – was soon to reveal himself as an entire comedian and something of a liability to the church. He is the merchant, or *unguentarius*, who sells ointment to the Maries on their way to anoint Christ's body. In his earliest appearances he is silent, but soon he is haggling over the price in a style of contemporary realism which was to become one of the glories of the mystery cycles. His typical qualities of a comedian, combined with the odd fact that in some versions his lines echo almost exactly those of the Doctor in the mummers' plays, make it probable that here the Church was directly influenced by the mimes and folk performers who had survived surreptitiously through the centuries.[5] The merchant in a much later manuscript (Fig. 55) is in fact selling his spices to Nicodemus but he is essentially the same secular character.

---

[1]246, 17;   [2]342, II, 401;   [3]273, 184;   [4]294, 52 v.;   [5]42, 102

Fig. 52 Exultet Roll, eleventh century

Fig. 53 Quem Quaeritis trope, *c.* 1100 (*left*)

Fig. 54 Angel and Maries in the sepulchre, eleventh century

Fig. 55 The merchant, *c.* 1520 (*below*)

The merchant leads towards the great flowering of the religious plays outside the churches from the thirteenth century onwards, but although the famous mystery cycles eclipsed the liturgical plays – or those still attached to church services – they in no way eliminated them. The original liturgical drama continued to develop in its own way, becoming both more elaborate and more free. During the eleventh and twelfth centuries a very wide range of themes from both the Old and the New Testaments had been added. Settings became more numerous, so that the houses sometimes filled the choir and spilled out into the nave; and individual houses were large enough to contain the supper at Emmaus[1] or Daniel being threatened in a cage by performers in lion masks.[2] Machinery became popular. Angels descended, doves – sometimes real, sometimes artificial – flew down from the roof at Pentecost, and Christ ascended up through the roof at the Resurrection.[3] The Pentecost accounts for St Patrick's in Dublin include several items connected with this large scale puppeteering, such as 'iv*s* vii*d* paid to those playing with the great and little angel and the dragon; iii*s* paid for little cords employed about the Holy Ghost.'[4] And in Florence in the early fifteenth century a machine descending from the roof of a church, large enough to contain twenty-one boys as angels, was attributed to no less an artist than Brunelleschi.[5]

Considerable boisterousness was tolerated too, particularly from the character of Herod who raged round the church under the special licence of the Christmas period. At Padua, from the thirteenth century onwards, he was even allowed to interrupt the service of Matins on Epiphany. He stormed in, threw a spear at the choir, and then proceeded *cum tanto furore* to read the ninth lesson while his attendant belaboured the bishops, canons and choristers with an inflated bladder.[6] And all the while the simplest little plays continued to be performed as part of the church year. Records survive of a canon in France who left a sum of money in 1521, at the peak of the splendours of the mystery cycles, for the annual performance by two choristers of a little Annunciation play which is as simple as anything done in the tenth century.[7] So the great civic plays were an offshoot of the liturgical drama in the churches, not a replacement of it.

The mystery cycles

It was during the late twelfth and the thirteenth centuries that the plays started to move out of the Church, and at much the same time they began to be performed in the vernacular instead of in Latin. Having been almost identical throughout Europe while they were part of the standard services, they now began to develop along regional lines.

The most spectacular of the mystery plays, particularly in terms of staging, come from France – as does the earliest known example of a performance outside the Church. This was the *Mystère d'Adam*, which was written to be played in front of the porch of a church, probably around 1170. This magnificent play is remarkable both for its very convincing characterisation and for stage directions which describe ambitious stage effects. The play ends when three or four devils tie Adam and Eve with chains and pull them off to Hell, from which smoke belches out and a great clatter of pots and kettles can be heard.[8]

With the new freedom outside the churches, the devils quickly became highly popular characters – they had appeared in the liturgical drama, but certainly not accompanied by pots and kettles. Like the best villains, they were funny and frightening at the same time. The devils

---

[1]273, 192; [2]342, II, 276; [3]342, I, 484; [4]245, II, 66; [5]12, VI, 1198; [6]342, II, 99; [7]247, 170; [8]245, II, 82

Fig. 56 Devils in French play, 1508
Fig. 57 Devil in German play, fifteenth century (*above right*)
Fig. 58 Harrowing of Hell. German play, fifteenth century

illustrating the page of a mystery play in Fig. 56 are in the middle of a satanic conference, but their positions suggest that they will at the same time make the audience laugh. By contrast the devil in Fig. 57, who also illustrates a play, is a much more alarming apparition. As in the *Mystère d'Adam* he is hauling someone off to Hell, and the fireworks became an essential part of the devil's wardrobe. A manuscript note in the fifteenth-century English play, *The Castle of Perseverance*, says; 'he that schal pleye Belyal loke that he have gunne-powder brennynge In pypys in his handis & in his eris & in his ars whanne he gothe to battel.'[1] The devil in Fig. 57 can be seen to have gunpowder burning in all the right places. A good example of the Grand Guignol flavour of the devils' behaviour comes in a French play where they take a woman out of a cauldron and taste her, then put her back because she is not cooked through.[2]

Again like all good villains, their downfall looms very clearly ahead. Towards the end of each mystery cycle Christ harrows Hell, overthrows Satan, and leads out Adam and the other patriarchs whom the spectators have already met in earlier plays. In the more lavish productions the Hell from which the devils swarmed was the traditional hell-mouth, a monster's gaping jaws, but the patriarchs were imprisoned in a tower nearby since Christ broke down the 'gates' of Hell

---

[1] 321, 19; [2] 247, 273

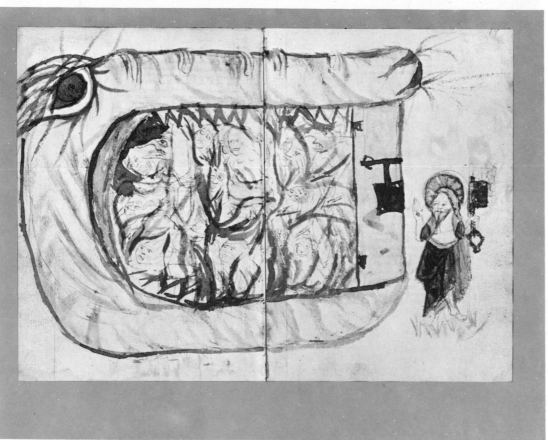

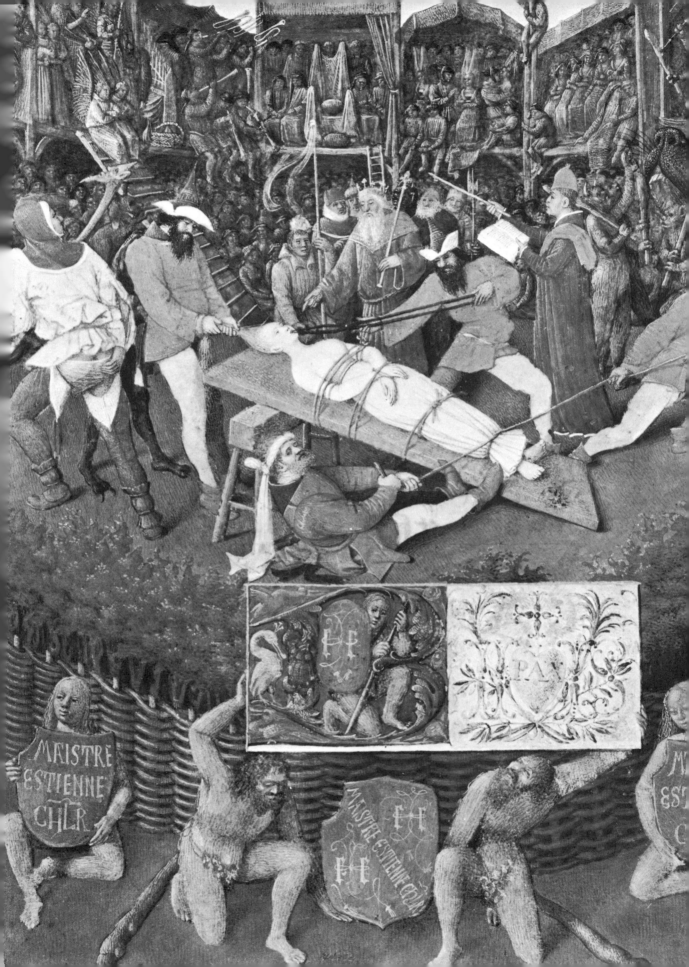

MAISTRE
ESTIENNE
CHLR

MAISTRE ESTIENNE CON

PAX

to release them. Fig. 58, from the same fifteenth-century German play as the devil with fireworks, represents a charming compromise for a cheaper production – a hell-mouth supplied with a padlock to which Christ holds the key.

The open hell-mouth can be seen on the right in the most famous of all medieval illustrations, and indeed the only one to show a mystery play in performance – Jean Fouquet's painting of the martyrdom of Saint Apollonia, dating from about 1460 (Fig. 59). The play is being presented in an area completely surrounded by scaffolds – we only see half of them, but the glimpse of another one on the extreme left shows that the circle continues. Under these scaffolds, and sitting on the ground in front of them, are spectators; the upper levels of some of the scaffolds are occupied by performers, and of others by spectators. On the left is Paradise with God and his angels, two of whom are sitting on a ramp down to the ground; beside them are the musicians; in the centre is an empty throne and the ladder by which the king has climbed down to supervise the torture; and then come two scaffolds with women in contemporary dress. It has been argued that these must be performers, thus giving the entire upper level to the cast, and certainly their costume is no firm proof that they are spectators. But the fact that they have no steps down to the acting area would seem to be conclusive, and this mingling of audience and cast was familiar in mystery plays. At Rouen in 1474 the scaffolds of the prophets were among the audience,[1] and a fifteenth-century diagram survives for the English *Castle of Perseverance* which shows the audience in a circle all round the central acting area, with five tall scaffolds for various characters placed at intervals among them.[2] The king's scaffold in the Fouquet painting is particularly interesting as it shows the curtain which could be drawn to hide the characters when they were not involved in the action – a technique deriving from the earliest Easter sepulchres and running throughout the mansion system of the mystery cycles.

The dominating figure in the centre, with his book and his conductor's baton, is both prompter and narrator. His book contains the actors' entrances and he will cue them in, but he will also introduce them to the audience. Such a figure appears in many types of primitive drama all over the world – his place is often taken in mummers' plays by Father Christmas – and he was widely known in mystery plays. As early as about 1225 the *meneur de jeu* of a French play explains a fairly elaborate set to the audience with the words:

> There is the crucifix, there the sepulchre, there a prison. Here Hell, over there Heaven and on one of the scaffolds, Pilate; on the other Caiaphas and the Jews, then Joseph of Arimathaea. A fourth place belongs to Nicodemus; a fifth is for the disciples of Christ. In the middle of the area, Gallilee and the inn at Emmaus.[3]

And in the so-called *Ludus Coventriae*, which probably comes from Lincoln, a stage direction describes a figure almost identical with Fouquet's; 'what tyme that procession is enteryd in to the place and the herowdys taken his schaffalde and annas and cayphas here (*their*) schaffaldys Also than come ther An exposytour in doctorys wede thus seyng . . .'.[4] This prompter-narrator would also be the play's director. By the sixteenth century the leading directors, such as Jean Bouchet in France, were much in demand and cities were competing for their services.[5]

The actual scene of the saint's teeth being drawn out with tongs would have been greatly to the audience's taste, and the more prolonged the better. In a Danish play of the sixteenth

---

[1]5, 29; [2]321, Fig. 1; [3]246, 50; [4]217, xvi, 2, 60; [5]247, 166–7

Fig. 59 Fouquet, a play in performance, *c.* 1460

century, *Dorotheae Komedie*, the saint is whipped, partially burnt at the stake, then stretched with tongs, after which the executioner calmly announces to her;

> I shall now hang you by your feet,
> And with the strongest rope you tie
> To twist your arms and legs a-wry,
> And stifle your mouth from all breath,
> And finally torture you to death.[1]

The stage directions of a Spanish play instruct those performing the soldiers to cut off a saint's breasts 'with the greatest possible cruelty'[2] and to achieve this same effect at Metz in 1468 a young man playing a saint had special breasts of cardboard.[3] The techniques used to make the tortures appear real were quite elaborate. The usual trick, as probably with Saint Apollonia, was a dummy substituted at the last moment. At Bourges in 1536 the prompt book said; 'let there be a naked or partly naked body for the skinning of Saint Bartholomew . . . Saint Bartholomew will be placed on a revolving table with the naked body underneath, and in covering him with a shroud let the table be secretly turned'.[4] In a fifteenth-century French play some monks were to be martyred in an oven. To convince the audience of the heat of the oven a baker puts in some dough, and when he opens the door again it comes out as bread.[5]

The unique aspect of the Fouquet picture is that it alone, among the paintings of the period, seems to reflect accurately the realities of a performance. Medieval art is full of devils prodding people into hell-mouths, but such paintings are theatrical only by analogy; the artists are using an image shared by the theatre. Nevertheless theatre historians regularly reproduce such paintings as theatrical, justifying themselves with the argument that the art conventions derive from theatrical practice – a fairly improbable proposition, since in the case of many of the images the opposite can be shown to be true and the theatre has almost invariably been a very conservative art where visual imagery is concerned. A good example of the dangers in medieval illustration is the magnificent manuscript in the Bibliothèque de l'Arsenal of Arnoul de Greban's *Mystère de la Passion*. The illuminations here are much nearer to theatrical practice than most, often using the same interior again and again in a way that suggests a theatrical mansion. But a page of the manuscript, such as Pl. IX (p. 81), shows that the artist was not thinking in terms of recording a performance: the setting has remained much the same, as have the costumes of two of the characters; but the third, for no reason to do with the text, has undergone two complete changes of costume during the scene. In the same way the brilliant red and blue draped cloths and the green chequered floor reappear so often throughout the manuscript that it is tempting to assume that they represent some sort of permanent setting for the scenes, perhaps as used by a travelling company. But, in fact, they are part of the basic convention of the medieval miniaturist and can be found in a wide variety of non-theatrical manuscripts.

The most that such illuminations, beautiful as they are, can offer in terms of theatrical reality is some hint of the feeling of the simultaneous or multiple style of staging, in which characters moved from one mansion to another, acting as they went. The illuminators of manuscripts used a similar convention, and so Figs 60–2 – three consecutive miniatures showing Jesus harrowing Hell – do give an idea of how the actor would have rescued the souls of the

---

[1]289, II, 5; [2]196, 63; [3]345, 41; [4]266, 19; [5]247, 150

Figs 60–2 Jesus harrows Hell, and leads Adam and Eve and
the patriarchs to Paradise, *c.* 1520

De Le offretoure des Rois · et purification de marie

prologhe

Fig. 63 Valenciennes, the fifth day, 1547

patriarchs from their prison mansion, after its door had fallen down, and would then have led them across the stage to another higher mansion, Paradise. But again this is only theatrical by analogy. It was not the miniaturist's intention to show us a performance. His way of showing us the event itself merely happened to coincide to some extent with the theatre's way.

The full system of simultaneous staging, by the time of the fifteenth and sixteenth centuries, was a far more elaborate affair than Fouquet's rather simple circular theatre – in which a character could speak from his individual scaffold but, if he needed to take part in any action, would have to descend to the central area. The great simultaneous stages carried many separate mansions, large enough for scenes to take place inside them. The only reliable illustration of such a system is the magnificent painting by Hubert Cailleau (Pl. X, pp. 82–3), of the stage at Valenciennes in 1547. The manuscript of the play, to which this painting is the frontispiece, describes in detail the more spectacular mansions. It points out that paradise had 'a golden ray

78

et le orrision des Jnorens ○ et la mort du Roy Herode ○

Nond sommes tont presse bref et romt | Et de qmel pays dont vous

behind God the Father which turned continually' – this was done with a wooden machine covered in gilt or gold paper, and the Seville accounts for 1497 refer to 'eighteen little gilded lamps and two hundred and thirty roses gilded and plated with leaves of tin to adorn the sky in which is God the father'[1] – but the Valenciennes manuscript is most proud, as always, of its hell. 'Opening its gullet it let out fire and smoke with devils of horrible shape, and Lucifer rising up high on a dragon shooting fire and smoke from its mouth; then one saw the boiling cauldron full of the damned, and others too being broken on wheels'.[2] All these can be seen in the painting and they would have been achieved with practical machinery rather than mere painted effects. This stage is lavish enough to have both the traditional hell-mouth and the tower beside it for the 'limbo of the patriarchs', with gates to be broken down – and the text done at Valenciennes

---

[1]306, 6;   [2]292, fol. 4 v.

was based closely on Arnoul de Greban's *Mystère,* which was also the source of the three miniatures of this scene in Figs 60–2.

Even more interesting, from the staging point of view, are the less spectacular parts of the Valenciennes setting. The picture gives an excellent idea of how such a stage can be arranged to provide all that a mystery cycle needs. The suggestion of towns and exteriors along the back gives each entrance a definite meaning. If a character comes out of Jerusalem for a scene in one of the mansions, we know that that mansion is in Jerusalem. A simple wattle fence provides for all countryside scenes and is situated where it will most often be needed, near the Nazareth entrance. The sea is used for a wide variety of purposes: the disciples fish in it, the Gadarene swine run into it, Jesus preaches to the five thousand beside it, and – in a highly apocryphal touch – the infant Judas sails across it in a tiny boat controlled magically by Satan. It contained real water and floated real boats. Finally the mansions themselves provide for all normal interior uses; a palace for those in authority, a temple for the religious, and a room for the rest. The result is a superbly adaptable permanent stage.

Mystery plays often lasted several days – the average was three, though at Bourges in 1536 the performance actually took forty days to complete – and there is evidence that at some places the mansions were changed each night to suit the next day's scenes.[1] Certainly Rouen in 1474 showed an almost nineteenth-century horror of using the same piece of scenery for two different locations. There were twenty-four different mansions, not counting those for the prophets which were among the audience, and the nine which made up Rome included not only *The Emperor's Room* but also *The Emperor's Throne* and *The Capitol,* and even *The Place where the Tribute is paid* – any one of which could have served for all the others.[2] But Valenciennes shows that a more imaginative use of the mansions was possible and probably normal, and it also raises an interesting point about the number of days of performance. We tend to think of the cycles being performed all day, from dawn to dusk, as indeed they often were. But the Valenciennes play spreads out over twenty-five days material which was elsewhere performed in three days, with the result that each day's text would last only an hour or so in performance. An hour a day for nearly a month would be an ideal way of digesting the huge narrative of the Bible, and no doubt a similar system held for the forty days at Bourges.

The Valenciennes manuscript also contains twenty-five other paintings by Cailleau showing the incidents in each day's plot, but with these he has merely set the events in a landscape – in the normal way of illustrators – instead of showing them precisely on the stage. His note in the manuscript implicitly admits this difference when he says of the frontispiece that he has 'given a portrait of the theatre or stage (*hourdement*) . . . as it was for the said play', but of the other scenes merely writes that he 'has painted the stories'.[3] But if these other scenes say little about the actual staging, they are nevertheless fascinating as showing many of the tricks or '*secrets*' which were clearly one of the greatest joys of these productions. Miracles provide the most perfect excuse for theatrical tricks, though when the Valenciennes Jesus suddenly makes himself invisible to avoid being thrown down from a high mountain, one can perhaps validly complain that the master-machinist was rather less reticent about his secrets than was Jesus himself.

The fifth of these scenes (Fig. 63) contains many such tricks and is also interesting because it includes self-portraits of Cailleau himself, who played several roles in the production –

[1] 329, 200; [2] 5, 29; [3] 292, fol. 378 v.

Pl. IX Illuminated page of French mystery play, *c.* 1520

Pl. X The stage at Valenciennes: painting by Hubert Cailleau, 1547 (*overleaf*)

Gamaliel scribe

Par me voit [...] eloquence
Et de grande suspicion
[...] vous faire question
Qui a respondre de legier
Ne [...] mais aultrement [...]
Du roy des Juifs [...]
Comme au [...] font rien [...]
Ce par nous [...] de bois commun
[...] en est nommée [...]
Dictez moy respondre [...]

Roboam ij sebe

Quant est prom homme [...] nommé
[...] Roy de [...]
A [...] est litterre [...]
[...] homme de [...] part
[...] clame Roy des Juifs
[...] a la pointe de l'espée
[...]
Et la terre dessoubz l'empereur
[...] qui en est le seigneur
[...] le monde [...]
[...] maintient en son [...]
[...] peur à [...] nulle ont
[...] lui et [...] ne nous [...]
En tant que a moy saint [...]
Et a [...] roy qui pre [...]
Herode par nom est nommé
[...] se tant est knomme
[...] son knom sur [...]
[...] en lieu dont estre venu
[...] le bon monstre vous

Jaspar

Ce n'est point [...] que nous
Mais [...] seroit il bon
Que [...] sa raison
[...] il en soit [...] chose

Zorobabel pharisien

[...] nommée en est [...]
[...] or la bonne
[...] de vos [...]
[...] bonne [...]
En force et honneur [...]
[...] noblesse [...]

Herode Roy

[...] bien que vous [...]
[...] le Dieu de [...]
[...] nommée Zorobabel
[...] le font nos [...]
[...] et les pharisiens
[...] en paine leur fault [...]

Zorobabel

[...] je ne sçay que tout bien
[...] vous amenez
[...] notables [...]
[...] ont [...] et propos
[...] Dieu [...] ou vostre mot

Le Temple

Nazareth

Hierusalem

Lieu pour
iouer sitere

vne salle

A fut iouer le Mistere de la passion nostre Sr Iesus christ. A° 1547.

Le limbe des peres

Le palais

L'enfer

La porte dorée.

Maison de euesques.

La mer.

rimement fist la mise
de Reins. Apres seoit
lempereur. Apres seoit
le Roy dinstitoine ou milieu
du sont de la sale. Apres
le Roy de sianee seoit le roy

des romains. Et auoit autant de dist
du Roy au Roy des romains come
Roy a lempereur. Et auoient lempri
le Roy et le Roy des romains chasain
pirement vn ciel de drap dor torde de
au aus armes de sianee et par dessus

among them one of the three kings, the moor, who can be seen twice in this illustration.[1] The description of the scene reads:

> On the fifth day of this mystery there were seen many other beautiful secrets, such as the star which appeared to guide the three kings, then some idols which broke and fell down of their own accord, while Mary and Joseph were going into Egypt. In falling they made a sound like a cannon shot, which they did by means of a squib or fuse which flew through the air and touched the columns on which the idols stood. Item, for the massacre of the innocents, one saw blood spurting from their bodies; then, when Herod killed himself, a devil flew away with his soul carrying it to hell.[2]

The star for the Magi was the oldest of all the machine effects in religious plays; even in the eleventh century it had been made to move along the nave to guide the travellers. And carefully planned explosions are a natural development from the gunpowder and squibs of the devils. The accounts from Amboise in 1497 mention the ingredients for precisely this effect:

> To purchase of thirteen fuses full of gunpowder and of one pound of powder for use in the said mystery, twelve of which fuses were placed in an idol and the other fuse in Paradise, and then thrown from the said place to the said idol to burn it up.[3]

Blood coming from an animal's bladder concealed under the costume, and punctured when the character is stabbed, is a favourite trick of primitive performances. And the devil at Valenciennes, flying across to Herod to collect the soul from his mouth, had at least less to cope with than in the usual procedure for the death of Judas. Lips which had kissed Christ could not have a soul such as Judas's passing through them, so it was arranged for his stomach to explode and for his guts to roll out, from which the devil would extricate his soul, again in the form of an infant.[4] Since Judas also had to hang himself before this, the part was a hazardous one and actors were known to have died playing it.[5]

But the splendours and technical achievements of Valenciennes in 1547 turned out to be the swan song of France's mystery cycles, because in the following year the new religious unrest was such that the mysteries were banned. They did linger on in the more remote parts, but never again at this level.

I have dwelt at length on the French mysteries, partly because the staging reached its most spectacular peak in France but also because only in France do any authentic illustrations survive. But almost every country in Europe had its own mystery plays. In some places the staging was similar to Valenciennes – such as London and the South of England, or Ferrara where a huge stage was built along one side of the cathedral piazza.[6] In Rome, Parma and Modena plays were done in a slightly different manner, on many separate stages and mansions placed all round a city square, and it is this type of staging which is shown in the only surviving ground-plans of medieval productions – for the play performed at Villingen[7] and for the two days of the play at Lucerne.[8] The only radically different way of producing mystery plays was the processional method, connected primarily with the north of England and with Spain, in which the mansions were placed on separate carts or pageants so that they could be wheeled round the city to give a succession of repeat performances.

York provides a highly developed example of this system. At 4.30 a.m. the Barkers wheeled

---

[1]292, fol. 378 v.; [2]292, fol. 60 r.; [3]5, 42; [4]247, 146; [5]5, 53; [6]12, VI, 646; [7]reprod. 12, VIII, 1591; [8]31, Figs 57–8

Pl. XI Charles V entertaining the Holy Roman Emperor: miniature, late fourteenth century

Fig. 64 Schembart ship pageant, *c*. 1500
Fig. 65 Austrian mountain pageant, seventeenth century

their pageant into the first place or station and there played the Fall of Lucifer. This took some ten or fifteen minutes, after which they moved on through the streets to the second station to play the same play before a new audience – while at the first station the Plasterers were now playing the second play of the cycle, the first five days of the Creation. There were at least twelve stations, and forty-eight scenes in the cycle, each with its own pageant. So, during one day, twelve separate audiences saw a complete presentation of a forty-eight-scene play which in each place lasted nearly the whole day. A few of the stations were traditionally fixed, but the corporation raised money by siting the rest in front of the houses of the highest bidders, who could then either enjoy the prestige of showing friends the play in comfort or could make a profit by letting out window space.[1]

In a stationary performance of a mystery cycle one actor would play many parts, as Cailleau did at Valenciennes, but with this processional system each playlet needed a separate cast. The system was only likely to be adopted, therefore, where the guilds had gradually taken over the plays from the clergy and had each become responsible for their own special play – in London, where the play was stationary, the performance remained in the hands of the parish clerks. As far as possible each play had some thematic link with the guild performing it. At Dublin in 1528, even after the subject matter of the plays had been heavily infiltrated by Renaissance themes, the link still held; 'the taylors acted the part of Adam and Eve; the shoemakers represented the story of Crispin and Crispinianus; the vintners acted Bacchus and his story; the

Carpenters that of Joseph and Mary; Vulcan, and what related to him, was acted by the Smiths; and the Comedy of Ceres, the goddess of Corn, by the Bakers'.[2]

The processional plays were connected with the Corpus Christi procession, an early fourteenth-century innovation in which the sacrament was paraded through the streets with suitable *tableaux vivants* in yet another attempt to make the Church's symbolism more vivid to the people. In England the scattered plays of the Church's year gradually grouped themselves round this very appropriate summer festival, and thus were able to form into complete biblical cycles. In Spain the festival led to the writing of separate plays specially for it, the famous *autos sacramentales*.[3]

There has been much argument about the exact nature of the English pageants or scenic carts, and we have no illustrations of them. The most lavish was usually Noah's ark – in Lincoln the charge for storing it was 12d as opposed to 4d for each of the other pageants.[4] It had the form of a ship, and – as we have seen – ships on wheels are part of a long processional tradition. It must at least have been similar to the ship in the Schembart processions (Fig. 64), though it was probably roofed in like the conventional ark in paintings.

Pageants less distinctive than the ark could sometimes be used for more than one play. At Chester, where the cycle lasted three days, the same pageant was used by the Painters for the play of the shepherds, by the Coopers for the trial and flagellation of Christ, and by the Skinners for the Resurrection.[5] Each of the plays required a hill or mound – large enough in one case for the shepherds to wrestle on – and two of them needed some sort of heaven above, where angels could appear and into which Christ could ascend.[6] A pageant which very nearly meets these requirements appeared in an Austrian procession in the seventeenth century, showing Jacob's dream (Fig. 65). It even has an elementary heaven, with someone apparently opening a window in the cloud. The Chester heaven was probably a larger and more definite superstructure, since Christ had to be hauled up into it, but the effect would have been similar. And the Austrian pageant suggests also another possible interpretation of the painted 'cloths round the pageant' mentioned in English records.[7] These would often have been round the superstructure, capable like the curtains of ordinary mansions of opening to reveal a scene within, but such cloths must also sometimes have hung to the ground. A ship on wheels, with tradition behind it, is one thing. A mountain on wheels might be far less acceptable.

The earliest description of the English pageants is that of Archdeacon Rogers, which refers to Chester but was written after the performances there had ended. Rogers said the 'pagiantes were a highe scafolde with two rowmes, a higher and a lower upon 4 wheeles (*6 wheels in another version of the manuscript*). In the lower they apparelled themselves, in the higher rowme they played, being all open on the tope, that all behoulders might heare and see them'.[8] This account has been much ridiculed by scholars and even branded 'notorious',[9] largely because certain pageants are known to have had roofs and because such a double-decker arrangement seems too awkward. Yet the only other early account talks of 'theatres for the several scenes, very large and high, placed upon wheels',[10] and both descriptions tally exceptionally well with the pageant carts which were used for the *autos* in Spain in the sixteenth and seventeenth centuries and which are far better documented than their English equivalents.

The two-tiered cart in Fig. 66 was built for the *autos* in Madrid in 1646, and these Spanish carts were virtually gigantic boxes of tricks. The upper storey could open in an almost infinite

---

[1]245, II, 410; [2]245, II, 365; [3]196, 81; [4]217, XXI, 3, 132; [5]314, 64; [6]137, I, 170; [7]251, 145–6; [8]272, v;
[9]137, I, 169; [10]272, iii

Fig. 66 Cart for Spanish *autos*, 1646
Fig. 67 Cart against scaffold stage, 1644

variety of ways – to reveal a scene within, or to fold out machinery for apparitions and for descents to the stage.[1] That the very top of the structure was used is shown by one *auto* of Calderon's in which a pillar of cloud rises from the cart and then an actress rises from the middle of the pillar.[2] Nearly all the spectacular effects happened in the upper storey. The lower level could open to reveal apparitions within, but in general its painted cloth curtains were used as a background to the stage, a *frons scaenae*.[3] It also contained the machinery for the effects above, but this had to be fairly compact because 'it was from the inside of these carts that all entrances and exits were made, where the actors and actresses had to dress and where they stood awaiting their cue'.[4] The stage on to which they entered was a platform, empty of scenery, where nearly all the action took place. Again Spain is able to illustrate this. The drawing in Fig. 67 shows a pageant up against such a stage in 1644, with a scaffold for the audience attached to a house facing the stage. The cart this time still has the enclosed area below, but a double tier above of a much more open design.

This flat stage in front of the pageant also had its counterpart in England, though we have no illustration of it. Rogers said that 'scafoldes and stages (were) made in the streetes, in those places where they determined to playe their pagiantes'.[5] He implies that these were fixed as in Spain, but records show that sometimes plain carts on wheels were taken round with individual pageants, to provide them at each station with their own special acting area.[6] The platform was the stage, and the pageant was the practicable setting.

Rogers was certainly wrong in implying that all the pageants were open at the top, but it is equally false to insist that none were. Some would certainly have been open on all sides, like the middle tier in Fig. 67 (and Rogers could have meant this), and others may even have been wholly open – as in the basic stage of the popular theatre of the time (Pl. XIV, p. 104), where the stage unit consisted of an open platform in front of a closed-in area for dressing in and entering from, out of the top of which an actor could also appear for scenes 'above'. The first known mansion outside the church was of precisely this type. The raised and flower-bedecked Earthly Paradise in the *Mystère d'Adam* was a framework made of silken cloths, in which Adam and Eve stood and were visible from the shoulders up.[7]

Pageants were designed as much as possible to meet the needs of individual plays, and audiences were used to extremes of simplicity or complication. The Brussels pageants, in the festival known as the Ommeganck, were the simplest open mansions on wheels,[8] while for one of Calderon's *autos* a cart was sufficiently elaborate to represent a tower of Babel which grew and grew and then suddenly fell to pieces. From a German ship to an Austrian mountain or Spanish architectural cart, the surviving illustrations of European pageants offer a wide variety of images – but the type of variety, I suspect, with which the citizens of Chester or York would have been perfectly familiar.

Pageantry

From the early fourteenth century there had been developing, side by side with the religious performances, a new strand of secular theatre in the entertainments which surrounded kings. At times they were even more ambitious in their effects than the mystery plays, and they may well have influenced the staging of the mysteries. The earliest illustration that we have of a performance at court (Pl. XI, p. 84) is almost a century earlier than the equivalent painting, by Fouquet, of a religious performance. It shows the spectacle arranged by Charles V of France at the banquet which he gave for the Holy Roman Emperor and his son, and the painting is an almost exactly contemporary record. The manuscript containing it dates from the fourteenth century, and the banquet took place in 1378.

The subject of the performance was the capture of Jerusalem by Godfrey de Bouillon in 1099. The end of the hall had been curtained off as a dressing-room, and from this there appeared a great ship containing twelve crusaders. The ship glided along the great hall – it was moved by men concealed within it – and stopped at one end of the high table. There then appeared a castle representing Jerusalem, also moved by men inside, which took up its position at the other end of the table. The Turks uttered some heathen chants from the battlements, the crusaders stormed the bastions with ladders – apparently also amusing the guests greatly by the way they fell off the ladders – and finally conquered the castle and threw down the Turks. In the miniature the three monarchs are behind the table with three bishops: Peter the Hermit is in the ship praying; Godfrey de Bouillon and the Count of Auvergne are half way up the ladders; at the foot of the ladders, awaiting their opportunity for heroism, are the King of England (an unhistorical touch) and the Comte de Flandre; and one actor has duly fallen off. After the show both the ship and Jerusalem slid away as smoothly as they had come.[9]

In its staging this shares with the mysteries the system of separate scenic units, the mansions of ship and castle, and in theme it looks forward to a long tradition of history plays. Here the

---

[1]196, 477; [2]196, 457; [3]196, 95–6; [4]196, 477; [5]272, vi; [6]137, I, 171; [7]245, II, 80; [8]reprod. 126, 19; [9]253, II, 236 ff.

Fig. 68 Allegorical float, Stuttgart, 1616

event was three centuries in the past, but soon history plays would become more topical and political. Long before Shakespeare had shown the heroic Talbot through English eyes, the French had been able to enjoy such celebrations as *The Discomfiture of Talbot at Bordelais* or *The jealous and perfidious English leopard subdued by the French*.[1]

Performances like this one for Charles V became common within the courts as private masques – with stimulating variations, such as the knights storming a castle full of ladies who pelted them with sweets and flowers[2] – but the wider theatrical influence of royal pageantry came from public processions, in which the various carts and floats used theatrical symbolism even more imaginatively than the religious pageants. Since the cloth around them is painted with waves and fishes, it is easy to accept that the trombonists in Fig. 68 are in the sea – in the same way a Spanish Saint Christopher put on a costume of waves and fishes before walking across the dry ground with Christ on his back[3] – and the shrouded little figure called *Dormiens Anima Cupidinis* (The Sleeping Spirit of Love) has considerable dramatic potential and demonstrates how the morality plays of the sixteenth century, composed of just such allegorical abstractions, were far from being as dry as they may sound.

More exclusively connected with royal pageantry were the street theatres and *tableaux vivants* which, from the early fourteenth century in France and a little later in England and the Low Countries, became a familiar feature of a king's entry into a city. A great variety of allegorical shows would be placed along the route the procession was to take, sometimes even

Fig. 69 Entry into Brussels, 1596

defining the route through an open area – as for the entry of the Archduke Albert into Brussels in 1596 (Fig. 69). The procession here has passed under the trumpeters on the city gates in the top left corner, has then gone under a tower with a show above it, past a two-tiered theatre, under two triumphal arches, then past a more open theatre and a ship and an obelisk. To the archduke these superb temporary structures were the show. To the audience, of whom we see a glimpse bottom left, the real show was the archduke's procession. Sometimes the audience could be part of the show too. For a Paris entry of 1530 the city fathers ordered that there should be in all the windows of the street 'some beautiful young women and girls as tapestry'.[4]

The splendour of the individual street theatres can be seen in one for the entry of the French king's brother, Francis, into Antwerp in 1582 (Pl. XII, p. 101). The event was to celebrate Antwerp's freedom from the Spanish and her new allegiance to France. Appropriately, the left hand scene shows Samuel tearing a piece off Saul's clothing to signify that the kingdom shall be taken from his family because of his disobedience; the central scene shows the young David being chosen as his successor; and, in case Francis should be in any doubt as to what was expected of him, on the right he could see David killing Goliath and some verses reminding him that he must 'protect his own from the inhuman tyrant'. Underneath, in something similar to a Shakespearian inner stage, Discord is in prison, tormented by Furies and Serpents.[5]

---

[1]5, 15–18; [2]44, 77; [3]196, 70–1; [4]5, 88; [5]275, 27–8

Fig. 70 Varied stages at Avignon, 1600

Fig. 71 Water pageant, Florence, 1608
Fig. 72 Entertaining Marie de' Medici, Amsterdam, 1638

Political hints to the ruler were an essential part of these *tableaux*. When Henry VII visited Bristol in 1486 the legendary founder of the city, King Bremius, stepped forward to tell him of the dire state of the ship-building industry and the next day Henry took steps to save it.[1]

During the procession from his ship to the centre of Antwerp Francis passed seven magnificent floats, four triumphal arches and eight such theatres – into the last of which he himself climbed as the central figure, confronted by a huge crowd including a line of bound criminals beseeching mercy, which they predictably received.[2]

These street theatres represent the first theatrical use of the proscenium arch – though the device itself was borrowed from painting, from sculpture, from tombs and even from frontispieces to books – and they also in some cases prefigure the two-tiered façade of the public theatres in Shakespeare's time. But the great variety of shape in the street theatres should be a warning to those who try to insist on one exclusive style of staging in the Shakespearean theatre. In 1600 – perhaps appropriately the year of *Much Ado about Nothing* and *As You Like It* – Avignon received Marie de' Medici with seven street theatres (Fig. 70), each with a short play performed on it. Nos 1 and 3 approach the 'normal' Shakespearean stage, a three-sided promontory; these are admittedly outnumbered by 'arena' or 'in-the-round' stages, nos 2, 5 and 6; but no. 7 is a tower, with the actors appearing out of the top, and the reason – says the text – is that by then they could think of no other new shapes. Clearly the actors of the time were open-minded.[3]

Another favourite area for royal pageantry was the water, and the whole aquatic paraphernalia of sea monsters and Neptune, scallop shells and ships, was to become very popular in

[1]137, I, 71–2; [2]275, 38; [3]337, 187 ff.

Fig. 73 Tournament theatre, Rome, 1565
Fig. 74 A court dance, 1612

seventeenth-century Italian theatre. Fig. 71 shows part of the spectacle on the Arno in 1608 for the wedding of Cosimo de' Medici. Two years later the great Burbage himself was afloat on the Thames on a dolphin, speaking a poem of welcome to Henry, Prince of Wales.[1] These sea-creatures were propelled by people hidden uncomfortably inside; the float, for example, which carried the king and queen on the Seine in 1581 was drawn along by 'sea horses made of several boats in which oarsmen were hidden'.[2]

When Marie de' Medici visited Amsterdam in 1638, water pageantry and theatre were directly combined (Fig. 72). She arrived on the Amstel in the burgomaster's boat and was greeted by Neptune in his cockle shell and by a second craft containing 'a beautiful virgin representing Amsterdam' and Mercury, who was appearing rather appropriately in Amsterdam as 'the patron and protector of merchants'.[3] The queen then saw two *tableaux vivants* in the theatre, which was itself on a floating island constructed for the occasion. One of the *tableaux* was about her own great family and the other about Amsterdam, after which she sailed round to the other side of the island where there was another proscenium with five more *tableaux* on the history of France.

An aspect of pageantry which had great influence on the shape of later theatres was the tournament. Even in their simplest form the temporary stands put up for spectators contain the germ of the wooden theatres of Elizabethan times,[4] and the great tournament arena of 1565 which lay between St Peter's and the Castel Sant' Angelo in Rome (Fig. 73) heralded even more sophisticated developments. The semicircular arrangement of seats at the far end is very close to the auditorium of Palladio's Teatro Olimpico, which was not begun till fifteen years later; and the boxes in the architectural façades to either side are repeated in many Italian tournament theatres over the next hundred years[5] and lead towards the basic design of Europe's seventeenth- and eighteenth-century auditoria.

One final type of entertainment is worth mentioning. Ever since the Middle Ages dancing had been an important part of courtly life, and a public dance by the king and queen combined the importance of ritual with the pleasures of performance. Fig. 74 shows the Holy Roman Emperor Matthias I and his wife dancing after his coronation in 1612. They are merely taking the first dance together, and others will follow them; but the degree to which this is essentially a performance can be judged by the tiers of seats built for spectators. In many seventeenth-century courts, and particularly at those of Louis XIII and XIV, this form of royal exhibitionism was to play an important part in the development of ballet.

[1]244, I, 134; [2]43, I, 236; [3]230, 67 ff.; [4]e.g. 137, I, Pls. VIII–IX; [5]e.g. 12, II, Tav. CXVII

5

THE RENAISSANCE

Classicism

Beyond any doubt the peak of European theatre was the century from 1575 to 1675. This period saw a double flowering in England, first of Shakespeare and his contemporaries and then of the Restoration dramatists; in Spain there were the plays of Lope de Vega and of Calderon; in France the development of ballet at the court and then the perfection of classical tragedy and comedy with Corneille, Molière and Racine; in Italy the invention of opera and of the Italian changeable scenery within a proscenium, which was to be Europe's standard stage setting for over two centuries; and in all these countries this period saw the first development of permanent public theatres.

These extraordinarily varied seventeenth-century achievements were entirely national in character but they shared a European heritage, not only in the two oldest strains of mystery plays and public pageantry, but also in the more recent sixteenth-century influences – the development of the new classicism, which was closely linked with the growing custom of performing plays in schools, and the sudden return to prominence of a thriving popular theatre. Before moving on to each of the higher national developments, I shall deal with these remaining common sources – although, since Italy led the Renaissance, it is true that the real roots are there.

The fifteenth century saw a growing interest in Terence, reaching almost the status of a cult. His work had been known throughout the Middle Ages – a tenth-century nun, Hroswitha, preferring his style to his themes, had even written Christian versions of the six plays – but now his influence suddenly spread into many new fields. The manuscripts became collectors' items; the plays were read aloud, discussed and set for study; by the early sixteenth century they were widely performed in schools; Erasmus pronounced that 'no one has ever become a good Latinist without Terence';[1] Melancthon added that 'Terence is an important example of bourgeois morality';[2] and by 1600 his plays had been printed in over five hundred editions.[3] Editions of Plautus and of Vitruvius added fuel to this new passion for the classical theatre, but the extent to which the influence was exclusively Roman can be seen in the late sixteenth-century theorist Leone di Somi: he wrote with complete accuracy that Terence and Plautus were Rome's best playwrights and Livius Andronicus her earliest, but solemnly announced that Greek theatre began with 'Aristophanes, Menander, and possibly the still more ancient Eupolis'.[4]

Performance of the plays was a natural development from the study and recital of them, and the first recorded production is of Terence's *Andria* by the students of the school of Vespucci in Florence in 1476.[5] At much the same time there were performances at the academy founded

---

Sources (*see* p. 317)   [1]212, V, 1, 33;   [2]20, 160;   [3]283, 251;   [4]31, 241;   [5]218, IV, 2, 103;   [6]245, 10;   [7]212, III, 3, 247;   [8]12, V, Tav. 14;   [9]159, 284 ff.;   [10]32, 157

in Rome by Pomponius Laetus, a professor of Latin who cultivated his garden according to the precepts of Varro and Columella[6] and lectured in toga and *cothurni*.[7] By the turn of the century such performances were fairly common in Italy, and during the sixteenth century they spread throughout Europe.

The many illustrations in the volumes of Terence and Plautus provide a rich but treacherous source for theatre historians. Two of the earliest and best known are almost identical frontispieces to late fifteenth-century manuscripts in Paris – one (Fig. 75) in the Bibliothèque Nationale, the other in the Bibliothèque de l'Arsenal.[8] These have often been used as evidence for contemporary productions of Terence, but in fact they are purely attempts to reconstruct a performance in ancient Rome. A drawing by Francesco di Giorgio of exactly the same period (Fig. 76) shows that Roman theatres were confused with the full circle of the circus amphitheatre. And the presence in the little central mansion of Calliopius – himself much like a medieval 'presenter' with his book – has been shown to derive from a series of misunderstandings about Roman theatre in various medieval commentaries on Terence.[9] The real interest of the painting is an accidental one. The *gesticulatores*, though intended as Roman actors, instead give an interesting glimpse of medieval buffoons,[10] and their masks and antics look forward to those of the Commedia dell'Arte.

Of the many early printed editions with woodcuts, the one which seems most nearly to illustrate actual contemporary staging is the magnificent Terence printed by Trechsel at Lyons

Fig. 75 Frontispiece to Terence MS, fifteenth century (detail)

Fig. 76 Francesco di Giorgio, Roman theatre, *c*. 1490

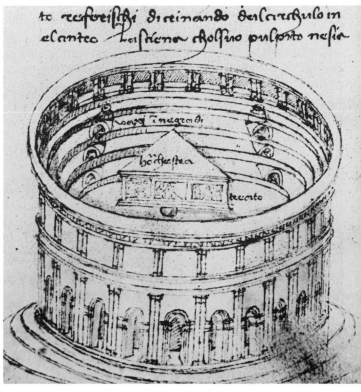

Fig. 77 Woodcut from Terence, 1493
Fig. 78 Woodcut from Plautus, 1518

in 1493 (Fig. 77). Here each of the six plays has its own different setting, composed of various arrangements of curtained doorways, each of the doorways being identified with the house of a certain character – thus 'Do. Lachis' in Fig. 77 stands for 'Domus Lachis', the house of Laches. Each setting looks fairly workable; and since the editor, Jodocus Badius, had just returned from Italy and personally supervised the making of the woodcuts, it has been suggested that these may show actual stages that he had seen.[1] But the fullest and most recent discussion of the woodcuts concludes convincingly that their obvious carefulness is concerned less with theatrical reality than with good book illustration,[2] combined presumably with a scholarly attempt at classical reconstruction – Vitruvius had talked of the *frons scaenae* having various doors in it which became identified with separate houses.[3]

Certainly what we know of Renaissance productions does not tally with these neat little structural stages. Pomponius Laetus produced plays in front of some sort of painted façade, and a Ferrara performance of 1486 attempted a fascinating combination of medieval and classical: five mansions, each containing a door and a window above, were placed side by side in a deliberate attempt to recreate the *frons scaenae* of Vitruvius, whose work had first been printed that very same year.[4] Since the plays of Plautus are full of characters coming from or returning to their *domus* – a name also used for the mansions in mystery plays – it seems natural that this most familiar scenic unit should find a place in recreating the classical stage. It can perhaps be seen in one of the woodcuts in a 1518 edition of Plautus (Fig. 78), where the little house is clearly a temporary structure and is probably in front of a painted arcade. But even if this does show the authentic earlier style, as used at Ferrara and elsewhere, it should be added that the 1493 woodcuts were often imitated in other editions and their influence may well have created a later style of production. When Plautus's *Poenulus* was performed in Rome in 1513 there was a 'scene-front, divided into five compartments by means of four columns . . . in each compartment is a doorway . . . at the doors of the scenes were placed curtains of gold cloth'.[5] And school performances at Leipzig in 1530 seem to have used a stage inspired by these same woodcuts.[6]

Quite early in the sixteenth century the Renaissance painters' interest in perspective drove off the stage any more antiquarian concern with the precise *frons scaenae* of Vitruvius. The

---

[1]212, III, 3, 258;   [2]20, 1–21;   [3]108, 234 ff.;   [4]218, IV, 2, 105–8;   [5]quoted 31, 82;   [6]159, 354

ornationis. q̃ cū aut fabulaꝝ mutationes sunt future seu deorũ aduentus cū tonitribus repentinis uersent mutentꝗ spetiē orna tionis in frontes. Secũdum ea loca uersuræ sunt procurrétes q̃ affi ciũt una a foro altera a peregre aditus in scœna.

De Tribus Scœnaꝝ Generibus.

Enera autem sunt scœnaꝝ tria unũ quod dicit tragicum Alterũ comicũ · Tertiũ satyricũ. Hoꝝ autem ornatus inter se dissimiles sũt. dispariꝗ rōne. q̃ tragicæ deformant colũnis & fastigiis signis reliquisꝗ regalibus rebus. Comicæ autē ædifitioꝝ priuatoꝝ & menianoꝝ habent spetiē pfectusꝗ fenestris dispositos imitatiōe cōium ædifitioꝝ rōnibus. Satiricæ uero ornā tur arbobus spelũcis mōtibus reliquisꝗ agrestibus rebus in topi celi spēm deformati. In grecoꝝ theatris nō omnia iisdem rōnibus sunt facienda. q̃ primũ in ima circinatione ut in latino trigonoꝝ ꝗtuor in eo quadratoꝝ triũ anguli circinationis lineā tangunt & cuius quadrati latus est pximũ scœnæ prehendit curuaturam præ circinatiōis ea regione designat finitio pscenii & ab ea regione ad

Fig. 79 Marginal drawings in Vitruvius, *c.* 1545
Fig. 80 Peruzzi, sketch for stage setting, *c.* 1530 (*below left*)
Fig. 81 Serlio's scene for comedy, 1545

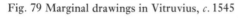

first record of a perspective setting is at Ferrara in 1508.[1] This may only have been a perspective backcloth but during the following years, and particularly at Urbino in 1513 and Rome in 1514, the perspective became more and more three-dimensional until it had developed – by the time of Peruzzi's set for the *Bacchides* in 1531 – into two complete rows of very elaborate and steadily diminishing painted houses. The simple house at one side in Fig. 78 had turned out to be the ancestor of a whole glittering street. All that remained of the interest in Vitruvius, apart from the use of his *periaktoi* as a method of changing scenery, was his famous classification of the three types of scenes – the comic, the tragic and the satyric. Fig. 79 shows the comic and the tragic, each by now a street of appropriate houses, as drawn by Battista da Sangallo beside the relevant passage in his copy of Vitruvius.

Although the Ferrara setting of 1508 is attributed to Pellegrino da Udine, the first great artist to design perspective scenery was Baldassare Peruzzi, who was connected with shows in Rome between 1513 and 1536. His drawing in Fig. 80 shows a typical series of houses designed to make one side of a perspective street. Sometimes in comedy, though never in tragedy, characters would talk through the window of a house with people on the stage,[2] but it is more probable that Peruzzi's butcher's boy is a figure painted on the house; partly because his foot stops so precisely at the bottom, and the line across suggests that this is where the painted backcloth was to come, continuing in two dimensions the effect of the three-dimensional houses further downstage; but also because Sebastiano Serlio, a friend of Peruzzi's, included this butcher's shop in his woodcut of the scene for comedy (Fig. 81) but left out the butcher's boy; and Serlio explained in his text that he disliked the custom of painting people in doorways 'because they cannot move and yet they represent living creatures; but a person who is asleep is acceptable; or some sleeping dog or other animal, for then they have no need to move'.[3]

Serlio was the first published theorist of the Renaissance theatre. His six chapters on how to build stages and scenery appeared first in Paris in 1545 under the title *Le second livre de la perspective*, and it was his woodcuts of the three Vitruvian scenes which first spread wide the image of Italian perspective scenery – together with an explanation of how the houses were to be made of painted linen stretched over frames, with cut-out pieces of wood added for cornices, balconies or chimneys, and of how lights could be made to sparkle in the windows or on the roofs.[4] Serlio's woodcuts are elaborate and empty of performers but they suggest well the style of the new stage, although it was not in fact by this time all that new. As early as 1513 Urbino had seen a glittering set by Girolamo Genga, which took four months to build and had houses made of stucco relief, glowing with jewel-like lights and with alabaster panes in the windows.[5]

Serlio's painted canvas is a more practical version of this, but the average production would have been simpler still as the style began to spread and to find less lavish patrons. The Venice Terence of 1553 (Fig. 82) gives perhaps the most convincing picture of a typical sixteenth-century perspective setting, as well as showing performers within it. As with Serlio, the perspective here reaches an abrupt end in a transverse building, but by the middle of the century this technique too was already becoming old-fashioned. The new style, looking forward to the Italian scenery of the early seventeenth century, encouraged the eye to wander away into the distance, often up diverging streets – as in Buontalenti's Florentine setting in the 1580s (Fig. 122). But then Serlio was seventy when his book was published, so it is hardly surprising that his style was a little conservative.

---

[1]69, 16;   [2]218, IV, 2, 99;   [3]317, II, fol. 29 r.;   [4]317, II, fol. 27 r.;   [5]218, IV, 2, 116–8

Pl. XII Street theatre in Antwerp: hand-coloured print, 1582

Pl. XIII Scene from the Commedia dell' Arte: oil painting, *c*. 1580 (*overleaf*)

VET, ET DISC

FO

Abstulit vt regni Dominus
moderamina Sauli etc

Fig. 82 Woodcut from Terence, 1553
Fig. 83 Teatro Olimpico, the auditorium

Although real interest in the Vitruvian *frons scaenae* had by now vanished there was one magnificent exception – the Teatro Olimpico, which was designed by Palladio for the Accademia Olimpica in Vicenza and is Europe's oldest surviving theatre. Palladio's intention, as one of the members of the first night audience in 1585 explained, was 'to construct a theatre according to the ancient use of the Greeks and Romans'.[1] And with its ceiling of sky and clouds, and the unbroken line joining the top of the auditorium with the top of the elaborate architectural *frons scaenae*, the interior does look remarkably like an open air Roman theatre (Fig. 83). It has even been described as 'more Vitruvian than Vitruvius'.[2]

The only non-Roman aspect of it is the perspective streets which recede behind each of the openings in the façade: the central one can be clearly seen in the oldest illustration of the theatre (Fig. 84), a 1620 etching by Ottavio Orefici of which only one copy survives, at Drottningholm. It is thought that Palladio intended to have doors or curtains in his arches, but he died in 1581, a year after the building was started, and Vincenzo Scamozzi completed the work and added the streets. These streets are extremely steep, with very rapid shortening of the houses along them, and this makes them useless for acting in – an actor walking the few steps from the far end to the front would start level with the roof tops and then rapidly shrink to the height of a door. But the streets did have the democratic advantage of allowing each spectator in the semicircular auditorium a good view up at least one of them – an important matter in an academy where each member was equal. In most theatres of the time perspective effects were easier to arrange since only one seat, the prince's, had to be seriously catered for.

The houses in Scamozzi's streets are nearer to sculpture than to paintings – the same first-nighter wrote that they were 'of solid wood so that they may last for ever' – and they therefore look all the way back to Genga's stucco houses at Urbino in 1513. They sum up in permanent form the Italian perspective street of the sixteenth century, just as Palladio's auditorium and

[1] 44, 169; [2] 20, 60;

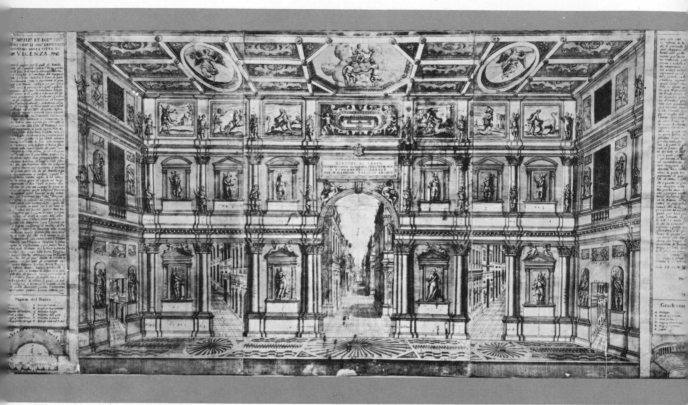

Fig. 84 Teatro Olimpico, etching, 1620

frons scaenae finally complete the quest to recreate the Roman theatre. But Scamozzi was turning Serlio's painted houses into stucco and relief again at precisely the period when other Italian artists were doing the very opposite – were beginning to flatten them more and more, and so to move towards the flat wings and purely painted marvels of seventeenth-century stage illusion. The Teatro Olimpico was still-born and is like a beautiful museum at the end of a *cul-de-sac*, but it serves as a most excellent monument to Classicism in the sixteenth-century theatre.

School plays

The Italian perspective scenery travelled through Europe during the sixteenth century – it was seen, for example, at Lyons in 1548,[1] at Valladolid in Spain in the same year,[2] and possibly at Christ Church in Oxford in 1566[3] – but on all such occasions it was no more than a fascinating foreign oddity. Only in the next century did it begin to conquer European theatre. Meanwhile the school performances of Terence and Plautus, which also began exclusively in Italy, were proving more immediately widespread in their influence. But there was also one other important line of school drama during the Renaissance which thrived largely outside Italy, and in particular in Germany – the performance by students of moral and religious plays.

In origin this was older than the performances of Terence – even in the twelfth century the

106

pupils at an English choir school were performing a *Play of Saint Catherine*[4] – but the most active period came with the ideological struggles of the Reformation and Counter-Reformation in the sixteenth century. Luther himself approved of plays in schools as a good way of learning both Latin and morality at the same time.[5] The Protestants were the first in the field, and the early decades of the century saw many anti-papist plays; but by 1550 the Jesuits were leading a theatrical counter-attack in Italy, France and Germany. For the next two centuries Jesuit schools were to make an important contribution to the history of the theatre.

The plays were acted frequently in market places or town squares – unlike the producers of Terence, these committed schoolmasters were determined to reach and thereby to improve a large public. The style of production varied from the simple to the very elaborate, and the best surviving illustrations show both extremes.

One of these can be seen in Johann Rasser's *Christlich Spil von Kinderzucht*, which was first performed at Ensisheim in 1573 and was printed the following year at Strasbourg with forty-four woodcuts of scenes from the play. The woodcuts are not entirely consistent, but they show a stage consisting of a simple platform with curtains behind it – arranged probably in a straight line along the back with short extensions projecting forward at the two ends. The audience seems to have stood to the front and half way along the two sides. Fig. 85 shows the Herald, dressed very much in the style of the Renaissance, introducing the play. Fig. 86, which by contrast seems entirely medieval, depicts the end of the play when the Devil is taking away the Jew Ulman, who has corrupted one of the leading characters. The play's theme is moralistic, about the different things that happen to an industrious and to an idle schoolboy, and its prologue reveals that it was written for Catholic children – but its dominant religious attitude is anti-Semitic. A study of the play's text shows that the curtains along the back of the stage in Fig. 86 were used as separate houses for different characters, following therefore the tradition of the Terence woodcuts.[6]

The much more elaborate type of school production survives in the stage design for Broelman's play, *Laurentius*, performed by Catholic students in Cologne in 1581. This design (Fig. 87) shows Rome constructed in a fascinating combination of medieval and Renaissance houses. Cloths now hang on three sides and within them there are Terentian arches and doorways, with curtains to close them and with the householder's name above – such as *Domus Hippoliti*. But standing free of these cloths can be seen the familiar units of the mystery plays – the thrones, the gaol with its open-work gate so that the prisoner can be seen inside, and the obelisk which in true mystery style will fall to pieces when Saint Laurentius curses the pagan gods. The two trees are real ones which were already in the courtyard when the stage on its barrels was put up around them.[7]

In most places the school drama died away in the seventeenth century with the ever increasing success of the professional players, but one interesting survival still continues today. In 1560 Queen Elizabeth decreed that every Christmas the scholars of Westminster should perform a Latin play 'that the young may spend Christmas with greater benefit and become better acquainted with proper action and pronunciation'. With the one exception of 1846, a Latin play has been performed every year since then – surely the European theatre's longest unbroken tradition. The repertoire has been almost exclusively Terence and Plautus. At first the stage was always set up in the dining hall, a favourite site for the English school and university

---

[1]44, 202; [2]306, 21; [3]123, 90; [4]293, 1; [5]22, II, 303; [6]169, 110–148; [7]20, 194

Fig. 85 Rasser's school play, 1573
Fig. 86 The same
Fig. 87 School play with multiple setting, 1581

Fig. 88 Westminster school play, 1839

performances, but from 1730 until recently the plays have been in the 'new dormitory'.[1] A watercolour of 1839 shows them there (Fig. 88). The setting was still a modified version of the sixteenth-century Italian perspective street, and the front pieces on each side – three-dimensional, with doors in them, and of a type to please Serlio himself – were referred to in the school as 'houses'. Moreover these two front houses, sixteenth-century in style though replaced at various times since, still survive.[2]

Popular theatre

In the Middle Ages the minstrels had been familiar figures at all levels of the community. They were an important part of great court functions – the expenses for Prince Edward's Whitsuntide feast at London in 1306 show payments to nearly two hundred named minstrels, including one with the delightful pseudonym *Pearl in the Egg*[3] – and they travelled the countryside visiting

[1]293, 85–99;   [2]217, III, 3, p. 46 & Fig. 6;   [3]245, II, 234–8

the manors, where it was the custom that they should be well received and allowed to sing for their supper. They also naturally stopped in market places on the way, interrupting their performances just before the climax to take a collection.[1] Their repertoire consisted originally of songs, jokes and stories, acrobatics and rope-dancing, but by the fifteenth century they were also performing plays and interludes.[2] Their performances were to lead to the many familiar booth stages of the wandering players in the sixteenth and seventeenth centuries, but we get a glimpse of professional actors at a much more primitive level in an engraving after Brueghel (Fig. 89) which shows players in the countryside, wearing the most elementary costumes supplemented by kitchen utensils, and performing a play about the wedding of Mopsus and Nisa which was probably called *The Dirty Bride*. Any doubt that these are actors is removed by the collecting box held by the boy on the left, which is identical with the ones being used in the Brueghel woodcut of Orson and Valentine in Fig. 9.

Other favourite performers of the late Middle Ages were the fools – though usually they were amateur whereas the minstrels were professional. They probably originated in the Church's Feast of Fools at Christmas, when for a brief season of licence priests were allowed to put on masks and indulge in every sort of foolery; but by the fourteenth century the fools were laymen and were wearing the famous fool's costume of a hood with asses' ears, in which they would dance around at carnival time satirising authority. Their costume is best known from the many editions of Sebastian Brant's *Ship of Fools*, first published in 1494. The book is an allegory about a shipload of fools, and the woodcuts have nothing to do with actual performances. However, one of them (Fig. 90) does show the fools in a situation perhaps a little nearer to the reality of their mocking antics in the streets. Their asses' ears had a direct Roman ancestry. Martial said that there was in Rome a market where house fools could be bought and that they had a 'pointed head and long ears that moved like those of asses'.[3]

In many places these fooleries were performed by specially organised societies, called *sociétés joyeuses*. The most famous of these, the Infanterie Dijonnoise, numbered rich burghers and even noblemen among its members, and sometimes let loose as many as two hundred fools in the streets of Dijon during carnival. At other times of the year they were also allowed to perform satirical plays on topical events in the city's life, such as 'larcenies, murders, unusual marriages, sexual seductions, etc.'.[4] The society had been founded in the fifteenth century, but was abolished in 1630 because of the 'disorders and debaucheries which it has produced'.[5] Their banner (Fig. 91) neatly sums up their mood. It seems highly unlikely that any two Dijon burghers, or indeed anyone else, would be capable of this acrobatic *double entendre*. But if they ever had managed it, it would undoubtedly have delighted both themselves and their audience.

The same happy scurrility is a regular feature of the Commedia dell'Arte (Fig. 92), which emerged in Italy in the sixteenth century and rapidly achieved enormous success throughout Europe. The earliest collection of illustrations of it, from which Fig. 92 comes, was in fact made in France. Fossard, a musician at the court of Louis XIV, gathered together various late sixteenth-century prints and his collection, known as the *Recueil Fossard*, is now in the theatre museum at Drottningholm.

The Commedia dell'Arte, with its special technique of improvising within the framework of a simple plot, quickly became popular in the courts of Europe as well as in the villages, and this has often led writers to argue that either the courts must have been depraved or the

---

[1]245, I, 44; [2]245, II, 186; [3]32, 108; [4]335, 65; [5]335, iv

Fig. 89 Early professionals, engraving after Brueghel, sixteenth century

Fig. 90 Sebastian Brant's fools, edition of 1506 (*below right*)

Fig. 91 Fool's banner, sixteenth century

Pantalon. Harlequin. Francisquina.

Ie suis des-honnoré, ce ruffien pipereau,
M'ayāt disné par cœur, encores me tourmēte,
Et fait de ma maison vn clapier & bordeau,
Auec ceste putain que i'ay prise à seruante.

Leuer le cotillon, & la chemise aussi,
Sa Dame renuerser comme l'amour l'apreuue,
Et couler sur la motte apres sa main ainsi,
Frācisquine mon cœur, en ce point con se treuue.

Ma vie & mon honneur entre vos mains ie mets,
Harlequin mon amy, prenez la iouyssance, v.
Que tant vous desirez, mais faictes que iamais,
Hōme aucū quel qui soit, n'en aye cōgnoissance.

Fig. 92 The Commedia dell'Arte, sixteenth century
Fig. 93 David Vinckeboons, booth stage, 1608

performances must have been different for the aristocratic audience. But certainly court and vulgarity were not incompatible. Somi, in the late sixteenth century, described a great banquet with many masques where the greatest success was won by two buffoons 'who had been called in specially for this purpose' and who brought in as props 'certain vile, lecherous or vicious things' with which 'they aroused great laughter by the variety of their witty remarks'.[1] Sexual innuendo is a very basic ingredient of theatre, and not only in our own tradition deriving from Greece and Rome. For example, in a surprising echo of the Greek comedians, the Cherokee Indians in their Booger dance 'distort their figures by stuffing abdomen, buttocks or shins'; 'some carry an imitation phallus of gourd neck or wrapped cloth'; and the traditional names of the dancers include Black Buttocks, Big Testicles, Sooty Anus and Rusty Anus.[2] When the English Puritans closed the theatres in 1642, partly because of their disgust with this element of theatre, they instead found themselves left with this alone. One of the most popular moments in the short 'drolls', which was all the actors were allowed to perform during the Common-wealth, was when Robert Cox came on as the Simpleton carrying a somewhat suggestive long French loaf. It can be seen in Fig. 98, and a member of the audience recorded that he had 'frequently known several of the Female Spectators and Auditors to long for some of it'.[3]

But even more typical than the bawdiness of the Commedia dell'Arte's content was the essential theatricality or playfulness of its style. The famous improvisation could be physical as well as verbal. One of the beautiful sixteenth-century oil paintings of the Commedia dell'Arte at Drottningholm (Pl. XIII, pp. 102–3) shows old Pantalone riding on a hastily improvised horse in his eternally frustrated courtship of the lady – seen here looking out of the side house which derived from the very beginnings of the Renaissance perspective stages and remained a perma-nent feature of the Commedia dell'Arte. In Fig. 92 it was Pantalone who was looking out of the house, as Arlecchino once again deceives him. Both in style and in content these two scenes suggest the very essence of popular theatre.

The typical booth theatre of the wandering players of northern Europe was slightly different from the setting preferred by the Commedia dell'Arte. One of the best pictures of it, among the many that survive, is Pieter Brueghel the Younger's painting in the Fitzwilliam Museum, *The Village Fair* (Pl. XIV, p. 104). This, as I suggested earlier, relates fairly closely to descriptions of northern pageant carts in mystery plays – consisting of an open platform in front of a room formed by hanging cloths, inside which the prompter can be seen standing with his book, props such as the stool can be kept and organised, and actors can dress before entering on to the platform or climbing up the ladder to appear out of the top for an elementary scene 'above'. At the moment the ladder in Brueghel's painting is badly placed for such a scene, but it can be shifted forward when needed; and a drawing by the elder Brueghel does show an actor per-forming out of the top of the booth, this time on a specially constructed little platform.[4] The subject matter of the scene on the stage in Pl. XIV, with flirtation at the supper table and a jealous face watching from the baker's basket, is in very much the same vein as the Commedia dell'Arte.

Playing so close to a village audience in the open air brought its own problems, which were no doubt enjoyed as part of the general entertainment. A painting by David Vinckeboons at Braunschweig includes a booth stage set up in front of a house (Fig. 93) where, in spite of special barriers put up against them, spectators are invading the stage and having to be driven

---

[1] 31, 262; [2] 324, 29; [3] 279, preface; [4] 43, II, Pl. XIII

Fig. 94 Travelling players visit a manor, 1610

off. Even in the much more sophisticated London playhouses this could at times present difficulties. A butcher, watching *Troilus and Cressida*, once felt such sympathy for Hector when he was about to be murdered that he leapt up on to the stage and drove off the terrified extras who were playing the Myrmidons; he then 'strooke moreover such an especial acquaintance with Hector, that for a long time Hector could not obtaine leave of him to be kill'd, that the play might go on'.[1]

As we shall see later, the Commedia dell'Arte and the travelling popular theatres had a healthy existence through the seventeenth and eighteenth centuries, and even some of the activities of their medieval predecessors survived for a surprisingly long time. Like many of his contemporaries Moyses Walens of Cologne kept an *Album Amicorum* – a sort of autograph book, in which friends were encouraged to write poems or draw pictures – and one friend painted in it in 1610 a sketch which provides a late but perhaps unique picture of travelling players actually arriving in a manor to present their performance (Fig. 94). And even in *War and Peace*, another two centuries later, the Rostov household still employs its own private buffoon, Nastasya Ivanavna.

---

[1] 220, 99

6

THE GOLDEN AGE

England

London's public theatres in the reigns of Elizabeth and James I were the most successful in all history, yet they are also – unfortunately – among the least well illustrated. At a time when the new plays were by Shakespeare, Marlowe, Ben Jonson and half a dozen other dramatists of at least comparable quality, it has been calculated that this city of 160,000 people was providing a weekly audience of 21,000.[1] One Londoner in every eight was going to the theatre each week, a rate certainly never matched in the history of entertainment except by the cinema between the wars. And yet the entire pictorial evidence of the inside of theatres in England up to their closing by the Puritans in 1642 can be printed with ease, to the exact original scale, on one page (Figs 95–7).

By far the most important of this trio is the first, which has come down to us only by a series of lucky accidents. Around 1596 a Dutch traveller, Johannes de Witt, visited London and wrote down his impressions – which included an account, with a drawing attached, of the inside of the Swan theatre. His manuscript is lost, but his friend Arend van Buchell had copied both the description and the drawing into his own commonplace book. This was found in the 1880s and from it comes the famous de Witt drawing of the Swan (Fig. 95).

De Witt wrote that there were four theatres in London – these were the two in the fields to the north, the Theatre and the Curtain, built in 1576 and 1577 after the city fathers had forbidden plays within the city boundaries, and the more recent Rose and Swan to the south on the opposite bank of the Thames – but of these four, said de Witt, the Swan was 'the largest and the most magnificent'. Its wooden columns were painted with superb marbling, and it would hold three thousand people.[2] This large figure for the audience has sometimes been dismissed as a wild exaggeration but it tallies fairly well with other contemporary evidence, and opposition to it is rooted in the widely held but false assumption that Elizabethan theatres were small. The contract for the Fortune, built in 1600, survives. It shows that the stage was 43′ wide and between 30′ and 40′ deep, depending on how much inner stage was used,[3] and this is larger than comparable 'open' stages built recently in Britain. The stage at Chichester is 32′ wide by 39′ deep. The stage at the Mermaid in London is 39′ wide and of variable depth.[4] The stage of the Globe, built a year before the Fortune, has recently been calculated to have been of 'a size rarely equalled today except for Metropolitan Opera companies'.[5]

The de Witt drawing shows many details which are confirmed by other sources. The flag flew all morning if there was to be a play that afternoon, and three separate blasts from the trumpeter in the roof let the people know – in an age without watches – that the playing time of two o'clock was approaching. This brazen self-advertisement was particularly offensive to

---

Sources (*see* p. 317)   [1]270, 41;   [2]244, II, 362;   [3]244, II, 436 ff.;   [4]332, Vol. 24 (1966), 2, pp. 17 & 39;   [5]220, 173

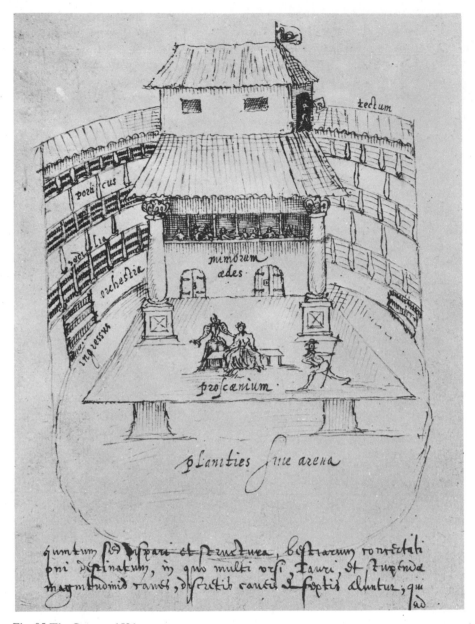

Fig. 95 The Swan, *c.* 1596

Fig. 96 From title page to *Roxana*, 1632 (*below left*)

Fig. 97 From title page to *Messalina*, 1640

the Puritan opposition. 'Those flagges of defiance against God, & trumpets that are blown to gather together such company, will sooner prevail to fill those places than the preaching of the holy word of God . . . to fill Churches';[1] and when the people had gathered, instead of hearing an edifying sermon they would enjoy 'loathsome and unheard-of Ribauldry, suckt from poysonous dugs of Sinne-sweld Theaters'.[2] De Witt's only inaccuracy here is that he has telescoped time. The trumpeter would have finished by the time the players were performing.

The spectators would all come through the only public entrance to the theatre, which was opposite the stage and immediately below the position from which de Witt made his sketch. The method of payment was interesting and impressively simple. Each person would put a penny in the box held at the entrance by a 'gatherer', who would incidentally often appear as an extra in the second half of the play.[3] This penny let the spectator into the pit, where he could stand for no further payment if he was prepared to be known as a 'penny stinkard'.[4] If he wanted more comfort and a better view, he could pay another penny at the foot of stairways to the left and right – these are what de Witt has labelled *ingressus*, though he has probably placed them too far round from the main entrance in order to get them into his drawing – and this second penny enabled him to climb up to the top gallery. A third penny into a third box allowed him into the first and second galleries. The system was most succinctly described by another foreign visitor, Thomas Platter from Basle, in 1599; 'Whoever cares to stand below only pays one English penny, but if he wishes to sit he enters by another door, and pays another penny, while if he desires to sit in the most comfortable seats which are cushioned, where he not only sees everything well, but can also be seen, then he pays yet another English penny at another door'.[5]

The only exceptions to this system were the few aristocrats who were allowed, probably for twelve pennies, to enter through the players' own door behind the stage and then to sit in the 'gentlemen's room' – the area marked *orchestra* by de Witt, to the left and right of the stage.[6] The price was high and the view was poor, but at least they had avoided rubbing shoulders with the rest of the public – precisely the reasons which, in the Victorian theatre and even well into this century, still encouraged the select few to pay the highest prices for the worst seats, in the boxes. Yet the presence of these Elizabethan and Jacobean gentlemen was an important influence on the quality of the plays, which combine so superbly the sophisticated and the popular. A Puritan, in more tolerant mood than usual, summed up pleasantly the universality of Shakespeare's audience: 'In deede I must confesse there comes to playes of all sortes, old and young; it is hard to say that all offend, yet I promise you, I will swear for none .'[7]

The other two illustrations, both tiny etched panels in the title-pages to plays (Figs 96–7), are much less reliable evidence than de Witt's drawing because they are unlikely to be more than generalised impressions of the theatre of the time. Even so, they do suggest some interesting details about the stage area. Both show the low railings round the stage for which there is evidence at the Globe and at other theatres.[8] They also show inner stages which can be opened and closed by curtains, whereas de Witt's Swan – if it had such an area at all – had two inner stages which were concealed by doors. Although curtains were probably more convenient and more usual, both systems were possible; and in Spain, where the public theatre of the time had so many similarities with that of England, there is evidence of both curtains and doors being used to conceal inner stages.[9]

---

[1]244, IV, 219; [2]244, IV, 254; [3]282, 95; [4]220, 65; [5]270, 24; [6]220, 71–2; [7]244, IV, 205; [8]220, 99–100; [9]196, 221

Even more interesting is the area above the stage. The *Messalina* etching (Fig. 97) shows a sort of upper inner stage, or basically just the curtained window which is an essential part of so many different types of stage. By contrast Figs 95 and 96 show people in a gallery or balcony behind the stage. Exponents of theatre-in-the-round and arena staging have argued that these must be spectators. They certainly appear to be spectators in Fig. 96, but in de Witt's drawing they are more likely to be characters in the scene, watching the action on the stage below: one of the figures is gesturing in a rather histrionic manner; de Witt specifically wrote on this area *mimorum aedes*, the house of the actors; and it would seem odd to show one part of the auditorium with spectators in and the rest empty, but not at all odd to show the performers without an audience. The probable truth is that in a theatre as practical as the Elizabethan, the players would keep this gallery for themselves if they needed it in a particular play but would naturally let it out to spectators if they did not. This sensible double use of the gallery was certainly the custom in at least one Spanish theatre,[1] and a good compromise between the functions can be seen in the frontispiece to *The Wits* (Fig. 98). This dates from after the Commonwealth and was printed in a collection of drolls, the short plays or extracts from plays which were all the actors could perform during the years of prohibition, but the style of its stage does hark back to the earlier period. It is perhaps a temporary stage put up in a hall – the chandeliers prove it to be an interior – and if so it is making good use of the stairs and gallery which would normally be found at one end of such a hall. Whether temporary or permanent, what the actors have arranged for themselves is a curtained entrance below – perhaps with a small inner stage behind it – and above, a gallery full of spectators with one curtained area reserved in the centre for the actors' upper window.

Although these four illustrations make up the only direct pictorial record of the time, there are also various European prints which can help to give some idea of how the interiors of the theatres may have looked and may have been used. Easily the best of these are two extremely rare German woodcuts, never before reproduced, which show the Fechthaus at Nuremberg (Figs 99–100) and which have more than an accidental connection with the English theatres of the time. An early offshoot of the thriving new London theatres had been the companies of English actors who began to take plays on tour in Europe and particularly in Germany, where in the early years of the seventeenth century they provided almost the only available dramatic entertainment. The repertoires were ambitious. That of John Green's company, for example, consisted of thirty plays and included *Romeo and Juliet*, *Hamlet* and *King Lear*.[2] And until the serious outbreak of the Thirty Years War in 1620 it was Nuremberg which had been visited more than any other city by these companies.[3]

It is extremely likely, therefore, that when the citizens of Nuremberg decided in 1627 to build themselves a theatre, their design was largely influenced by the customs of the English actors; and certainly the Fechthaus does fit very closely with what we know of the London theatres of the time. It had just the one main entrance opposite the stage; it contained three galleries; and it even held three thousand spectators.[4] The magistrate ordered that it should be an all-purpose theatre, to house 'all sorts of fencing shows, comedies, and animal baiting',[5] and there is a complete precedent for this type of adaptable building in a London theatre, the Hope, which was built in 1613–14. The Hope contract survives, and it instructs the builder to provide a play house or game place 'of suche large compasse, fforme, widenes, and height as the

---

[1]196, 194;   [2]244, II, 286;   [3]12, VII, 1207;   [4]269, 197–200;   [5]280, 27

Fig. 98 Frontispiece to *The Wits*, 1673

Fig. 99 Animal baiting at Nuremberg, seventeenth century (*overleaf*)

Fig. 100 Performers at Nuremberg, seventeenth century (*overleaf*)

Changling

Simpleton

Sr I Falstafe

Hostes

Clause

Fig. 101 Hetzamphitheater in Vienna, *c.* 1780

Plaie house called the Swan' and to make it 'fitt & convenient in all thinges, bothe for players to play in, and for the game of Beares and Bulls to be bayted in the same, and also a fitt and convenient Tyre house and a stage to be carryed or taken awaie, and to stand uppon tressells good, substanciall, and sufficient for the carryinge and bearinge of suche a stage'.[1]

In Fig. 99 the Nuremberg Fechthaus can be seen without a stage in it, being used for the baiting of a bull and a rather ape-like bear, and the view in Fig. 100 shows it with an elementary stage put up at the far end for acrobatics. Even this simplest of stages has the basic ingredients of stages in the English illustrations – the curtain behind, and the squarish stage jutting out into the yard with a canopy over it. The area beneath the stage is left open as in de Witt's drawing, but this soon ceased to be the normal custom in the London theatres. It had to be boarded in once actors began entering from beneath the stage through trap-doors.

However, it is reasonable to suppose that the Fechthaus in its earlier days could be used with a grander stage than the one belonging to these acrobats. It was opened in 1628; the English

[1]244, II, 466

Fig. 102 Temporary theatre in piazza, Bologna, 1632

players returned in strength after the end of the war in 1649; and it remained the only play-house in Nuremberg until 1668 when an indoor theatre was built to house the serious plays.[1] The woodcuts date from 1689 by which time only inferior entertainers, like these acrobats, would be putting up a stage in the Fechthaus. But just as the Hope contract demanded 'a fitt and convenient Tyre house' behind the stage, the Fechthaus appears to have provided one too. In Fig. 99 there is an area where complete rooms, with doors and windows, interrupt the spectators' galleries. All except the large door at the bottom are useless for animal baiting; but in Fig. 100 the temporary stage is put up against precisely this part of the theatre and the clown putting his head through the curtains would seem to have come through the door which is level with the first gallery. If a more elaborate stage were set up, the bottom door could lead under the stage for entrances through traps; the middle door could be level with the stage itself; and the pair of windows at the top could serve for appearances above. The three together correspond to the three levels known to have been used in the English theatre, and they may well constitute the skeleton of an adaptable tiring-house façade.

The Hope would have looked different from the Fechthaus in one important respect, since it was based on the Swan and was therefore round. However, the Fortune, like the Fechthaus, was square; and Europe does also provide one glimpse of a round bear-baiting arena in action, in an eighteenth-century print of the Hetzamphitheater in Vienna (Fig. 101). Two round arenas of precisely this sort appear in miniature on a map of London published in Cologne in 1572, four years before London's first theatre was built.[2] There is a glimpse of the animals inside them, one being captioned 'The Bowll baytyng' and the other 'The Beare bayting', and it is these – rather than the often quoted inn-yards – which were to give the early London theatres their characteristic shape.[3] Five or six round theatres had been built before the first square one, the Fortune, appeared in 1600.

Before leaving the English theatre of this period and moving on to Spain, it is worth pointing out that although these two countries were the ones to make the most of this type of theatre, it was far from exclusive to them. As the Nuremberg woodcuts show, it travelled from England to Germany. But already in 1581 there were two public theatres in Venice, 'one oval in shape, and the other round', which may well have been similar in many ways to those in England.[4] Tournament theatres in Italy, such as the one put up in Bologna in 1628,[5] often approximated to the London pattern – as indeed any structure of galleries round a central area is likely to – and the theatre erected for Bologna's annual civic festivities in 1627 not only provides a fascinating combination of an oval theatre formed of galleries round a 'pit' with a painted illusionistic show at one end (Fig. 102), but is also unique in this period in showing gatherers at the various entrances and at the bottom of the steps to the galleries. Similarly, a central European religious performance of the mid-seventeenth century (Fig. 103) uses very much the same sort of stage as the one for Kirkman's collection of drolls in Fig. 98.

Spain

It is a commonplace that the public theatres in Spain and England at the end of the sixteenth century shared many interesting details. Madrid's first permanent public theatre, the Corral de la Cruz, was built in 1579 – just three years after the Theatre in London – and was followed

---

[1]269, 215;   [2]220, Pl. I;   [3]137, II, 157;   [4]69, 33;   [5]12, II, Tav. CXVII

Fig. 103 Religious performance, seventeenth century

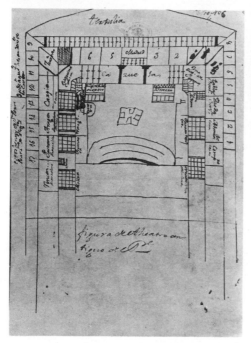

Fig. 104 Plan of the Corral del Principe, eighteenth century
Fig. 105 The corral theatre, Almagro

by the Corral del Principe in 1582.[1] Madrid found its Lope de Vega even sooner than London discovered Shakespeare, and both men wrote for theatres which used a stage on three levels with trap-doors from below, a gallery or balcony above, and some sort of inner stage at the back (there is in fact far more detailed evidence of the Spanish inner stage and it was a more ambitious affair, opening up as early as the 1580s to reveal such delights as a city lit up with candles[2]). In both cities the theatres were open to the sky, though the Spaniards had a canvas covering against the sun; the plays started at two or three in the afternoon; the spectators stood on the ground in the pit or sat in three tiers around this central area; they entered through the one large door opposite the stage; and they paid their money piece by piece to gatherers in different parts of the theatre.[3]

But there were also important differences. The Spanish theatre was a more gradual and natural development from earlier temporary playing places. From the middle of the century the players used many corrals which were merely the open courtyards formed by the backs of a square of houses ('corral' means an enclosed place or a yard); the spectators either stood in the courtyard or watched from the back windows of the houses. The first permanent corrals were a deliberate recreation of this area. On the top two floors they kept this same arrangement of ordinary rooms with windows on to the yard (the *aposentos* and the *desvanes*), but the ground floor did acquire several rows of raised steps and seats (the *gradas*) against the side walls.[4] Deriving so directly from courtyards the corrals were rectangular, just as the London theatres, based on bear-baiting arenas, were nearly all round. And unlike London, where the sexes mixed all too freely for the Puritans' liking, Spanish women were forced to sit alone in a special gallery at the back of the auditorium, known as the *cazuela* or 'stew-pan'.

126

There were differences, too, in the shape of the stage. Unlike the English promontory, with the audience in the pit on three sides of it, the Spanish stage filled the entire end wall of the courtyard and its edges came right up to the seats in the *gradas* on either side. It was perhaps this extra width in the rear wall which allowed scenes on the inner stage to become more important in Spain than in England. Before the end of the sixteenth century Somi, in Italy, had reported that in the Spanish theatre one could see 'an open, well-appointed room in which, for example, a lover has an interview with a bawd', but he then went on to point out the ultimate naturalistic problem which was to cause so much concern in the late nineteenth century; such a room, he said, can give 'a strong impression of verisimilitude, yet it goes so contrary to reality – in that the room is lacking (as it must) a fourth wall – that it appears to me rather awkward'.[5]

The interior of these Spanish theatres is even less well illustrated than that of their English cousins – there are in fact no illustrations at all – but there is instead something which the English theatre entirely lacks, a group of diagrams showing how the buildings were laid out. One of the most interesting is a rough drawing, possibly dating from about 1730 and only discovered in the 1960s (Fig. 104). It shows the inside of the Corral del Principe in Madrid. The central rectangle is a straightforward ground-plan of the pit and stage, and the three rows of named and numbered boxes round the sides are the artist's way of depicting the rooms which were above each other in three storeys round the corral, together with the names of their occupants; in the side facing the stage one can see, for example, the box where the women sat (the *cazuela*) and above it the box belonging to the city of Madrid. The line across the bottom half of the drawing represents the back wall of the corral, and the line just above it across the stage is where the edge of the balcony came, forming below it the very spacious inner stage. The curved lines in front of the stage are not an apron but are an ancestor of the 'front stalls' – a raised area called the *luneta* where spectators could sit on stools without blocking the view of those standing behind. The square in the middle of the pit is probably a well, which is known to have stood there.[6]

Besides its diagrams, Spain has one other unique relic of this style of theatre building – an actual small corral theatre at Almagro which was discovered and restored in the 1950s. Its precise date is not certain, but the dressing-rooms behind the stage were found still to contain a seventeenth-century pack of playing cards. The view in Fig. 105 is taken from the women's gallery looking towards the stage with its three separate little balcony areas for appearances above. It can be seen how the projection of this balcony provides space for an inner stage almost the entire width of the main stage, though in this case rather shallow; and the beams still contain the hooks for the curtains.[7]

This auditorium has moved a long way from a courtyard formed by the backs of houses, and it corrects the simple courtyard image which the term corral suggests. Documents show that already in the seventeenth century galleries of this sort grew up above the old ground floor rows of covered seats, in front of each of the upper storeys of rooms.[8] The result was something very much more like the open galleries of the London playhouses. Modern scholarly reconstructions of the London stages will incorporate more accurate individual details, but there is no actual building in existence which can offer, as successfully as this little theatre in Almagro, both an authentic image of the seventeenth-century public theatre in Spain and at the same time a convincing idea of the feeling inside the rather similar English theatres of the same period.

---

[1]306, xi; [2]196, 202; [3]306, 47; [4]306, 42; [5]31, 260; [6]196, 410; [7]219, IV, 34–6; [8]20, 268

France

Since at least the fourteenth century a favourite pastime in European courts, and in particular in France and Italy, had been a type of entertainment in which gentlemen and ladies, wearing exotic costumes and masks, entered the hall on magnificent floats from which they descended to perform a dance. It was while taking part in such a performance in 1393 that Charles VI of France very nearly burnt to death, when he was dancing as a wild man and his costume caught fire.[1]

A late but typical example was the ballet put on by Catherine de' Medici in Paris in 1573 in honour of the Polish ambassadors (Fig. 106). The performers had entered reclining on a mobile mountain, which made a complete circuit of the hall before they descended to dance. This type of spectacle could have been seen at the time in most of the richer European courts, but in 1581 France produced a ballet which was distinctly new. It was the *Balet Comique de la Royne*, devised by Baltazar de Beauioyeulx for Henry III's queen, Louise de Mercoeur, to celebrate the marriage of her sister. Beauioyeulx explained that he had invented a new *genre*, the *ballet comique*, because he thought a comedy by itself would be too dull for the occasion and because ballet, after all, is nothing but 'geometric patterns of various people dancing together'.[2] His solution was to mix the two, and in doing so he provided the first dramatic ballet in which the various performers arriving on their floats were all part of a fairly loose plot about Circe.

This ballet is rightly famous, not only for its originality, but also for the superb series of etchings in the published edition of 1582. Fig. 107 shows the hall where it was performed; it was the Salle du Petit Bourbon, where the dance in Fig. 106 had also taken place. At the bottom Henry III is sitting with his mother, Catherine de' Medici, since his wife was performing in the ballet. The etching includes the three permanent pieces of scenery. On the right is a wood with Pan in it, on the left a cloud containing the musicians – both of these very much in the style of mansions in the mystery plays – and at the far end is the garden of Circe, full of flowers, fruits and animals, and behind it 'a city in perspective', which together form a unit very similar to the *tableaux* of the street theatres for royal entries. All the other floats and pieces of scenery were in the processional style of street pageantry: they glided in when needed through the two trellis arches on either side of Circe and made their tour of the hall, stopping in front of the king for a song or a recital which made plain their connection with the plot. Fig. 108 is one of these mobile units – a grove containing four Dryads, played by four of the queen's own ladies. Their leader, Mlle de Victry, rose to her feet when they were in front of the king and recited some verses 'so distinctly, and with such grace and modest self-assurance, that the gentle spectators, who until this moment had known nothing of her, could appreciate instantly that her vivacity of mind was capable of the highest achievements in every science or discipline'.[3] She must have particularly touched Beauioyeulx, for he speaks of nobody else in quite this vein. After Mlle de Victry's recital the grove moved on to join up with Pan, the glories of whose own wood were now fully revealed when the semi-transparent curtain partially hiding it was allowed to fall. In true pageant tradition all these various floats and mansions were sparkling with many lights.

At the end of the story the queen came forward to present the king with a medallion, and each of the ladies in the ballet did the same to her own chosen gentleman in the audience. They

---

[1]303, 3; [2]232, fol. e. iiii v.; [3]232, fol. 37 v.

Fig. 106 Ballet for the Polish ambassadors, Paris, 1573

Fig. 108 *Balet Comique*, 1581, a grove
Fig. 109 Court ballet, 1617, opening *tableau*

then drew the men on to the floor to dance with them the final *grand ballet*.[1] So ended a very remarkable show, which created a new form out of at least three separate strands of earlier pageantry.

From now on ballets became increasingly popular at the French court. Louis XIII in particular loved to dance in them, having apparently acquired a taste for performance at a very early age. His tutor recorded in his diary that when Louis was three he saw a company of English comedians perform at Fontainebleau. Soon after he said 'let's dress up as actors'. So his tutor 'made him a cap of his pinafore, and he began saying "tiph, toph, milord" and walking about with large strides'.[2]

From 1610 onwards a rather primitive type of changeable scenery began to supplant the simultaneous staging of the *Balet Comique*. The best illustrated court ballet of this new type is the *Ballet de la délivrance de Renaud*, danced in 1617 in the Grande Salle in the Louvre with Louis XIII, now sixteen years old, in a supporting rôle to his favourite, M. du Luynes, who sang and danced the lead. Fig. 109 shows the dancers as they were revealed at the start of the ballet, with M. du Luynes reclining at the bottom and the king and twelve gentlemen perched on the wall of a grotto above him. This uniquely awkward setting does nevertheless suggest very well its true function – that of a shop window in which to exhibit the fine gentlemen in their gorgeous costumes. The audience was suitably impressed. 'There was no one who saw this mountain, decorated with such strange beauty and filled with people so imaginatively masked and clothed . . . who did not believe himself to be in some delightful dream.'[3] When the gentlemen had descended to dance in the hall, the scenery on the small stage changed on a revolving platform.[4]

[1]232, fol. 64 r.;   [2]244, II, 293;   [3]260, 4;   [4]303, 153

Fig. 107 *Balet Comique*, 1581, the hall

Fig. 110 Costume in court ballet, 1628

This type of scene-changing may have come to seem merely clumsy, because during the 1620s the ballets danced by Louis XIII reverted to a type of masquerade with only the simplest permanent setting behind it, sometimes provided by a single backcloth. The dancers appeared in a succession of different *entrées* of which the main point was the costumes, often imaginative but almost invariably in the direction of the grotesque, such as *Perrette La Hazardeuse* in Fig. 110. Perrette herself would have been danced by a man, and her cat by a child, and typical roles danced by the king were a wandering musician, a Dutch captain, a grotesque warrior, a farmer, a woman; 'he danced fairly well' reported Tallemant, 'but he never performed anything but ridiculous characters'.[1]

These *ballets à entrées*, with the dances linked only very loosely by a theme, were a temporary digression from the dramatic ballets which had been the fashion from the *Balet Comique* to the *Délivrance de Renaud*. The earlier style was to prove more influential in the history of theatre, but for a few decades from the 1620s the *ballets à entrées* held sway. While the Duc de Nemours was devising them in Paris for Louis XIII, the Count Filippo d'Aglié was doing the same for the court of Savoy in Turin – which of course had very strong links with France. Records of the Turin ballets survive in a superb series of manuscripts, which contain paintings of all the costumes and sets and which amount to the most complete and charming pictorial record that we have of any period in the theatre's history. Pls XV and XVI (p. 137) show two of these

132

Fig. 111 Louis XIV as a Bacchante, 1651
Fig. 112 Louis XIV as a Muse, 1651
Fig. 113 Louis XIV as a Fury, 1654
Fig. 114 The Duke of York as a coral fisher, 1654

watercolours for the ballet *Il Carnevale Languente*, danced in 1647. In the opening scene Aesculapius, god of medicine, announces that Carnival is languishing because his humours are disordered. This immediately allows for twelve entries attached loosely to the four humours and their corresponding elements, Fire, Water, Earth and Air. So, in Pl. XV, we see the Marquis of San Damiano in his magnificent costume as the Choleric Fiery Humour; and in Pl. XVI we see him dancing in an appropriately fiery setting, the City of Dis. The Turin costumes were considerably more elegant than the Paris ones, but otherwise the main difference between the two schools of ballet was that the Turin entries were performed in front of the Italian perspective scenery.

However, the French ballets were soon to follow this same path. In 1641, soon after Richelieu had opened his new theatre in the Palais-Cardinal, the *Ballet de la Prospérité des Armes de France* was performed there in Italian scenery.[2] And by the time of *Les Noces de Pelée et de Thétis* in 1654 Louis XIV, who as a young man inherited his father's love of dancing, was performing his *entrées* with his noble friends in between the scenes of an opera by a professional Italian company, and in settings designed by the great Torelli.

The costumes worn by Louis XIV in his various roles were very slightly more elegant than those of his father's time, but the roles themselves were almost as 'ridiculous'. In 1651, when he was only thirteen, he danced five parts in the *Ballet du Roi des Festes de Bacchus*; they were a divine, a Bacchante (Fig. 111), a man of ice, a Titan and a Muse (Fig. 112). The diarist Evelyn saw the performance and reported that 'the glory of the Masque was the greate persons performing it . . . but the habites of the Masquers were stupendiously rich & glorious'.[3]

The printed text shows that Louis was also billed as playing a Coquette, in which role he had to speak the lines:

---

[1]303, 174;   [2]20, 377–403;   [3]May 11, 1651

Ie doute qu'avec moy pas une Demoiselle
  Entre en comparaison,
Car je suis belle enfin, jeune, spirituelle,
  Et de bonne maison.[1]

(I doubt whether any maiden can compare with
me, for I am beautiful, young, witty, and
from a good house.)

This was suppressed, perhaps understandably, but self-congratulation of a less *risqué* nature was very much the essence of all the king's lines. In the ballet for *Les Noces de Pelée et de Thétis* he danced a very frantic Fury (Fig. 113) and appeared also as Apollo, introducing himself as 'more brilliant and better formed than all the other gods put together', and then praising himself for having recently defeated the Fronde.[2] The poor Duke of York, in exile at the French court with his brother Charles II, had rather more pathetic lines – in keeping with his political situation. He appeared as a coral fisher (Fig. 114) and said:

Loin de ne faire icy que pescher le coral
  Il faut que d'un endroit malheureux et fatal
    Que la vaste mer environne,
Ie m'applique en homme expert
A pescher tout ce qui sert
  A refaire une Couronne.[3]

(Instead of just fishing for coral, I must apply
my expert skill in a fatal and unhappy place, which
the vast sea encircles, in fishing for anything
which will help re-make a crown.)

As James II, the poor coral fisher was to return at the end of his life for yet another spell of exile at this same court of Louis XIV.

In the court ballets a medieval style of staging had survived until the *Balet Comique* in the late sixteenth century, and it was to last even longer in France in the public theatres. Paris had an unbroken tradition and style of indoor public performances which ran from the late fourteenth century, when the *Miracles de Notre Dame* were performed in the hall known as the Puy Notre Dame, until about 1635 when modern plays were still being presented at the Hôtel de Bourgogne in a remarkably similar manner. In 1402 one particular guild, the Confrérie de la Passion, was granted the privilege of being the only company of actors in Paris; in 1548 they built themselves in the Hôtel de Bourgogne an auditorium which was probably a rectangular hall with the stage filling one end, and with standing space the whole length of the floor and two galleries along the walls; they played here until 1578, when they began letting it out to visiting companies; and in 1629 the actors who were renting it were given the official title and position of Comédiens du Roi.[4] The Hôtel de Bourgogne remained the home of the Comédiens du Roi until 1677, and it was for their productions here in the 1630s that the designer Mahelot kept wash drawings of the various settings, together with instructions as to how each setting should be arranged, in the remarkable volume in the Bibliothèque Nationale known as the *Mémoire de Mahelot*.

Fig. 115 Setting by Mahelot for *La Prise de Marcilly*, 1631

The continuity of production style over almost three centuries can be seen in the requirements for two settings. For the thirty-second miracle of Notre Dame in the fourteenth century
there was needed:

a palace of two rooms, a forest, a prison, an inn, a house for the *charbonnier*, a temple or church, a
boat on the sea, and the house of the *tabellion*.[5]

For *La Prise de Marcilly* in 1631, Mahelot's drawing of the setting (Fig. 115) is accompanied
by this description:

In the middle of the stage stands the fortress of Marcilly, five feet high, where the assault takes place
in the fifth act; also some standards, trumpets, drums, fireworks and squibs. Below the fortress a
further fortification on the counterscarp; in the said fortification there must be a grill which can
open and close. To one side of the stage there must be a tent of war, a passage, a tower, a knotted
rope for climbing down from the tower, a drawbridge which can descend when necessary. On the
other side, a wood and a grotto, a shepherdess's hut, a sea. A boat, two oars, some nightingales, some
cocks, some dogs, a night, a lance and a dummy head.[6]

[1]229, Entrée Supprimée;   [2]297, 6;   [3]297, 20;   [4]281, Part I, Vol. II, 709;   [5]329, 81;   [6]288, 81

If anything it is Mahelot's requirements which seem the more medieval of the two, with the fireworks and the trick beheadings. Mahelot's drawings show that the design of his individual houses of wood and canvas was often influenced by the classical motifs of Serlio, but the un-medieval arrangement of the houses in two receding rows had probably grown up not from deliberate Serlian principles but as a practical result of indoor performance in halls, where a stage's width is limited but its depth can be extended.

In the 1630s this late form of multiple staging was at last about to vanish under pressure from the French interest in the three Unities, and particularly the Unity of Place. The trend was perhaps started by the Hôtel de Bourgogne's only rival, the Théâtre du Marais, which Mont-dory and Charles le Noir had built for themselves in a tennis court in 1634. In January 1637 they presented Corneille's *Le Cid*, by far the greatest single success of the period and a play which could well have been performed in one of Mahelot's multiple sets. Corneille himself said of the play's setting; 'Everything happens in Seville, it is true, and therefore it keeps to a sort of Unity of Place; but the particular place changes from scene to scene, and is variously the royal palace, the Infanta's appartment, Chimène's room, a street or a public square.'[1] We have no precise details of the setting for this original production, but Scudéry violently attacked the play, complaining among other things that 'the staging is so muddled that a single place repre-sents the king's apartment, then the Infanta's, Chimène's house and the street, almost without any change of appearance, so that most of the time the spectator has no idea where the actors are supposed to be'.[2] The setting was certainly simple enough for spectators to be able to sit on the stage – an innovation in France at the time, and something that would have been difficult among Mahelot's houses. And when the Hôtel de Bourgogne produced *Le Cid* a few years later, they used a setting very different from Mahelot's; 'The stage is a room with four doors. There must be a chair for the king.'[3] It would tally with Scudéry's criticism if Montdory's stage in 1637 was already of this type. And if so, the famous *palais à volonté*, the single neutral setting which would serve as a background for the tragedies of Racine, had arrived.

An important part of the entertainment at the Hôtel de Bourgogne, from the days of the Confrérie onwards, was farce – which seems to have been performed in a shallower and more unified permanent setting than tragedy or comedy. The three enormously popular performers of farce in the early years of the seventeenth century, Gros Guillaume, Gaultier-Garguille and Turlupin (Fig. 116), are depicted in several etchings of the period and always in very much the same scenery. At first sight it seems hard to understand how this setting, an elegant version of the basic Commedia dell'Arte scene with its two side houses, could be used on the same stage as Mahelot's creations. The answer is that these were merely a single pair of houses, instead of the two or three on each side used by Mahelot, with a cloth behind them cutting off the rest of the stage. Almost the precise setting of the farce – the chair, the architectural background, the side houses and even the low balustrades – can be seen further upstage in one of Mahelot's designs (Fig. 117). Abraham Bosse, in his etching of the farce in Fig. 116, has drawn these details with far more care than Mahelot in his quick sketch. But since such houses and all the various other pieces would be valuable items, used again and again in many different plays, it is likely that their appearance – at any rate in intention – was nearer to Bosse's polished version than to the rough impression they give in the sketches.

These farce players were French, but their style as well as their stage was much influenced by

[1]5, 191;   [2]5, 191;   [3]288, 12

Pls XV & XVI Costume and setting for Turin ballet: watercolours, 1647

Pl. XVII Interior of the Teatro Ducale in Turin: watercolour, 1681 (*overleaf*)

L'HVMOR COLLERICO IGNEO

Dann springen sie von einander, und ihrer dreÿ heben den 4ten beÿ Händ und füßen in die Höhe, tragen ihm also hinein, hat also der ganze tantz ein Ende.

the Commedia dell'Arte – which through the seventeenth century was to become more and more important in French theatre, contributing in some respects even to the brilliance of Molière with whom the Italian players shared a theatre for fourteen years from 1658.[1] Figs 118 and 119 suggest how close the two companies could at times come to each other's style, and how much both of them were willing to borrow from the traditions of Italian opera and the French *pièces à machines*. Fig. 118 is the frontispiece to Molière's *Amphitryon*, first performed in 1668; it shows Jupiter on a cloud, explaining to Amphitryon how he has just seduced his wife,

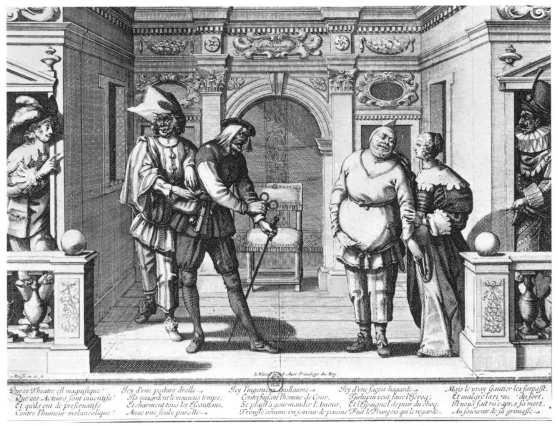

Fig. 116 Farce at the Hôtel de Bourgogne, *c.* 1630

while Mercury, who has acted as pander to his divine companion, flies away behind. Fig. 119 is the frontispiece to *Le Mercure Galant*, first performed in 1682 and one of the many plays, each with its own frontispiece, in Gherardi's famous collection *Le Théâtre Italien*; in it Harlequin as Mercury, mounted on Jupiter's eagle, arrives to assist his master in the seduction of Rosalba.

In such comic mockery of the gods, albeit now safely distant and unlikely to retaliate, the Italian players were following once again the long tradition stretching back to the Phlyakes. Unfortunately their jokes, in keeping with the tradition, were still a little broad for the purest

[1]12, VII, 1637

Pl. XVIII Acrobatics on a perspective stage: hand-coloured etching, 1716

Fig. 117 Setting by Mahelot for *La folie de Clidamant*, *c*. 1630

French classical taste and in 1697 Mme de Maintenon managed to have them expelled from the city. But by 1716 they were back and now, to judge by designs done for them at this time by Claude Gillot, they were putting the machinery of the contemporary theatre very much to their own individual purposes. Fig. 120 is an etching of one of Gillot's inventions. Harlequin must often have lit a squib in the past, but he could not always have relied on such spectacular results. In 1723 the Hôtel de Bourgogne was officially renamed 'Hôtel des Comédiens Italiens ordinaires du Roi' and in the mid-century the Commedia dell'Arte gave Paris's oldest theatre its last brilliant period. The auditorium can be seen in 1772 (Pl. XIX, p. 173), still preserving its rigidly rectangular shape even after the introduction of more elegant boxes. Ten years later it was out of use, and it was soon pulled down – but by then the Italian players too had made their final departure from Paris.[1]

Outside the official theatre the French *charlatans* (Fig. 121), the local version of the Italian *ciarlatini*, had for long been equally successful, spreading yet further the influence of the Commedia dell'Arte in the French entertainments of the time. Their various preparations, and in particular orvietan, were offered as little short of a universal panacea. As the poster in Fig. 121 solemnly explains, orvietan is sovereign against 'every sort of poison. Against the bites of poisonous creatures, and wild dogs. Against the plague. Against the worms which eat us. Against the smallpox and other ills'. The powders were invariably kept in the chest with a barrel lid, which appears in literally dozens of prints of charlatans, and the performers' function

[1] 12, VII, 1638

Fig. 118 Frontispiece to Molière's *Amphitryon*, 1684

Fig. 119 Frontispiece to *Le Mercure Galant*, 1721 (*above right*)

Fig. 120 Gillot, machinery for Commedia dell'Arte, *c.* 1730

Fig. 121 French charlatans, *c*. 1650

was not only to attract an audience – the medicine was sometimes even the subject of the act. Thomas Platter, in 1599, saw a street show at Avignon in which Zani opened the chest and boasted of a marvellous Turkish remedy which he had bought for a hundred crowns a packet but was willing to sell for ten; the Doctor then indulged in a comic argument with him, claiming that it cured nothing (an argument which Zani was presumably allowed to win), and then objecting to the price; on this score he managed to beat Zani down to five crowns, then two, then one, and finally, after a great deal of haggling, to one hundredth part of a crown; and at this level, representing one ten-thousandth of the original price, a vast number of packets were sold.[1]

Italy

Just as towards the end of the sixteenth century ballet had developed in France from earlier traditions, so at much the same period in Italy opera was born from other long-standing types of entertainment. Almost as soon as classical plays had begun to be performed in the various Renaissance courts, the custom grew up of enlivening them with more spectacular items between the acts; and from the beginning the *intermezzi* seem often to have pleased the audiences rather more than the plays themselves. At Ferrara in 1502 the comedies of Plautus were sweetened with moors carrying lighted torches, satyrs chasing wild beasts in time with a musical clock, harvest activities performed to bagpipes, Swiss soldiers in a war dance, and a golden ball which melted away in the air to reveal four Virtues who sang a quartet. Isabella d'Este's comment on the entertainment was that 'neither the verses nor the voices struck me as very good, but the *Moresche* dances between the acts were very well danced, with great spirit'.[2] An early *intermezzo* even closer in style to the delights of seventeenth-century opera was a view of the river Arno with sirens swimming in it with fishes' tails, which interrupted the performance of *Il Commodo* at the wedding festivities of Cosimo I in Florence in 1539.[3]

144

As the *intermezzi* became more elaborate their own scenery had to be alternated with that of the play, and some form of changeable setting became necessary. As early as the 1490s Leonardo da Vinci had designed a revolving stage with two static settings on it,[4] but this was more in the medieval tradition of the machinery in the street theatres. The introduction of changeable perspective scenery has been variously claimed for Castro in 1543 (rather doubtful), for Ferrara in 1561, and for Florence in 1566.[5] All the earliest systems used variations of the Vitruvian *periaktoi* – houses which could revolve to reveal another face.

The first settings for *intermezzi* which survive in illustrations are the famous designs by Bernardo Buontalenti at Florence in 1589. They are often presented as a point of departure, though with a long tradition behind them of similar *intermezzi* they were not intrinsically new. But as they were the first *intermezzi* settings of which etchings were made, they rightly have a special fascination and must certainly have contributed to the spread of Italian scenery. The festivities of 1589 were for the wedding of Ferdinando I and Christine of Lorraine. The dramatic highlight was the performance of a comedy by Girolamo Bargagli, *La Pellegrina*, with six *intermezzi*, in a theatre built by Buontalenti in the Uffizi underneath the picture gallery – an area now occupied by the department of prints and drawings. A theatre had first been constructed here in 1585/86 by Buontalenti for a play with very similar *intermezzi* for the marriage of Ferdinando's sister, Virginia.

La Pellegrina was performed in front of a perspective which was remarkable, in the words of an eye-witness, Bastiano de' Rossi, for having 'three open vistas; the one in the middle on a straight axis, and the other two curved'.[6] This background is certainly the one seen in a contemporary etching by Scarabelli (Fig. 122). The Serlian houses to either side in front of it were probably not used for *La Pellegrina*, since Rossi says that the houses were recognisable buildings from Pisa, where the play was set, and that they included the leaning tower; but at any rate they would have been of much the same type as these houses. Oddly enough this very same setting, with only minor alterations, is much more widely known from the plates etched thirty-one years later by Callot to illustrate the first edition of *Il Solimano* (Fig. 123), published in Florence in 1620. It is perhaps possible that the original canvas houses designed by Buontalenti still existed and were put to use again in a production of Bonarelli's play – later centuries would use the same settings for considerably more than thirty years. But the 1620 edition makes no mention of any specific production in Florence and the play had been first performed at Ancona in 1618, so it is much more likely that Callot merely copied the earlier Florentine etching to illustrate the book.

This type of street setting, still basically Serlian, reappeared for every act of *La Pellegrina* between each of the six *intermezzi*. It is not known how the changes were effected. The houses may have been *periaktoi*, with the Pisan architecture on two sides and a new flat panel fitted to the third side during each act, to turn into view for the next *intermezzo*. But a few ambiguous hints by Rossi suggest that the houses for the play were perhaps fixed and that flat panels slid out in front of each of them for the *intermezzi*.[7] If so, this was a very early foretaste of the sliding flat wings of the future.

The *intermezzi* had the usual complement of cloud machines from above and horrific apparitions from below, and the locations of the scenes were equally typical. The full sequence of six consisted of a cloud scene in the heavens; a delightful garden; a rocky cave and a dragon; a hell

---

[1]301, 392–4;   [2]243, 206–7;   [3]5, 199;   [4]12, VI, Tav. CLXXXVIII;   [5]12, VIII, 1596;   [6]312, 33 ff.;   [7]181, 79–82

Fig. 122 Buontalenti, setting for a play, etched *c.* 1589
Fig. 123 Plate from *Il Solimano*, Florence, 1620

scene; a sea scene with mermaids, dolphins and a ship (Fig. 124); and finally a return to the clouds.[1] Precisely these ingredients had already provided the *intermezzi* in Florence in 1585, when the permanent setting for the comedy had been a view of Florence itself rather than Pisa,[2] and for many years the basis of all scenery would be five general types established in the sixteenth century – heaven, hell, the countryside, the sea, and a street or courtyard. And in the seventeenth century these delights would no longer be confined merely to the *intermezzi*. They would constitute the entire show in one happily unending series of *intermezzi*, separated by

Fig. 124 Buontalenti, setting for intermezzo, 1589

nothing more arduous than intervals, under the title of opera. Isabella d'Este's preference for the interludes had won the day.

The *intermezzi* of 1589 are particularly relevant in this respect since the first opera – *Dafne*, done in Florence in 1597 – was an expansion of the third *intermezzo*.[3] A century later a stage direction neatly sums up the world of seventeenth-century opera: 'The Scene is partly in Heaven, partly on Earth, partly on the Sea and partly in Hell.'[4] This apparent offer of total freedom merely instructs the set designer to produce once again the hallowed ingredients of the sixteenth-century *intermezzi*.

The sky, the sea and hell were the most popular of the group because they provided the best

---

[1]181, 74–89; [2]181, 61–9; [3]69, 23–4; [4]227, intro.

147

Fig. 125 Guitti, *Andromeda*, 1638

opportunities for spectacular machinery and effects; and in terms of plot the story of Andromeda, with Perseus flying in on Pegasus to rescue her from the sea monster, became an obvious favourite. Fig. 125 shows the scene from an *Andromeda* performed in Ferrara in 1638 with sets by Francesco Guitti. A year before, when Venice's first public opera house, the Teatro San Cassiano, had opened with yet another version of the Andromeda story, the sea monster was 'made with such beautiful cunning that, although not real, he put people in terror. Except for the act of tearing to pieces and devouring, he did everything as if alive and breathing'.[1]

The method by which such a miracle was achieved can be seen in Fig. 127, one of a series of drawings in Parma of seventeenth-century stage machinery. The man working the monster climbs in through the hatch and then controls the tail, jaws and eyes by pulling various strings, while the whole apparition moves across the stage in its wooden runway. Another runway further upstage is occupied by a delicate marine seat in which some nymph or goddess will probably travel. The mechanism beneath these machines was concealed from sight by mechanical waves which stood in front of them and which can be seen in another of the Parma drawings (Fig. 126). In this particular method flat boards, painted and cut out like waves, oscillated in front of each other. The first theatrical designer to leave a detailed account of how the scenes and machines worked was Nicola Sabbattini, whose *Pratica di Fabricar Scene* was

148

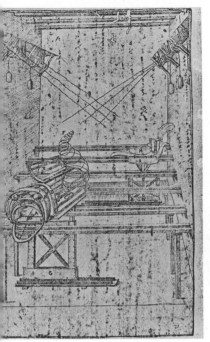 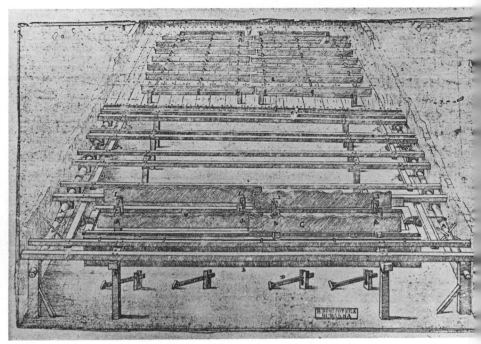

Fig. 126 Machinery for sea monster, *c.* 1650
Fig. 127 Wave machine, *c.* 1650

published in two volumes in 1637 and 1638, precisely the years of the Venice and Ferrara *Andromedas*. He describes two more ways of making waves, the more usual of which was a series of long cylinders, again moulded and painted like waves, each of which revolved on its own axis to combine into one rolling sea.[2]

Monsters were highly effective in the air as well as in the sea. A page of drawings in Stockholm, probably French and from the late seventeenth century (Fig. 128), shows at the top a flying dragon in which the movement of the jaws and the tail is controlled by cords from above the stage. Below this can be seen another way of fitting the driver into a sea monster. Here his hands work the front flippers, he controls the head with a metal band round his own head, and the stirrups under his feet probably affect the tail. Again the wave machine will cover his legs, hanging down from the monster's chest. This particular creature could move more freely in the sea than the Parma version in Fig. 127, since it could pivot on its own axis, pushed round by someone crouching underneath and holding the handle. Sometimes this task of revolving the machine was left to the less important members of the cast. A French scallop-shell throne of about 1700, accompanied by dolphins and tritons (Fig. 129), has beneath it a note; 'the two tritons could turn the machine crawling on their knees'. There must have been lively competition among the extras not to be cast as a triton.

The chief delight of scenes in the heavens were the enormous and amazing cloud machines, often carrying vast numbers of carefully selected deities. The stage directions for the prologue of an opera in 1685, *Servio Tullio*, begin: 'The Heavens. On a huge cloud machine, neatly

[1]185, 27;   [2]313, 110

Fig. 128 Machinery for monsters, late seventeenth century
Fig. 129 Revolving scallop-shell, *c.* 1700

arranged, appear Jupiter, Juno, Neptune, Vesta, Apollo, Venus, Mars, Pallas, Mercury, Diana, Vulcan and Ceres, who in the opinion of Herodotus and Pythagoras are the twelve principal deities. The rest of the scene is filled by a huge cortège of other deities.'[1] In this case heaven and its cloud effects would have filled the whole stage, but on slightly less impressive occasions it was accepted as perfectly normal that a cloud should float down in an ordinary street and even contain within itself considerable action – as, for example, between the trio who are aloft in Fig. 130 in another scene from the Ferrara *Andromeda*. The true reason for the great use of clouds in the theatre is that they provide the best possible way of concealing the mechanics of flying machines, and as such their use goes all the way back to the mystery plays. There are various records of cloud machines from the late fourteenth century[2] and in 1562 a place as small as Chelmsford found it necessary to buy fifty fathoms of linen to make clouds.[3]

The Italian cloud machines of seventeenth-century opera were in effect suspended platforms, each like a tiny stage carrying its own arrangement of painted scenery, and equipped with boards in front, cut out and painted like clouds, which could open to reveal the interior. A French drawing (Fig. 131) shows a front view and cross-section of a fairly simple 'glory', with its cut-out clouds and banners; this particular one is designed to seat only one woman, yet even it has five rows of borders hanging below it. Such a machine had its own internal lights, behind the cut-out shapes, and the manuscript notes on Fig. 131 say that the pillars on either side of the façade were transparent. The covering clouds could be parted either on a fan principle or on long hinged arms – and both methods can be seen in the rear view of a cloud machine in Fig. 132. Such devices had a long theatrical pedigree. A medieval Cornish play starts with the stage direction: 'The father must be in a clowde, and when he speakethe of heaven let the levys open.'[4]

[1]334, Prologue;   [2]137, I, 94;   [3]314, 70;   [4]245, II, 391

Fig. 130 Guitti, *Andromeda*, 1638

Fig. 131 Flying apparition machine, front view and cross section, French, *c.* 1700

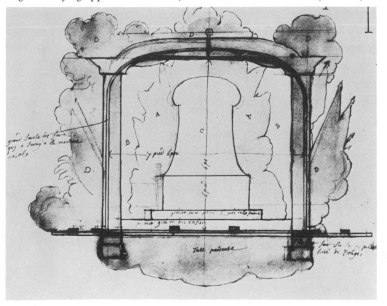

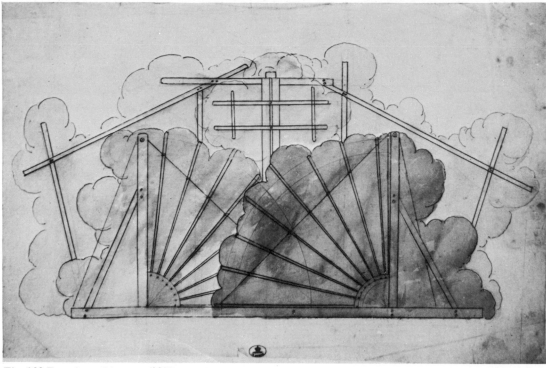

Fig. 132 French machinery, *c*. 1700

The cloud in *Andromeda* in 1638 (Fig. 130) appears to be floating above a typical stage street of two-sided houses, of the type which had been familiar since the time of Peruzzi and Serlio a century before; and Sabbattini, writing in the same year, assumes that the scenic units will be either complete *periaktoi* or at least two-sided houses. Sabbatini does admittedly go on to acknowledge, in a rather grumbling vein, that 'it seems nowadays that nothing is considered good . . .unless all the Scenes, or at least part of them, change'; and he then describes two ways of changing them, which are so extraordinarily clumsy that he recommends that a diversion should be caused at the back of the auditorium at the appropriate moment so as to distract the audience's attention.[1] But Sabbatini was already far out of date, for at some time in the first quarter of the century the system of stage design had been discovered which was to last with only minor modifications for nearly three hundred years. The secret was to paint the setting on flat panels or wings, standing parallel to each other on either side of the stage. This had an aesthetic appeal – it was even more of a challenge to the painter's skill in creating the illusion of depth – and it offered also one very clear practical advantage; other sets of wings could be placed immediately behind the ones seen by the audience, and to change the entire setting it was only necessary that the first set of wings should be pulled back and the second set pushed out in their place.

The introduction of scenery painted on flat wings is usually credited to the architect G. B. Aleotti, who built a theatre at Ferrara in 1606 as well as the famous Teatro Farnese – the first theatre to be equipped with a permanent proscenium arch – at Parma in 1618. It is not known precisely where or when his first wings made their appearance. In a volume of his

Fig. 133 Torelli, *Il Bellerofonte*, 1642

drawings, mainly architectural, in the library at Ferrara there are two very interesting studies for a forest setting made up of flat wings (Figs 134 and 135), which are probably the earliest surviving diagrams of this very important type of setting. There is no suggestion in these drawings of any system for moving the wings, but once they existed in a flat form this became an obvious next step.

Until the late 1630s the development of opera, with its spectacular scenery and machines, had been achieved through occasional performances in the courts of princes – as an example of just how occasional, Aleotti's great Teatro Farnese was not used for a performance until 1628, ten years after it had been built[2] – but in the following decades it was the public opera houses in Venice which took the lead. The first, the Teatro San Cassiano, was opened in 1637. It was so successful that within four years it had been followed by four others and it was at the last of these, the Teatro Novissimo, that the next step forward in Italian scenery occurred. The opening production, *La Finta Pazza* in 1641, introduced an invention of Giacomo Torelli by which the eight pairs of wings were all linked to a counterweight system and could be changed instantaneously when one person, even 'a single boy of fifteen years', released the weights.[3] Previously each wing had needed its own stage hand to push it forward in its groove or rail. Torelli cut through the stage and hung each wing on a tall framework, which moved backwards and forwards on a trolley beneath the stage – much like the trolley under the sea monster in Fig. 126 – and the trolleys were all connected by ropes to a central drum. This invention soon

---

[1]313, 71–2;   [2]12, I, 273;   [3]69, 109

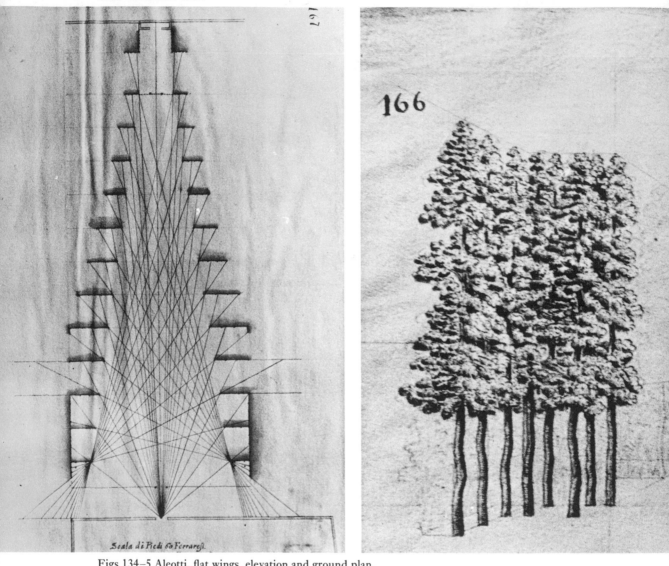

Figs 134–5 Aleotti, flat wings, elevation and ground plan,
early seventeenth century

swept through Italy and later through much of Europe, though London and Amsterdam and various German cities kept faithfully to the earlier method of grooves on the surface of the stage. A complete example of Torelli's system of machinery can still be seen under the stage at Drottningholm.

Torelli was a very original designer as well as a brilliant machinist, and in the following year – with his final setting for *Il Bellerofonte* – he introduced in Venice the perspective stage's first true 'interior' (Fig. 133), in which the canvas borders above the stage were included in the illusion to represent a ceiling. A contemporary description suggests that he may also, for this particular setting, have placed panels between the wings, and at right angles to them, to form continuous interior walls along both sides, giving something of the effect of a box-set.[1]

154

In 1654 Torelli went to Paris for a series of productions which introduced the splendours of changeable scenery to the French, and his example in taking the new style abroad was soon followed by several other designers from the public theatres of Venice. The Burnacini family, who went to Vienna, and Franceso Santurini, who chose Munich, were extremely important figures in the rapid conquest of Europe by the Italian scenery. But in chronological terms it was the English court which was the first to be converted. And there the reason was not the visit of an Italian designer, but the return from Italy of an English one – Inigo Jones.

[1]69, 72

THE EUROPEAN STYLE

Italian scenery spreads: to England

In 1600 the public theatres in London were firmly established, with their free form of staging in front of a permanent neutral façade, but other forms of entertainment – particularly the masques at court and the performances of boy companies in the private theatres – still remained much closer to a medieval form of multiple setting.

A payment for properties at court in 1574, recorded in the Revels Accounts, is for such items as 'Monsters, Mountaynes, fforestes, Beastes, Serpentes . . . dishes for devells eyes, heaven, hell, & the devell',[1] and the deployment of these props in the entertainment certainly suggests a more primitive version of the style of France's *Balet Comique* in 1581. In a similar vein William Percy, a dramatist writing for the boys of St Paul's towards the end of the sixteenth century, describes his scene as requiring:

> A Kiln of Brick. A fowen Cott. A Hollowe Oake with vice of wood to shutt to. A Lowe well with Roape and Pullye. A Fourme of Turves. A green Bank being Pillowe to the Hed. Lastly A Hole to creepe in and out.

This is like Mahelot without even the orderly influence of Serlio, but Percy realises that his stage may become a hopeless clutter and continues:

> Now if so be that the Properties . . . will not serve the turne by reason of concourse of the People on the Stage, Then you may omitt the sayd Properties . . . and supplye their Places with their Nuncupations onely in Text Letters.[2]

It is perhaps worth adding that if the producer at this private theatre followed such early Brechtian advice and labelled parts of the stage, the event would be very untypical of any other known type of Elizabethan staging; and that the term 'private' theatre is a misnomer, the precise reason for which is unknown; they differed from the public theatres only in that they were smaller, were indoors, and charged more for their seats.

Around 1600, then, the court and the private theatres were decidedly backward in terms of staging, but very soon the court was to forge ahead – almost entirely owing to Inigo Jones. In his twenties, around the turn of the century, Jones spent a few years in Italy and he went back there at least once in later life. As an architect he was much impressed by the work of Palladio – he came back with a copy of Palladio's *Architettura*, and inside it a drawing of his own, closely imitating the Teatro Olimpico[3] – but as a set-designer the real influence on him was Florentine, in the work of Giulio Parigi, himself a pupil of Buontalenti's and his successor as the chief stage designer for the Medicis.

156

Fig. 136 Alfonso Parigi, *La Flora*, 1628
Fig. 137 Inigo Jones, *Chloridia*, 1631

Many of Jones's designs seem directly inspired by those of Giulio or his son Alfonso, most of whose work was immediately etched and published – so that even when Jones was not in Italy their influence would have continued to reach him. As an example, Fig. 136 is a setting by Alfonso Parigi for *La Flora* in Florence in 1628, and Fig. 137 is a scene by Inigo Jones for a masque, *Chloridia*, at the English court three years later. Nevertheless, even if many of his

Sources (*see* p. 317)   [1]123, 111–2;   [2]244, III, 137;   [3]31, Fig. 150

ideas were borrowed, Jones pushed the techniques of English staging forward at an amazing speed. From 1605 onwards he experimented with *periaktoi*, with Serlian two-sided houses, with back 'shutters' which opened to reveal two-dimensional cut-out scenes 'in relieve', and finally in the late 1630s with a fully fledged system of flat wings in grooves.[1] By himself he had taken England in thirty-five years through a whole century of Italian scenic development – and in doing so had been roundly abused by Ben Jonson for making 'painting and carpentry . . . the soul of masque'.[2] His most spectacular production, *Salmacida Spolia*, is also the first in which he can actually be proved to have used flat wings in grooves, since the stage diagrams survive.[3] It took place in 1640, or almost exactly the period when even Sabbattini, working in Italy, had shown that he still knew nothing of this new system.

Inigo Jones also designed the costumes for the English masques and here too his style was largely Florentine, following very closely a tradition which is common to Vasari, Buontalenti and the Parigis. Typical is the costume to be worn by the queen, Henrietta Maria (Fig. 138), also for *Chloridia* in 1631. It still carries a handwritten note by Jones which suggests most vividly the usual last minute rush in preparing any entertainment:

> This dessigne I conceave to bee fitt for the invention and if it is leafe hir Majestie to add or alter any thing I desier to receave hir Majestie's command and the dessigne againe by this bearer. The collors also are in hir Majestie's choise; but my oppinion is that several fresh greenes mix with gould and silver will be most propper.

It is certain that these new developments at court would gradually have spread to the theatres, and there seem to have been a few special productions at the private theatres between 1635 and 1640 with expensive painted settings,[4] but any such natural process was ended abruptly in 1642 when the Puritans closed the theatres. However, when serious performances began again, tentatively, in the form of a private production of *The Siege of Rhodes* given by Davenant in 1656, it was with rather elementary Italian scenery; and in the London theatres built after the Restoration such scenery was normal, though always on a much smaller and less impressive scale than in foreign courts or in the public opera houses of Venice. Indeed for the whole period only one group of settings ever achieved the usual accolade of being etched – the five scenes for Settle's *Empress of Morocco* in 1673, of which the prison (Fig. 139) is the most elaborate.

Nevertheless the degree to which the Italian manner eventually became general, with its proscenium arch and flat pieces of scenery, can be seen in Fig. 140 where even a country performance of 1788, in something much like a barn, does its best to approximate to the pattern. The cut-out trees will be pushed on from the wings, even though without grooves; and the outline of drapes and tassels above the proscenium will look to the audience like a proper curtain (a technique which was also used in much more expensive theatres). An interesting detail of the production, and one that is possible only in this type of staging, is the row of cut-out kings mounted on a plank, which can be seen among the jumble of drums, shields and banners in the loft above the prompter, who sits on a barrel with his book; this row of models will be pulled across the back of the stage when Macbeth sees the future descendants of Banquo in a vision. The patrons of this little playhouse look as if they would have been most flattered by a description of a similar theatre at Margate in the 1770s: 'Notwithstanding the neighing of horses, and

---

[1]12, VI, 793–5;   [2]30, 155;   [3]31, Figs 78–9;   [4]224, 14

Fig. 138 Inigo Jones, the queen's costume, *Chloridia*, 1631

Fig. 139 *The Empress of Morocco*, 1673 (*above right*)

Fig. 140 A country performance, 1788

yelping of dogs in the stable over which the stage was built, the place occasionally overflowed with the best company.'[1]

The witches, entering on their trap, are typical of Italian methods, but this time not exclusively so; they could always have entered in this way, because the Globe had similar machinery and Macbeth, just before seeing the vision of kings, says 'Why sinks that cauldron?' as it begins to be lowered through the floor. The type of machinery which achieved these effects can be seen in an etching of 1844 by George Cruikshank (Fig. 141), which claims to show how two actors had tortured a colleague at Drury Lane by whipping his legs while he was slowly lowered during the final impressive lines of his speech as a ghost. As almost all types of stage use traps, one can say that the only distinctive feature of Shakespeare's theatre to survive the arrival of the Italian system was the permanent stage doors, which were built in front of the proscenium in English theatres throughout the eighteenth century. Through them the actors made their entrance on to the main acting area, the part of the stage in front of the proscenium known now as the apron. These doors can be seen at Covent Garden in Fig. 208 and they remained exclusively British – until, as such, they formed a natural part of the earliest American theatres, both in Philadelphia (Fig. 249) and in New York (Figs 250–1).

To France

The first Italian perspective setting with flat wings to be seen in France was the one designed for *Mirame* (Fig. 142), with which Richelieu in 1641 opened the expensive theatre which he had built in his own palace. However, although the wings were flat, they never changed during the entire play. There were flying machines and apparitions, but the only variations in the setting itself were lighting changes from night to day and the gradual movement of the sun through the sky. This was due not to any lack in the Cardinal's new stage equipment but to the French concern with the Unity of Place, which had become increasingly important since the quarrels about Corneille's *Le Cid* in 1637. A few weeks later a ballet was presented in the theatre, *Le Ballet de la Prospérité des Armes de France*, which – unlike a play – was not bound by the new classical rules and therefore did have several changes of scenery. The settings have recently been shown to have been much more lavish than was previously assumed, and they seem to have been painted on flat wings which could change within view of the audience.[2]

Richelieu, who had loved classical drama and the ballet, died in 1642; and Louis XIII, whose passion had also been the ballet, died the following year. Under the Italian cardinal, Mazarin, and the queen, Anne of Austria, the emphasis in Paris turned suddenly towards opera. In 1645 Anne wrote to the Duke of Parma, asking him to send her his set designer, Camillo.[3] Instead he sent Torelli, and in that same year Torelli built an Italian stage, complete with his own scenery and machinery, in the large hall of the Petit Bourbon – the very room which had housed the *Balet Comique* in 1581. The opening opera was *La Finta Pazza*, with which Torelli had introduced his system of scene-changing and had established his reputation in Venice thirteen years before. It was a huge success, with the *Gazette* enthusing over its 'admirable changes of scene, until now unknown in France'[4] – a sentence which has caused the scene-changes in the *Prospérité des Armes de France* four years earlier to have been disregarded. The explanation may be partly that Richelieu's ballet had been a private performance, seen by comparatively

---

[1]265, I, 176; [2]20, 381 ff.; [3]69, 121; [4]69, 123

Fig. 141 Trap mechanism, 1844

Fig. 142 *Mirame*, 1641

Fig. 143 Torelli, *Andromède*, 1650

few invited guests, and partly that Torelli's scene-changing was undoubtedly swifter and more magical than anything the Palais-Cardinal could provide.[1]

In 1647 Torelli designed scenes and machines for an opera, *Orphée*, which only had six performances, and so Corneille was commissioned to write a play which would make further use of Torelli's expensive machines. The result was *Andromède*, yet another version of the best of all machine stories, which was presented in 1650. Fig. 143 is one of Torelli's five settings.

These two productions, *Mirame* in 1641 and *Andromède* in 1650, represent the two main strands of French theatre for the rest of the century. Both used Italian scenery, but for entirely different purposes. The setting for *Mirame* has been called 'the first *palais à volonté* on the French stage'.[2] Though probably not the very first, it is certainly the first to be illustrated; and it leads towards Racine and Molière and the powerful traditions of French classical drama, so widely influential throughout eighteenth-century Europe, in which Unity of Place demanded a single setting but Italian scenery could be used to make it look attractive and realistic. An insular traveller from England, where the Unities had been taken seriously only by a few, fell foul of the style when he saw such a production as late as 1833 in Naples and commented:

> They follow that abominably stupid rule of never changing the first scene thro'out the whole piece! What stuff! – So if the first scene is 'a street', perchance the whole of the actors make it convenient to dine . . . all in the street!! Oh what tomfooling . . . I think old Aristotle did not show his philosophy when he laid down this rule for dramatic composition.[3]

The other strand, that of the *pièce à machines*, had been eagerly taken up even before *Andromède* by the Théâtre du Marais – the company which had grown up in the 1630s as the only rival to the Hôtel de Bourgogne, and which after a fire in 1644 rebuilt its theatre with fairly elaborate machinery. As early as 1648 they clearly realised the appeal of the spectacular, when they gave a revival of Chapoton's *Descente d'Orphée aux Enfers* having rechristened it *La Grande Journée des Machines ou Le Marriage d'Orphée et d'Eurydice*.[4] The vogue for machine plays lasted until the 1680s[5] and by 1669 the Académie Royale de Musique, which later became the Opéra, had been founded and was able to satisfy all future demands for lavish productions. So the strict French devotion to the Unities in straight drama never deprived Paris entirely of the spectacular pleasures from Italy.

To Austria and Germany

Although there were occasional operatic performances in the German-speaking countries from as early as 1618, when the Archbishop of Salzburg presented an opera at his palace,[6] the first energetic influence from Italy came through the work of an enthusiastic theorist, Joseph Furttenbach, a student of engineering and architecture who spent some time at Giulio Parigi's academy in Florence. He returned to Germany in 1621, and in 1627 published an account of his travels, *Newe itinerarium Italiae*, with a description of the theatre built by Buontalenti in the Uffizi and a print of a scene on its stage.[7] In 1640 he followed this with a much fuller account, in *Architectura Recreationis*, of how settings should be constructed on a stage; and this, together with later passages on theatrical lighting and machinery fitted here and there into his many

[1]20, 389; [2]20, 401; [3]221, 172; [4]69, 120; [5]281, V, 17; [6]240, 7; [7]reprod. 167, 42

Fig. 144 Cross-section of stage by Furttenbach, 1640

Fig. 145 Wing flat, *c.* 1700

books on architecture, fortifications, fireworks, artillery and garden design, makes him the German Sabbattini. But he was like Sabbattini also in being a little out of date. In 1640 he was still earnestly explaining how three-dimensional houses should be turned as *periaktoi* (Fig. 144) – the very method which Sabbattini had recommended two years earlier as the best way to change scenery. Furttenbach did have a chance to put his theories into practice when he was invited to build a theatre at Ulm in 1641, the first public theatre in Germany with changeable scenery.[1] But he was only involved in two productions there, both school productions, and he complained continually that everything in Germany was on too small a scale to match the theatrical glories he had known in Italy.

However Vienna, closely rivalled by Munich, was soon to provide the most spectacular Italianate productions of the entire century. The immediate cause was the Emperor Leopold I himself. The princes of almost every European court of the time were eager to show a leg in a masque or to appear in triumph at the climactic moment of an opera, but Leopold was also a prolific and ambitious composer – a fact, however, not much likely to benefit native German opera, since he said he would prefer 'an Italian aria sung by a horse to a German aria in the mouth of the most beautiful of singers'.[2]

The superbly spectacular quality of the Viennese court operas was due entirely to the Burnacini family. The father, Giovanni, was brought from Venice in 1651 by Leopold's father, Ferdinand III, himself also a composer. But it was Giovanni's son, Lodovico, who was to design the most lavish productions, including the greatest of all, *Il Pomo d'Oro* in 1668, with its twenty-two complete changes of setting. Lodovico Burnacini brought much more fanciful detail to the painting of the wings than any stage artist before him, and greatly enlarged the type of subject which the wings might represent. A setting for *Il Fuoco Eterno* in 1674, for example, where the wings incorporated elaborate and intriguing machinery (Fig. 146), was highly original at the

164

time – and remained rare even after Burnacini, since most set-designers were usually content with the few well-established types. An interesting exception is an anonymous series of drawings in Stockholm for the wings of a hell scene, dating from about 1700, where machines of torture and jagged red hot steps are neatly combined with the usual flames of the inferno (Fig. 145). The flames are painted on the flat wing, which is cut out so that it will merge almost imperceptibly with the one behind it. Sabbattini had said that the way to make a set appear to burn was to sprinkle it with *aqua vitae* and to set fire to it; this, he insisted, was not 'extremely

Fig. 146 Lodovico Burnacini, *Il Fuoco Eterno*, 1674

dangerous, though there is always a certain risk attached'.[3] In this respect too, the painters' new skill with flat wings must have seemed a welcome advance.

Another excellent example of Burnacini's extension of the rôle played by the wings, involving them more in the action, is a setting for *Il Ratto delle Sabine* with rows of lively spectators painted in their boxes for a tournament, during which the rape occurs (Fig. 147). This time it is possible to see even more clearly how the figures were painted on separate flat wings, since in the extensive collection of drawings by Johann Oswald Harms at Braunschweig there are sketches for precisely such wings (Fig. 148). The similarity is so great that Harms may have

[1]12, V, 778; [2]12, VI, 1406; [3]313, 85

Fig. 147 Lodovico Burnacini, *Il Ratto delle Sabine*, 1674
Fig. 148 Harms, wing flats, late seventeenth century

been inspired directly by the etching of Burnacini's scene. Harms was the first native German set-designer of any merit, though he too had received his training in Venice in about 1670.[1]

The most impressive productions of the seventeenth century in Germany itself had taken place a little earlier, in the 1660s, at the court of Bavaria in Munich, with settings by another Venetian, Francesco Santurini. The extremely theatrical quality of Santurini's imagination makes him one of the most interesting of all the great seventeenth-century designers, though he has been considerably neglected – partly perhaps because no drawings survive of his sets

Fig. 149 Santurini, *Berenice Vendicativa*, 1680

and the etchings are technically of very poor quality. He was the only set-designer to apply his imagination to the entire playing area of the stage; no other designer had attempted to divide up the stage, using the setting to create different theatrical areas, but Santurini did this both horizontally and vertically. His division of the stage down the centre into two separate rooms, for *Berenice Vendicativa* at Piazzola in 1680 (Fig. 149), is an ambitious but rather awkward use of seventeenth-century scenery – though this type of treatment of the stage, not considered

[1]309, 15 ff.

Fig. 150 Santurini, *Fedra Incoronata*, 1662
Fig. 151 Jesuit school opera, 1654

again for a hundred years, would return to fascinate designers from the nineteenth century onwards. But Santurini's division of the stage into two vertical areas, for *Fedra Incoronata* at Munich in 1662 (Fig. 150), is entirely and triumphantly successful. Flat wings are ideally suited to cope with the surface of the water running along the eye-line; and a platform half way up the back scene, which was generally used for the much more routine business of supporting an apparition of gods, makes an obvious place for the rowing boat to move along, setting its seal on the illusion. The hero is free to wander about in the open air among the painted shells and weeds, and yet seem perfectly submerged.

It was in Vienna and Munich too that the Jesuit drama – having started more humbly a century earlier – reached the giddiest heights of baroque theatricality. The Jesuit schoolboys were in the main aristocratic, and so their annual productions became closely associated with the entertainments at the two courts. The texts were in Latin, the themes were suitably pious, and the performers were all amateurs; but apart from this, as Fig. 151 shows, the result was much like any other expensive opera. This particular scene is from *Theodosius Magnus*, done in 1654 in Vienna. The Genius of Theodosius (played by Ioannes Fridericus Hoffer, Gram.) is very properly tipping the Genius of the tyrant Eugenius (Ioannes Doll Hassus, Rhetor) off his dragon, while fifteen schoolboys of only slightly less academic distinction cavort as satyrs below. The cast list at the end is always a prominent part of Jesuit plays, and usually the larger the part the greater the number of academic achievements after a performer's name. Theodosius himself, when he finally appears, is played by no less than R. D. Paulinus Mayr, A.A & Phil. Mag. SS. Theol. Aud.

To other countries

Changeable Italian scenery arrived early in Spain, when Cosimo II de' Medici sent Cosimo Lotti – yet another designer who had worked with Buontalenti and the Parigis – to the court of Philip IV. He arrived in Spain in 1626, and his first spectacular production was of Lope de Vega's *La selva sin amor* in 1629, for which his moving sea was so convincing that it was said to have made the women in the audience sea-sick.[1] From then on the style was well established at court, and in 1640 Lotti was also employed by the Jesuits in Madrid for a production to celebrate the centenary of their order.[2] Fig. 152 is one of two Dutch etchings of about 1680 showing Charles II and his new French queen, Marie Louise, watching a court opera. The cloud machines are familiar enough, but at the side of the stage the artist has painted the illusion of the wings, as seen from the front, rather than the wings themselves.

During the course of the seventeenth and eighteenth centuries the Italian scenery spread to every country in Europe. Among those not already treated individually the most interesting are Holland, which is dealt with separately in a later chapter, and Sweden, where by a lucky accident an entire court theatre of this type, with its complete stock of scenery and machinery, survives to this day at Drottningholm. Although not built until 1764–6, the scenery painted for it was still firmly in the style of the seventeenth century. The theatre was used continuously until the end of the eighteenth century, but only very occasionally during the nineteenth, finally becoming a store-room for court paintings. It was this disuse which saved it from alteration, and the scholar who re-discovered it, Agne Beijer, was in fact looking for a painting there in

---

[1] 196, 275–6; [2] 196, 449

Fig. 152 Opera at the Spanish court, *c.* 1680
Fig. 153 *Li Buffoni*, 1641 (*above right*)
Fig. 154 A street setting, Drottningholm

1921 when he found, stacked against each other on the stage, the complete groups of wings and backcloths for a great many different settings. Apart from the process of cleaning them and the renewal of the ropes in the machinery, no actual restoration was needed before the theatre could be used again in precisely the way it had been designed for; and every summer now seventeenth- and eighteenth-century operas are performed in it. It is appropriate to end this section, after so many prints of the Italian settings, by showing one in reality – a street of classical buildings leading down to the sea (Fig. 154). Although they look exactly like Serlian two-sided houses, the straight bottom edge to each wing reveals that this is only the result of the scene-painter's cunning illusion.

Fig. 155 Stage in Nuremberg Fechthaus, *c.* 1730

The mixing of styles

Around 1600 England, Spain, France and Italy all had very distinct national styles in their entertainments and it was therefore convenient to treat them as separate strands until, by the end of the seventeenth century, the Italian system had established itself throughout Europe. But it is wrong to suggest that each strand was entirely isolated or self-contained.

For example, I chose France to describe the gradual inclusion of the Commedia dell'Arte within the permanent indoor theatres, because it was in France that the process was most striking and most influential. But in other places too, and in other ways, the figures of the Commedia

171

Fig. 156 Stage in amphithe
at Verona,

172

Pl. XIX Interior of the Com
Italienne: wash drawing by P. R. Wille?, 1

Pl. XX Design for a fan showing Bartholom
Fair: watercolour by Thomas Loggon? c. 1740 (overle

COMEDY IN THE COUNTRY.

TRAGEDY IN LONDON.

Pub May 29 by Tho? Tegg N° 111 Cheapside — One Shilling colour'd

Rowlandson Sculp

dell'Arte found themselves incorporated in more formal types of theatre. In 1641 Margherita Costa wrote a literary comedy, *Li Buffoni*, of which the subject was 'zanies, buffoons and dwarfs', and therefore in Stephano della Bella's frontispiece (Fig. 153) the figures of the Commedia dell'Arte are seen in a formal Serlian setting. Della Bella has drawn the performers in the angular prancing positions which derive from Jacques Callot's *Balli di Sfessania* in about 1625, a much copied series of little etchings which made the Commedia dell'Arte performers one of the most popular of seventeenth-century graphic images.

At the same time as some of the strolling performers were moving into the regular theatre, others were taking the apparatus of the regular theatre with them on their travels. The simple platform of the booth stages survived now only in the fairs – as a balcony outside temporary enclosed theatres, on which the actors would appear in their full costume to try and entice people to visit the show inside. They can be seen doing so at Bartholomew Fair in about 1740 (Pl. XX, pp. 174–5), and at two French fairs of the eighteenth century.[1] The real travelling theatres, performing still in market places or in any open area, began in the eighteenth century to deck themselves out with various arrangements of wings. A mobile theatre set up once again in the Fechthaus at Nuremberg in about 1730 (Fig. 155) has as many pairs of wings as the smaller permanent theatres of the day, and yet still keeps the old Commedia dell'Arte arrangement of the two houses downstage with a practicable door and window in each. The advance from the old type of booth stage set up by tumblers on the same Nuremberg site only forty years before (Fig. 100) is considerable. In subject matter, too, the players in Fig. 155 have borrowed from the serious theatre, confronting Harlequin with the plumed hero and heroine of tragedy.

More elaborate still is the temporary stage set up in 1772 in another older and larger arena – the Roman amphitheatre in Verona (Fig. 156). Here, as well as the excellently painted wings and backcloth, there are even some very fashionable boxes. Yet while so energetically imitating the present, the whole scene also strikes an echo from a very distant past. Not only are the canvas strips, for providing shade, a version of the old Roman *velarium* (Fig. 31), but the Phlyakes, remote ancestors of the Commedia dell'Arte, would themselves have set up their temporary stages in the middle of theatres or amphitheatres in just this way.[2] Even the puppet theatre, animating the same familiar Commedia dell'Arte characters, and with the puppeteer looking out through his curtain above the stage (Fig. 157), makes very effective use of the flat Italian wings.

These popular scenes are all from the eighteenth century, when the Italian style had had plenty of time to spread in the normal course of events. But during the seventeenth century one important element in the rapid spread of the new scenery throughout Europe was the vast number of opera settings which were etched and published – for the most part with a literal attention to theatrical detail which is unequalled before or since, except in Holland during the eighteenth century. We have seen how etchings of Parigi influenced Inigo Jones and how Harms could be inspired by a print of Burnacini, and even the princes themselves seem to have deliberately tried to outdo the published splendour of each others' theatricals. Fig. 158 shows Louis XIV watching an open air performance at Versailles in 1664. Fig. 159 shows his great rival, Leopold I, watching an open air performance in Vienna in 1700. Admittedly the gap between the two events is a long one, but can Leopold really have been unaware of the comparison?

---

[1] both 12, V, Tav. LII; [2] 42, 67

Pl. XXI Satirical etching by Thomas Rowlandson, *c.* 1810

177

Des Policinello
Abentheurliche
Reise.

Fig. 158 Louis XIV, Versailles, 1664
Fig. 159 Leopold I, Vienna, 1700

The Low Countries and Amsterdam

In a history of theatrical illustrations the Low Countries, and Holland in particular, play a uniquely important role. Not only did they reflect nearly all the important developments in European staging between the sixteenth and eighteenth centuries, but they recorded them in paintings and etchings with unparalleled completeness and accuracy.

In the sixteenth century there were more frequent royal entries into cities of the Low Countries than anywhere else in Europe – largely because these cities came under a rapidly changing succession of foreign princes, each of whom felt it politic to put in a spectacular appearance – and the street theatres, with their allegorical *tableaux* or playlets, were a special feature of these northern entries. Closely linked with these little theatres were the famous Chambers of Rhetoric, amateur societies something in the style of the medieval *confréries*. Every town had its Chamber of Rhetoric and periodically the Chambers gathered together for a theatrical festival, lasting many days, in which they competed by acting allegorical plays on set themes. For the greatest of these competitions ever held, the Landjuweel at Antwerp in 1561, which lasted a whole month, the plays all had to answer the eternal question which plagues all those who wish to promote culture: 'What can best awaken man to the liberal arts?' The first prize went to a Chamber whose play answered 'Praise, honour & reward' and the second to 'The hope of eternal glory in this world and the next'. Second-grade Chambers had a separate competition on a more practical theme: 'Which profession not now highly esteemed would bring the most reward and nobility?' The winners enacted 'The reclamation and cultivation of the land'.[1]

Prints survive of the stages on which these rather earnest moralities were performed at both Ghent in 1539 and Antwerp in 1561,[2] and it has often been pointed out that their architectural façades, with a form of inner stage and a balcony above, bear a close relationship to the later public stage in England. A very similar type of stage was used in the street theatres in many of

---

[1]44, 116–122;   [2]31, Figs 139–140

Fig. 157 Puppet theatre, *c.* 1730

Fig. 160 Rhetoricians' stage, Amsterdam, 1609 (*overleaf*)

D'hoveerdighe Tarquyn velt d'hooghste Bloemen nu,
Dats slaet de hoofden de Ghemeente is van der weer

Den dwinghelant Tarquyn het volck vertredt het,
En Brutus speelt den Set, al gh'hem wel gheret

Van Lucretius Eere getuyghen zyn gheneeft,
Maer Needt voor haren Man, en voor de Goon haer

ALDVS WAS HET TOONNEEL, STAEN

Tarquin en syn gheslacht van d'allerhooghste trap
versoeken, moeten uyt en gaen in ballingschap

Wil boven eyghen baet elck een de Vryheyt min

De vryheyt van syn lant slaet Brutus voor soo waardt
Dat hy zyn Soons daer voer niet van de doodt en spaert

the royal entries, which is not surprising since it was the Chambers of Rhetoric who were usually asked to provide them.[1] Typical is a street theatre in Brussels in 1594 (Fig. 161). The Rhetoricians are known to have used the balcony in their productions, as well as the inner stage below it – as an area for scenes or *tableaux* to be 'discovered' when a curtain is drawn.[2] They also used very substantial props. In Antwerp in 1561 there was brought on 'an arbor, made all open that what happens within may be seen from all sides'; Man goes to sleep in this arbor, and

Fig. 161 Street theatre, Brussels, 1594

is only wakened by Fear of Poverty after Self-Satisfaction, Desire for Knowledge, and Industry have all failed to rouse him.[3] This is virtually still a medieval mansion, of much the same type as Pan's grove in the *Balet Comique* in Paris in 1581, and there is evidence that this type of scenery was used also on the public stages in London – forming yet another link, together with the façade, the balcony and the inner stage, between the Elizabethan theatre and its predecessors in the street shows of the Low Countries.[4]

By 1609 the Rhetoricians had moved towards a proscenium theatre. One of the most fascinating of all theatrical prints shows the stage which the Chamber called *De Eglantier* put up in Amsterdam in 1609 (Fig. 160), and the stage is surrounded with ten scenes from the play. The scenes show that, in spite of the proscenium and curtain, the production was still in an abstract setting and still retained a vestige of a slightly raised inner stage at the back. In the top left-hand

182

Fig. 162 Deceitful people, 1631
Fig. 163 Temporary stage in tent, 1683

scene there is a rare glimpse of the type of small piece which was brought on to suggest a setting, in this case a very portable bank of flowers. The bottom scene on the left shows that the old medieval conjuring trick of decapitation still had its appeal, and in one of the scenes on the right a panel of the curtain is put to a very theatrical and non-literal use in providing a hiding place behind an arras.

Soon these particular Rhetoricians were to take part in the founding of a permanent theatre in Amsterdam. In 1617 Samuel Coster founded a new-style Chamber of Rhetoric, leaning more towards the Italian academies of the Renaissance, which he called the Nederduytsche Academie. It concentrated on theatrical activities and in 1635 the new academy joined with *De Eglantier* to build, in 1637/38, Amsterdam's first theatre.[5] With this we begin the story of the famous Amsterdam Schouwburg, but – before moving into it – it is worth looking at the more popular forms of theatre which had co-existed with the Chambers of Rhetoric and would continue to do so with the Schouwburg. For popular theatre, too, is better illustrated in the Low Countries than anywhere else.

As we saw earlier, it is from these areas that the Brueghel family provided the best surviving illustrations of truly primitive theatre in Europe (Figs 9 and 89) and also of the most basic form of the booth stage (Pl. XIV, p. 104). As the conditions of the wandering players improved, they more often found themselves able to set up their stages indoors. This happened in every country, but illustrations showing them indoors with their audiences are almost unknown except in Holland and Flanders, where there are several examples. A small book of popular homilies,

[1] 44, 60–1;   [2] 44, 121–2;   [3] 44, 121–2;   [4] 308, 85;   [5] 12, I, 502

Fig. 164 Tennis-court theatre in The Hague, 1635

dated 1631, fortunately chooses as its illustration of 'deceitful people' a troupe of Commedia dell'Arte performers (Fig. 162) on a simple indoor stage made of curtains, with two puppets performing 'above'. Apart from defeating the weather, the obvious advantage of playing indoors is that one can collect money more efficiently from the spectators. But the supply of light through the window is more important than the one girl who is getting a free glimpse.

A watercolour by Peeter Bout from 1683 shows the eternally popular rope-dancers on a similar platform, this time with a more definite inner stage (Fig. 163), but the most elaborate and revealing of all the Dutch or Flemish interior stages is an etching of 1635, published in a book describing a couple's experiences at the fair in the Hague (Fig. 164). As the scene in the Nuremberg Fechthaus showed (Fig. 100), there was nothing unusual in having two separate stages – in this case a conjuror's at this end and the players' stage at the other. The trick of walking a tightrope over the heads of the audience was still being performed by Blondin and others in nineteenth-century theatres, though undoubtedly if the tightrope-walker is a lady in skirts an extra excitement is offered to the pit. The artist's only probable distortion is to show all these activities happening at once, all lessening each other's appeal, but each separate act is mentioned in the text and he wanted to include them all in his illustration.

Behind the exaggerated flurry of activity the building itself is of extraordinary interest. The throne or projecting inner stage, with its canopy and the curtain which can hide or discover whatever is within, is in a well-established Dutch and Flemish tradition. It relates to the throne in the street theatre of 1594 (Fig. 161); it appears in the first Amsterdam Schouwburg in 1637 (Fig. 165); and it is seen in the more elaborate open air theatres of wandering performers of the period, as at Louvain in 1594.[1] The long curtain behind is merely an extension of the normal booth stage curtain, though by now it contains an entrance on either side of the throne. On one side of the stage there is still the old ladder, perhaps for occasional appearances at an upper level as well as to reach the slack rope for more antics; and on the other side can be seen an example of the more solid type of platform for appearances above. The trees visible behind, which have no reason to be growing in here, are almost certainly property trees which can be brought out on to the stage.

Even more interesting, the building itself is the most common of all temporary theatres in the seventeenth century, a converted tennis court. It was first suggested on the evidence of the print alone[2] that this must be a tennis court, with its long horizontal windows, here partially boarded up, and with the steeply-rising rows of spectators on the left who could be sitting on the sloping roof of the spectators' gallery. The identification is proved by the fact that comedians performing at the fair in the Hague during the first half of the seventeenth century had a choice of two buildings – the Piquerie, a brick building which was lit by ten individual windows, and a tennis court, presumably wooden, which had been built beside it in 1624.[3] It is reasonable to suppose that Fig. 164 must show one or the other, since the book was published in 1635 in the Hague and considerable accuracy is likely in such a detailed illustration of a local event; and of the two it must clearly be the tennis court. For the period of the early 1660s contracts even survive employing the master carpenter Hendrik van Erp to convert the inside of the tennis court so that comedians could play in it during the four weeks of the fair. It seems to have taken him each time about a week to put up the stage and the seating arrangements, and about two days to take them down again. He was also always required to close up the tennis court all round, which presumably meant boarding up the windows.[4]

This makes Fig. 164 the only surviving illustration of a tennis court theatre, although it was certainly one of the most common types of indoor playhouse. In France Hendrik van Erp's methods of conversion would have seemed unnecessarily laborious, since travelling companies often played in the evening after the day's tennis matches were over. And the buildings themselves were extremely numerous; in Paris, in 1600, there seem to have been about two hundred and fifty tennis courts.[5] Their use as theatres is most often associated with France, and it is in French theatrical history that the *jeu de paume* plays its most important role – Paris's second permanent company adapted several from 1629 onwards, before finally converting one more thoroughly in 1634 into the first Théâtre du Marais[6] – but they were common elsewhere too. The first theatres in London after the Restoration were hurriedly adapted tennis courts,[7] and the one in the Hague was only one of several which were used by players in Holland.[8]

But Amsterdam's first permanent theatre was something much more ambitious than a converted tennis court, and luckily the Schouwburg of 1637 begins the excellent tradition which the later Schouwburg was to continue so superbly in the eighteenth century – that of leaving behind a series of illustrations of unparalleled interest and reliability. Not only is the 1637 building the first theatre for which there are prints of the view both towards the stage (Fig. 165) and into the auditorium (Fig. 166), but these are even accompanied by a ground-plan of the entire building (Fig. 167).

This Schouwburg also happens to have been a most unusual and significant theatre, combining many separate influences in an awkward but not unintelligent manner. The native influence of the stages of the Rhetoricians is predominant – in the formal arrangement of pillars,

---

[1]22, II, Fig. 23;   [2]217, IX, 1, 5 ff.;   [3]263, 39;   [4]263, 107–112;   [5]154, 159;   [6]12, VII, 768;   [7]17, 236;   [8]263, 460

Fig. 165 Stage of the 1637 Schouwburg

Fig. 166 Auditorium of the 1637 Schouwburg

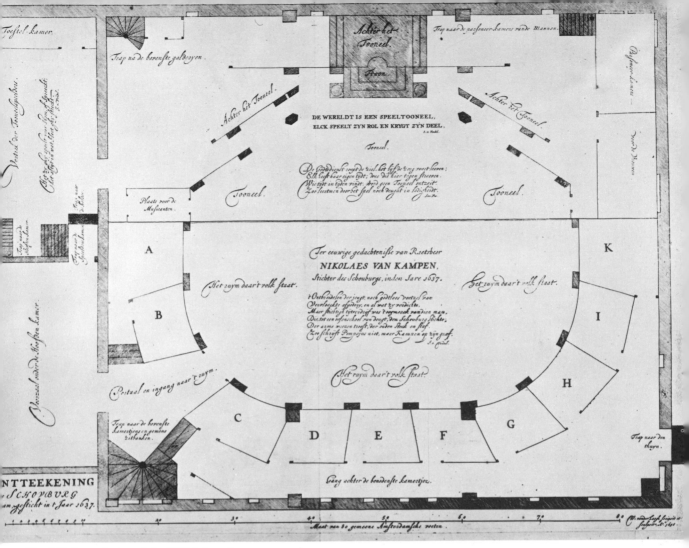

Fig. 167 Ground-plan of the 1637 Schouwburg
Fig. 168 Ground-plan of the 1665–1772 Schouwburg

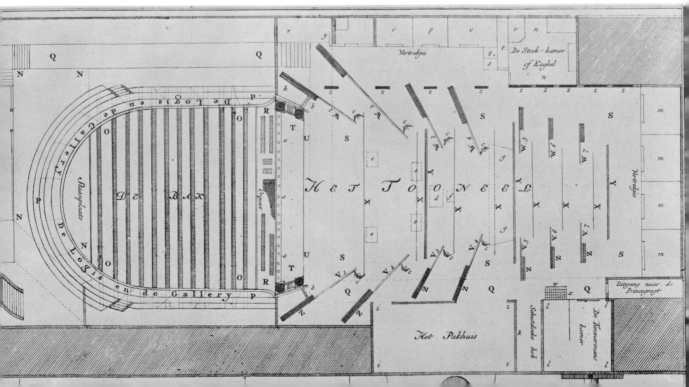

in the practicable galleries above, and in the throne at the back with its own canopy and curtain. But the Italian style had won a foothold in the painted flats which were fitted between the pillars. These flats could remain in keeping with the stage façade when they were purely ornamental, like the first pair in Fig. 165 with their pattern of medallions, but they could also introduce a very different element when they showed a view in perspective, like the Italian street on the second pair of panels in Fig. 165. The positioning of the panels can be seen more clearly on the diagram (Fig. 167), and in a way they make the stage strangely adaptable: if they are all neutral, the area is as generalised as the Elizabethan stage façade; if they are all pictorial views of one place, then the whole stage becomes that place; and if each panel represents a different place, then a system of multiple staging like Mahelot's in Paris becomes feasible. All three styles were current elsewhere when the Schouwburg was built, and it is able to make use of them all. The only limitation is that although the panels were changeable, they were not yet capable of the Italian system of visible and instantaneous changes of scenery. There is therefore an innovation, the curtain, which is an enlarged version of the individual curtain for the throne or for a mansion, but which can now be drawn to hide all four panels while they are changed and yet leave the forestage available for acting – a technique associated almost exclusively with the nineteenth-century stage, but here introduced as a practical solution to a problem two hundred years earlier and without even a proscenium arch. Never have so many different elements been forced to co-habit on one stage. But the result, though ungainly, is surprisingly practical.

The auditorium in Fig. 166 is at least as interesting and rather more typical of its time. Contemporary Paris theatres had standing room in the pit, rows of boxes along the two side walls and across the back, and long benches in an open gallery above them.[1] Nikolaes van Kampen's design for the Schouwburg is in advance of theirs because they, with their origins in halls and tennis courts, were rectangular whereas his curved row of boxes was to become – in an extended form and with sloping rows of benches in the pit below – the typical pattern for auditoria of the eighteenth century. As such, if one allows it the date of its construction in 1637/38, this is the earliest illustration of a 'modern' auditorium. The great barrelled ceiling, which makes room for the large semicircular window at the back of the auditorium and carries light from it towards the stage, is another of van Kampen's entirely practical solutions to a problem; but this particular detail remained uncopied – a relic of a past age, when daylight was expected to light the play, at a period when most indoor theatres were already relying on lamps and candles.

In 1664/65 this Schouwburg was demolished and a new one was built on the same site, the stage now being entirely organised 'in the Italian style as used in Venice'.[2] For this theatre too there is a detailed ground-plan of the stage and auditorium (Fig. 168). This time the ground-plan dates from a whole century later, since it was printed just after the theatre had burnt down in 1772, but there had been only minor alterations between 1665 and 1772 and the diagram's accuracy is confirmed by documentary sources and by other etchings. It shows the first four pairs of wings set at an oblique angle, and then three pairs behind them parallel to the front of the stage. This arrangement was certainly in use in Italy in the seventeenth century,[3] but there was one important respect in which these Amsterdam wings were not based on the system of the leading Venetian theatres – they did not use Torelli's mechanism for scene-changing, with the framework of the wings running on trolleys under the stage. Instead, like England, Amsterdam kept to the older system of grooves on the floor of the stage; a description of 1774 explains

Fig. 169 Forest scene, 1749

that the wings 'were pushed in and out, that is to say moved backwards and forwards, by means of raised slots or grooves . . . of which some used copper but the other wings ran on rollers between wooden slats and were in this way pushed in and out'.[4] A slightly earlier account reveals that it was the longer and therefore heavier downstage wings which needed the grooves to be lined with copper, but that they too ran on a pair of rollers or wheels.[5] The first illustration of these grooves in any theatre is again a Dutch one – an etching by S. Fokke, dated 1749 (Fig. 169), where the slats of the grooves can be seen at the bottom of the wings, particularly on the left of the picture.

Fokke's etching is typical of the Dutch theatrical prints of the eighteenth century. It is artistically accomplished and yet is also supremely accurate and literal. Each of the three pairs of forest wings and sky borders can be clearly identified in front of the cloud machine which

---

[1]281, Part I, Vol. II, 712; [2]172, 131; [3]see diagrams reprod. 175, pp. 105 & 111; [4]226, V, 12; [5]338, 757

Fig. 170 A long gallery

occupies the centre of the stage. The setting could be accurately reconstructed from the print alone. The most impressive series of such etchings – and probably the greatest of all theatrical prints from any period – are the thirteen views of Schouwburg settings published by J. Smit between 1738 and 1772. All these prints show the same precise awareness of each separate wing in every setting. So for example Pl. XXII (p. 193) reveals how an interior was achieved with two pairs of wings and a backcloth – the nineteenth-century box-set will merely fill in a few gaps. Pl. XXIV (p. 194–5) shows how a pleasantly domestic street scene is created with three pairs of wings and a backcloth, together with practicable doors in a few of the pieces. Only a few of the prints were coloured, naturally by hand, but even the colouring seems to have been done with the same conscientious accuracy. In all the coloured versions the pillars on either side of the stage are marbled red and white, which is precisely what they were said to be in a 1765 description of the theatre.[1]

The accuracy of the Dutch prints makes it possible to see just how an eighteenth-century theatre mingled and adapted existing settings to put them to new uses. Painted scenes were expensive, and it was generally accepted that with about a dozen complete settings a theatre was equipped for all contingencies. Figs 170–3 show four different uses for one of the Schouwburg sets. In Fig. 170, one of Smit's series, the setting is seen in its fullest original form – that of a long gallery stretching away to a distant vanishing point, though in fact the

[1]338, 756

Fig. 171 A general's tent
Fig. 172 A throne room (*above right*)
Fig. 173 A general's tent and the camp

perspective after the first four wings was painted on a backcloth.[1] Fig. 171, also by Smit, shows it when a different backcloth – a view of receding tents – has been dropped in, this time behind the first two wings. They themselves are still exactly the same as before, but the new backcloth turns them easily from the walls of a gallery to the interior of a general's very lavish tent, from which we see the vista outside. Figs 172 and 173 are two etchings done later than the Smit series; but, although of much more primitive craftsmanship, they still retain something of the old accuracy. In Fig. 172 the same two first wings have become the walls of a throne room, sealed off this time by a large set-piece representing the throne. But the most cunning transformation of all comes in Fig. 173. Here only the first pair of wings is kept. The statues which are painted on them have been temporarily covered by panels of military trophies; the border above has had a curtain and tassels added to it; in the next three sets of grooves the stock pairs of tree wings are used and, as the accompanying text explains, small painted tent-pieces have been placed in front of them;[2] and the backcloth is a stock piece from a sea setting. So, merely by mingling different settings and by adding just a few special pieces – such as the trophies and the tents, which were both no doubt used also in other combinations – an almost unrecognisable new setting has been created.

A delightful example of the hurried provision of a small panel to alter a stock scene survives from Bristol in 1770. The performance on July 13 was of *Romeo and Juliet*. It appears that the stock prison setting was to be used for the tomb scene, but a few minor prison details were not exactly appropriate. On the very day of the performance Michael Edkins was therefore employed 'painting paper to cover a Bottle and Glass in the Prison Scene'.[3]

The painting of furniture on the wings was common practice in eighteenth-century theatres. Fig. 175, one of the settings for the Schouwburg when it was rebuilt soon after the fire of 1772, shows a farm interior in which everything except one chair, one table and the spinning-wheel is painted on flat canvas. The prints after 1772 continue the earlier accuracy – the two pairs of oblique wings can again be seen – though something of the charm of the earlier prints is lost in the later more grandiose settings. At first sight, however, it may seem that the artist in Fig. 175 is allowing the effect of the painted scenery to be too convincing. One's instinctive reaction is that the details could not possibly have looked so real in the theatre, and that the painted ceiling on its two vertical strips of cloth (the borders) could never have appeared so flat and so solid. One tends to expect such painted interiors to have looked in practice much more like the delightful but ludicrous version offered by Lambranzi in 1716 (Fig. 174). But a very similar setting at Drottningholm proves that even here the Dutch artists were accurate. Fig. 176 is an actual photograph of it on the stage. Every single piece of furniture, every beam, is painted.

It is appropriate, for two reasons, to end this section on the extraordinary Dutch illustrations with an English one – the design by Michael Angelo Rooker for a frontispiece to one of the plays in a collected edition of Beaumont and Fletcher in 1778 (Fig. 177). This is an exceptionally interesting watercolour. First, it is as accurate and literal as the Dutch etchings, and it shows how the mingling of different settings could sometimes be very much more clumsy than anything we have seen. The mixture in Fig. 173 was so tactful that the result almost passed as a complete design, but here the wing on which one of the characters has hung his hat and coat – while sitting in the street outside a cottage – is in fact a stray part of some very splendid rococo interior. Contemporary quotations reveal that such incongruities were not uncommon. A critic

---

[1] 338, 757; [2] 226, VI, 13; [3] 217, XVI, 2, 44

Pl. XXII Interior setting at the Amsterdam Schouwburg: hand-coloured etching, *c.* 1765

Pl. XXIII Animal heroes in Viennese drama: hand-coloured etching, 1830

Pl. XXIV Street setting, Schouwburg: hand-coloured etching, *c.* 1765 (*overleaf*)

La öisamecitia.

Fig. 174 Lambranzi farmhouse, 1716

reviewing Kemble's *Coriolanus* in the late eighteenth century complained that 'a pretty exact representation of *Hanover-square*, and some very neat *Bond-street* shops appeared two, or three times, as parts of Rome'.[1] Even closer to the subject of the watercolour, it was reported in 1822 that 'in the farce of Bombastes Furioso on Friday last, the wing of a Palace was left during an entire scene in a cottage'.[2]

The other fascinating aspect of the English design is that it explains precisely why the accuracy of the Dutch prints was so extraordinarily rare. The majority of theatrical illustrations, like Rooker's watercolour but unlike the Dutch etchings, were designed for printed editions of

[1]295, III, 35; [2]135, 311

Pls XXV & XXVI Before and after the disaster at Pompeii: coloured aquatints of settings by Alessandro Sanquirico at La Scala, 1827

Fig. 175 Schouwburg farmhouse, after 1774

Fig. 176 Drottningholm farmhouse, late eighteenth century (*below*)

Fig. 177 Rooker, design for frontispiece, 1778

plays or operas. During the seventeenth century illustrators had been content to provide a fairly literal view of what was seen on the stage, though they never did it so accurately as the Dutch. But from the eighteenth century onwards the attitude changed. Part of the reason may have been that seventeenth-century prints were mainly done in a horizontal format, which coincided with the shape of the proscenium, and were then folded into books – with the result that they rapidly became creased and torn. In the eighteenth century this type of etching vanished, replaced by the ordinary upright format of book illustrations – a shape certainly far more suitable for books, but one in which it is difficult to represent accurately a proscenium stage. The artists began illustrating the story of the play, as they might illustrate a novel, instead of depicting the play itself in performance. Confronted with *King Lear*, they drew their impression of an old man on a heath. He might well have the features and even the costume of Garrick, but his surroundings were those of nature rather than of the theatre. And it is this – often though they are reproduced – which makes most eighteenth-century theatrical frontispieces virtually useless as serious theatrical evidence, except for occasional details of costume or stance.

Rooker's watercolour, since it is a theatrically realistic frontispiece from 1778, appears to refute this argument. Instead it confirms it. It is the only frontispiece among the many in this collected edition of plays which does show any theatrical reality, and the reason is a simple one. It illustrates *The Knight of the Burning Pestle*, a play which actually takes place in a theatre. A citizen and his wife come to the theatre with their son Ralph; they then clamber on to the stage, call for stools, and insist that Ralph is given a leading part in the play; and in the watercolour they can be seen on their stools, while Ralph performs in armour as the Knight of the Burning Pestle. So, again, the illustrator has depicted not a performance of the play but a moment in the plot – though for once the two coincide. In other plays it is precisely this emphasis on the plot, instead of on the performance, which invalidates so many eighteenth-century prints. And it is the lack of it, together with their careful precision, which makes the Dutch etchings a source of such rare and valuable evidence.

The 'scena per angolo'

While Sweden and Holland and many other countries were still perpetuating the scenic style of the seventeenth century, with the perspective receding to a central vanishing point, Italy had already moved on in new directions and was developing the famous *scena per angolo*. The introduction of this system, by which the lines of perspective could seem to move obliquely across the stage towards vanishing points out of sight on either side, is usually credited to Ferdinando Galli-Bibiena. The members of the Bibiena family have been established by successive historians as the most brilliant set-designers in theatre history – among the many famous families of designers it is they, spanning the whole of the eighteenth century, who stand as the undisputed aristocrats. In terms of art history the decision is a valid one. Few stage artists have been such excellent draughtsmen and watercolourists; their sketches are rightly pursued in the sale rooms, and they have an endless fascination to art experts since it is almost impossible to distinguish between the styles of the various members of the family, and therefore the game of attribution need have no end. But in more purely theatrical terms their brilliance has been greatly exaggerated.

Certainly the pictorial evidence would seem to deprive Ferdinando of the credit for having

Fig. 178 Chiarini, *Scena per angolo*, a prison, 1694
Fig. 179 Ferdinando Bibiena, *Scena per angolo*, a prison, 1703

introduced the first *scena per angolo*. The first etchings of such scenes by him are dated 1703, a year which is therefore often quoted as marking the arrival of the new scenery on the stage.[1] But nine years earlier, in 1694, a very confident and impressive *scena per angolo* had been designed by Marcantonio Chiarini at Bologna for *La Forza della Virtu* (Fig. 178). Compared to this, Ferdinando Bibiena's prison design of 1703 (Fig. 179) is a feeble affair. The one quality which it does have, and which is undoubtedly distinctive of the Bibienas, is a tendency to soar upwards and to suggest undiscovered heights above – allowing for a new type of romantic scenery which would, a century later, be echoed in some of the more cavernous and oppressive of nineteenth-century creations. This upward aspiration can be seen in its most extreme form in the etchings of scenes published by Ferdinando's son, Giuseppe, in his *Architetture e Prospettive* (Fig. 180). My own feeling that such a design is oppressive and unattractive is purely a matter of opinion, but at best this is just a spectacular drawing-board dream. As a record of what might actually have appeared to an audience in the theatre it is clearly an exaggeration.

But both it and the rather hasty sketch in Fig. 179, which goes if anything to the other extreme, raise the interesting question of how the Bibienas tried to achieve on the stage the effect of the *scena per angolo*. Some scholars have assumed that they actually hung a backcloth at an oblique angle across the stage;[2] others that it was all done by skilful painting on ordinary wings with a backcloth parallel to the front of the stage.[3] Certainly when Ferdinando Bibiena described how to paint a set, in his *Direzione della Prospettiva Teorica* in 1732, his diagram showed an entirely conventional row of flat wings down each side (Fig. 181).

Yet already by 1710 other Italian designers were using far more ambitious techniques – in particular Filippo Juvarra, who in 1708 built a theatre for Cardinal Ottoboni in Rome and

[1]e.g. 69, 234;   [2]44, 191;   [3]219, II, 73–4

designed the sets for it. A manuscript volume of his settings between 1708 and 1712 is in the Victoria and Albert Museum and is of unique interest, since on many of the designs Juvarra has added a diagram showing how the flats were arranged on the stage. These show that Juvarra's technique was to place flats anywhere that might suit him across the width of the stage, but always to stand them parallel to the proscenium. So, for example, in the *Libreria Reggia* (Fig. 184) the line of parallel flats strides across the stage obliquely from front to back.

Fig. 180 Giuseppe Bibiena, stage design, 1719

This system introduced a great new freedom into set design, though the Bibienas themselves seem to have been slow to follow it. The evidence of the conventional wings in Fig. 181 does admittedly give an unjust impression of their conservatism, because there are at Fano a series of nine diagrams of the settings designed for the theatre in 1718–19 by Ferdinando and another son, Antonio. These do move a certain way towards the new ideas typified by Juvarra, although the most revolutionary of the settings, *Il Carcere* (Fig. 182), still only uses the free arrangement of flats to a very shallow depth. The other diagrams, which use the full depth of the stage, fall much more into the old pattern of conventional wings with various attachments.

It is also worth pointing out that by this time the device of painting oblique perspectives on the ordinary flat wings at the side of the stage cannot still have been very rare or new, since precisely this arrangement (Fig. 183) appears in 1716 in Lambranzi's *Deliciae Theatrales*, a book of dances in which the settings are only important as a background to the figures. This system could have been used to achieve Giuseppe Bibiena's soaring creation in Fig. 180, which has just such receding perspectives at each side, though the result would inevitably have been much

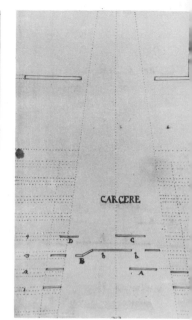

Fig. 181 Ferdinando Bibiena, constructing a set, 1732
Fig. 182 Ferdinando and Antonio Bibiena, a prison, 1718

less impressive than the etching. The majority of the Fano diagrams, with their conventional wings to each side of the stage, show that this is certainly the way in which Ferdinando Bibiena would have created such a setting – whereas another sketch in Juvarra's volume contains a much more ambitious method for achieving the same effect, with two actual alley-ways of flats receding on each side.[1]

The comments of a French visitor to Italy, Charles de Brosses, reveal that by 1739 Juvarra's system was fairly general; 'instead of placing the various parts of the scene evenly, as we do, in the wings, they spread them out right across the stage; if there are colonnades or galleries, they arrange them obliquely on several diagonal lines which greatly increases the effect of the perspective'. At the same time the shortened stage of the Bibiena prison in Fig. 182 must have been proving itself another effective step towards the box-set of the next century, since de Brosses continues: 'if the place is meant to be cramped, they reduce the stage and close it in so well on all sides that one feels oneself to be in a cave or a tent, or under a vault'. Both these developments – the free placing of pieces of scenery, and the enclosing of a space downstage – were to become important elements of nineteenth-century theatre, and de Brosses already noticed the inherent snag: it took so much more time to change than the old system of wings. 'There are', he wrote, 'two or three changes per act; these are done without much skill, and with less co-ordination and speed than we are used to. And yet, when all is done, the reality of it is such that I had to pay very close attention to be sure, when the time came to change them again, where the joins were in those pieces which I had just seen put separately into place.'[2]

If de Brosses was right in saying that this system was unknown in France in 1739, it was

---

[1]31, Fig. 177;   [2]239, 390

certainly soon to arrive there. When Diderot and d'Alembert published in 1772 the volumes of plates for the *Encyclopédie*, they included two fat sections on theatrical scenery and machinery, in which they naturally showed various cross-sections of the Comédie Francaise – and on its stage they showed a typical *scena per angolo* (Fig. 185). But this angled scenery spread only partially in eighteenth-century Europe. It made little impact in England or Holland and is not found among the scenes at Drottningholm, though the two surviving court theatres of the

Fig. 183 *Scena per angolo*, Lambranzi, 1716

late eighteenth century in Czechoslovakia, at Krumlov and Leitomischl – each almost as interesting as Drottningholm, and each with a stock of original scenery – do have several drop cloths giving at least a *prospettiva per angolo*.[1]

Taking a longer view of the history of stage scenery, it was not so much the angled image itself which was important, as the accompanying freedom to place painted flats in any position on the stage – whether in the sweeping style of Juvarra's royal library or in the newly confined space of Ferdinando Bibiena's prison. Here, in the first decades of the eighteenth century, the scenery of the nineteenth was already heralded.

---

[1] 22, V, Figs 49–50

Fig. 184 Juvarra, royal library, *c*. 1710

Fig. 185 *Scena per angolo* for the Comédie Française, 1772

Lighting

I have dealt with the development of European staging from the sixteenth to the eighteenth centuries largely, so far, in terms of scenery and machinery. Various aspects of the story remain which are best treated on their own – in particular lighting and costume, but also the more social aspects of the theatre, such as life backstage, the audience itself and the developing shape of the auditorium.

In a stage tradition which aimed for both splendour and illusion, lighting had a very important part to play. In the sixteenth century, when a perspective street of Serlian two-sided houses could remain in position for the whole evening, the setting was often festooned with lights until the stage was one sparkling jewel – at any rate in intention. Serlio explains how his houses should be studded with coloured lights shining through ornamental holes in the façade, and how such lights were achieved by placing candles behind bottles full of different liquids.[1] But he also described a technique which in the long run was to prove more useful in the theatre – how to project a light in a given direction by placing a reflector behind it. In Serlio's case a new

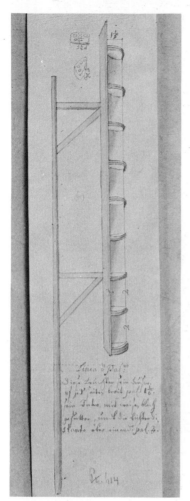

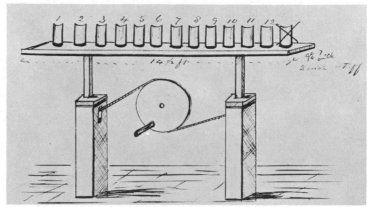

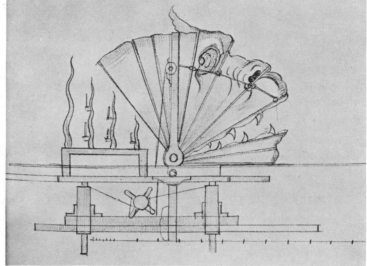

Fig. 186 Lighting stand, *c.* 1700
Fig. 187 Machine for lowering footlights, nineteenth century (*above right*)
Fig. 188 Dragon's mouth, *c.* 1700

and shiny barber's basin was recommended.[2] Somi, towards the end of the same century, used mirrors which would direct light from the wings towards the centre of the stage – in this way, he said, you get more light without any extra smoke.[3] The fact that it was impossible to generate light without smoke, whether with oil lamps or tallow or wax candles, was to remain a constant theatrical problem until the arrival of gas. Sabbattini in 1638 advised against the use of footlights, partly because they light up the costumes of the performers while making their faces so pale that they appear to have risen from a sick-bed, but also because 'more is lost than gained' since the extra brightness is counteracted by the cloud of smoke between spectators and settings, not to mention the vile smell. Like nearly all the early commentators he agrees that the only thing to do about the smell of lamps is to mix sweet perfume with the oil.[4]

---

[1]317, II, fol. 31 r.;   [2]317, II, fol. 31 r.;   [3]31, 259;   [4]313, 62–5

Once the seventeenth-century stage with its proscenium and its changeable flat wings had become established in Italy, the most effective method of lighting it was found to be reflectors attached all round behind the proscenium, with others on vertical stands between the wings (Fig. 186). These stands, practical though they clearly were, seem to have travelled through Europe rather slowly. They were only introduced into England, for example, by Garrick in 1765.[1] Northern countries made much more use of chandeliers hanging openly over the stage (e.g. Figs 98 and 169), and of footlights (e.g. Pl. XIX, p. 173).

The amount of light on the stage could be increased or reduced during the performance in various ways. The reflectors in Fig. 186 could be turned on their supporting pole so that they shone into the wings instead of on to the stage; the pole itself often passed through a hole in the stage to be supported on a floor beneath, so that the movement of the dancers should not shake

Fig. 189 Panorama and moving sky, eighteenth century

the lights. Less accessible lights could be dimmed by a system of ropes, which lowered a tubular metal shade over each candle or lamp – the best known illustration of this is Sabbattini's frequently reproduced etching of 1638,[2] but an almost identical system survived well into the nineteenth century as a way of dimming the footlights. An English encyclopedia of about 1803 explains that the first gap in the stage floor was for 'raising and lowering the foot-lights'[3] and Fig. 187 shows the machinery with which it was done – in this case in a theatre in Ipswich, where this system was used until 1857.[4] The only difference from the Sabbattini device of two centuries before is that instead of a shade being lowered on to the lamps, the lamps themselves are lowered into a hole.

A lighting effect which became very popular during the seventeenth and eighteenth centuries

Fig. 190 Moonlit scene, *Servio Tullio*, 1685

was the 'transparency', in which lights glowed, or a scene was viewed, behind some transparent surface. It has a long pedigree. In a Resurrection play of about 1400 the tower of Limbo had transparent walls and Jesus's spirit could be seen inside,[5] and Fig. 188 shows the use of lights in a transparent effect which would have delighted both medieval and baroque audiences. From the auditorium red flames will appear to dance in the dragon's gullet.

A much more ambitious combination of lights and machinery can be seen in an Italian water-colour of the eighteenth century (Fig. 189). This not only shows a stage hand waiting to operate a continuously moving sky, but also provides a unique glimpse of an arrangement for making and lighting a distant scene in relief at the back of the stage. Although we only see the small lamps at the end of each row, there will be others attached to the back of it along its whole length.

From the start playwrights and stage managers were eager to adopt any effects which the lighting expert could provide. In the late sixteenth century Somi was already using lights for evocative purposes. He presented the happy scenes at the start of a tragedy in a blaze of light, but with the sudden and unexpected death of a queen the lamps were dimmed; 'this created a profound impression of horror among the spectators and won universal praise'.[6] Storms provided an obvious occasion for such effects. In Shadwell's version of *The Tempest* in London

---

[1]295, III, 38–9;   [2]reprod. 12, VI, 499;   [3]135, 283;   [4]217, XIII, 4, 132;   [5]247, 94;   [6]31, 258

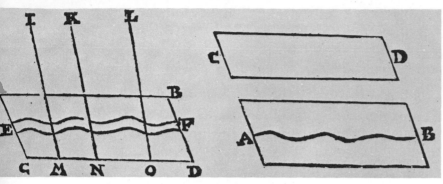

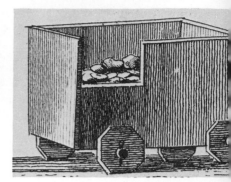

Fig. 191 Lightning, Sabbattini, 1638
Fig. 192 Thunder, *Encyclopédie*, 1772

in 1674, 'when the Ship is sinking, the whole House is darken'd, and a Shower of Fire falls upon 'em. This is accompanied with Lightning, and several Claps of Thunder, to the End of the Storm'.[1]

An even more ambitious use of light was seen in an opera in Munich in 1685, *Servio Tullio*, where the changing light was put to the service of the plot. The scene is a moonlit garden (Fig. 190), and characters move about in it unobserved whenever clouds come in and cover the moon, darkening the stage. A typical cloud machine can be seen around the moon, waiting to close in and conceal it. The etching is also interesting as showing a practicable balcony, one of the various pieces which were sometimes set between the flat wings. The stage directions say that at the start of the scene Tullia is 'on a balcony playing her lute' and that later she descends to the garden.[2]

During the nineteenth century lighting effects were to become more varied and more easily controlled with the arrival of gas. It was introduced on the stage in London in 1817,[3] spread to Paris by 1822,[4] and in the following years rapidly replaced oil and candles in all major theatres. Apart from the fact that lights could now be raised or dimmed at the mere turn of a valve, gas was also capable of producing unprecedented brilliance in the form of limelight, achieved by burning a combination of gas and oxygen on lime. Limelight was powerful enough to provide the first really effective spotlights; one can probably be seen in Fig. 3, although since the date of this production is 1876, it could even be an electric spot. An elementary form of electric light had been used for a few spots and floods in the Paris opera as early as 1860, but gas remained the normal method of stage lighting till the 1880s, when it was widely supplanted by electricity.[5] The earliest view of a stage lit by electric lighting is from Munich in 1881[6] but by 1893 Miss Sita was singing in Monte Carlo lit by a hundred and fifty electric bulbs carefully concealed about her person.[7]

Before leaving the subject of stage lights it is worth adding two closely related effects – thunder and lightning, both of which followed the dimming of the lights in Shadwell's *Tempest*. Sabbattini describes one way of making lightning (Fig. 191). A plank must be cut in two along a zig-zag line. It is then placed in the sky over the stage. Another plank, covered in tinsel and carrying a row of candles, is placed behind it. When the lightning is needed, the two halves of the front plank are quickly parted and then re-joined. He goes on also to describe the basic and most usual technique for thunder – merely an inclined wooden trough, set high above the stage

210

and preferably with some shallow steps in it, along which cannon-balls are rolled at the appropriate moment.[8] Diderot and d'Alembert, in the plates to their *Encyclopédie* in 1772, offer an intriguing alternative but one which looks rather harder work to operate (Fig. 192).

Like those on the stage, the lights in the auditorium were sometimes oil lamps and sometimes candles; they either hung from the roof in chandeliers or were attached to the fronts of boxes; and they were alight throughout the performance. In the sixteenth century the prince's seat was often lit as brightly as the stage[9] – to the rest of the audience he was no doubt a spectacle almost as absorbing as the play itself. Probably the earliest theatre to adopt the modern principle of dimming the auditorium lights during the performance was the court theatre at Weimar, where in 1798 an arrangement was made for them to be drawn up into a recess in the roof.[10] Since the wicks of both candles and oil lamps need constant attention, the candle-snuffer was a familiar figure on both sides of the footlights. On the stage there was usually a special uniformed attendant, but a violinist can be seen briefly leaving the orchestra to do the job in the auditorium in Pl. XXI (p. 176).

Costume

For the performance of straight plays in the seventeenth and eighteenth centuries there was very little variety of costume. The innumerable Roman characters in tragedy were played in a full wig and a helmet surmounted by huge plumes, together with a special theatrical version of a Roman military tunic; illustrations of this costume are legion (it can be seen, for example, in Figs 130, 139, 146 and 155), but the most self-confidently ludicrous version is undoubtedly the much reproduced etching of Quin as Coriolanus in 1749.[11] For Eastern characters a turban would replace the helmet, and baggy pantaloons the Roman skirt. For everyone else a slight variation of contemporary dress was considered sufficient disguise, and the costume of the actresses – though often very charming – remained even closer to the fashions of the day. The players, for the most part, owned their own basic costume and the theatre merely provided any special trimmings – a sheet for a ghost, or a particularly impressive cloak like the one described by Steele as 'an imperial mantle, made for Cyrus the Great, and worn by Julius Caesar, Bajazet, king Harry the Eighth, and signor Valentini'.[12]

The real brilliance and fantasy of stage costume appeared only in ballet, where the bizarre oddity of the outfit was an essential part of each entry. The most basic type of costume here was the emblematic, in which the character's appearance is built up from details connected with his nature or occupation. This is a tradition which goes back at least to allegorical performances and *tableaux* of the late Middle Ages; for example, in a morality play performed by French students in about 1500, Truth could be recognised by the mirror she carried and Justice by her pair of scales.[13] The style became more playful and more elaborate in the *intermezzi*; Somi said that a suitable subject for an *intermezzo* was a group of artisans playing musical instruments which would be concealed in the tools of their trade, so 'a small lyre would be in the locksmith's pan, a violin in a boot belonging to the mender of old shoes, a flute in the handle of the broom borne by the chimney-sweep'.[14] This type of presentation of a character reaches its delightful peak in the costumes for the ballets at Turin in the mid-seventeenth century where, for example, the Watery Phlegmatic Humour (Fig. 193) has breeches and sleeves lined

[1]295, I, 44; [2]334, 35–40; [3]17, 466; [4]12, VI, 500; [5]17, 469; [6]1, Fig. 491; [7]68, 103; [8]313, 158; [9]12, VI, 494; [10]240, 310; [11]31, Fig. 216; [12]333, no. 42, July 16, 1709; [13]5, 71; [14]31, 261

Fig. 193 Ballet costume, Turin, 1647

with waves, a tunic of scallop shells, a ship on his head and a fish and a twig of coral in his hands.

A little earlier than this, the French ballets under Louis XIII had inclined to more grotesquely comic costumes. So in an entry of typically macabre-sounding characters, the Hocricanes and the Hofnaques (Fig. 194), a large part of the effect depends on the fact that two of the four are dressed entirely as the top half of men, all doublet, and the other two as the bottom half, all hose.

This style of comic costume was not exclusive to ballets at court. In Lambranzi's collection of dances in 1716 there are many variations on the theme, most of them considerably more assured than the earlier court versions. For example, the characters in Fig. 197 are in fact danced by one performer. The head of the man apparently sitting in the basket is the performer's own; the head and arms of the woman are part of his costume, attached to his stomach and chest. Several of the very beautiful designs in Lambranzi's book achieve the same mood of fantasy in a less contrived manner and so become even more timelessly delightful – such as the clown in the large hat (Fig. 198) whose appearance would charm audiences of any period. In Restoration London Nell Gwynn was a huge success performing a speech of Dryden's in a hat which had 'the circumference of a hinder coach-wheel . . . The whole theatre was in a convulsion of applause; nay, the very actors giggled, a circumstance none had observed before'.[1]

---

[1]257, appendix, p. 12

212

Fig. 197 Trick costume, Lambranzi, 1716 (*overleaf*)

Fig. 198 Fantastic costume, Lambranzi, 1716 (*overleaf*)

Fig. 194 Ballet costumes, Paris, 1629

Fig. 195 Garrick as an elderly lady, 1776 (*below left*)

Fig. 196 A French actress as a captured soldier, eighteenth century

Dieſer masquirte Bauer, ſtehet in einem korb ohne boden
und machet die pas riguadon, mit ſtarcken fuß ſtampffen
auf die Erde, hernach macht Er obengezeigte Figur mit
pas ballones e contretemps auf bäureriſche aber kunſt
mäßige art, und wird darbeÿ die Aria 4 mahl abgeſpielt.

Narcisin

Diese Figur, Narcisin di Malembergo genät, hat eine ströhne hut auf
de haupt, u. sind die auge von frischen Pomerantze Schelffe gemacht
die nase aber vo eine stuck kürbis, umb sie recht lächerlich vor zu
stelle, u. also tanzt sie die pas-contretemps et ranzegndi,
das ist mit gezogene knie u. aufgehebte füsse, u. steht hernach
auf eine fuss allein, schlägt mit de andern hin und
wieder auf die knie, Endlich macht sie die
pas rigaudon mit brave verdreh-
ungen, u. Continuirt mit aller
hand artigen posse, so lang
bis die Aria
zu Ende.

Fig. 199 Costume for a centaur, late seventeenth century

A very popular trick, particularly in eighteenth-century England, was to devise reasons in the plot for actresses to wear men's clothes – the famous 'breeches parts'. The obvious appeal of this can be seen in a French drawing of a charming actress (Fig. 196) wearing a version of male military costume – and pitifully chained as well. The reverse, actors in women's costumes, had been familiar in the court ballets (for example Louis XIV as a Bacchante and a Muse, Figs 111–12), but in the public theatre this was much less common and certainly far less attractive than actresses in breeches. When it did occasionally happen, though, it was considerably funnier. Garrick, in the character of Sir John Brute masquerading as a lady, can stand as an example (Fig. 195).

The more spectacular operas of the seventeenth century introduced many almost inimitable mythological creatures, and it is hard to believe that their appearance was not often slightly comic. Placing tritons and mermaids on their knees, behind the convenient screen of waves, was perhaps not too difficult. But the satyrs must have been expected to dance about the stage on at least an attempt at hooves. Even harder the centaurs, half men half horses, sometimes had to put in an appearance. A drawing of the late seventeenth century, in the style of Bérain (Fig. 199), suggests that these costumes were taken very seriously and that they may even have been surprisingly convincing. It shows how two men perform as a centaur. The technique is the obvious one of the pantomime horse, but the care used here is extraordinary. Not only is the skin padded in places round the body to give it a horse's shape, but the hooves are amazingly ingenious. Anticipating Darwin, they make the correct but far from obvious link between a horse's and a man's leg, so that all the joints now bend in the right directions.

Backstage

Glimpses of life backstage are rare, but they usually have much to reveal. One of the best known, Hogarth's engraving of strolling actresses dressing in a barn (Fig. 200), is often reproduced for the sake of the actresses and for the charm of the scene itself, but it is also a cornucopia of minor

216

Fig. 200 Actresses in a barn, Hogarth, 1738

details – around the walls of the barn almost every inch is filled with fascinating props and pieces of scenery, and the equipment suggests yet again how even the simplest of companies were by now expected to provide the full delights of baroque theatrical machinery. On the left is a pair of wave-rollers, complete with handles for turning them. Beside them is the edge of a set-piece, a classical gateway with roses creeping up it. Further back and up in the roof is a full-scale flying machine, drawn by a dragon and complete with clouds, on which Cupid has evidently been drying his stockings; the ropes by which the machine will be flown pass over a beam and are stretched across the barn as a clothes-line. Still aloft, and behind the flag, is a glimpse of a cloud apparition machine, and below that are two tree wings. The floor of the barn is littered with a vast variety of small props, mainly Roman or ecclesiastical, and several of the performers are already half-dressed in the type of costumes which are familiar in their finished form in other prints; in the bottom left corner a small eagle is carefully feeding a baby, and a little higher a mermaid – whose tail is kept in position by a string around her waist – is receiving finishing touches to her bodice.

The only other print which offers quite so many intriguing backstage details in such a small space is a view of a theatrical auction (Fig. 201) in Pierce Egan's *Life of an Actor*, dating from almost a century later. The text explains that the book's hero, Proteus, wants to set up as a theatrical manager and so tries to purchase 'a variety of scenes, dresses, coats of mail, skeletons, devils, fiery dragons, flying horses, ships, balloons, properties for thunder, lightning etc.'[1] In the plate we see him surrounded by these basic theatrical necessities, none of which – except

---

[1] 261, 249

217

Fig. 201 Theatrical auction, 1825

the balloons – would have been any different during the two previous centuries. Painted cut-out figures, like the devils on wheels in the left hand corner, were familiar on the English stage from the Restoration to the nineteenth century.[1] And once again Sabbattini's wave-rollers can be seen stacked up on the right.

Ever since the establishment of permanent theatres and professional actresses, a favourite part of theatre-going was a visit to the actresses in the dressing-room. The best illustration of this is a print of about 1830 showing gentlemen chatting with the cast in the green room of the Royal Theatre at Copenhagen (Fig. 202). Through the large door dancers can be seen rehearsing beside some tree flats; for an actual performance a backcloth would conceal the green room from the audience. A very similar area can still be seen behind the stage of the Copenhagen court theatre, now used as a theatre museum, with just such dressing tables and wig stands, and with small individual dressing-rooms leading off at each side. By 1830 the scene is rather calm and respectable, but in earlier crowded conditions – with just one general dressing-room – it had been less so. A seventeenth-century account of a Spanish rake follows him to the theatre's tiring-house, where he deliberately places himself in front of an actress when her maid is about to change her stockings. 'The poor actress must suffer this and does not dare to protest, for, as her chief object is to win applause, she is afraid to offend any one.'[2]

Naturally the special link between actresses and the most eligible members of the audience

218

is almost as old as the theatre itself, and at most periods the actresses have been well pleased with it. In 48 BC, and much to the disgust of Cicero, Mark Anthony hurried back from the battle of Actium purely to rejoin his mistress, who was one of the mimes.[3] In the sixth century AD the Emperor Justinian had to change the laws in order to be able to marry Theodora, an actress and performer of striptease, and to make her his empress.[4] And the first known French actress was an eighteen-year-old, at Metz in 1468 in the *Mystère de Sainte Catherine*, who played the part of the saint so fetchingly that she ended up with a nobleman for a husband.[5]

Fig. 202 Green room, Copenhagen, *c.* 1830

But timeless though the relationship has been, it probably reached its peak in the strange private world of London's Restoration theatres. Here the visiting of the actresses became so normal that a charge was instituted for admission to the dressing-rooms.[6] A large proportion of the audience was looking for a mistress, just as most of the actresses were looking for any advantageous arrangement. Thus the performances of Nell Gwynn and her rivals acquired a highly charged overtone of erotic interplay between themselves and the gallants in the audience – an element which the dramatists were quick to make use of in their scripts. Even in the rather more decorous theatre of George II's reign, the members of the royal party were known to prefer Covent Garden to Drury Lane: at Drury Lane the green room was on the opposite side of the stage to the royal box, but at Covent Garden it was on the same side, which made it easier for gentlemen of the court to visit the actresses between the acts.[7] After such aristocratic

[1]135, 199; [2]306, 335; [3]32, 96; [4]104, 240; [5]281, Part I, Vol. II, 731; [6]295, I, 13; [7]282, 149

Fig. 203 Actress and elderly gallant, France, 1830

excitements, the much more conventional nineteenth-century gentleman – offering his devotion beside a wing (Fig. 203) – has a decidedly seedy air.

Audiences

Life in the auditorium could be fairly social too. One of Fielding's characters, Lord Dapper, compliments himself on his qualities as a critic with the argument; 'as I am one half the play in the green room talking to the actresses and the other half in the boxes talking to the women of quality, I have an opportunity of seeing something of the play, and perhaps may be as good

Fig. 204 A box at the theatre, Amsterdam, c. 1820

a judge as another'.[1] Certainly, of the four people in the boxes in the foreground of Fig. 204, not one is looking at the dance on the stage (the tragedy queen between the proscenium pillars is a statue). In the excitement of the social moment even the tea things are temporarily unattended.

These boxes, separated only by a low partition, were typical of most public theatres in the seventeenth and eighteenth centuries. There was no question of reserving a box or even a bench in a box; spectators took a seat wherever one was free; the area was a public gallery which happened to be divided by partitions. It was the opera houses which introduced the individual sealed-off rooms which we now mean by the term 'box'. One can be seen in Fig. 205, an etching of 1789 which illustrates a salaciously sentimental story in which a prince asks for a lovely young dancer at the opera to be brought to his box, and only discovers just in time (he already 'was passing a slightly free hand beneath her chin'[2]) that she is the child he adopted as his ward several years before, and whom he put into a convent to be taught dancing. The hoary old goat's head outside the box is a carefully appropriate ornament, and the blind which can be drawn across the front of the box is a witness to the odd fact that at certain periods it was thought desirable to be able to shut out the performance. When the furnishings of Her Majesty's Theatre in the Haymarket were sold in 1853, the catalogue of the sale included '337 Yellow Satin Curtains'.

The degree of social activity going on in the auditorium of seventeenth-century theatres during the performance is well suggested by several entries in the diary of Samuel Pepys, a most energetic Restoration playgoer. In 1667, for example, he went to see *The Maid's Tragedy*. Sir Charles Sedley was near him in the audience and was flirting with an unknown masked lady:

> He would fain know who she was, but she would not tell; yet . . . did give him leave to use all means to find out who she was, but pulling off her mask. He was mighty witty, and she also making sport with him very inoffensively, that a more pleasant rencontre I never heard. But by that means lost the pleasure of the play wholly, to which now and then Sir Charles Sedley's exceptions against both words and pronouncing were very pretty.[3]

Pepys's tolerance of the activity all round him is clear also from another occasion. 'To the Theatre . . . and here I sitting behind in a dark place, a lady spit backward upon me by a mistake, not seeing me; but after seeing her to be a very pretty lady, I was not troubled at it at all.'[4] And it was not unusual for quarrels to develop among spectators which were serious enough to lead to duels outside.[5]

Apart from the turmoil going on in front of him, the actor had another problem to cope with on either side – spectators sitting or standing on the stage and blocking the wings. In England there had been spectators on stools on the stage in the Elizabethan public theatres, and the custom continued on the proscenium stage of the Restoration; Charles II made a few unsuccessful attempts to stop it, but it remained the fashion until Garrick abolished it in 1763.[6] In France the habit began in 1637 as a direct result of the success of *Le Cid*. So great was the demand to see the play at the Théâtre du Marais that Montdory allowed spectators on the stage, where they remained until 1759. In the better organised theatres they were provided with rows of seats to each side of the stage – in 1689 the Comédie Française built a dozen rows of such

---

[1]282, 159;   [2]307, 33 ff.;   [3]Feb 18, 1666/67;   [4]284, 38;   [5]295, I, 18;   [6]295, III, 15

Fig. 205 A box at the opera, Paris, 1789

banquettes on each side[1] – and in this form they at least provided less obstruction to the per-formances, since they were confined to a specific area which the actors could take into account. Such an arrangement can be seen in Fig. 206, a French print of the early eighteenth century, but very often spectators merely stood or sat on loose chairs in the wings, with the result that an actor might well have to push his way through them to make an entrance. The advertisement for a play in London in 1702 requested rather plaintively; 'It is humbly desir'd that no Gentle-man may Interrupt the Action by standing on the Stage the First day'.[2]

Fig. 206 Spectators on the stage, *c.* 1730

Yet another extra presence on many continental stages of the time was the prompter. In most places the covering over his head was only a nineteenth-century refinement, so he sat with his book and his candle in an open hole in the middle of the front of the stage, as in Fig. 207. Schlegel, describing an Italian company, wrote; 'it is exceedingly amusing to see the prompter, when, from the general forgetfulness, a scene threatens to fall into confusion, labouring away, and stretching out his head like a serpent from his hole, hurrying through the dialogue before the different speakers'.[3] It was generally agreed that it was the German and Austrian prompters who had to work hardest. According to Madame de Staël, the prompter at Vienna had more

Fig. 207 The prompter in his hole, 1796

to do than could be accomplished from any one position; he 'used to furnish most of the actors with every word of their parts; and I have seen him following Othello from one side of the scene to another, to prompt him with the verses which he had to pronounce on poniarding Desdemona'.[4]

Allowing for some obvious exaggeration on Madame de Staël's part, the weakness of memory of the German actors is not so surprising when one considers their repertoires. During Caroline

[1]154, 193;   [2]295, II, 36;   [3]282, 33;   [4]282, 34

Neuber's season at Hamburg in 1735 her company presented seventy-five full length plays and ninety-three one-acters,[1] and until fairly recently this type of feat was to remain a common part of the theatrical trade. In fifty-two months in the 1870s Squire Bancroft played three hundred and sixty-four different parts.[2]

The prompter in England has always remained in a less obtrusive position – behind the proscenium to the actors' left, where he can be seen in Fig. 140. From his own point of view this is a far more comfortable post, though perhaps also less effective. Since the continental prompters constantly spoke among clouds of dust from the stage floor, wrote Stanislavski, 'it is a well-known fact that three-quarters . . . end with tuberculosis'.[3]

In addition to the mere inattentiveness of Sir Charles Sedley and the unknown lady, audiences could also be quite dangerously aggressive towards the players. There is almost an artists' tradition of drawing caricatures of the typical boorish audience of the time; Hogarth's 'Laughing Audience' is the best known,[4] but Rowlandson's contrast between 'Comedy in the Country' and 'Tragedy in Town' (Pl. XXI, p. 176) is a good example of the convention and is also interesting as showing a candle in the auditorium being snuffed by one of the violinists. The intention of both Hogarth and Rowlandson in these cases was satirical rather than realistic, but the unruly air of their coarse spectators is confirmed by a mass of evidence. In certain moods audiences felt that it was well within their rights to stop a play during its performance and demand that a different one should be substituted. It was probably the zealots among the audience at the time of the French Revolution who provided the oddest examples of this type of interference. In 1792 the spectators stopped a scene in Paris for a ceremonial unfurling of the national flag, and the rhythm of many a noble alexandrine was disrupted by the audience's insistence that all forms of address, whether *duc*, *marquis*, *comte* or *seigneur*, should invariably be altered to *citoyen*.[5]

The most prolonged interruption by any audience was the O.P. (Old Price) Riot at Covent Garden (Fig. 208), which erupted on September the 18th, 1809, and continued for sixty-seven nights – during which the spectators yelled, blasted and whistled their way through every evening's play. An O.P. dance was devised for performance on the pit benches; the box fronts were festooned with placards; and there was a brisk trade in special O.P. medals, hats, handkerchiefs and waistcoats. The audience's chief complaints were a rise in the prices and the employment of too many Italians. After two months a compromise was reached.[6]

Such occasions were of course the exception, but a regular hazard in all theatres was the gangs of partisans determined to destroy a rival's play or an unpopular actor's performance. The English 'catcall' was an actual wind instrument designed and brought into the auditorium specifically to make a raucous and abusive noise, and precisely the type of rattle used by modern football crowds to express enthusiasm was reserved by London audiences for moments of particular hostility; both weapons can be seen in Fig. 208. The Spanish seem to have used whistles for the purpose as far back as the 1630s;[7] and a French print, *L'auteur sifflé*, shows a barrage of such instruments in use.[8] Even Boswell and some friends went to Drury Lane in 1763 armed with oak cudgels and catcalls, and determined to damn a brother Scot's play; but in the end they did nothing because the audience was 'disposed to let it pass'.[9]

The obvious solution for authors and performers was to ensure that an energetic portion of the audience should always be disposed to let it pass, and the eighteenth century saw the beginnings of really organised *claques*. There was nothing new in the principle. Nero is said to have carried it to extremes for his performances in the vast theatre at Naples, where he not only

Fig. 208 O.P. Riot, Covent Garden, 1809

trained five thousand strong men in the noble art of applause but also took the precaution of locking the audience into the theatre.[10] In eighteenth-century England the art remained essentially an amateur one, though sometimes on a fairly large scale. In 1786 a dramatist called Reynolds, who was a lawyer and had been educated at Westminster, scored a great success with a play at whose first performance there were 'at least one hundred Westminster boys' in the pit and boxes and 'about fifty young sprigs of the law' in the gallery, so as to 'maintain a proper circulation of applause through all parts of the house'. The manager later congratulated Reynolds on having 'more *real friends* than any other man in London'.[11]

It was in Paris that the business first became a profession, and in Fig. 209 a French *chef de claque* can be seen leading his troops. At the end of the eighteenth century Prudhomme described an individual, appropriately nicknamed Monsieur Claque, who 'has the enormous hands of a washerwoman, and is paid thirty-six pounds for his attendance if the play succeeds, and twelve pounds if it fails'. By 1830 there was even a special Paris agency called 'Assurance des succès dramatiques', and *claque* leaders were attending final rehearsals at the theatre in order to be able to plan more precisely their rehearsals with their own cast. A delightful glimpse of the care and detail of the operation can be seen in a letter from a *chef de claque* to Rachel, who had complained that she had received less applause on the second night than the first. Rather hurt by this, he replied: 'I cannot remain under the obloquy of a reproach from lips such as yours. At the first performance I led the attack in person thirty-three times. We had three acclamations,

[1]240, 12; [2]343, 211; [3]326, 297; [4]reprod. 22, IV, 174; [5]248, 81–96; [6]262, 92–5; [7]306, 118; [8]reprod. 12, IV, 971; [9]217, VII, 3, 67; [10]219, V, 1, 10 ff.; [11]295, III, 11

Fig. 209 A *chef de claque* and his troops
Fig. 210 Chenda, tournament theatre, Bologna, 1639

four hilarities, two thrilling movements, four renewals of applause and two indefinite explosions.'
He went on to explain that this had so exhausted his performers that they had had to decide
on some cuts for the second night. Amazingly, a professional *claqueur*, Mr John Bennett, still
organises support for the productions of the Metropolitan Opera Company of New York and
even goes on tour with the company. He provides a claque of some twenty to twenty-five people.
He joined the claque himself in 1907 and rose to its leadership in 1919.[1]

Auditoria

As we saw earlier with arenas for tournaments or animal baiting, the most natural way to give
a maximum number of spectators a good view of a playing area is to build rows of galleries or
boxes vertically around it. This simple fact led to the design of the Elizabethan public theatres
in the open air, but it was also the main influence on the auditoria of indoor theatres. In a
rectangular hall, where the stage is at one end and the floor of the hall has to be used also for
the performance – as for the *Balet Comique* (Fig. 107) in 1581 – the audience must clearly be
placed at the far end of the hall and along the side walls, in one or more tiers. And when the

floor of the hall can also be used for spectators, a flat pit surrounded by vertical galleries will still provide space for more people than any other arrangement. Galleries of some sort around the walls are a natural and central feature of the development of the auditorium.

In this respect the importance of the Teatro Farnese, built at Parma in 1618, has been greatly exaggerated. Aleotti's theatre was undoubtedly a central and highly formative influence in the history of the stage itself, with its permanent proscenium and changeable flat wings. But its audience sat on a single U-shaped tier of steps rising evenly to the walls behind. Like the Teatro Olimpico, this part of Aleotti's design derived from the Roman theatre and is a brief neo-classical *cul-de-sac* in the history of the modern auditorium. Such a seating arrangement has had a revival in certain open-stage theatres of this century, but the main tradition of our theatre interiors descends from another process in the early seventeenth century.

The two illustrations which best show the emergence of the modern auditorium are the etching of the 1637 Schouwburg (Fig. 166) and a painting of a theatre created by Chenda in 1639 for a tournament play in Bologna (Fig. 210). The Schouwburg interior shows curved tiers of boxes and an open gallery at the back, both of which were to become standard. Chenda's interior lacks these, but it adds other elements missing in the Schouwburg – the much more enclosed feeling created by the sheer wall of five tiers of boxes at the two sides, and the fact that these boxes continue to join the proscenium wall at the far end, thus completely enclosing the auditorium as an area quite separate from the stage behind the proscenium. For this particular show of 1639 the performers came down and performed beneath the audience on the floor of the theatre, since this was a *torneo*. But it is only necessary for the ramp to be replaced by an unbridgeable orchestra pit, and for the floor to be covered with benches, and the standard auditorium of the later seventeenth and eighteenth centuries has been created.

Where the theatres remained small, the effect of spectators in curved tiers round an enclosed area must have been very intimate and delightful, and a certain connection was retained between actors and audience since the stage boxes reached far enough forward to flank the acting area in front of the proscenium. A painting of the Warsaw court theatre, although dark and rather battered, suggests well this intimate relationship (Fig. 211). But during the eighteenth century the public theatres in most countries were growing larger and larger, chiefly for commercial reasons. One method of fitting in more spectators was to extend backwards the part of each gallery opposite the stage. This was the trend which led towards the deep dress circles and upper galleries of nineteenth-century theatres, and which destroyed the basic feature of the seventeenth-century auditorium – that of a unified and self-enclosing curve of people, most of whom could see each other. Wren's cross-section of a theatre in 1674, which is probably for Drury Lane, has four rows of curving benches in each gallery; in Holland's cross-section of Drury Lane one hundred and twenty years later one of the galleries extends back to a depth of sixteen benches.[2]

Meanwhile the other obvious ways of enlarging a theatre's capacity – adding yet more tiers of boxes at the top, and increasing the size of the pit – soon made any sort of subtle acting impossible. The Teatro Argentina in Rome (Fig. 212), built in 1732 but painted here in 1749, shows the vast new dimensions. Admittedly this was an opera house, and it would still be acceptable for grand opera today, but in the late eighteenth century the straight theatres quickly followed suit. Another problem to add to the size was that in the days before numbered seats

---

[1]219, V, 1, 10–25; [2]136, Pls. 2 & 5

Fig. 211 Court theatre, Warsaw, *c.* 1780

there was no fixed capacity to a theatre. On a popular night in an ordinary public theatre spectators would continue to squeeze in until they could squeeze no more. A note of Macready's in the nineteenth century reads; 'Acted King Lear to such a house as never was seen before in Birmingham. Acted my best, but the house, though attentive, was too full to enjoy the play.'[1]

Fig. 212 Teatro Argentina, Rome, 1749

The Teatro Regio in Turin in about 1740 (Fig. 213) was still of tolerable size, and it provides the best illustration of the activities of a rather more peaceful audience of the time. This is an opera and many of the gentlemen in the pit are following in their *libretti*. One in the back row on the left is using a telescope as an opera glass. The waiter in the centre is bringing round drink, and the one on the right a bowl of fruit – an occupation performed rather more seductively in London by the orange girls. The military figure in the aisle is a sentry. They were employed to keep order, or to try to do so, in most public theatres of the period – and in many they even stood on the stage. In London there was an armed sentinel on either side of the proscenium, staring at the audience and very occasionally, according to Steele, shedding a tear during a sentimental scene.[2]

---

[1]252, 44;   [2]282, 230

Fig. 213 Teatro Regio, Turin, *c.* 1740

THE NINETEENTH CENTURY

Weimar

The clearest turning point between the long classical tradition of the seventeenth and eighteenth centuries and the new romantic theatre of the nineteenth is in the work of Goethe and Schiller. The typical eighteenth-century repertoire had consisted of tragedies on the French pattern, in classical or in exotically Eastern settings, and sentimental comedies of middle-class life – both essentially complacent in mood. In his early twenties Goethe became the leader of a revolt against such plays with the production in Berlin in 1773 of *Götz von Berlichingen*. This was an extravagant and loosely shaped drama of which the hero was a sixteenth-century robber baron in revolt against tyranny; its acknowledged stylistic influence was Shakespeare rather than Corneille; and it became the spearhead of the theatrical movement known as *Sturm und Drang* (Storm and Stress). Eight years later Schiller's first play, *Die Räuber*, also written when he was only twenty-two, followed the same mood of revolt and like *Götz* was set in the sixteenth century. The breach made by these plays in the classical rules of dramatic composition was to prove a lasting one, and a passion for picturesque historical drama was to continue throughout the next century, but the *Sturm und Drang* movement itself had faded away as a serious crusade by the time of the late 1790s, when Goethe and Schiller were working together at Weimar.

Goethe went to Weimar in 1775, and for the next eight years arranged the amateur theatricals which his young master, Duke Karl August, so much enjoyed; a new passion for amateur play-acting had started in France in the 1760s and soon spread through much of Europe.[1] Goethe and his courtly patrons achieved many of their most charming performances in the open air, and Fig. 214 shows a performance of *Adolar und Hilaria* in the park at Ettersburg in 1780. Goethe, reclining in the beam of a well improvised spotlight, was Adolar; and Hilaria, surrounded by a cheering crowd of aristocratic yokels, was played by Corona Schröter, the only professional in the cast.[2]

Between 1783 and 1791 Goethe was too busy with Weimar's affairs of state to take any part in running the court theatre and an inferior professional company was employed, but in 1791 he was reluctantly persuaded to organise and take charge of a new professional company. There was, however, nothing particularly distinguished about the repertoire he presented until his partnership with Schiller towards the end of the decade. In 1798 the interior of the court theatre was rebuilt, and the opening production in the new auditorium was Schiller's *Wallensteins Lager*. Between then and his death in 1805 it was to be followed in quick succession by *Maria Stuart*, *Die Jungfrau von Orleans*, *Die Braut von Messina* and *Wilhelm Tell*.[3]

These historical plays were to be much imitated in the following decades, and Goethe's and Schiller's approach to their production was one which was to become typical also. One of the

---

Sources (*see* p. 317)   [1]240, 288;   [2]12, VII, 1720;   [3]240, 296 ff.

Fig. 214 Goethe performing, Ettersburg, 1780

actors recorded that for *Wallensteins Lager* Goethe gathered together 'all the available woodcuts which showed scenes of life in the army camps of the Thirty Years War'. Also 'the costumes were cut out according to pictures which survived from that period', but unfortunately the Weimar theatre was so small that 'large crowds of soldiers could of course only be suggested on our stage symbolically, through just a representative few'.[1]

There is no surviving illustration of the inside of this theatre, nor of any of Goethe's productions on the stage. There are, however, at Weimar many of Goethe's rough sketches containing ideas for settings, for he was essentially an all-round man of the theatre – not only author, director and company manager but also scene-designer and even at times, according to one of his own verses, candle-snuffer.[2] Fig. 215 is one of his designs, an eminently practical one and an interesting early example of an adaptable structural setting. It was for a production of *A Midsummer Night's Dream*. On the left the structure is used as a flight of steps up to a door with a gallery above; on the right the steps lead to a path meandering up a rocky hillside. The size of the prompter's box in each gives a good idea of the smallness of the stage.

Also among Goethe's own papers is a pleasant caricature of the court theatre (Fig. 217),

Fig. 215 Goethe, adaptable structural setting, early nineteenth century

contrasting the gaiety caused by ordinary strolling players on the right with Goethe's three Graces on the left, who are inducing little but sleep. The cartoon dates from about 1800, when Goethe and Schiller both started translating French classical tragedies into verse – mainly as an exercise for the company, though it was precisely this French influence in German theatre which they had both originally rebelled against. Goethe was clearly sufficiently amused by the caricature to keep it, but criticism from the audience was not so well received. When the duke had a courtier arrested in his seat for hissing, Goethe's only objection was that it would have been more seemly to wait until the offender had left the auditorium.[3] Goethe behaved as a virtual dictator to his company, and by doing so he stifled some of his own more advanced ideas. He was, for example, far ahead of his time in emphasising the importance of actors working as a team, each individual performance being subordinated to the effect of the whole – an attitude which implies the much later emergence of the modern type of director – but at Weimar towards the end of Goethe's life it led instead to the complete submission of the actors until they were little more than puppets.[4]

Nevertheless, at his and Schiller's hands, various important changes had been set in motion. By 1830 the romantic assault had reached the very citadel of the old rules, Paris itself. The occasion was the first night of Victor Hugo's *Hernani* (Fig. 216). Hugo had taken the precaution of enlisting a claque some three hundred strong to defend the principles of romanticism against the reactionary forces of classicism.[5] Chaos broke out with the very first couplet, when it was discovered that a phrase ran on without a break from the end of the first alexandrine to the beginning of the second:

> Serait-ce déjà lui? C'est bien à l'escalier
> Dérobé.

Théophile Gautier was sporting his famous red waistcoat, Balzac was hit in the face by a portion of cabbage,[6] and as the caption to Fig. 216 admits, 'if the play had had six acts, we should all have collapsed asphyxiated'. But it was the romantics who won the day.

---

[1]22, V, 185; [2]240, 289; [3]240, 319; [4]240, 595; [5]219, V, 1, 10 ff.; [6]274, 7

LES ROMAINS ÉCHEVELÉS A LA 1re REPRÉSENTATION D'HERNANI.

Si le drame avait eu six actes, nous tombions tous asphyxiés.

Fig. 217 Caricature on Goethe's repertoire, *c.* 1800

Spectacle and archaeology

With their study of old prints for *Wallensteins Lager*, Goethe and Schiller were only carrying
one step further a concern for historical accuracy which was becoming fairly general throughout the theatres of Europe. The Renaissance, deliberately deriving its inspiration from the past,
had been very interested in accuracy and towards the end of the sixteenth century Somi argued
that 'in costuming tragedies a careful producer must not be satisfied with modern clothes, but
must dress his actors after the fashion of antique sculptures or paintings'.[1] The producer of a
university play in England in 1595 even took the trouble to borrow old costumes from the
Tower of London, 'there being in that Tragoedie sondry personages of greatest estate to be
represented in auncient princely attire which is no where to be had, but within the office of the
Roabes at the Tower'.[2]

It was the seventeenth and eighteenth centuries which considered such attempts at accuracy
less important than the impropriety of being seen in public without a full wig, but by the middle
of the eighteenth century the reaction had already set in. When Caroline Neuber attempted
some genuine classical costumes in Germany in 1741, the experiment was before its time and
was treated by the audience as a great joke,[3] but in 1776 Charlotte Brandes scored a success by

[1] 31, 254; [2] 31, 234; [3] 31, 183

Fig. 216 The first night of *Hernani*, 1830

appearing at the Gotha court theatre in Greek costume.[1] In the same decade in London Macklin was much admired for his Macbeth in 'the old Caledonian habit'[2] and he was soon to be rivalled by Garrick's Lear in 1776, of which it was said that 'the play received considerable improvement . . . from the characters being judiciously habited in old English dresses'.[3] The greatest compliment which such a reformer could wish for is said to have been paid accidentally to Talma. As a very young man in the Comédie Française in 1789, when he was playing the seventeen line part of a tribune in Voltaire's *Brutus*, he collaborated with the artist David in copying from sculptures an authentic Roman costume in which, without warning, he suddenly took his place on the stage among all the leading actors in their wigs. The audience was delighted, but on the way through the green room an actress had caught sight of him and had exclaimed in horror: 'Look at Talma! How ugly he is! He looks just like one of those old statues!'[4]

Half a century later everyone was trying to look like an old statue, but with each actor responsible for his own appearance reform was bound to be a slow business. From costumes, the desire for accuracy spread to the scenery. In 1779, for *The Wonders of Derbyshire*, de Loutherbourg reproduced on the London stage actual sketches which he had made in Derbyshire; and in the 1790s, when Goethe and Schiller were studying their woodcuts, William Capon was making detailed research among old buildings in London in order to anchor his designs firmly in the correct period.[5]

One obvious appeal in this new approach was that it provided magnificent opportunities, on an ostensibly serious basis, for spectacular displays of scenery and costume. Managers have always recognised the appeal of lavish processions and great numbers of people on the stage, and the theatres of the eighteenth century willingly provided their share. Within weeks of George III's coronation in 1761 both Drury Lane and Covent Garden had incorporated in their productions coronation processions which involved more than a hundred extras.[6] Perhaps less justifiably, Kemble's *Macbeth* in 1794 included a chorus of fifty singing witches.[7] But from the beginning of the nineteenth century these excesses were suddenly to be given a new and respectable aura. They were to become genuine glimpses of history, of clear educational value.

Goethe and Schiller at Weimar, where 'large crowds of soldiers could only be suggested symbolically', were unlikely to be troubled by the dangers of historical spectaculars, though they must certainly have been aware of them – as is shown by the fortunes of Schiller's *Die Jungfrau von Orleans*. The play was ready in 1801, but was not performed at Weimar till 1803 – largely because the only person in the company who could play Joan, Caroline Jagemann, was also the duke's mistress, and the parallel with Voltaire's *La Pucelle* was thought at first to be dangerously tactless. When the play finally was produced, the unspectacular nature of the production is well suggested by the fact that Goethe and Schiller strongly objected when they found that a blue curtain was to be used as the coronation robe; they managed to arrange the special purchase of an imitation velvet one, which became the chief item in the theatre's wardrobe and was used for all stage royalty from then on.[8]

But the play had already been produced by Iffland in Berlin in 1801, and in a manner very different from the parsimony of Weimar. Two hundred and four people walked in the coronation procession, which was visible at three separate points on the stage as it wound backwards and forwards, and was watched by a stage crowd of another forty-three.[9] Berlin was entranced, and hardly noticed the slaughter being perpetrated by the cast on Schiller's lines. One of the actresses, when she later came to play Maria Stuart, had the part written out for her in prose to help her memorise it.[10]

Fig. 218 Beuther, *Die Jungfrau von Orleans*, Weimar, 1815

Nevertheless even Weimar, in spite of its tiny stage, did try to move in the new direction. In 1815 Friedrich Beuther was employed as resident set-designer, and Goethe praised his work for both the fashionable reasons – its accuracy and its impression of size. Beuther, he said, 'studied in the Weimar library both Egyptian and early German architecture'; and he 'knew how to use perspective so as to create on our tiny stage a feeling of boundless space'.[11] Fig. 218 is Beuther's new setting at Weimar in 1815 for *Die Jungfrau von Orleans*. No doubt the scenery for Iffland's Berlin production had been similarly grandiose in style, but inevitably the procession here is still of more modest Weimar proportions.

For an entire century, from about 1770, the move towards historical accuracy continued to astound audiences, because as the research became more and more serious it made all the

[1]240, 197; [2]31, 183; [3]295, III, 36; [4]248, 44–5; [5]295, III, 29–30; [6]217, XIV, 1, 10–12; [7]217, XXI, 2, 69; [8]240, 311–3; [9]12, VI, 481; [10]240, 357; [11]22, V, 215

Fig. 219 Schinkel, *Die Jungfrau von Orleans*, Berlin, 1817

previous attempts seem unrealistic. One of the most earnest researchers was the distinguished architect, Karl Friedrich Schinkel. The introduction to the first printed collection of designs by him, published in Berlin in 1819, points out that in the past a talent for perspective was all that a scene painter needed, but that nowadays only a learned man can be a designer of theatrical scenery. New settings must be such that 'painters, archaeologists, sculptors and architects, yes even specialists in natural history and botany, are able to find satisfaction in them'. And when Schinkel designed the setting for *Die Jungfrau von Orleans* in Berlin in 1817 (Fig. 219), 'one of the most felicitous ideas was undoubtedly that of allowing the spectators, during Joan of Arc's

240

magnificent monologue, to see a part of the city and cathedral of Rheims. The latter, moreover, was painted from a precisely accurate sketch'.[1]

Already implicit is the idea that one of the functions of a theatrical production, taken over more recently by lavish films in exotic locations, is to give the spectator the pleasure and improvement of being an armchair traveller. To support Schiller's words – and especially during a monologue, however magnificent – what could be more interesting than an authentic glimpse of a famous foreign cathedral? And the audience, knowing the seriousness of the artists involved, can rest assured during the coronation that this is all exactly how it was four centuries ago. An even more ambitious recreation was provided in 1827 by Alessandro Sanquirico at La Scala – and one that brought in also all the old pleasures of explosive stage effects. Pl. XXV (p. 196) shows

Fig. 220 *The Workshop of Quince the Carpenter*, 1856

a reconstruction of a Pompeii street in the normal life of the city; Pl. XXVI (p. 196) guides us excitingly through the disaster itself.

In England this tendency reached its peak rather late, in the productions of Charles Kean in the 1850s; but these do illustrate better than any others the laughable excesses of this theatrical fashion, and fortunately Kean had pictorial records made of his productions in a very complete series of watercolours, now in the Victoria and Albert Museum, which show all the scenes and

[1]316, Vorwort

Fig. 221 *Hamlet*, A Room in the Castle (III, 1), 1858
Fig. 222 *Hamlet*, 'A Room in the Castle (III, 2), 1858 (*above right*)
Fig. 223 *Hamlet*, A Room in the Castle (V, 3), 1858

242

even most of the props. London so admired Kean's earnestness that in 1857 he was elected a Fellow of the Society of Antiquaries, and in terms of hard work he certainly deserved the honour. His main productions were Shakespearean, but Shakespeare merely provided the springboard. Where *The Winter's Tale* demands a prison, Kean provided 'one of the Latomiae or Prisons of Syracuse, excavated out of the Rock, and known as the Ear of Dionysius';[1] when it calls for a feast, 'a representation of the celebrated *Pyrrhic Dance*, so popular throughout the principal states of Greece for its martial character, has been attempted';[2] and as the famous sea coast of Bohemia would have been out of place among so much exactitude, Kean 'followed the suggestion of Sir Thomas Hanmer, in his annotations on Shakespeare' and changed the country to Bithynia.[3] No scene in *A Midsummer Night's Dream* takes place in 'The Workshop of Quince the Carpenter' (Fig. 220), but the working area of an Athenian carpenter is something no serious tourist would willingly miss, so Kean not only provided it in 1856 but guaranteed that 'the Furniture and Tools introduced in this Scene are copied from discoveries at Herculaneum'.[4]

One disadvantage of this approach, apart from the obvious harm to the plays themselves, is that the audience expect many different scenes but certain plots are very ill-suited to providing them. Clearly Elsinore had many rooms, and equally clearly the characters would have used them, so in Kean's 1858 production of *Hamlet* the audience had to see at least a reasonable selection. Fig. 221 is *A Room in the Castle* for Act III, Sc. 1: Fig. 222 is *A Room in the Castle* for Act III, Sc. 2: and Fig. 223 is *A Room in the Castle* for Act V, Sc. 3. Amazingly, while the first two are by H. Cuthbert, the third is by Jones, for by this time the scenery was so much a succession of interesting paintings that it would have been unreasonable to limit the exhibition to one single artist. In addition to these three rooms in the castle there were also other settings called *A Hall in the Castle*, *The Queen's Chamber*, another *Room in the Castle*, *A Room in Polonius's House* and *A Room of State in the Castle*.

But the real truth about all this earnest reconstruction had already been neatly summed up by an author who wrote in 1840 that '*correctness of costume* was a phrase invented to excuse pageantry, as was *accuracy of locality* for spectacle'.[5]

The structural setting

Like the seventeenth-century etchings of opera settings, the lithographs of Schinkel and Sanquirico and the watercolours of Charles Kean's productions were all made after the event as impressive pictorial records of famous scenes. As such, one would expect to find that they glamourise very considerably what an audience actually saw on the stage, and the evidence suggests that the nineteenth century was considerably less capable of realising in wood and canvas the artists' grandiose dreams than the seventeenth century had been of capturing the more purely perspective illusion of Torelli or Burnacini. Pl. XXVII (p. 277) is Charles Kean's official record of the magnificent effect of Henry V, played by himself, addressing the army in 1859: Pl. XXVIII (p. 277) is an unofficial and far more literal view of another scene in the same production, where Pistol eats the leek. It is the second which has the more authentic air, with the few characters standing in front of a drop-cloth which meets a bare stage, reducing the river suddenly to planks. In fact the *Art Journal* in 1853, discussing Charles Kean's productions,

---

[1]278, 36;   [2]278, vii;   [3]278, vi;   [4]277, 12;   [5]295, IV, 41

Fig. 224 Basoli, Zoroastrian temple, 1847

specifically complained that the methods of placing scenery on the stage were 'still highly inefficient for artistic illusion, and have not kept pace with other improvements; indeed there has been hardly an advance at all for the last half century'.[1]

The 'other improvements' were probably the new historical seriousness, and the great practical problem of the nineteenth century was how to present more and more realistically on the stage these carefully gathered details of such archaeological importance. The inevitable answer was a gradual move towards a more structural form of setting. Slowly the visible and instantaneous changes of flat wings, which had delighted audiences for two centuries, were replaced by elaborate fixed settings, erected by a host of stage hands working out of sight behind drop-cloth or curtain. England was behindhand in the process – as late as the 1850s Charles Kean was still relying basically on flat wings and back-scenes – but throughout Europe the two systems were to co-exist a little awkwardly and in various degrees throughout the entire century.

A tendency of the designs of the first half of the century was to bring dark and heavy features of the setting far downstage, to suggest a weighty and mysterious quality. A scene like Antonio Basoli's in 1847, called *Tempio misterioso del culto astrifero di Zoroastro* (Fig. 224), is clearly not well suited to the old arrangement of wings and back-scene, though Juvarra's free arrangement of flats anywhere on the stage could have attempted it. An interim and extremely unpractical method of putting such a setting on the stage survives in an interesting maquette for a scene, made by Gaspare Galliari some time before 1823 (Fig. 225). The design, mounted in a miniature theatre, consists simply of three cut-out cloths, each filling the entire width and height of the stage. For at least two centuries a system of cut-out flats, or scenes 'in relieve', had been used

244

at the back of the stage to give added interest to the distant part of the prospect. Here the system has been moved down to occupy the whole stage, but has thereby rendered it virtually useless as an acting area. Players could stand on a platform between the first and second cloths, but they would not be able to move from there since the steps both in front of them and behind them were merely painted on vertical canvas. Effectively, the whole action has to take place in front of the first cloth; and in Basoli's design it looks as though this may well have been the intention, since the figures beyond look painted.

Fig. 225 Gaspare Galliari, maquette, *c.* 1820

For a long time this type of arrangement remained useful for certain spectacular effects, as can be seen from a print of 1895 (Fig. 226) in which, appropriately, there are no actors at all at stage level. The heroine imprisoned on top of her tower (she and it have risen together from under the stage) waves for rescue to a passing ship, navigated by three stage hands along its groove behind the flat row of waves.

The system which was to prove most generally useful was a free structural arrangement of steps, platforms and set pieces. In the Drottningholm Theatre Museum there are a remarkable

[1]135, 328

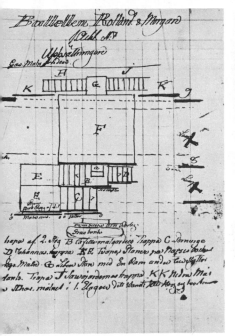

Fig. 227 Stockholm ground-plan, *c*. 1820
Fig. 228 Robbers' underground cave, Vienna, 1828

series of volumes called the *Maskinmästarejournalen* (literally 'machine-master's journals'), in which groundplans were kept for all the settings at the Royal Theatre in Stockholm between 1814 and 1888. These provide a unique record of the gradual change in staging methods in a nineteenth-century theatre. One of the earliest ground-plans, from about 1820 (Fig. 227), shows to what extent minor structural pieces were already a part of the everyday scenic equipment. The various steps leading to the areas marked E and F are themselves lettered A, B, C and D, and the script below gives the following description of them: 'A. Little flight of 2 steps. B. *La Fille Mal Gardée's* steps. C. Panurge steps. D. Johanna's steps.' So, except for the little flight of two steps, the others were all more important stock pieces which were known by the play or character for which they had first been built. From now on, identified always by this name, they would be used again and again in different combinations. Where the eighteenth-century manager had mingled old wings and back-cloths to make a new setting, his successor in 1820 was now beginning to do the same with old platforms and flights of steps. So far it was limited to the upstage area, since Fig. 227 shows that the structure was flanked by the seventh, eighth and ninth pair of wings; and the next page of the manuscript reveals that the front part of the setting consisted exclusively of flat wings in their normal position on either side of the stage.

Structural effects as part of the back wall of the setting had been known even in the seventeenth century (such as the boat rowing across in Fig. 150), but they were now becoming far more elaborate. The magnificent series of prints of Viennese settings, published by Bäuerle in his *Theaterzeitung* between 1827 and 1832, provide many examples of this – such as Fig. 228, dated 1828, where there is a two-level stage of considerable depth and solidity. Above, a great

Fig. 226 *La Tour Enchantée*, Paris, 1895

Fig. 229 *La Ronde du Commissaire*, Paris, 1884
Fig. 230 Backstage at Booth's theatre, 1870

many robbers are bringing a prisoner before their chief, while 'below is the robbers' cave, where a robber is on the look-out in case anyone is approaching'.[1]

An obvious extension of this is the gradual movement towards the box-set for interiors. Already in the eighteenth century in France there had been experiments with two or more open rooms in the upstage area, and prints of these survive for 1775 and 1779.[2] In England in 1833 this idea was developed into a setting often used today, that of the open façade of a house with two rooms up and two down[3] – the cast disliked it intensely, and asked during rehearsals that this 'perplexing, unexampled, undramatic, unactable four-roomed scene' should be omitted, but it was left in and was a great success with the public.[4] But these were still single structural devices upstage. The *Maskinmästarejournalen* show how during the century the arrangement of wings and flats downstage gradually closed together, until a genuine box-set was created in which the whole scene was one unit. In a French print of 1884 such a setting can be seen in a finished form (Fig. 229), complete with a structural staircase and sufficiently sturdy doors to make the most of the precise mechanics of French farce of the period.

A necessary part of any free-standing setting, which needs to be light enough to be changed quickly, is the braces which are still used in the theatre today to hold flats upright. An article in 1870 about Booth's new theatre in New York shows such braces being used (Fig. 240) and suggests that they were an innovation; the 'wings are not run in on grooves, as in other theatres, with slides above to support them, but are held in place by long braces, which we see men busily placing in our first illustration'.[5] It was not till 1881 that Irving finally abolished the old system of wings in grooves at the Lyceum and replaced it with a free-standing arrangement of flats supported by braces,[6] but nevertheless free-standing flats had for a long time been used in all theatres in conjunction with wings in grooves, and there must considerably earlier have been some form of brace to hold them up. The attitude of a nineteenth-century manager appears to have been that he would certainly make use of the grooves whenever they could help with any

 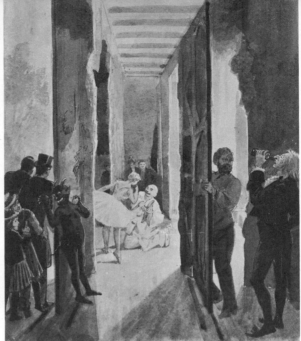

Fig. 231 Paris Opéra, 1892

Fig. 232 Danish pantomime, *c.* 1900

part of a setting, but if the setting demanded otherwise he was quite prepared to disregard them entirely: in the Stockholm *Maskinmästarejournalen* settings using the old wing system can be found over several decades side by side with others using almost exclusively set-pieces. And Figs 231–2 show the peaceful co-existence of the old and the new systems continuing right up to the beginnings of this century. Fig. 231 is a view of the Opéra in Paris during the 1890s, on an occasion where the structural setting has won the whole stage for itself. Yet Fig. 232, a watercolour from about 1900, depicts a Danish pantomime still being performed with the wings in their grooves, just as they could have been seen in European theatres at any time during the previous two hundred and fifty years.

Melodrama

Structural settings were particularly well suited to two favourite types of nineteenth-century entertainment, fairy extravaganzas and melodrama – and again Bäuerle's prints show them being put to good early use in Vienna. Excellent examples are the two prints, dated 1829, of scenes from *Der Apfelkönig und der Menschenfeind*. The villain, Rappelkopf, comes to a hut in a wood to meet an accomplice (Fig. 234) but in front of the door stands the ghost of his first wife, Viktorine; he tries to get in through the window, but finds there the ghost of his second wife, Walburga; he tries to climb in through the roof, when who should appear but the ghost of his third wife, Emerentia; finally he sees in the moon the face of his present wife. Shouting 'Hellish Quartet', he assaults the door, when a flash of lightning sets the hut ablaze and a torrential downpour begins, which turns the whole forest into a sea. Rappelkopf and his servant Habakuck (who is Pierrot) are about to drown when the Apfelkönig himself comes rowing out

[1]228, 2 Jhrg. no. 19;   [2]reprod. 11, IV, 131 & 77;   [3]reprod. 217, VIII, 4, Pl. 1;   [4]217, VIII, 4, 81–6;   [5]223, 591;   [6]135, 217

Figs 234–5 Scenes from Viennese melodrama, 1829

in a boat to rescue them (Fig. 235). Habakuck falls out of the boat and has to swim for safety, while 'on the hills there appear Swiss boys and girls in pairs'.[1]

Such a mixture of spectacle and magic was to have an undying appeal throughout the century, using many of the old tricks and adding some new ones as well. A fascinating page of stage effects for such shows appeared in *The Illustrated Dramatic News* in 1886 (Fig. 233). The text explains that no. 1 is how to produce a snow storm from the flies; 2 is a simple lift, mainly for stage hands; 3 is one way of achieving a vanishing lady; 4 and 13 are magic supplies of wine; 5 and 11 are appropriate rat effects for *Dick Whittington* or *The Piper of Hamelin*; 6 is a running spring; 7 a fairy queen skimming magically over the stage; 8 mysterious music from below; 9 how the spirit of the mountain vanishes and reappears among rocks; 10 a stormy passage; and 12 the manufacture of steam under the stage to represent smoke. The only interesting detail not mentioned in the text is the stage hand in no. 8, who is using his bellows to blow up a bright flame which will add an eerie light to the apparition and will support the 'mysterious music from below'. This was a primitive way of producing an effect which was achieved much more efficiently by the limelight lamp, devised by Drummond, which produced a very bright light by burning lime in an oxyhydrogen flame.

Like all stage effects when seen from behind, the overall impression of Fig. 233 is how amazingly primitive and yet laborious most of the techniques are. One nineteenth-century technique seems even to have been considerably more primitive than its predecessors – the system of making the waves of the sea, as depicted by Daumier (Fig. 236), which involved herding dozens of extras on all fours under a blue cloth and instructing them to heave about. Although this was more laborious than the various systems recommended by Sabbattini in 1638, its one advantage was that unlike them it could be used convincingly right downstage, in this case under the very nose of the prompter.

---

[1]228, 3. Jhrg., nos 14 & 19

Fig. 233 Stage effects, 1886

251

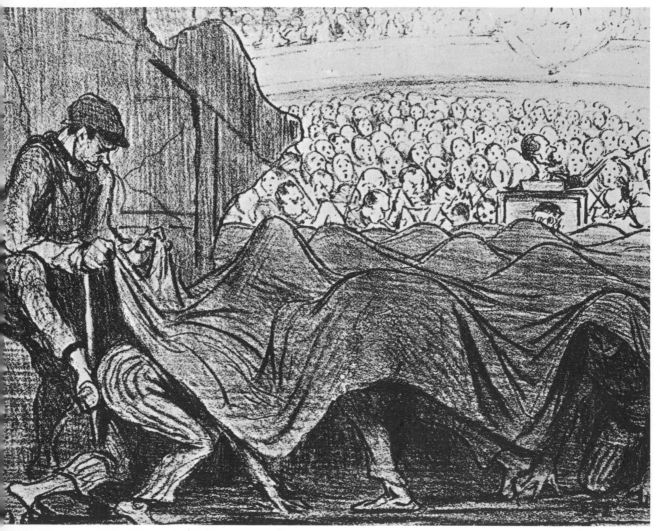

Fig. 236 Daumier, human wave machine

Figs 237–8 Pepper's ghost, the effect and the technique

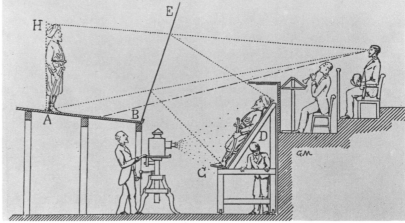

Fig. 239 *Mazeppa* on a poster, *c.* 1860
Fig. 240 *Mazeppa* from the wings, 1851

In other areas the march of science did bring some definite refinements to theatrical magic. A new method of making a ghost appear, known as *Pepper's ghost* and invented in the 1860s, was clearly an advance on the old system of cranking the spectre up on a trap, though it proved too complicated for use in any normal play. Fig. 237 shows what the spectators saw, and Fig. 238 reveals the system. There was a sheet of plain glass between the audience and the stage, and on it could be seen the reflection of an actor, very brightly lit and supported at the appropriate angle beneath the stage. The actor in Fig. 238, in spite of his awkward position, is free to move his head and arms and to draw his scimitar; and he will seem to glide across the stage when the stage hand pushes him along on his trolley.

Melodrama used a vast number of spine-chilling stage effects, but usually of a more traditional nature. The wide range can be seen in a famous book in the Harvard Theatre Collection, entitled *Specimens of Show Printing*. It is a collection of melodrama posters, reproduced in miniature, which a firm of printers sent to theatrical managers in the 1860s and 1870s to tempt them to order the actual posters. Probably the best known of these are the picture of wolves pushing down the door of the hut in *Davy Crockett*[1] and that of the hero tied to a railway line in the path of an advancing train in *Under the Gaslight*.[2] These and several others from the volume are often reproduced as actual illustrations of melodrama in the theatre, but in fact the poster artists usually accepted the stage illusion entirely and were not too concerned with precise theatrical details. So, for example, the poster for *Mazeppa* – one of the most successful of all melodramas – gives a powerful romantic impression of Mazeppa strapped to the back of the horse and pursued by wolves (Fig. 239), but gives little idea of how this might have been performed in the theatre.

When the practical details are added, in a cartoon by Tenniel in *Punch* (Fig. 240), the overall effect becomes a little less flamboyantly dramatic. Mazeppa had been tied to a wild horse by a Polish nobleman, who discovered him in a love scene with his wife; the horse galloped for two days and two nights, and at this point is seen wading in the Dnieper, with the wolves on

---

[1] 12, IX, Tav. XXI;   [2] 12, IV, Tav. V

the bank and a vulture overhead. It is worth quoting a few sentences from Mazeppa's mono-logue at this terrifying moment to give the extraordinary flavour of such melodramas:

> Though nigh exhausted by the strong exertion, yon group of ravening wolves scare the affrighted beast from off the bank – already have their gnashing teeth been buried in my flesh; and I could almost wish again to feel their horrid grip – if perchance it might free me from the cruel thongs that eat into my flesh, and squeeze my swollen veins almost to bursting – . . . yon horrid bird of prey, now hovering over its destined victim, forewarns me that my torments soon shall end. . . . It brings me, too, the sacred consolation that I have reached my native Tartary, to which its form and plumage are peculiar . . .[1]

The square paper hats worn by the men manipulating the group of ravening wolves were peculiar to stage carpenters.

Animals

The horse was an important part of the success of *Mazeppa*, and animal performers became increasingly popular on the nineteenth-century stage. Audiences have always loved animal effects in plays, but at most periods they have been property animals. The mysteries used many and the play at Bourges, for example, introduced a dromedary which 'moved its head, opened its mouth and stuck out its tongue'.[2] Stephen Gosson, writing in 1582, complained that many a play consisted of 'nothing but the adventures of an amorous knight, passing from countrie to countrie for the love of his lady, encountring many a terrible monster made of broune paper',[3] and the inventory of the Rose theatre in about 1595 included 'i lyone skin . . . i bears skyne . . . i bores heade . . . i dragon . . . i lyone . . . ii lyon heades . . . i great horse . . . i black dogge'.[4] Serious playgoers throughout the seventeenth and eighteenth centuries regularly objected to these effects – though they were accepted as a proper part of the more spectacular court operas and ballets – and a caricature attacking Drury Lane in 1808 (Fig. 241) provides a revealing glimpse of some of these brown paper monsters in a half-finished state.

It also includes, beside the animal which is being ignominiously pumped up with a pair of bellows, a Newfoundland dog called Carlos which had appeared with great success in *The Caravan* in 1803, and it was in fact the live animals which were to dominate such spectacles in the nineteenth century. Again, theatre people have always known that any animal trained to take part in some sort of performance will bring in the crowds, and the more surprising and dangerous the better. Trinculo's first reaction on seeing Caliban in *The Tempest* is that if he were back in England he could make good money exhibiting such a monster, and in 1610 a licence was issued in London to 'shew a strange lion, brought to do strange things, as turning an ox to be roasted etc.'.[5] Something nearer to a theatrical entertainment was offered by the various companies of dogs which appear in many prints dressed in the full costume of the day (e.g. Fig. 241), and an enterprising Venetian showman combined this in 1762 with the more alarming appeal of a lion (Fig. 242), in a performance of which the main attraction was clearly that sooner or later the lion would be unable to resist one of his tiny colleagues.

Within the theatres themselves the menagerie of animals woven into the plot could at times be fairly exotic, or such at any rate is implied by a satirical attack on Covent Garden in 1752,

---

[1]315, 198 ff.; [2]247, 147; [3]244, IV, 215; [4]31, 233; [5]244, I, 320, n.2

Fig. 241 Drury Lane's animals, 1808
Fig. 242 Animal performers in Venice, 1762 (*above right*)
Fig. 243 *Timour the Tartar*, Dublin, *c.* 1820

Fig. 244 Racing drama, late nineteenth century

announcing a pantomime in which 'the principal parts . . . will be performed by a wonderful *Armadillo* from *Brasil*, a *Serpent* from the river *Oronoque*, the famous *Lanthorn-Fly* from *Peru*, a *Mermaid* from the *Ladrones Islands*, a surprising *Camel*, a *Rhinoceros*, and many horrible animals, *being their first appearance on the English stage*'.[1] Schinkel would surely have approved of the educational value to zoologists.

Camels, rhinoceroses and elephants had appeared in seventeenth-century operas and ballets, but these were lifesize models pushed around on wheels. Except where managers were purely taking the opportunity of exhibiting a rare species, the only regular animal performers had been dogs and horses. Horses were in frequent demand to provide the pleasures of spectacular equestrian feats in a confined space – they still excite audiences in *Aïda* – and there was a special theatrical form known as the *balletto a cavallo* (horse ballet), but this was a courtly entertainment and usually in the open air. It was in the nineteenth century that a passion developed in the public theatres for 'hippodrama', in which the horses were carefully incorporated in a melodramatic plot.

Fig. 243 shows the purely spectacular appeal of horsemanship, during Monk Lewis's *Timour the Tartar* in the Crow Street Theatre in Dublin, but by now considerably more was also required of the animals; they had to learn their own parts and play a decisive role in the plot. Some turned out to be surprisingly talented. Parry saw a horse in Paris in 1833 which 'fired a pistol and then walked all about as if it was lame – and at last it laid down . . . and died – with its 4 legs in the air!'[2] The type of melodramatic climax which these skills made possible can be

256

seen in Pl. XXIII (p. 193), a Bäuerle print of 1830 for a play called *Die Räuber in den Abruzzen, oder, der Hund, seines Herrn Retter*. Not only is the dog tackling the villain downstage centre, but a horse has carried its master over a bridge upstage and then up some rocks to the window of a house. For this type of performance the new structural sets were an obvious necessity. In a similar way the fame of the dog Carlos in 1803 at Drury Lane had been largely due to its gallant rescue of the heroine from a tank of water.[3] Such moving moments have a long history stretching back from the Lassie films at least to the time of Vespasian, when a dog entertained the emperor himself with a fairly elaborate little plot involving a supposedly poisoned piece of cake.[4] But undoubtedly it is the nineteenth century which carries away the laurels, both for the number of performers employed and for the seriousness with which their art was taken. The owners of the famous horse which played Rosinante in *Don Quixote* in Paris announced that the horse had voluntarily given up eating in order to be better fitted for its mangy role, and when it died of starvation in 1843 Théophile Gautier justifiably acclaimed it as a 'sad victim of the theatrical art'.[5]

While concentrating on the sentimental side, the century was careful at the same time to improve considerably on the spectacular aspects. George Sanger recalled in his memoirs that a pantomime of 1876, called *Gulliver on his Travels*, included one scene which 'used three hundred girls, two hundred men, two hundred children, thirteen elephants, nine camels, and fifty-two horses, in addition to ostriches, emus, pelicans, deer of all kinds, kangaroos, Indian buffaloes, Brahmin bulls, and, to crown the picture, two living lions led by the collar and chain into the centre of the group'.[6] And finally there was developed the most dramatic form of animal spectacular ever devised in a theatre – the 'racing drama'. In 1899 New York was even offering the chariot race in *Ben Hur*, and Fig. 244 shows how the effect was achieved – this time for a normal horse race. The horses galloped on moving belts set into the stage, and the man on the right of the stage controlled the speed of each belt to keep the horse on it. Behind the horses the landscape flashed by on a moving panorama, and in front of them a series of vertical white posts hurtled along beneath a horizontal white bar to suggest the railings.

Audiences and auditoria

At the beginning of the nineteenth century audiences were perhaps more unruly than ever before; by the end of the century the meek and orderly behaviour of modern audiences, with nobody standing on the seats or shouting at the actors, had become established as normal. The change was a gradual one and several causes contributed to it, one of the most important being a steady improvement in the arrangement of seating in the theatres. The pit had been the main area for riotous behaviour – it was both nearest to the stage and the best place for being seen by the rest of the audience – but during the century it slowly moved from its old status as one of the cheapest parts of the theatre to its present one as the most expensive, changing its name on the way from 'pit' to 'orchestra stalls' or just 'stalls'. In London the march of respectability went roughly as follows: in the late 1820s a few rows of more comfortable seats appeared in front of the ordinary benches of the pit and were called stalls; at much the same time a system of reserved seats was introduced, which would lead to a far more organised arrangement of the auditorium instead of the old system by which a spectator battled for any space he could secure

[1]295, III, 25; [2]221, 92; [3]295, IV, 25; [4]32, 120; [5]315, 73–4; [6]315, 237

Fig. 245 Interior of the Dagmar Teater, Copenhagen, 1887

on unnumbered benches;[1] also around this time the galleries with their open boxes began to split into two very distinct areas, closed boxes near the stage for those who wanted privacy and a more convenient open gallery for the rest; the term 'dress-circle' was first used in 1822.[2] By about 1880 the stalls reached to the back of the more important theatres, though the auctioneer's catalogue of the Royal Court Theatre, when it was sold in 1932, shows that some theatres even then still had both pit and stalls. When the Prince of Wales's Theatre in 1865 introduced comfortable carpeting throughout the stalls, it could be said that the familiar habitat of the modern middle-class theatregoer was finally and firmly established. Apart from the costumes, Fig. 245 could be a theatre in any western city today. It is in fact a view of a Danish theatre in 1887.

The new quietness of the audiences was noted by an author in 1859, who wrote; 'modern audiences are less easily worked up to demonstration than they were at the beginning of the present century . . . Audiences now-a-days are more numerous than ever; but they sit, for the most part, in silent admiration . . . The stalls, boxes, and even the pit, are too genteel to clap their hands; and the Olympian deities are awed into silence by their isolation, and the surrounding chill'.[3] By the end of the century, life in even the steeply-raked upper galleries was extremely respectable. A wash drawing of 1900 (Fig. 246) gives a delightfully evocative glimpse of this part of the audience during an interval, in a theatre still lit by gas.

Of course the whole period was more self-consciously respectable than before, but another possible reason contributing to the new mood was that the old theatrical audience had split in two. During the eighteenth century the public theatres had tried to cater for all tastes. During

---

[1]295, IV, 12, n.5;   [2]295, IV, 10;   [3]295, V, 13–14

Fig. 246 In the upper circle of the Kongelige Teater, Copenhagen, 1900

Fig. 247 Cruikshank, *Café de la Paix*, Paris, 1822

the nineteenth there grew up special variety theatres – or in England the music halls – and the more boisterous spectators preferred to patronise these, leaving the straight theatres to concentrate on supposedly more serious matters. Even in small details the split was apparent. In many earlier theatres a moderate amount of eating and drinking had been a normal accompaniment to the play. Now food and drink vanished from the serious theatres during the performance but became an essential part of the enjoyment in variety theatres; indeed the English music hall came into being largely because publicans found that if they provided entertainment they could sell more drink. A print by Cruikshank (Fig. 247) is an unusually early view of such a place of entertainment in Paris. It illustrates David Carey's *Life in Paris*, published in 1822. Our hero, Dick Wildfire, is paying a visit to the famous Théâtre de la Paix, also known as the Café de la Paix, where 'the performances, which consist of rope dancing, light *vaudevilles*, music, etc. are given gratis, while the visitors are refreshing themselves with whatever the *Café* affords . . . In front was the stage, where damsels of the most zephyrine lightness, no ways encumbered with dress or modesty, delighted and astonished all eyes by their feats on the rope and slack wire'.[1]

Cruikshank had never been to Paris, and though his aquatint is faithful to all the details of Carey's text he has given it a very English mood. This was still before the birth of the real music hall in England, but the entertainment on the stage would have been a familiar sight to pantomime audiences at Sadler's Wells at the time, and the clown is even wearing a costume specially associated with Grimaldi. In London the music hall was to become the special preserve of the working classes; and it seems that this was already the case in Paris, since Carey says the chief patrons of the Café de la Paix were 'the Paris cockneys'.

260

There were also in the capital cities of the industrial age a vast number of tiny makeshift theatres, catering for the roughest and poorest section of the audience and offering garbled little plays several times nightly. In England these were called 'penny theatres', because the patrons only paid a penny each, and it was calculated in the 1830s that there were between eighty and a hundred such places operating in London.[2] Fig. 248, a rough etching pasted into a scrap-book

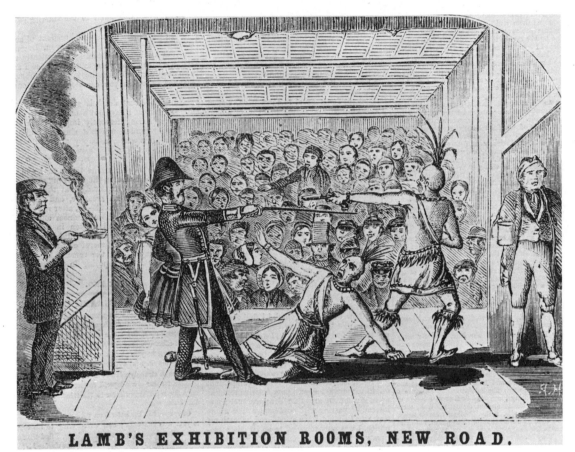

LAMB'S EXHIBITION ROOMS, NEW ROAD.

Fig. 248 A penny theatre, *c.* 1850

in the Boston Public Library, is a rare illustration of one of these tiny theatres. The play being performed seems to be an early Western, with the heroine being rescued from the Indians. The man behind the wing with a flaming pan in his hand is providing light. The repertoire was usually an even more crude version of the melodrama in the larger theatres; for example the cast of a play called *The Red-Nosed Monster, or the Tyrant of the Mountains* consisted of the Red-Nosed Monster himself, the Assassin, the Ruffian of the Hut, the Villain of the Valley, the Wife of the Red-Nosed Monster, and the Daughter of the Assassin.[3] Such theatres should perhaps be seen as successors to the outdoor theatres of the strolling players, who had virtually vanished by the

---

[1]242, 305; . [2]268, 6; [3]268, 26

Fig. 249 Chestnut Street Theatre, Philadelphia, built 1791 (etching 1794)
Fig. 250 Park Theatre, New York, 1821

nineteenth century; and like their predecessors, the penny theatre actors often carried in their heads no more than the outline of the simple, if lurid, plot, around which they improvised.

American theatres

In general terms European theatres during the eighteenth and nineteenth centuries followed a broadly similar pattern of development, but the theatres of the United States deserve a brief section of their own because the whole process was sandwiched there into a much shorter period, of less than a hundred years.

During the early part of the eighteenth century there was very little theatre in America, provided only by occasional companies on tour from England who played in temporary buildings, but during the second half of the century permanent playhouses began to be built. The earliest surviving illustration of an interior is of the New Theatre which had been built on Chestnut Street in Philadelphia in 1791 (Fig. 249). Its capacity was only 1,165, and in style it was similar to the London theatres of about a century earlier. Being directly influenced by the visiting English players, it kept the doors in front of the proscenium which were peculiar to the English stage. The theatre's nickname among Philadelphians, 'Old Drury', was appropriate.[1]

The earliest illustration of a New York playhouse, the Park Theatre, dates from thirty years later. The first Park Theatre had been built in 1798 but was burnt in 1820. It was immediately rebuilt and the new interior was shown in a woodcut frontispiece (Fig. 250), attached to the *Rejected Addresses* for the opening in 1821. Again the English stage doors are included. A delightful watercolour by John Searle (Fig. 251), dated only a year later, shows the auditorium from a different angle but the details tally exactly with the earlier woodcut. With its greater capacity (between 2,000 and 2,500), and its four tiers as opposed to the Chestnut Street Theatre's three, this playhouse was now nearly in line with the vastly oversized auditoria in Europe at this period.[2] Drury Lane officially held 3,611 in 1794 and 3,060 in 1812.[3]

By the middle of the century it was New York which was beginning to show Europe the meaning of luxurious and expensive theatres, and Broadway was soon to become and to remain

---

[1] 12, V, 298;   [2] 12, VII, 1125;   [3] 344, 64

Fig. 251 Park Theatre, New York, 1822

Fig. 252 Vaudeville, Wyoming, 1877
Fig. 253 Harvard, Hasty Pudding Club, 1856

the real home of the extravaganza. When Booth opened his new theatre in 1869, it was compared by Joseph Jefferson to a 'church behind the curtain and a countinghouse in front of it'.[1] No Victorian manager, many of whom made vast fortunes out of deeply earnest spectaculars, could have wished for a more flattering description.

Meanwhile theatre of a sort was spreading west as well. A plate in *Frank Leslie's Illustrated Newspaper* in 1877 (Fig. 252) depicts a variety show or vaudeville at Cheyenne, Wyoming – in a considerably more genteel saloon than the average Western would allow, with its fairly full orchestra and lace curtains over the boxes. And university drama was making a tentative start, but one which would lead a long way. During our own century, as Broadway grew more and more cautious because of the vast sums of money involved, the home of experimental theatre in the United States became increasingly the universities. Between the wars, said the set-designer Mordecai Gorelik, 'hundreds of "little theatres" led an artistic rebellion against the stereotypes of the older Naturalistic theatres. These community and college playhouses devoted themselves ardently to the New Stagecraft'.[2] Their number continues to grow, and off-Broadway is their most distinguished offspring.

It is as an early, though somewhat less serious, college playhouse that I include a watercolour of Harvard's Hasty Pudding Club in performance in 1856 (Fig. 253). The club was founded in 1797, began acting plays in 1845 and is still in existence. In 1856 the poster promised that the club would 'on this splendid occasion . . . draw the Claret from the Conk of Tragedy, and horribly expand the Mug of the Comic Muse' with such items as the 'thunderous, hell-fiery, polysyllabic, ear-piercing, spirit-stirring, bowels-of-compassion-moving, pompous and morally-virtuous *Chrononhotonthologos*'.[3]

Such a burlesque approach might suggest that the university players were already at odds with the commercial theatre, but this would rate their detachment too high. The professional theatre of the time offered very similar fare. A London playbill of 1852 promises 'A Grand Operatico, Tragico, Serio-pastoralic, Nautico, Demoniaco, Cabalistico Original Christmas Pantomime'[4] – a description at which neither Polonius nor the Hasty Pudding Club would sniff.

[1]30, 566;   [2]267, 207;   [3]264, May 23, 1856;   [4]320, 131

9

THE MODERN THEATRE

The half century from 1880 to 1930 was a period of extraordinary inventiveness in the theatre, presenting in aesthetic terms a rapidly changing kaleidoscope of revolution and counter-revolution. It is almost impossible to find any stylistic feature of *avant-garde* theatre, however new it may still seem, which had not already been carried to more extreme lengths before 1930. The theatre today is in a period of consolidation. The many avenues opened by pioneers at the turn of the century have gradually won acceptance and have become a part of the theatrical repertoire. I exclude from this generalisation the two fields of subject-matter and dialogue – a playwright may still shock an audience with either of these – but no stylistic device, whether in the field of writing, directing or set-designing, will today alienate an audience by its strange-ness. Spectators waiting for the curtain to rise, or waiting in full view of a stage with no curtain, will be equally willing to respond whether the production turns out to come under the heading of naturalism, theatricalism, symbolism or one of a host of other modern techniques. Each had been the latest *cause célèbre* at some time between 1880 and 1930, and each has left its mark.

A critic writing in 1928 wrote that 'in its course from the first realism of the 1900 period to the stylised realism of the Reinhardt epoch, and from that point, by a constantly increased synthesis, to the architectural setting, then on to expressionism, to scenic dynamism, to con-structivism and, finally to a return to Neo-Realism . . . the stage setting seems to have com-pleted a cycle'.[1] He concluded from this that in modern theatrical art each new development seems to die immediately. His facts were right, but his conclusion wrong. The error was in assuming that each new development must replace its predecessors. Instead, forty years later, it is clear that these styles can co-exist. Each, usually in a more practical form than its first revolutionary flourishes, is with us still. It therefore becomes a distortion to tell the last part of this history in a strictly chronological manner. Instead I shall treat each style separately, as a continuous thread running from its beginnings between 1880 and 1930 up to the present time.

Naturalism

The earliest and probably the most influential of the modern theatrical movements was Naturalism, dating from the 1870s. In a sense it was a logical development from the earlier passion for accuracy in settings and costume, but it added a new element. Schinkel, Charles Kean and all the other archaeological men of the theatre had been interested in creating im-pressive and educational pictures on the stage, in front of which the actors would perform. The new trend, deriving largely from the Duke of Meiningen's company, went beyond this. The duke – at once patron, director and designer to his company – saw the set not so much as a background to the actors as an environment of which they are part. Instead of scenery he wanted

Sources (*see* p. 317)   [1]77, 5

Fig. 254 Meiningen, Mark Anthony's oration, 1867

a setting. Unlike earlier sketches for stage designs, his show the actors themselves more promi-
nently than the scenery. The grouping, particularly of a crowd, was all-important, and by the
use of structural settings the shape made by the crowd could be extended vertically as well as
horizontally to give plastic expression to the content of the scene – something familiar to any
modern director, but a new concept in the theatre of the late 1860s. Typical is Meiningen's
drawing for Mark Anthony's speech to the Roman mob in *Julius Caesar* (Fig. 254).

  Meiningen wanted his groupings to be dictated by natural requirements and not by those of
the stage. This meant avoiding the conventional pattern, balanced on either side of stage centre.
It also meant discarding the theatrical convention by which characters invariably speak towards
the audience. From now on it gradually became a point of honour to disregard the audience.
Meiningen's actors were forbidden to look directly at the spectators and a reasonable proportion of even important speeches had to be played facing upstage.[1] More and more in the
productions of the late nineteenth century the actor was in his own world, unwittingly spied on
by hundreds of strangers. 'It is essential,' wrote Jean Jullien in 1892, 'that the position of the
curtain should be a fourth wall, transparent for the audience, opaque for the actor,'[2] and various
ways were found to fortify this missing fourth wall; sofas and chairs were arranged with their

backs to the audience; fire-irons were placed against the proscenium and actors warmed their hands at them, or appeared to study pictures on the wall to either side of them; the pattern of a window frame was painted on the stage near the footlights, as though cast there by a sun shining somewhere among the spectators;[3] a mirror on the wall facing the audience was painted so that it seemed to reflect patterned paper on the missing wall.[4]

Though slightly ludicrous, these devices were at least grappling with naturalistic illusion in an area where it was a feasible proposition – that of interior scenes. A room on the stage can be wallpapered, curtained and furnished with precisely the materials that are used in a real room. Except for the fourth wall, the illusion is no longer even an illusion. But when the same intentions are applied to exterior scenes, particularly in the countryside, the results are very different. The helplessness of the designer who tries to imitate nature is well suggested in an English stage manager's rehearsal note for Charles Kean's *Tempest* in the 1850s; 'canvas aprons wanted to the feet of both large working trees, to hide wheels – Act 4'.[5] A good example of the extreme improbability of such exterior scenes is a 1900 photograph of a setting in Paris, entitled 'The Abandoned Camp of the Greeks', for Berlioz's opera *La Prise de Troie* (Fig. 255).

It was through Zola that naturalism became Naturalism and was raised to the level of a carefully formulated theatrical crusade against stage romanticism. Even Meiningen's new realistic groupings, within his mainly classical repertoire, were designed to achieve heroic images on the stage. Zola, in his dramatisation of his own *Thérèse Raquin* in 1873 and in his essay *Le Naturalisme au Théâtre*, introduced a new sociological seriousness. The value of the realistic setting was to be that it presented the real environment in which real modern people could be presented and analysed. Like the Naturalistic novel, the Naturalistic stage setting was to capture contemporary reality by an accumulation of carefully observed details. Zola wanted 'the living drama of the interaction between character and context'. 'We are', he wrote, 'in an age of method, of experimental science; we need, above all, precise analysis'[6] – words echoed fifty years later by Brechtians arguing in favour of aesthetic principles which are diametrically opposed to Naturalism, but which are designed to achieve aims similar to Zola's.

Zola professed to want to study all people in their real environments, but inevitably – in reaction against middle-class romanticism – the bias of the new Naturalistic drama was towards working-class life and the more sordid aspects of contemporary conditions. The arguments about 'kitchen sink' drama in the 1950s were but pale shadows of seventy years before, when the outraged middle-class audience usually had more cause for complaint – in the realm of the sordid it was all too easy for realism to degenerate into melodrama, as in a play called *Conte de Noël*, in which the child of an adulterous liaison is killed and its body is thrown to the pigs on Christmas Eve to the sound of carols.[7]

In a period which had long been dedicated to the illusion of reality on the stage, the new subject matter of Naturalistic drama brought definite aesthetic advantages. Romantic drama had introduced a high proportion of those exotic settings for which stage illusion is invariably inadequate, but since Naturalistic drama studied man in his natural habitat, and since for the most part his natural habitat is indoors and in cities, the most laughable failures of illusion were now more often avoided. The typical Naturalistic scene is in the style of the *café-bar* in Zola's *L'Assommoir* (Fig. 256), and this photograph of a scene in the play could almost pass as a photograph of people in an actual café.

---

[1]68, 120–1; [2]68, 121; [3]68, 121; [4]295, V, 47; [5]319, 12; [6]68, 107 ff.; [7]267, 134–5

Fig. 255 *La Prise de Troie*, Paris, 1900
Fig. 256 *L'Assommoir*, Paris, 1900

Fig. 257 *La Clairière*, Paris, 1901

Such a café on the stage is Naturalism at its most pure, most uninspired and most dull. The illusion is complete, precisely because care has been taken to exclude any distinctive touch of design which would set this café apart from every other typical café; and this style has become the standard for uninspired directors and set-designers of ordinary living-room dramas ever since. But among the more creative men of the theatre this pure Naturalism had a surprisingly short run. The high priest of Naturalistic production was Antoine, since his Théâtre Libre was the first to weld into successful productions the new ideas which had been mainly theory in Zola and which had then partially developed, side by side with other elements, in the plays of Ibsen and Strindberg in Scandinavia. Yet Antoine himself, while insisting along correct Naturalistic lines that furniture and props should be not only real but visibly used and old,[1] was for the most part too great an artist to exclude the element of distinctive design. The school-room setting for his production of *La Clairière* in 1901 (Fig. 257) is in one sense a naturalistic schoolroom, but is at the same time an unusually elegant one. It includes a formal patterning which is still believable in naturalistic terms, but which is lacking from the café scene in *L'Assommoir* and from most schoolrooms in real life. An artistic element has been introduced by the selection of the pattern, just as a good photographer by his choice of camera angle can uncover a spatial beauty in an ordinary schoolroom today – revealing an image which to the casual eye was not there, and which in the objective view of Naturalism should not be there. Already, therefore, in Naturalism itself the next scenic developments are prefigured, since the majority of the theatrical styles of this century have emphasised the importance of the artist's personal vision in scene design. Antoine, armed with this return to an aesthetic sense, can even avoid the old pitfalls and succeed with an exterior scene in the country, such as his figure crossing a farmyard in driving rain (Fig. 258) in *La Terre*, a play based on a story by Zola.

[1] 267, 124 ff.

Fig. 258 *La Terre*, Paris, 1902

Significantly, although this is again a photograph of the actual scene, the force with which it strikes one is not so much that of naked reality as of an impressionist painting.

Appia, Craig and spatial design

One of the earliest rebels against Naturalism was Adolphe Appia, but several of his designs involve the same process of simplifying and patterning as Antoine's ostensibly Naturalistic sets. The castle in Fig. 259, for example, is still a recognisable castle, but it is treated as a juxtaposition of structural forms to provide an atmospheric design.

Appia arrived at his ideas through an admiration for Wagner's operas, combined with disgust at the clumsy illusionistic scenery in which even Wagner himself had intended them to be performed. The Rhine maidens on the first night of *Das Rheingold* (Figs 2 and 3) suggest well what Appia found so offensive, and his ideas were first published in 1895 in *La Mise en scène du drame wagnérien*. Others had already begun to rebel against the exaggerated contemporary interest in

270

Fig. 259 Appia, *Parsifal*, 1896

historical accuracy. The text of *La fille aux mains coupées*, presented in Paris in 1891 by Paul Fort, states that 'the action takes place no matter where and more or less in the Middle Ages', and the programme described the play as the drama 'of the human soul, constant and true to itself through the useless succession of epochs and the insignificant variety of countries'.[1] A little later, in 1900, Gordon Craig in a programme note to *Dido and Aeneas* dedicated himself to being 'totally incorrect in all details'.[2]

Where the Duke of Meiningen and the Naturalists had tried to integrate the actor and the setting, Appia went further and subordinated the setting to the actor. He emphasised that the actor was the whole point and life of the theatre, and the only function of the setting was to provide a space which would best reveal the actor and would reflect his emotions. So the stage must show not a forest with Siegfried in it, but Siegfried in a forest. 'When the forest, gently stirred by the breeze, attracts Siegfried's attention, we in the audience shall see Siegfried bathed

[1] 68, 152;   [2] 68, 298

Fig. 260 Appia, example of 'rhythmic space' for *Götterdämmerung*, 1909

Fig. 261 Craig, *Scene*, 1907 (*below left*)

Fig. 262 Isaac Grünewald, *Samson and Delilah*, Stockholm, 1921

in light and flickering shadows, instead of cut-out bits of cloth jerked about on strings'.[1] Appia was the first to realise the great power of light in the theatre once the infinitely variable potential of electricity had been introduced. He saw its value for the suggestion of setting and mood, as with Siegfried in the dancing shadow of the leaves, and also for the simple definition of space. With light to provide variety, his concept of the scenery as being literally a setting for the actor led towards a simple structural stage, such as Fig. 260, on which actors could move freely and could take a wide variety of positions in relation to each other. From Appia onwards such settings gradually became part of the theatre's normal scenic repertoire. They are the modern *château à volonté*.

Soon after Appia, Edward Gordon Craig began working along very similar lines; he was, though, more of a mystic than Appia and his visions of the future ranged wider than matters of mere production and stage settings to embrace an almost religious concept of theatre, with the all-powerful Artist as high priest of a cult of beauty. This difference is reflected in the designs of the two men. Appia's sketches are for the most part extremely practical; they show sets which could be built without much difficulty in any theatre. By contrast many of Craig's settings soar to impossible heights, though his own reply to this comment used to be that he was presenting not a scale drawing but the impression which an audience would receive. An example is Fig. 261, one of the nineteen prints called *Scene* with which Craig developed in 1907 his system of 'screens'. The walls were to be composed of canvas screens which could be moved in view of the audience to innumerable different positions – this part of the system was tried out by Craig in his Moscow *Hamlet* of 1912[2] – and the floor and ceiling were to be made up of 'movable cubes' which could be individually raised or lowered.[3] Variety was to be provided by the lighting; 'during the whole course of the Drama the light either caresses or cuts – it floods or it trickles down . . . travelling it produces the music'.[4] The setting was to be the complete antithesis of the nineteenth century's love of precise historical detail, for Craig insisted that this variable scene was the 'essential habitation of man'. To discover it, he explained with mock solemnity, he had studied two hundred and fifty models of man's dwellings ranging from 5000 BC to AD 1900, and 'having rejected in the two hundred and fifty models any pieces which cannot be found in every other piece, I find I am then left with the essential parts which form the habitation of man. The walls remain: The floor. The ceiling . . . nothing else'.[5]

Though both Appia and Craig directed a few productions, their real influence was as theorists. Their vision of the stage spread through their sketches, many of which were not for any specific play but were generalised concepts of how the stage might look. Craig's 'scene' was Appia's 'rhythmic space'. They found followers very quickly. Even Stanislavski, whose productions of Chekhov and Gorki were among the most famous achievements of Naturalism, produced Maeterlinck's *Blue Bird* in 1908 in a setting reminiscent of Appia.[6] And when the Künstlertheater opened in Munich in the same year, Fritz Erler's settings consisted of movable blocks combined with lighting effects.[7] From the 1920s on, innumerable examples could be found. Pl. XXX (p. 280), dated 1927, borrows Appia's platform and steps in their simplest form, and Fig. 262 shows an excellent use of light to create a sculptural shape, in this case a changing one. In 1921 the American set-designer, Robert Edmond Jones, travelled through Europe, visiting leading theatres and making sketches of the more impressive new styles of production and design. Fig. 262 is his sketch of a setting by Isaac Grünewald for the Royal Opera in Stockholm.

---

[1]68, 250;   [2]68, 323;   [3]68, ms. note on Fig. 138;   [4]250, 21;   [5]250, 22;   [6]12, IX, Tav. XIX;   [7]267, 177

Fig. 263 Jo Mielziner, *Winterset*, New York, 1935

It shows Samson at the mill. 'A slanting shaft of light strikes the millstone in a vivid crescent. As the wheel travels in its track this crescent widens to a disk of blinding light, and then shrinks again.'[1] Another American designer, Donald Oenslager, emphasised that 'the twentieth century stage designer can paint with light; invention has made him a fellow of infinite jest, of most excellent fancy, able like Prospero to create in a moment the baseless fabric of a vision'.[2]

Perhaps even more influential was another idea shared by both Appia and Craig – that the designer should pick out the one or two most dominant images of the play, and construct of these a setting which will symbolise the whole. So, in 1895, Appia wrote that a setting for *Das Rheingold* should merely express the three elements at the centre of the drama – water, air and fire.[3] And Gordon Craig explained:

> Come now, we take *Macbeth*. . . . In what kind of place is that play laid? . . . I see two things. I see a lofty and steep rock, and I see the moist cloud which envelops the head of this rock. That is to say, a place for fierce and warlike men to inhabit, a place for phantoms to nest in. Ultimately this moisture will destroy the rock; ultimately these spirits will destroy the men.[4]

---

[1] 286, opp. p. 122;   [2] 267, 223;   [3] 68, 268;   [4] 249, 27

Fig. 264 Mikulas Kravjansky, *La Casa de Bernarda Alba*, Bratislava, 1957
Fig. 265 Edward Carrick, *Macbeth*, Stratford-upon-Avon, 1949

So the mist and the rock not only determine the particular pattern of the setting, but also embody in themselves an image of the impending drama itself – and this form of scenic symbolism, merging with the more nearly naturalistic settings of the commercial theatre, has provided one of the most familiar of contemporary styles. An excellent example is Jo Mielziner's setting for *Winterset* (Fig. 263). The plot specifies a house beneath a bridge, but Mielziner's bridge also broods like doom over the tragedy below. A Czechoslovakian setting of 1957, by Mikulas Kravjansky (Fig. 264), shows the same symbolist approach still providing a very powerful setting. The play was Lorca's *The House of Bernarda Alba*, about five daughters imprisoned at home, with explosive and tragic results, by their mother's determination to wait for sufficiently well-born husbands. Kravjansky's setting is extremely beautiful in the simplicity of its design, but it is also most carefully built up on symbolist principles; the black clothes against the hot blinding white of the sun on the courtyard walls; the spindly green tree reaching up towards the air above; and the single-barred gate to the outside world.

So the visions and theories of Appia and Craig, launched from ivory towers against the ordinary theatre of the day, became lastingly incorporated in the ordinary theatre of the next day. Both men would no doubt have rejected violently many of the compromises involved, but the practical theatre has benefited. There can be no better example of how far the compromises could go than Fig. 265, a design for *Macbeth* in 1949 by Craig's son, Edward Carrick, in which the new images are blandly combined with the old methods. The 'lofty and steep rock' is here, with even a hint at the top of the 'moist cloud', and the almost geometric blocks of the cliff face and the slanting rays of light across them are very much in the Craig style. But the father would hardly be pleased by the manuscript note at the bottom of the son's sketch; 'To be painted on drop with entrance through cloth in centre.' Nothing was more anathema to Craig, as also to Appia, than the painted canvas scenery of the nineteenth century.

Diaghilev and the painters

Simultaneously with the rejection by Appia and Craig of painting in the theatre, and their replacement of it by structural forms, other innovators were trying to break away from the Naturalistic stage in precisely the opposite direction – towards more rather than less painting. The idea was to throw the stage open as an area to be filled with the fantasy and invention of genuine painters, established names of the *avant-garde* art galleries. In the 1890s this was already happening in a few small theatres – Lugné-Poe at the Théâtre de l'Oeuvre, for example, used settings painted by his own friends, among them Bonnard, Munch, Toulouse-Lautrec and Vuillard,[1] though unfortunately nothing survives of their work except one rather vague sketch by Toulouse-Lautrec.[2] But productions of this type only began to reach a wider audience after 1900. Reinhardt produced *Ghosts* in Berlin in 1906 with a setting by Munch,[3] and 1909 saw the beginnings of the *Ballets Russes*, in which Diaghilev was eventually to present to a world-wide audience the work of many extremely distinguished painters. In the early years they were mainly Russian, and were still primarily men of the theatre, though their approach to stage design was essentially that of painters. The most successful was Bakst, and his sketch for *Schéhérazade* in 1910 (Fig. 268) shows well the freedom with which the luxury of an Eastern potentate's court is now interpreted in terms of paint – something familiar enough to any painter at the time, but

---

[1] 68, 157; [2] 68, Fig. 48; [3] 68, Fig. 58

Pls XXVII & XXVIII Two scenes from Charles Kean's *Henry V*: watercolours, London, 1859
Pl. XXIX Interior setting: watercolour by Leon Bakst, 1922 (*overleaf*)

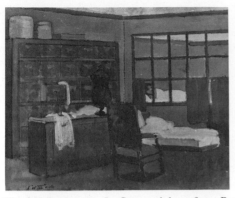 

Fig. 266 Dethomas, *Le Carnaval des enfants*, Paris, 1910

Fig. 267 Leslie Hurry, *Hamlet*, Sadler's Wells, 1942 (revived 1958)

still new in the theatre. When Bakst was tied down to the old naturalistic subject of an ordinary interior (Pl. XXIX, pp. 278–9), he dutifully kept to the prosaic requirements of the setting but was still able to release a painter's love of colour in a superb collection of exotic furnishings and upholstery.

In Paris in the 1920s Diaghilev used a much wider range of artists; including Picasso, Matisse, Braque, Derain, Juan Gris, Miró, Max Ernst, Léger and de Chirico.[1] Unlike Bakst, these were painters for whom stage design remained essentially an interesting side-line – though fortunately, since in ballet the centre of the stage has to remain empty and the scenic emphasis therefore falls on the backcloth, it was often sufficient for the artists to treat the backcloth as a huge canvas on which they could paint their own comment on the mood of the dance.

The *Ballets Russes* provided the most flamboyant opportunity for the painters in the theatre, but elsewhere too there was appearing a more sober version of the same painterly response to stage design. Fig. 266, for example, is a 1910 setting by Maxime Dethomas who had been an established painter for ten years before working in the theatre. At first sight it is a conventional interior setting, but its pattern of shapes and tones is essentially the careful composition of a painter and even points ultimately towards Mondrian. Dethomas was working for the Théâtre des Arts in Paris, a theatre dedicated to the new anti-realist principles of stage scenery, but this design has precisely the same sense of style as Antoine had achieved under the banner of Naturalism. In a more abstracted form, the open and simplified stage house designed by Strohbach in about 1930 (Pl. XXXI, p. 280) is a natural development of the same style and one that has had many successors.

The one danger in giving the painters a free hand in the theatre is that their fantasies, like the elaborate painted scenery of the last century, may tend to compete with the actor rather than support him. This section ends with a design which would certainly have convinced Appia and Craig that their crusade had been in vain – Leslie Hurry's 1942 setting for *Hamlet* (Fig. 267). Admittedly this *Hamlet* was a ballet, but even so the photograph suggests that it may have been something of a problem for the performers on the stage to compete with the performer on the backcloth.

[1]68, 186 and 12, VIII, 1605

Pl. XXX Setting for Handel's *Belshazzar*: watercolour by Hans Wildermann, 1927

Pl. XXXI Stage set: watercolour by Hans Strohbach, *c.* 1930

Fig. 268 Bakst, *Schéhérazade*, Paris, 1910 (*overleaf*)

Constructivism and expressionism

Zola had called science to the aid of the theatre in the form of sociological analysis; in the 1920s its help was again enlisted, but this time it was to be salvation through mechanics. In a mood of extreme seriousness, directors and designers began to see the theatre in terms of geometry; the actor was to be reduced, or rather raised, to the status of a machine. The extraordinary mock-scientific solemnity of the movement can be seen in Fig. 269, a diagram which appeared in a book about the new theatre put out by the Bauhaus in 1924, and which was supposed to reveal the relationship between spectator and performer; 'this contrast between the passive spectator and the active performer determines also the form of the stage, of which the most monumental example has been the ancient arena and the most primitive the booth stage in the market place'.[1] The book also contains the costumes by Oscar Schlemmer for *Das Triadische Ballett* which was performed in 1922, though the costumes had been conceived ten years before. The designs were soundly based on mystical-geometrical principles. Fig. 270 shows the pure concept of one of them in diagram form, and Fig. 271 the resulting costume itself. Schlemmer's notes to the diagram go as follows: 'The laws governing the movement of the human body in space: here are the forms of rotation, alignment, intersection of space: gyroscope, Archimedes' screw, spiral, disk. Result: a technical organism.'[2]

Similar avenues were being investigated in Italy by the movement known as Futurism, and the general philosophy found even more ponderous expression in a statement by Enrico Prampolini, director of the Teatro Magnetico:

> From painting, *sceno-synthesis*, to plastic, *sceno-plastic*, from this to the architecture of plastic planes in movement, *sceno-dynamic*. From the traditional three-dimensional scene to the creation of *poly-dimensional scenic-space*, from the human actor to the new scenic personality of space, the actor, from this to the *polyexpressive magnetic theatre*; which I see already outlined architectonically in the center of a valley of spiral terraces, dynamic hills on which rise bold constructions of *polydimensional scenic-space, center* of irradiation of the futuristic atmospheric scenery.[3]

In slightly more practical hands the main result of this line of thought was the style known as Constructivism, particularly associated with the theatre of Meyerhold in Moscow in the 1920s. Meyerhold's early training had been with the Moscow Art Theatre, but he soon rejected the introspective drama of Chekhov and Stanislavski and moved towards a stage composed of machinery and abstract arrangements of scaffolding. To be able to match the machinery and clamber about the scaffolding, the actors had to undergo rigorous physical training according to Meyerhold's famous principle of 'bio-mechanics'. This system, it was explained, 'assumes that the actor is a rather wonderful engine composed of many engines. The new problem of the theatre is how to get the engine in full motion, with all its parts – muscles, sinews, tendons, representing flexible piston rods, cylinders etc. – working at their full capacity'.[4] The principle of the actor as gymnast was one which Meyerhold had consciously derived from the Commedia dell'Arte, but the machine-age jargon was purely of the 1920s.

Alexandra Exter's design for Calderon's *La Dama Duende* in 1919 (Fig. 272) is an example of a Constructivist setting, though it is less stark than many, and its disturbing and unreal angles introduce the extra element of Expressionism. This can be seen as a close relation of

[1] 231, 8; [2] 231, 17; [3] 267, 206; [4] 267, 345

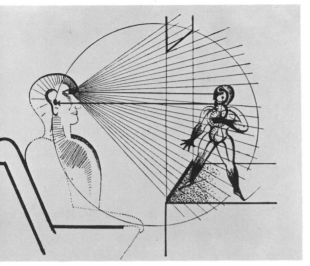
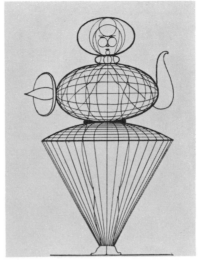

Figs 269–71 Bauhaus drawings and designs by Oscar Schlemmer

Fig. 272 Exter, *La Dama Duende*, Moscow, 1919

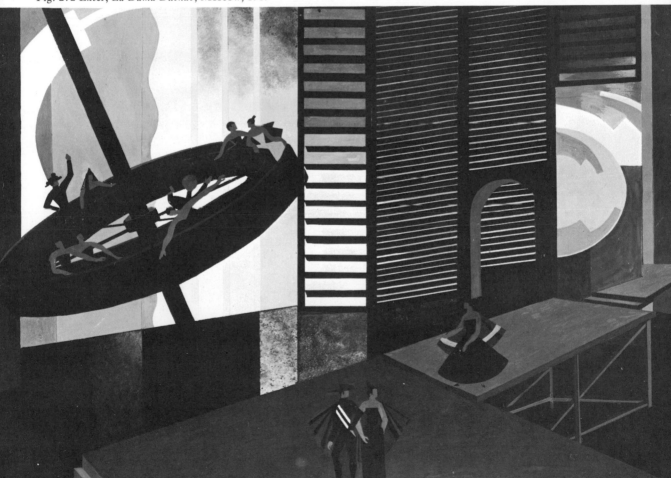

285

Fig. 273 Exter, *Don Juan*, Cologne, 1929

Constructivism, since the two can be used effectively in conjunction, but their basic principles
are quite different. Constructivism is an arrangement of the actors' playing space; Expressionism
is a use of the scenery and costumes to comment on the meaning of the play. Early Expressionist
plays, such as Strindberg's *Dream Play*, used extraordinary combinations of settings as part of
the play's bizarre narrative. In later years Expressionism became also a technique by which
directors and designers could provide a new and literally angled version of plays written for
quite other settings – as with this play of Calderon's, which was presented in one of the four
studios attached to the Moscow Art Theatre.

Another of the studios belonged to the Hebrew theatre, the Habima, and the company's
world-famous production of *The Dybbuk* still uses the original Expressionist settings from 1922.
Unlike the earlier styles of modern scenery, whether by Antoine or Appia or Bakst, the stilted
distortions of *The Dybbuk's* sets now seem a fascinating but very dated curiosity. Expressionism
is almost the only important production style of this century not to have found a lasting place
in the mainstream of modern theatre. Constructivism has fared a little better. A modern
audience will certainly accept a stark arrangement on the stage of unadorned scaffolding, though
its uses are more limited than other types of setting. And modern scenery using simple open
frameworks can be seen as a very distant and prettified descendant of Constructivism. Another
design by Alexandra Exter, done only ten years later (Fig. 273), serves to suggest the possible
link. Her later design would seem entirely familiar on a modern stage, whereas the earlier one
would now seem very odd indeed.

Brecht

The only influential style of production to have been developed more recently than the 1920s
is the style created by Brecht while directing his own later plays in East Berlin after the war.

Fig. 274 *L'Assommoir*, Paris, 1900

All the modern trends we have discussed have been in some form or another revolts against Naturalism, but it is the Brechtian theatre which is linked with Naturalism most closely of all, being both its bitterest enemy and its natural successor. The various other styles pursued the elements which Naturalism excluded – whether fantasy, mystery, poetry, or merely colour and luxury. But where the others were simple opponents of Naturalism, Brecht was its rival. Like Zola he wanted to bring real social and moral problems on to the stage, but Zola hoped to make the spectator take the problem seriously by involving him in it, whereas Brecht wanted to surprise him into taking it seriously by detaching him from it, until he could view it coolly with unmisted eyes. Both had, first of all, to convince the spectator that the problem was a real one. The Naturalists believed that this could be achieved by an accumulation of detail. Brecht maintained that it could only be conveyed by a selection of detail. And with selection comes the element of style which is lacking in pure Naturalism.

Both theories were essentially right for their own time, which is why both have had such influence. Images of reality vary. Eighty years ago people saw reality in pre-Raphaelite paintings and in the illustrations to family Bibles. Today, when the camera surrounds us with images of surface reality, the current image of reality in art tends to be found in more 'primitive' painters, whose work is stylised by their careful selection of detail. There is precisely the same difference between the Naturalistic and Brechtian images of reality on the stage. Fig. 274 is another photograph from the 1900 production of *L'Assommoir*; Fig. 275 is a design, strongly influenced by Brecht, for *El Nost Milan* at the Piccolo Teatro in 1955; and Fig. 276 shows the central part of the same setting, as seen on the stage. The laundry in *L'Assommoir* is brilliantly created in Naturalistic terms; the grouping is extremely natural; the utensils look both used and usable; and the structure and the piping of the building are sufficiently ramshackle to be fully convincing. By contrast, the workhouse of 1955 is entirely formal. Quite apart from the fact that the walls, basin and water-tank are sliced through so that a cross-section of the room is laid bare,

287

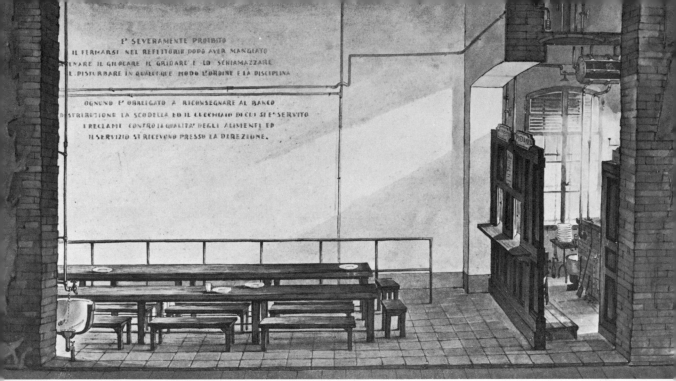

Fig. 275 Luciano Damiani, *El Nost Milan*, Milan, 1955
Fig. 276 *El Nost Milan* on the stage, 1955

Fig. 277 Karl von Appen, *Pauken und Trompeten*, Berlin, 1955
Fig. 278 V. E. Egorov, *The Life of Man*, Moscow, 1907

the tables and chairs are themselves a striking piece of abstract design and the plumbing could have been fitted by Mondrian. Yet to my eye it is the formalised workhouse which gives the stronger impression of reality. The 1900 laundry is trying so hard to seem real, without actually being real, that an impression of falsehood is inevitable. It offers an imitation of reality, where the Brechtian workhouse provides, more acceptably, an image of reality.

Brecht's writing achieves its effect in precisely the same way – by selecting and heightening the crucial elements in a scene, instead of allowing it to be cluttered with other details – and it is this, rather than the more famous Alienation Effect, which is his real contribution to modern theatrical tradition. His determination that the audience must always be aware that it is in a theatre had been anticipated in the early years of the century by several directors and designers. Fritz Erler insisted at Munich in 1908 that a play 'must take place on a stage, in the proper sense of the word, and in such a way that it is always recognisable as such',[1] and Reinhardt often used a revolving stage which turned in full view of the audience, a purely theatrical device much favoured by Brecht. In the longer perspective of theatrical history this acceptance of the stage as a mere stage has been the normal state of affairs; contemporary theatre has only returned to it after the brief oddity of pure Naturalism. The objections of the old guard to Naturalism before its heyday were much the same as those of the *avant garde* after it. In 1827 James Boaden, the biographer of Mrs Siddons, argued that it was not desirable 'that the spectator should lose his senses to the point of forgetting that he is in a regular theatre, and enjoying a work of art invented for his amusement and instruction by a poet, and acted by another artist of corresponding talent called a player. All beyond this is the dream of ignorance and inexperience',[2] and he added later that 'the modern stage affects reality infinitely beyond the proper objects of dramatic representation'.[3] In any case the argument has raged around a fallacy. The real Naturalistic illusion was to suppose that audiences ever might forget they were in a theatre. If they did, would they have sat silently by while the body of a child was thrown to the pigs?

It is possible to maintain that the style of production and scenery which I have described as Brechtian was also anticipated by others. Fig. 277, for example, is the Berliner Ensemble's setting for a scene in *Pauken und Trompeten* (Brecht's adaptation of Farquhar's early eighteenth-

---

[1] 68, 365;   [2] 236, II, 297–8;   [3] 236, II, 355

Fig. 279 Annenkov, *The Storming of the Winter Palace*, Leningrad, 1920

century play, *The Recruiting Officer*), and an extraordinarily similar mood can be seen in Egorov's setting for a Moscow Art Theatre production of 1907 (Fig. 278). But in art it is almost always possible to find individual antecedents for every new style. The fact is that it was due to the brilliant productions of the Berliner Ensemble that this particular style spread through the world.

Images from the past

No period in theatrical history has thrown up so many new styles in such a short space of time as the years since 1880, and artists have added yet another dimension to this development by becoming far more interested in the theatre of the past than any of their predecessors – with the possible exception of the Renaissance stage designers, but then they were interested in only one section of the past, Rome.

There are a few types of modern setting which derive in an unbroken line from the past – patrons of grand opera, for example, are often still confronted with settings which might just have seemed daring in the early nineteenth century – and other forgotten styles sometimes become revived accidentally, to meet a specific need. Fig. 279, Annenkov's design for *The Storming of the Winter Palace*, performed in the Winter Palace Square in Leningrad with 8,000 actors and 150,000 spectators, happens to use precisely the same system of multiple settings on a permanent stage as was seen at Valenciennes in 1547 (Pl. X, pp. 82–3). The problem was similar, and so was the solution.

But what is new in recent times is a conscious and sophisticated borrowing from the past by set-designers. The International Theatre Institute's two collected volumes of modern set designs[1] contain many settings where the flat wings of seventeenth- and eighteenth-century stages are used to excellent effect as deliberately archaic touches. The debt to the past is an even closer one when Donald Oenslager, a famous collector of theatrical prints and drawings as well as a most distinguished set-designer, produces a setting in 1960 (Fig. 280) which is a direct imitation of one by Burnacini in 1668 (Fig. 281); appropriately, it was for a revival of an early seventeenth-century opera, Monteverdi's *Orfeo*. The same fondness for the theatre's past can be seen in a setting by Peter Rice at Sadler's Wells in 1961 (Fig. 282). The design is deliberately

[1] 78 and 79

Fig. 280 Donald Oenslager, *Orfeo*, New York, 1960
Fig. 281 Lodovico Burnacini, *Il Pomo d'Oro*, Vienna, 1668

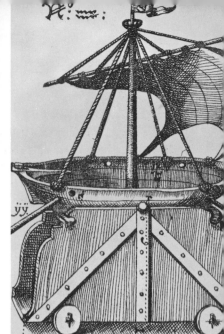

Fig. 282 Peter Rice, detail of sketch for *Ariadne in Naxos*, London, 1961

Fig. 283 Furttenbach, *Jonah's Ship*, 1663 (*above right*)

Fig. 284 Casino Teater, Copenhagen, 1933

theatrical, with the drop-cloth hanging loose and with wings and wing frames standing about; and, again entirely appropriately, there is in the middle of it a detail, the ship machine on wheels, which for total authenticity is most precisely copied from the theatrical section of a manual of 1663 by Furttenbach (Fig. 283). Never before has such variety been available to directors and set-designers; apart from the unprecedented range of modern styles, all the images from the theatre's own past are now at their disposal too.

Stages and auditoria

When, as today, new scenery is designed for each new production, it is natural that theatrical settings should change more rapidly with the times than the permanent parts of the theatre building – the stage itself and the auditorium. As a result, in most of our theatres, audiences stare at specifically twentieth-century settings from the comfortable darkness of nineteenth-century auditoria, much like the one in Fig. 284 – an oil painting of 1933, of which the content now seems decidedly dull because it is so familiar to us as theatregoers, but which is nevertheless contemporary evidence of precisely the type which I have been using throughout this book.

But although this remains the old-fashioned norm which is for the most part automatically accepted by audiences, the reaction against it is one of long standing. It began in the nineteenth century, largely as part of the desire to be as accurate as possible, and particularly in relation to the plays of Shakespeare. As early as 1836 Ludwig Tieck was arguing: 'If we want to play Shakespeare genuinely, without distortion, we must begin with a theatre which is similar to his'.[1] In 1889 *King Lear* was produced in Munich on the 'Shakespeare-Bühne' (Fig. 285), an attempted reconstruction of the Elizabethan stage which was built within a proscenium but with an extension approximating to the apron stage of the English Restoration theatre. In 1893 William Poel produced *Measure for Measure*, having created an Elizabethan playhouse on the stage of a London theatre; in an attempt to improve the illusion he provided spectators in Elizabethan costume sitting on the stage and in galleries to each side.[2] Similarly when Antoine produced *Le Cid* in 1907, he realised that an authentic Naturalistic version of Corneille's image of ancient Spain was an impossibility, but solved the problem by presenting instead a Naturalistic view of the first night of the play in the proper setting of a seventeenth-century theatre, complete with candle-snuffer.[3]

The main motive of these experiments was the old wish for accuracy, but it soon merged with a more general interest – that of breaking away from the absolute separation between auditorium and stage, audience and performers, which had been typical of the nineteenth-century theatre with its sheer proscenium sealing off the entire acting area. The quest for a new integration of stage and auditorium was linked to the knowledge that this had existed in theatre up to the eighteenth century, and it therefore took the form of investigating different earlier systems. For this to be more than another Naturalistic recreation of past styles, virtually as historical *tableaux* within the villainous proscenium, it became necessary to stage the experiments outside the conventional theatres. So, for example, Lugné-Poe presented *Measure for Measure* in 1898 in a circus (Fig. 286), and the stage he used was little different from an ordinary booth stage in a sixteenth-century market place. Reinhardt, a director of extraordinary versatility who experimented with almost every conceivable style in the first quarter of this century,

---

[1] 68, 344;   [2] photo. 68, Fig. 162;   [3] photo. 68, Fig. 36

Fig. 285 *King Lear*, Shakespeare–Bühne, Munich, 1889
Fig. 286 *Measure for Measure*, Paris, 1898

Fig. 287 *The Miracle*, London, 1911

achieved one of his most spectacular successes with *The Miracle*, which had its première in 1911 in the great arena at Olympia in London (Fig. 287). Here the audience of many thousands were actually within the setting, since the walls of the hall had been turned into the walls of a cathedral, but in staging terms what they were witnessing was very similar to the methods of the *Balet Comique* in Paris in 1581 (Fig. 107). The Olympia design specifically shows the 'rails on which the hill and trees moves into the arena', much as the grove with its nymphs (Fig. 108) had moved on to the open floor of the Petit Bourbon three hundred and thirty years before. In the previous year Reinhardt had turned the Schumann Circus in Berlin into something approximating to a Greek theatre for his production of *Oedipus Rex*,[1] and a contemporary account proves that his purpose went deeper than the old interest in historical reconstruction; 'in pursuit of the intimacy idea, space was cleared in front of the stage by removing rows of stalls for the chorus and crowd to act in and mix with the spectators'.[2]

This desire to create a new communion between players and spectators, and to do so by

[1] 68, Fig. 176;   [2] 225, 220

Fig. 288 Project for plastic stage, Vienna *c.* 1925

altering the relationship between the stage and the auditorium, soon led to specific designs for new types of theatre. Figs 288 and 289 are two of several projects presented in Vienna in the 1920s, and although these particular designs were not built at the time, the ideas which they embody found concrete form in several theatres built thirty or more years later – as at Stratford in Ontario, at Chichester, and at Minneapolis. Most countries now have one or two theatres where the stage is either a peninsula; or the complete island of the arena stage, which is also known as theatre-in-the-round; or an adaptable combination of both. Each system has its own disadvantages. On a peninsular stage, with the audience spread around in an arc of 180°, the actor who wants to address them all will have to press himself against the back wall. On an arena stage, where the spectators sit in a full circle, he can only share out his favours by slowly rotating. Oddly enough the arena stage is best suited to naturalistic plays, even though these were written for elaborate scenery and this type of stage is limited to props. The reason is that the actors in a naturalistic play are supposed to disregard the audience and on an arena stage they virtually have to do so. The spectators are being offered a slice of life, but instead of peering at it through a hole in the wall they are now observing it at the bottom of a well. Considerable heat is engendered in arguments for and against these two types of stage. The truth is that both are extremely limited in their purest forms. Quite apart from the paradoxical fact that they actually hinder direct communication between actor and audience, they also deny themselves the very considerable pleasures of stage scenery. The proscenium stage, for all its faults, has proved far more adaptable than any one of its successors.

But just as each new and aggressively different style of modern scenery became more generally useful when it was slightly diluted and could merge with the broader trends of theatrical development, so the most effective theatres of the future will take the best features of the various contenders and will combine them – not merely by providing something which can be adapted from night to night, for except in the smallest studio theatres this is invariably a poor compromise, but by devising ways to incorporate the advantages without the disadvantages.

296

The most hopeful sign of this process happening is the theatre designed by John Bury for the Royal Shakespeare Company, soon to be built at the Barbican in London. The chief originality of this design is that instead of the stage being at one end of a rectangle (the proscenium system), or at the centre of a circle or semicircle (arena and peninsular stages), it is in one large corner of an irregular diamond – or perhaps more precisely in the broad apex of a triangle with a curved base. In this way the feeling of close contact between audience and stage is achieved, because the walls of the stage are a straight continuation of the walls of the auditorium, yet an actor can address the whole audience because it fills an arc of only 130°; and, since the stage does actually recede in one direction from the entire audience, a wide range of scenic effects is still possible.

So that this book should end with a glimpse of the future, after moving through some 4,000 years of the past, Elizabeth Bury has very kindly drawn an impression of the inside of her husband's theatre (Fig. 290), which conveys perfectly the open feeling created by the broadly triangular stage without a proscenium. Besides amalgamating the various rival shapes of stage into what would seem a very promising synthesis, John Bury has also – whether consciously or instinctively – incorporated several excellent ideas from the theatre's past. His stage, for example, is bounded by movable gridded screens, direct descendants of Gordon Craig's, which serve a wide variety of purposes:

> Set back they leave a large free area behind the acting area, set forward they completely enclose the acting area and create a complete one-room area with the auditorium. There are also intermediate positions in which wings can be created . . .
>
> The gridded surface of these screens serves a practical as well as decorative function. Scenery can be attached (*in the sketch only the large disc has been attached*), balconies hung, doors and windows

Fig. 289 Theatre project, Vienna, *c.* 1925

can be created. These are the permanent working surfaces of the stage. Thus large areas of masking scenery are unnecessary unless they are specifically required for a given production.[1]

The auditorium, too, makes good use of the past. The three balconies visible on either side in Elizabeth Bury's sketch continue round the entire auditorium, but each contains only three rows of seats. So, instead of the separate layers of people which make up the audience in a standard nineteenth-century theatre, this auditorium returns to the vertical rings of people around an open central area – an arrangement which contributed greatly to the intimacy of both Elizabethan and Restoration playhouses. Even the central area itself takes a new hint from the past, in that the pit is apparently to rejoin the stalls. The front rows of the sloping auditorium are to revert to being cheaper seats, and in order to provide informality, together with greater capacity on a crowded night, they will probably be equipped with benches instead of individual seats. This will bring a younger section of the audience into the centre of the theatre; and, since the excesses of the old pit are extremely unlikely to return, this lightening of the sedate mood of the stalls is likely to prove a definite change for the better. The groundlings have twice been banished up to the gods – with the change from the Elizabethan to the Restoration theatre, and again with the supplanting of the pit by the stalls in the last century – and their return to the centre of things is to be encouraged.

John Bury's design makes an ideal ending to a book of theatrical history, because it uses a natural and imaginative synthesis of past and present to provide a very promising theatre of the future.

Fig. 290 Elizabeth Bury, impression of theatre under construction at the Barbican, London, 1968

---

[1]quoted 332, Vol. 24 (1966), no. 4, 35

NOTES ON
THE ILLUSTRATIONS

BIBLIOGRAPHY

NOTES ON THE ILLUSTRATIONS

The notes include numerical references to a great many comparable illustrations published in other modern works: the system of numbering is the same as that in the footnotes and relates to the *Bibliography* (p. 317 ff.), where the full details of the works referred to, in **bold**, can be found. Where more than two of my own illustrations come from the same museum or collection, I have used the following abbreviations:

A.C.   Author's collection.
A.F.C. Archivio fotografico dell'Istituto di Lettere, Musica e Teatro della Fondazione Giorgio Cini, Venice.
A.N.   Archives Nationales, Paris.
B.A.1. Bibliothèque de l'Arsenal, Paris.
B.A.2. Bibliothèque de l'Arsenal, Paris: Collection Rondel.
B.C.A. Biblioteca Communale Ariostea, Ferrara.
B.M.1. British Museum: Printed Books.
B.M.2. British Museum: Prints and Drawings.
B.M.3. British Museum: Oriental Antiquities.
B.M.4. British Museum: Manuscripts.
B.M.5. British Museum: Classical Antiquities.
B.M.6 British Museum: Coins and Medals.
B.M.7. British Museum: Egyptian Antiquities.
B.N.1. Bibliothèque Nationale, Paris: Estampes.
B.N.2. Bibliothèque Nationale, Paris: Manuscrits.
G.M.W. Goethe National Museum, Weimar.

H.M.W. Historisches Museum der Stadt Wien, Vienna.
H.T.C. Harvard Theatre Collection.
M.M.   Metropolitan Museum, New York: Prints and Drawings.
M.N.N. Museo Nazionale, Naples.
N.M.S. Nationalmuseum, Stockholm.
R.M.   Rijksmuseum, Amsterdam: Prentenkabinett.
T.M.A. Toneelmuseum, Amsterdam.
T.M.C. Teatermuseet, Copenhagen.
T.M.D. Drottningholm's Teatermuseum.
T.M.M. Theatermuseum, Munich.
T.M.S. Museo Teatrale alla Scala, Milan.
V. & A.2. Victoria & Albert Museum, London: Prints and Drawings.
V. & A.3. Victoria & Albert Museum, London: Indian study room.
V. & A.4. Victoria & Albert Museum, London: Gabrielle Enthoven Collection.

Colour photographs: acknowledgments

AMSTERDAM T.M.A. XXII, XXIV

DROTTNINGHOLM T.M.D. XIII

LONDON
John Freeman I, V, VI, VII, VIII, XII, XX, XXI, XXV, XXVI;
Derrick Whitty XIV, XXVII, XXVIII, XXIX, XXX, XXXI;
British Museum IV

MUNICH T.M.M. XVIII

NAPLES Angelo Murale III

NEW YORK Eric Pollitzer II

PARIS Josse-Lalance IX, X, XI, XIX

TURIN Chomon-Perino XV, XVI, XVII

VIENNA H.M.W. XXIII

Colour plates

26. The best known view of a London Fair at this time is Hogarth's print of Southwark Fair in 1733 (**38**, Pl. 23). There are also two prints deriving from a lost watercolour of May Fair in 1716 (**311**, opp. p. 114 and **323**, 149).

XXI Comedy in the Country and Tragedy in London: satirical etching, c. 1810, by Thomas Rowlandson. (A.C.) *see* p. 176.
Other good views of uncouth audiences of the time: **12**, II, Tav. 29; **14**, II, Tav. 16 & 24; **31**, Fig. 201; **126**, 119; **282**, opp. p. 122.

XXII Schouwburg setting known as *De Behangen Kamer* (the wallpapered room): coloured etching published by J. Smit, c. 1765. (T.M.A.) *see* p. 193.
Other late 18th-c. interior scenes clearly made up of flat wings: **12**, V, Tav. CXXIII; **22**, V, 553; **135**, Fig. 13; **167**, 115.

XXIII Setting for *Die Räuber in den Abruzzen, oder, der Hund, seines Herrn Retter*: hand-coloured etching, dated 1830, from Bäuerle, *Gallerie drolliger und interessanter Scenen der Wiener Bühnen*, 4. Jahrgang, no. 11. (H.M.W.) *see* p. 193.
For two horses, dressed as a soldier and his wife, sitting down to a meal, see **12**, IV, Tav. 20.

XXIV Schouwburg setting known as *De Gemeene Buurt* (the common neighbourhood): coloured etching published by J. Smit, c. 1765. (T.M.A.) *see* pp. 194–5.
Other settings with houses clearly painted on flat wings: **12**, II, Tav. 14; **17**, Pl. 34; **22**, III, 396 and IV, 643; **167**, Taf. IV.

XXV–XXVI Settings by Alessandro Sanquirico for *L'Ultimo Giorno di Pompeii*, Milan, 1826: coloured aquatints in Sanquirico, A., *Sceniche Decorazioni*, n.d. (B.M.2.) *see* p. 196.

XXVII–XXVIII Two scenes from Charles Kean's *Henry V*, London, 1859: watercolours. (V. & A.2.: nos D.1737–1901 and E.3222–1938) *see* p. 277.

XXIX Interior setting by Leon Bakst, dated 1922: original sketch. (V. & A.2.: no. E.841–1937) *see* pp. 278–9.

XXX Setting by Hans Wildermann for Handel's *Belshazzar*: watercolour, dated 1927. (V. & A.2.: no. E.91–1928) *see* p. 280.

XXXI Setting by Hans Strohbach: watercolour, c. 1930. (V. & A.2.: no. E.2312–1938) *see* p. 280.

Monochrome illustrations

1 Emblem of Cotswold Players: woodcut by Maxwell Armfield, 1911. (A.C.)

2 *Das Rheingold*, Bayreuth, 1876: painting by J. Hoffman. (T.M.M.)

3 *Das Rheingold*, Bayreuth, 1876: print. (B.A.2.)

4 Hunting mask of Cherokee Indians: leather with wildcat and horsehair trimmings. (Museum of the American Indian, Heye Foundation, New York.)
For a 19th-c. painting of American Indians dancing in buffalo masks, see **1**, Fig. 2. The best collection of illustrations of all aspects of primitive dance, mime and ritual is **41**, p. 41 ff.

5 Knights on men disguised as horses: black-figured vase, c. 550 BC. (Staatliche Museen, East Berlin.)
Similar Greek chorus with birds' wings, **105**, Fig. 123; with cocks' masks, **105**, Fig. 124; mounted on ostriches, **105**, Fig. 125. Terracotta statuettes of Greek actors with animal masks, **32**, Figs 21–22. Similar bird costumes in modern primitive performances, **291**, Fig. 74.

6 Performers in animal masks, 14th c.: miniature in ms. *Li Romans du boin roi Alixandre*. (Bodleian: ms. Bod. 264, fol. 181 v.)
Roman performers in animal masks, **32**, Fig. 76. Similar animal performers in French ms., **22**, I, Fig. 57 and **126**, 17.

7 Performer in stag's skin: miniature in ms. *Le Romans du boin roi Alixandre*. (Bodleian: ms. Bod. 264, fol. 70 r.)

8 Animal dance with audience: Bushman cave painting from Orange Spring. (Tongue, M. Helen, *Bushman Paintings*, Oxford (Clarendon Press), 1909, Pl. XXXVI.) (B.M.1.)

9 Masquerade of Orson and Valentine: woodcut after Pieter Brueghel the Elder. (B.M.2.) ('There is an almost identical scene in the top left-hand corner of Brueghel's painting *The Tournament of Carnival and Lent*.)
Mummers surviving today in the same tradition: in Italy, **336**, Figs 67–72; in Greece, **222**, XVI (1909–10), Figs 8–10; in England, **218**, VIII, after p. 92.

10 Girls performing: painting from the tomb of Nebamun at Thebes, c. 1400 BC. (B.M.7.)
Other Egyptian girl dancers: **12**, I, Tav. 12 and II, Tav. CLVIII & CLIX, and pp. 118 and 1330.

11 Horus and the scribe Ani: painting in the papyrus of Ani, a Theban book of the dead, c. 1250 BC. (B.M.7.)

12 A dance by young men: painted relief from Gizah, c. 3560 BC. (B.M.7.)

13–14 Part of coronation ritual, from Ramesseum papyrus: original and reconstruction. (Sethe, K., *Dramatische Texte zu Altaegyptischen Mysterienspiele*, Leipzig (Hinrichs), 1928, Taf. 9 & 20.) (A.C.)

15 Sileni and maenads: detail from Greek vase. (Furtwängler, A., *Griechische Vasenmalerei*, Munich (Bruckmann), 1900–32, Series 1, Taf. 45.) (B.M.1.)

16 Satyrs, possibly as early chorus: from Duris Satyr vase. (Furtwängler, A., *Griechische Vasenmalerei*, Munich (Bruckmann), 1900–32, Series 1, Taf. 48.) (B.M.1.)
Satyrs slightly more clothed and more clearly a chorus, **105**, Fig. 16.

17 Dionysus in ship cart: drawing from Greek vase. (Judica, Baron Gabriele, *Le Antichità di Apre*, Messina, 1819, Tav. XXXVI.) (B.M.1.)

18 Actors and chorus for a satyr play: from the Pronomos vase. (Furtwängler, A., *Griechische Vasenmalerei*, Munich (Bruckmann), 1900–32, Series 3, Taf. 143–4.) (B.M.1.)
The most reliable vase paintings of Greek tragic costume, though all incomplete in various ways, are **105**, Figs 79–91, 112–13 & 115–17.

19 The remaining stones of the classical Theatre of Dionysus. (Fiechter, E., *Das Dionysos-Theater in Athens*, Stuttgart (Kohlhammer), 1935, Vol. I, Abb. 27.) (V. & A.1.)

20 Theatre of Dionysus at Athens. (Mansell-Alinari 24566.)
There are now high modern buildings behind the stage area. I have used an old photograph because it shows better the open hillside site.

21 Theatre at Epidaurus. (German Archaeological Institute, Athens: Epidaurus 193.)

22 Theatre of Dionysus at Athens: Roman coin from Athens in the Imperial Period. (B.M.6.)

23 Dionysus with Phlyax, wearing Karneian basket crown: from vase by Asteas, *c.* 350 BC. (B.M.5.)

24 Terracotta statuettes of comic actors, *c.* 370 BC. (M.M.)
Technically these are actors of Middle Comedy rather than Old Comedy, since Old Comedy ended around 400 BC, but the difference in costume is slight. For the best selection of such statuettes, see **105**, Figs 133–78.

25 Comic actor: a terracotta jug. (M.N.N., Hall LXXXVII, showcase III.)

26 A mime dancing Perseus before two spectators: Attic vase, *c.* 420 BC. (*Journal of Hellenic Studies*, 65 (1945), Pl. 5.) (B.M.1.)
Scholars have variously argued that this is an official comedy performance in the public theatre, a private performance in a rich man's house, and a more simple travelling stage (for the arguments see **238**, 196–7). If the sweeping lines to the right represent a curtain (suggested **109**, 20), it is also the earliest illustration of this. For an early view of an audience watching circus activities, see **11**, I, 159 top.

27 Dionysus, a female tumbler and two Phlyakes; Phlyax vase. (Museo Eoliano, Lipari.)
Similar female acrobats: **32**, Fig. 24; **105**, Figs 579 a–c (including one tumbling among knives set into the floor).

28 Herakles tempts Apollo: Phlyax vase. (Hermitage, Leningrad.)
For the best selection of Phlyax vases, see **105**, Figs 481–539.

29 Performances in amphitheatre: ivory relief. (Staatliche Museen, East Berlin.)
Other similar reliefs: **2**, I, Fig. 161; **12**, VIII, Tav. CXXXVIII; **105**, Figs 834–8.

30 *Frons scaenae* with actors: terracotta relief from tomb of P. Numitorius Hilarus, 1st c. BC. (Museo Nazionale, Rome: Mansell-Alinari 29953.)
Drawing from similar relief, **108**, Fig. 78.

31 Amphitheatre at Pompeii: wall painting from Pompeii. (M.N.N.)
The painting depicts not an actual performance, but a riot which took place in the theatre in AD 59 (**105**, 179).

32 Roman tragic actors: relief in theatre at Sabratha *c.* AD 200. (Museum of Antiquities, Sabratha.)
A very similar impression is given by the famous Rieti statuette of a Roman tragic actor, **22**, I, Fig. 32.

33 Theatre at Sabratha *c.* AD 200: the stage and bottom tier of the *frons scaenae*. (Museum of Antiquities, Sabratha.)
Reliefs of stage façades without actors, **105**, Figs 480 & 634.

34 Possibly a scene for comedy: wall painting from villa at Boscoreale, *c.* 40 BC. (M.M.)
For other interesting wall paintings, quoted as theatrical but probably only sharing a theatrical style, see **12**, VIII, Tav. 23; **13**, Figs 41–2; **105**, Figs 775–8.

35 Scene from a comedy: marble relief. (M.N.N.)

36 Possibly an interior scene, set between pillars of *frons scaenae*: mosaic from villa of Cicero at Pompeii. (M.N.N.)
The mosaic is a copy made in about 50 BC from a Greek original, probably dating from two centuries earlier (**108**, 223 ff.). There is a pair to it, showing some dancing musicians, **105**, Fig. 346.

37 Roman mime: terracotta statuette, *c.* 1st c. AD. (B.M.5.)

38 Pulcinella: etching from Bertelli, F., *Il Carnevale Italiano Mascherato*, 1642. (Raccolta Bertarelli, Milan.)

39 Bharata Nhatyam dancers: stone relief, 10th c., from Purāna Mahādeo Temple, now in Sikar Museum. (Kramrisch, S., *The Art of India*, London (Phaidon Press), 3rd ed., 1965, Pl. 118.) (A.C.)

40 Tanjore dancing girl and her Tickatoio men: painting. (V. & A.3.: I.S.176–1949.)

41 Chinese theatre: detail from scroll painting. (B.M.3.: scroll no. 40.)

42 Chinese theatre: detail from scroll painting. (B.M.3.: scroll no. 302.)
For a modern photograph of a Chinese audience in a theatre, which brings out well the similarity with the Elizabethan theatre, see **14**, II, opp. p. 736.

43 Chieh Chih-t'ui carries his mother to the hills: lithograph, from original by Chinese artist. (Arlington, L. C., *The Chinese Drama*, Shanghai (Kelly and Walsh), 1930, Fig. 182.) (A.C.)

44 Hsiang Yü's make-up: lithograph, from original by Chinese artist. (Arlington, L. C., *The Chinese Drama*, Shanghai (Kelly and Walsh), 1930, Fig. 114.) (A.C.)
Other Chinese faces, **110**, Pls 66–76 and **120**, 39–43.

45 *Nō* play on a *nō* stage: woodcut by Harunabu from *Ehon Shogei Nishiki*, 1763. (B.M.3.: woodcut book no. 56.)
Two of the most interestinging *nō* illustrations, both *c*. 1800, are of open air performances: a *kanjin-nō* performance on the estate of a feudal lord, **113**, Pl. 4; and a performance in an open air theatre of the Elizabethan type, surrounded by two rows of galleries, **111**, Pl. 1. An interesting woodcut of a *dengaku-nō* performance in 1742, on a stage very different from the usual *nō* version, is printed **298**, opp. p. 68. The painting of a *nō* play on the stage, published **119**, opp. p. 10 and later **13**, Fig. 200, appears to be modern. For a good explanatory ground-plan of the *nō* stage, see **116**, after p. xvi; and for photos of modern *nō* performances, **113**, Pls 5–6.

46 *Kyōgen* on a *nō* stage: woodcut by Harunabu from *Ehon Shogei Nishiki*, 1763. (B.M.3.: woodcut book no. 56.)

47 *Joruri* theatre from backstage: woodcut by Shokosai, 1800. (B.M.3.: woodcut book no. 153.)
For another view of a puppet theatre from backstage, with minstrel also visible as he sings the epic, see **115**, Pl. 11.

48 *Joruri* puppet: woodcut by Shokosai, 1800. (B.M.3.: woodcut book no. 153.)
Colour photographs of actual 18th-c. *joruri* puppets, **12**, VII, Tav. 6.

49 The *kabuki* stage: woodcut by Shokosai, 1800. (B.M.3.: woodcut book no. 153.)
The various labels describe the functions of the parts of the stage. For a translation and analysis of them, see **217**, VI, 4, p. 83 ff. There is in the same woodcut book a similar print of the closely related *joruri* stage, complete with even a 'flower walk' for the puppets (**217**, VI, 4, Pl. 4).
Various views of the machinery in action on a *kabuki* stage: the revolving stage, **2**, IV, Figs 369–70 and **115**, Fig. 11; the trap, **115**, Fig. 12; and a *kabuki* setting being put up, **115**, Fig. 17.

50 Minor and perhaps improvised *kabuki* stage: woodcut by Shokosai, 1800. (B.M.3.: woodcut book no. 152.)

51 Stage conventions: woodcut by Toyokuni, *c*. 1800. (B.M.3.: woodcut book no. 169.)

52 Priest chanting from Exultet Roll: miniature in roll itself, 11th c. (Biblioteca Vaticana, Rome; ms. Vat. Barb. Lat. 592.)

53 The Maries at the sepulchre: miniature for Quem Quaeritis trope, *c*. 1100. (Bibl. Capit., Piacenza: ms. 65, fol. 235.)
A famous illumination of this moment from a St Gall ms. shows also the empty cloths in the sepulchre, **342**, I, Fig. 1.

54 The Maries at the sepulchre: miniature in the Reichenauer Antiphonary, 11th c. (Badische Landesbibliothek, Karlsruhe: Cod. Aug. LX, fol. 93 v.)

55 The merchant selling spices: miniature in Arnoul de Greban, *Le Mystère de la Passion*, *c*. 1520. (B.A.1.: ms. 6431, fol. 202 v.)

56 Mystery play devils: Arnoul de Greban, *Le Mystère de la Nativité*, 1508. (B.N.2.: ms. Fr. 815, fol. 2 r.)
Selection of prints of devils, **159**, Abb. 112–13 & 122–5; surviving costume and masks, **159**, Abb. 126–9. A pair of miniatures from a manuscript of the *Renault de Montauban* (reprod. **11**, II, 96 and **12**, I, 1082), give every sign of showing an actor being costumed as a devil but in fact they illustrate a magical event in the story with no direct theatrical connection.

57–8 Devil drags away a sinner, and Christ harrows Hell: two watercolours from a German play of the Last Judgement, 15th c. (Kongelige Bibliotek, Copenhagen: Thott. ms. 112.)

59 Performance of the martyrdom of St Apollonia: miniature by Jean Fouquet in *Les Heures d'Etienne Chevalier*, *c*. 1460. (Musée de Chantilly, photo Giraudon.)

60–2 Jesus harrowing Hell and leading the patriarchs to Paradise: three consecutive miniatures in Arnoul de Greban, *Le Mystère de la Passion*, *c*. 1520. (B.A.1.: ms. 1431, fol. 196 r.–197 r.)

63 The fifth day at Valenciennes, 1547: painting by Hubert Cailleau. (B.N.2.: ms. Fonds Rothschild 3010, fol. 56 v.–57 r.)

64 Ship cart in Nuremberg Schembartbuch: later painting from original source of *c*. 1520. (B.M.4.: add. ms. 15684, fol. 68 v.)
For a magnificent illustration of the Nuremberg ship cart being stormed, an event which ended each year's pageant, see **167**, Abb. 4–5.

65 Austrian pageant, 17th c.: watercolour. (Albertina, Vienna: Bildarchiv, N.B.606.017.)

66 Two-tiered cart for autos, 1646: drawing. (Shergold, N. D., *A History of the Spanish Stage*, Oxford (Clarendon Press), 1967, Fig. 23.)

67 Cart for auto drawn up against stage, 1644: drawing. (Shergold, N. D., *A History of the Spanish Stage*, Oxford (Clarendon Press), 1967, Fig. 22.)

68 Allegorical float in procession, 1616: etching by Merian in Hulsen, E. von, *Repraesentatio der Furstlichen Aufzug und Ritterspil*, Stuttgart, 1616. (V. & A.2.)

69 The entry of Archduke Albert into Brussels, 1596: etching. (M.M.)

70 Street theatres at Avignon in 1600: details from seven etched plates in Valladier, A., *Labyrinthe Royal*, Avignon, 1601. (M.M.)

71 Water pageantry on the Arno, 1608: detail from one of nineteen etchings by R. Cantagallina after G. Parigi and others, under title *Battaglia Navale rappresentata in Arno . . . 1608*. (V. & A.2.)

72 Water pageantry and theatre, 1638: etching by S. Savry after S. de Vlieger in Barlaeus, G., *Medicea Hospes*, Amsterdam, 1638. (B.M.1.)
The 17th c.'s most spectacular combination of stage and water pageantry was at Parma in 1690. (12, VII, Tav. 18.)

73 Tournament theatre in Rome, 1565: etching by Lafreri. (N.M.S.)
For the gradual development of the tournament area into a fully theatrical type of arena, see 12, II, Tav. CXVII; 16, 335; 22, III, 30; 137, I, Pls VIII & IX. As an example of other types of courtly event acquiring the quality of theatre, see the baptism in 1668 of the Dauphin, 15, Port. XI, Pl. I.

74 The Holy Roman Emperor and Empress dancing: etching in Bry, J. T., *Electio et Coronatio*, 1612. (B.M.1.)
Precisely the same feeling of public spectacle can be seen in a print of Louis XIII and Anne of Austria dancing after their marriage in 1615 (reprod. 11, III, 229).

75 Renaissance image of Roman theatre: detail of miniature in Terence manuscript of late 15th c. (B.N.2.: Cod. Lat. 7907 A, fol. 2 v.)
The other very similar miniature is in the *Térence des Ducs* in B.A.1. (12, V, Tav. 14.)

76 Renaissance image of Roman theatre: drawing by Francesco di Giorgio, c. 1490. (Biblioteca Medicea Laurenziana; ms. laur. Ashb. 361, fol. 13 r.)
The same fallacy about the shape of the Roman theatre can still be seen a century later in several prints in Panvinus, O., *Antiquae Urbis Imago*, Venice, 1580.

77 Illustration to Terence's *Eunuchus*: woodcut in Terence, *Comoediae*, Lyons, 1493, fol. h7.v. (B.M.1.)
For woodcuts illustrating other plays in the same edition, see 31, Fig. 72 ff. The frontispiece to the edition (31, Fig. 74) is another very interesting and grossly inaccurate attempt to reconstruct the Roman theatre from varying sources.

78 Illustration to Plautus: woodcut in Plautus, *Comoediae*, Venice, 1518, fol. 277 r. (B.M.1.)
The woodcuts in this edition are repeated indiscriminately to illustrate different plays.

79 Comic and tragic scenes: drawings by Battista da Sangallo in margin of his copy of Vitruvius, c. 1540. (Biblioteca Corsiniana, Rome.)

80 One side of a stage setting, c. 1530: sketch by Baldassare Peruzzi. (Biblioteca Reale, Turin: Mansell-Anderson, 9861.) About ten theatrical drawings by Peruzzi survive (listed 12, VIII, 36–7) and they are the earliest iconographical record of the Renaissance perspective stage. A much earlier design by Bramante, dated 1495, has often been reproduced as a stage setting (e.g. 2, II, Fig. 28 and 22, II, Fig. 10), but there is no evidence that it is more than an architectural study.

81 The scene for comedy: woodcut in Serlio, S., *Second Livre de Perspective*, 1545. (B.M.1.)
Peruzzi may in fact have agreed with Serlio about painted figures; the butcher's shop appears yet again, this time without the boy, in a drawing by Peruzzi (12, VIII, Tav. CCXII) which shows every sign of having directly influenced Serlio's scene for comedy.
The clearest demonstration of how Serlian houses were placed on the stage is in Scamozzi's diagram for the Teatro Olimpico at Sabbioneta (12, VIII, Tav. CLXXVIII). For Serlio's other scenes and his full text, see 244, IV, 353 ff.

82 Illustration to Terence's *Eunuchus*, 1553: woodcut in Terence, *Comoediae*, Venice, 1558, fol. 54 r. (B.M.1.)
Like many Terence illustrations, these woodcuts were used again and again; their first use had been in the Venice edition of 1553 (283, 187). A similar and better known woodcut of 1552 is the frontispiece to *Il Pellegrino* (31, Fig. 84).

83 Teatro Olimpico at Vicenza: the auditorium. (A.C.)
For the best selection of photographs of the surviving Renaissance auditoria at Vicenza, Sabbioneta and Parma, see 6, Figs 245–52.

84 Teatro Olimpico at Vicenza, the stage: etching by Ottavio Orefici, 1620. (N.M.S., on loan to T.M.D.)
For a blurred and anonymous drawing of the façade, possibly earlier than this etching, see 44, Fig. 50: and for a good later cross-section of the stage and auditorium, 16, 216. The concept of separate perspective vistas at the sides of the stage was occasionally attempted again; e.g. at Hamburg in 1690 (44, 191) and at Imola in the late 18th c. (31, Fig. 158).

85–6 School play, Ensisheim, 1573: Rasser, J., *Christlich Spil von Kinderzucht*, Strasburg, 1574, woodcuts nos 2 and 44. (Bibliothek der Universität, Basle.)
For similar but less detailed woodcuts of a Shrove Tuesday morality of 1515, see 22, II, 271: and for photographs of a morality played till recently on a similar stage in Italy, 179, Tav. V & VI.

87 Stage for school play, Cologne, 1581: painting in ms. of Broelman's Latin play *Laurentius*. (Stadtarchiv, Cologne.)

88 Westminster school play, 1839: painting by Sargent. (Westminster school.)

89 Professional players, 16th c., about to perform *The Dirty Bride*: engraving by P. van der Heyden after P. Brueghel the Elder. (R.M.) (The same group of figures can be seen centre left in Brueghel's painting *The Tournament of Carnival and Lent*.)

Various glimpses of minstrels as jugglers, acrobats, dancers, etc.: **2**, I, Fig. 186; **11**, II, 107; **32**, Figs 110–13; **42**, after p. 23.

90 Fools performing in the street: woodcut in Brant, S., *Nevis Stultifera*, Basle, 1506, fol. i 5, v. (Private Collection, Clare Neilson.)

Roman figure of fool with ass's ears, **32**, Fig. 60. A very detailed print of a Feast of Fools within a cathedral (**22**, I, Fig. 48) looks suspiciously like a 19th c. reconstruction, but there is a print of *c.* 1520 showing priests in animal masks at carnival time (**290**, Part II, Vol. II, 627). The situation of the serenade and the chamber pot is adopted by the Commedia dell'Arte in **12**, III, Tav. CLI.

91 The banner of the Infanterie Dijonnoise, 15th c. to 1630: etching in Tilliot, M. du, *Mémoires pour servir à l'Histoire de la Fête des Foux*, Lausanne, 1741, Pl. 7. (B.M.1.)

92 Scene from the Commedia dell'Arte, 16th c.: woodcut from the *Recueil Fossard*. (N.M.S., on loan to T.M.D.)

The other early series of illustrations of the Commedia dell'Arte is the extensive mural in Burg Trausnitz in Bavaria (**212**, V, 1, Taf. I–IV and **212**, V, 2, Taf. V–VIII). Some of the most beautiful iconographical records are the fifteen collages of Commedia dell'Arte characters, made out of birds' feathers by the gardener to the governor of Milan in 1618 (**55**, Figs 32, 35, 39–40, 52–3, 57, 73–5, 78 and the frontispiece in colour).

93 Booth stage against house, 1608: detail from oil by David Vinckeboons. (Herzog Anton Ulrich Museum, Braunschweig.)

94 Players visit a manor: painting, dated 1610, in Moyses Walens's *Album Amicorum*. (B.M.4.: add. ms. 18991, fol. 11 r.)

For similar but more courtly entertainment during a meal, see **126**, 17; also the famous painting of Sir Henry Unton's wedding masque, **126**, 48.

95 The Swan Theatre, *c.* 1596: copy of de Witt's sketch, in Arend van Buchell's commonplace book. (Bibliotheek der Rijksuniversiteit, Utrecht.)

For the various title-page woodcuts which are usually accorded too much theatrical validity, see **11**, III, pp. 29, 67 & 80 and **132**, Pls 9 & 10. For a recent but unconvincing argument that a 'memory theatre' of 1619 is a view of the interior of the Globe, see **341**, Fig. 17 and p. 342 ff. And for an argument that the de Witt sketch may show a rehearsal in progress, see **217**, X, 80.

96 An English stage: etched panel in title-page to Alabaster, W., *Roxana*, London, 1632. (B.M.1.)

Chambers argued that this was a university stage, on the weak grounds that the play had been presented at Trinity College, Cambridge, *c.* 1592 (**244**, II, 519); but it would be a very academic engraver who would cast his mind back forty years before designing this tiny panel.

97 An English stage: etched panel in title-page to Richards, N., *Messalina*, London, 1640. (B.M.1.)

98 An English stage: engraved frontispiece to Kirkman, F., *The Wits*, London, 1673. (B.M.1.)

Throughout the 19th c. this was taken to be the Red Bull – a fallacy which has long since been disproved (**244**, II, 520), but which is still often repeated.

99–100 Two views of the Fechthaus in Nuremberg, built 1628: woodcuts in *Curiöser Spiegel*, Nuremberg, 1689, Pls XXXVI and XXX. (V. & A.2.)

The copy in V. & A.2. is the second edition, dated 1793; but the original woodcuts were used both for this and for the edition of 1812. The original edition is extremely rare – there is not even a complete copy of it in the Stadtbibliothek or the Germanisches Museum in Nuremberg. There is no mention of *Curiöser Spiegel* or of these woodcuts in the recently published Kertz, P. and Strössenreuther, I., *Bibliographie zur Theatergeschichte Nürnbergs*, 1964.

For a view of the Nuremberg courtyard where the English players performed before 1628, and which may also have influenced the design of the Fechthaus, see **325**, p. 3 of Plates.

101 The Hetzamphitheater in Vienna, *c.* 1780: hand-coloured etching. (Nationalbibliothek, Vienna: Bildarchiv, N.B. 607. 116.)

102 Temporary theatre in Piazza Maggiore, Bologna, 1627: painting in *Insignia degli Anziani del Commune*, Vol. V, fol. 102 v.–103 r. (Archivio di Stato, Bologna.)

The sixteen ms. volumes of the *Insignia* cover more than two centuries of public events and include many illustrations of theatrical interest: e.g. **12**, II, Tav. 13 & 14 and III, Tav. 33 and V, Tav. 8 and VI, Tav. 13.

103 Religious performance, central Europe, mid 17th c.: woodcut in Eisenberg, *Ein zweifacher Act und geistliches Spiel*, Bartga, 1652. (A.F.C.)

A.F.C. has only the photograph of this woodcut, together with the above reference; I have been unable to trace either the woodcut or the book quoted, in order to find out precisely what is represented.

104 Diagram of the Corral del Principe; drawing, probably 18th c. (Biblioteca Nacional, Madrid: Shergold, N. D., *A History of the Spanish Stage*, Oxford (Clarendon Press), 1967, Fig. 18.)

The drawing which is often reproduced as the interior of the Corral del Principe in 1660 (**20**, after p. 272, Fig. 1) is a reconstruction made by J. Comba in the 1880s, based on a diagram which itself derives from this recently discovered plan (**20**, 270). For other interesting diagrams of corral theatres see **196**, Figs 16, 17 & 19.

105 Corral in Almagro, recently restored. (Photo from Alcalde y Jefe local, Almargo.)

106 Ballet for the Polish Ambassadors: woodcut in Dorat, J., *Magnificentissimi Spectaculi*, Paris, 1573, second of two plates. (B.M.1.)

107–8 Ballet of 1581, the entire hall and a grove of Dryads: etchings in Beauioyeulx, B. de, *Balet Comique de la Royne*, Paris, 1582, pp. 4 & 35. (H.T.C.)

109 Ballet of 1617, opening tableau: etching in Durand, E., *Discours au Vray du Ballet Dansé par le Roy*, Paris, 1617. (H.T.C.)

110 Perrette la Hazardeuse in the *Ballet des Ridicules*, St Germain, 1628: watercolour. (B.N.1.: vol. Qb.3.rés., drawing numbered 6.) (This is a large volume containing watercolours of all the costumes for the court ballets of 1628, 1629 and 1630. For other costumes from it, see **149**, Figs 13–25.)

111–12 Louis XIV as a Bacchante and as a Muse: watercolours in ms. of *Ballet du Roi des Festes de Bacchus*, 1651. (B.N.1.: vol. Pd.74.rés., pp. 88 & 105.)
Louis XIV's most famous costume is as the Sun in 1653 (reprod. **22**, IV, 47), but an almost identical costume had been used nine years before in Turin (reprod. **63**, 6 and, in colour, **176**, back cover).

113–14 Louis XIV as a Fury and the Duke of York as a Coral Fisher: watercolours in ms. of *Les Noces de Pelée et de Thétis*, 1654. (Bibliothèque de l'Institut de France, Paris: ms. 1005, fol. 18 & 12.)

115 Mahelot's setting for *La Prise de Marcilly*, 1631: wash drawing in *Mémoire de Mahelot*. (B.N.2.: ms. Fr. 24330, fol. 42 r.)
The published title of the play was *Dorinde*, by Auvray, in which the central event is the taking of Marcilly (**288**, 81, n. 3). All Mahelot's sketches are reproduced in **288**. There is no authenticated illustration of the interior of the Hôtel de Bourgogne at this period, but a drawing of the mid 17th c. (**22**, IV, 106) and a later copy of it (**11**, III, 128) may both derive from this theatre.

116 Performers of farce at the Hôtel de Bourgogne: etching by le Blond after A. Bosse. (B.N.1.)
There are several slightly different versions of this scene: e.g. **16**, 286 and **22**, IV, 68 & 69. For earlier French farce, on a simpler stage with a background of curtains, see **233**, Pl. XLIV.

117 Mahelot's setting for *La Folie de Clidamant*: wash drawing from *Mémoire de Mahelot*. (B.N.2.: ms. Fr. 24330, fol. 26 r.)

118 Frontispiece to *Amphitryon*: etching in Molière, *Oeuvres*, Amsterdam, 1684, Tom. III. (B.M.1.) (This design had previously been used in the Paris ed. of 1682.)
In two charming paintings of 1670 Molière even appears in a composite stage group with the figures of the Commedia dell'Arte (**11**, III, 127 and **22**, IV, Fig. 11). He is also unique among playwrights in that many of the frontispieces to his plays include evident attempts at portraits of him in the roles which he played (e.g. **11**, III, 182–3); and there is an excellent portrait of him as Sganarelle (**11**, III, 185).

119 Frontispiece to *Le Mercure Galant*: etching in Gherardi, E., *Le Théâtre Italien*, Amsterdam, 1721, Tom. I. (B.M.1.)
Together with the great number of Gherardi frontispieces, the other most interesting prints of the Commedia dell'Arte in France at this time are the frontispieces to *Le Théâtre de la Foire* (e.g. **22**, IV, pp. 304, 314 & 319). Harlequin was fairly eclectic in his mockery of the more distant gods; he can even be seen as Mahomet in **22**, IV, Fig. 29 d.

120 Design by Claude Gillot for the Commedia dell'Arte, *c.* 1720: etching in Gillot, C., *Théâtre Italien*, Paris, n.d. (*c.* 1730). (FitzWilliam Museum, Cambridge: Dept. of Prints & Drawings.)
Gillot died in 1722, and these designs were etched later by Huquier and Joullain.

121 French charlatans selling orvietan, *c.* 1650: etching. (B.N.1.)
There are a great many illustrations of charlatans performing throughout Europe: e.g. **2**, II, Fig. 69; **12**, III, 730 & 1191 & Tav. 19; **13**, Pl. 97; **16**, 404–5; **22**, III, 271; **32**, Figs 148–9; **126**, 12; **156**, Abb. 18; **212**, III, 4, Bild XII. For a photograph of an audience in 1899 watching such an open-air stage, with passers-by on horseback among the spectators, see **12**, II, 7.

122 Bernardo Buontalenti, scene for a play: etching by Orazio Scarabelli, *c.* 1589. (M.M.)
Beijer has suggested that these side houses may have been used for the Commedia dell'Arte play which was performed at the same 1589 festivities, retaining the backcloth used for *La Pellegrina* (**218**, III, 3, 175, n. 18). The same *intermezzi* were repeated during the Commedia dell'Arte play (**181**, 90). Nagler makes no mention of this print in relation to Rossi's *tre fori* (**181**, 79).
Buontalenti may have based his first house downstage right on a Florentine setting of twenty years earlier by Baldassare Lanci (**12**, VI, Tav. LXXXVII), which is also the clearest example of how famous buildings were worked into these settings. Probably the earliest surviving designs with divided perspective streets are two attributed to Francesco Salviati, *c.* 1560, in B.M.2. One of them is published, **22**, II, 106.

123 Illustration to *Il Solimano*; etching by Jacques Callot in Bonarelli, P., *Il Solimano*, Florence, 1620. (B.M.1.)
There is no mention of the original designer on the plates or in the text, but the designs have been attributed to Giulio Parigi (**69**, 81) and to his son Alfonso (**31**, Fig. 96). It is more likely that Callot merely modified the Scarabelli etching.

124 Bernardo Buontalenti, design for the 5th *intermezzo*, Florence, 1589: etching by E. d'Alfiano. (M.M.)

125 Setting by Francesco Guitti, 1638: etching in Pio di Savoia, A., *Andromeda*, Ferrara, 1639. (B.C.A.)

126–7 Machinery for a monster and for waves: from a collection of thirty-nine drawings of scenes and machines, *c*. 1660. (Biblioteca Palatina, Parma: ms. Parm. 3708.)

A very similar series of 17th-c. drawings was reproduced in *Prospettive*, no. 19 (1959), p. 49 ff.

For an 18th-c. diagram from the *Encyclopédie* of a ship pulled along while a wave-roller revolves, see **2**, II, Fig. 228. For a photograph of the surviving 18th-c. wave-machine in position at Drottningholm, see **187**, 256; and of cut-out ships to pass along it, **187**, 262–3.

128 Machinery for monsters: drawings, *c*. 1700. (N.M.S.: Tessin coll., vol. S7, p. 203.)

129 Sketch for revolving scallop-shell, *c*. 1700: drawing. (A.N.: Vol. 01.3241, fol. 85.)

There are in A.N. five volumes of drawings of scenes and machines (vols 01.3238–42), which were bound together in 1752.

130 Setting by Francesco Guitti, 1638: etching in Pio di Savoia, A., *Andromeda*, Ferrara, 1639. (B.C.A.)

It is possible that these merely appear to be the old two-sided houses and that the etching shows the illusion and not the reality, because Guitti certainly knew about the new flat wings – see notes 138–9 below.

For a good colour photograph of the Drottningholm cloud setting on the stage, see **6**, Pl. X.

131 Two views of an apparition machine, *c*. 1700: drawing. (A.N.: Vol. 01.3239, fol. 76.)

For various aspects of machinery for flying, see **6**, Figs 168–71; **11**, IV, 12; **12**, I, Tav. 13 bis, and VI, Tav. LXXXIX, and VII, Tav. CXLVIII; **22**, IV, 51; **69**, 141; **212**, III, Bild V.

132 Machinery for apparitions etc., *c*. 1700: drawings. (A.N.: Vol. 01.3238, fol. 73.)

Techniques for opening and closing clouds, **12**, VI, Tav. VII and **22**, IV, 49.

133 Setting by Giacomo Torelli, 1642: etching in Nolfi, V., *Il Bellerofonte*, Venice, 1642. (B.M.1.)

Torelli's system of linked wing carriages below the stage can be seen in one of the Parma drawings, **69**, 111; and for various ways of making a continuous side wall on the stage, see **22**, III, 578–9; **60**, Fig. 111; **69**, 72; **212**, XII, 2/3, Taf. XII.

134–5 Flat wings for forest setting: sketch and diagram by G. B. Aleotti, *c*. 1620. (B.C.A.: ms. Cl.1.N.763, fol. 166–7.)

The earliest dated diagram of flat wings on a stage is by Francesco Mazzi and Francesco Guitti (**20**, after p. 158, Fig. 5; and p. 139) for the temporary theatre put up in 1627/28 in the Cortile di San Pietro in Ferrara; but Aleotti's undated drawings are almost certainly earlier.

136 Setting by Alfonso Parigi, 1628: etching in Salvadori, A., *La Flora*, Florence, 1628. (M.M.)

137–8 Setting and costume by Inigo Jones for *Chloridia*, 1631: drawings (Devonshire Collection, Chatsworth: by permission of the Trustees of the Chatsworth Settlement).

An important series of stage diagrams for court masques by Inigo Jones and John Webb, now in B.M.4., is reproduced **217**, II, 1, Pls 1–12. The volumes of costume designs by Vasari etc. in the Uffizi and Biblioteca Nazionale in Florence are fully described in A. M. Petrioli's Uffizi catalogue entitled *Mostra di Disegni Vasariani*, Florence, 1966; but the few by Buontalenti reproduced in **22**, II, Figs 14–18 are sufficient to show Jones's indebtedness.

Since Jones invariably worked with much shallower stages than those on the continent, a far greater emphasis in his settings falls on the furthest pair of flats which actually joined in the middle to form the back of the scene and which were known as 'back-scenes' or 'shutters'. He was using such shutters as early as 1608 (**135**, 34) and they are often thought of as being a special feature of the English stage. But the idea derived from the *scena ductilis* of Vitruvius which had been much discussed in Italy; and Furttenbach, who like Jones had studied with the Parigis in Florence, later carried the same idea to Germany (**69**, 22, n. 33). It is probable, therefore, that Jones found the system already in use in Italy. The earliest diagram of such shutters at the back of a stage is Italian (**20**, after p. 158, Fig. 5), and dates from 1627 (see note 134–5 above). And the Teatro di Tor di Nona, built by Fontana in Rome in the 1660s, has shutters at various distances from the front of the stage (see stage diagram, **175**, 111), which became a feature also of the English Restoration theatres.

139 Prison scene: etching in Settle, E., *The Empress of Morocco*, London, 1673. (V. & A.2.)

For the other *Empress of Morocco* etchings, see **126**, 63–4. The only other print of Italian scenery in England before 1700 is the very vague 1674 frontispiece to *Ariane*, **31**, Fig. 195. The 1699 frontispiece to Eccles's *Theater Musick* has been shown to be a copy of a French print after Bérain (**218**, III, 3, 222 and **217**, XIX, 2, Pls 1 & 2).

140 An English country performance: sepia aquatint by J. Wright after W. R. Pyne, 1788. (H.T.C.)

141 Trap mechanism: etching by George Cruikshank in Raymond, G., *Memoirs of Robert William Elliston*, London, 1844, opp. p. 280. (A.C.)

For an excellent late 19th-c. print of a clown about to be hauled up on a trap, see **134**, Pl. 12.

142 Scene for opening performance in Richelieu's theatre in the Palais-Cardinal: etching by Stephano della Bella in Desmarets, J., *Mirame*, Paris, 1641. (V. & A.2.)

The interior of this theatre can be seen in the famous print entitled *Le Soir* (**20**, after p. 401, Fig. 5), showing Richelieu and the royal family watching *Le Ballet de la Prospérité des Armes de France* which was presented later in the same year (**20**, 381).

143 Setting by Giacomo Torelli, 1650: etching by F. Chauveau from Corneille, P., *Andromède*, Rouen, 1651. (M.M.)

144 Cross-section of stage setting with *periaktoi*: etching in Furttenbach, J., *Architectura Recreationis*, Augsburg, 1640, Bk II, Pl. 23. (B.M.1.)

Furttenbach seems to have overlooked the considerable problems of turning *periaktoi* on a raked stage. Other illustrations showing the use of *periaktoi*: by Wren, **31**, Fig. 191; and as late as 1783 at Lemberg, **22**, V, 607.

145 Machine wing for hell scene: one of a series of drawings of wings, *c.*1700. (N.M.S.: Tessin coll., vol. S5, fol. 61–71.)

Sabbattini's recommendation of *aqua vitae* echoes Serlio a century before, and the satirical stage inventory in the *Tatler* in 1709 (no. 42) includes 'spirits of right Nantz brandy, for lambent flames and apparitions'.

146 Setting by Lodovico Burnacini, 1674: etching by Küsel from Minato, N., *Il Fuoco Eterno*, Vienna, 1674. (M.M.)

An 18th-c. setting with similar machinery painted on the wings survives in the castle theatre at Krumlov; photo of it on the stage, **22**, V, Fig. 48.

147 Setting by Lodovico Burnacini, 1674: etching by Küsel in Minato, N., *Il Ratto delle Sabine*, Vienna, 1674. (Kungliga Biblioteket, Stockholm.)

Torelli had used spectators painted on the wings in 1654 (reprod. **69**, 171), but they were more distant and more static.

148 Designs for wings by Johann Oswald Harms: drawings, late 17th c. (Herzog Anton Ulrich Museum, Braunschweig: no. AT. 119.)

149–50 Settings by Francesco Santurini, 1680 and 1662: etchings from Rapparini, G. M., *Berenice Vendicativa*, Padua, n.d. (A.F.C.) and Bissari, P. P., *Fedra Incoronata*, Munich, 1662. (B.M.1.)

The former, though printed at Padua, had been performed at Piazzola in 1680.

151 Anonymous setting, 1654: etching from *Theodosius Magnus*, Vienna, n.d. (B.A.2.)

152 Opera at the Spanish court: Dutch etching by Harrewyn, *c.*1680. (B.N.1.)

For the pair to this, a play at the Spanish court, see **196**, Fig. 7a. The most interesting Spanish illustrations of the period are the 24 drawings of sets for Calderon's *La fiera, el rayo y la piedra* in 1690: all are reproduced in *Archivio Español de Arte y Arqueologia*, no. 16 (1930), 1–16; and a selection of five in **196**, Figs 9–13.

153 Commedia dell'Arte figures on perspective stage: etched frontispiece by Stephano della Bella in Costa, M., *Li Buffoni*, Florence, 1641. (T.M.M.)

For Callot's *Balli di Sfessania*, see **54**, Figs 14–26. Commedia dell'Arte characters appear in much more primitive perspective settings, made up of very simple canvas houses, in the ms. *Scenari d'istrione*, *c.*1620, in the Biblioteca Corsiniana in Rome: published in full, **56**, V, 252 ff.

154 One of the Drottningholm settings, late 18th c. (photo T.M.D.)

All the surviving settings at Drottningholm, and at another Swedish court theatre, Gripsholm, are published in **187**.

155 Stage put up in Fechthaus at Nuremberg: hand-coloured etching from *Angenehme Bilderlust*, *c.*1730. (T.M.M.)

Similar temporary stage, **152**, Pl. 9. Various market-place theatres of the period: **6**, Fig. 38; **16**, 405; **22**, III, Fig. 14.

156 Stage put up in Roman amphitheatre at Verona, 1772: oil by Marco Marcola. (Art Institute of Chicago.)

For a very early temporary outdoor theatre complete with boxes, *c.*1620, see **83**, Fig. 76.

157 Puppet theatre with wings: hand-coloured etching by Martin Engelbrecht from *Nahrungsart von leichtem Sinn*, *c.*1730. (T.M.M.)

For a similar English puppet-stage of 1709, see **135**, Pl. 26. And the full scenic apparatus of an 18th-c. theatre can be seen as still used today in a modern marionette theatre, **304**, 103 ff.

158 Louis XIV watching *L'Isle d'Alcine* at Versailles, 1664: etching by Israel Silvestre in *Les Plaisirs de L'Isle Enchantée*, Paris, 1673. (V. & A.1.)

The vast series of prints made for Louis XIV, and known as the *Cabinet du Roi*, contains several sections of theatrical interest. The more important are grouped in the later editions under the title *Fêtes de Versailles*, which includes *Les Plaisirs de L'Isle Enchantée*, Paris, 1673, *Les Divertissements de Versailles*, Paris, 1676, and *Relation de la fête de Versailles*, Paris, 1679. A selection of these prints is reproduced in **15**, Port. XI.

159 Leopold I watching *La Costanza d'Ulisse* at Vienna, 1700: etching after Lodovico Burnacini from anonymous edition of libretto, Vienna, 1700. (M.M.)

160 Stage put up by the Chamber of Rhetoricians known as *De Eglantier*, Amsterdam, 1609: engraving by J. C. Visscher, after David Vinckeboons. (R.M.)

For an interesting but simpler stage of this type in Antwerp in the same year, see **11**, II, 220.

161 Street theatre for entry of Archduke Ernest into Brussels in 1594: etching from *Descriptio et Explicatio Pegmatum*, Brussels, 1594. (Bibliothèque Royale, Brussels: Imprimés.)

162 A booth stage indoors: etching in Bourgoingne, A. van., *Ghebreken der Tonghe*, Antwerp, 1631, p. 112. (R.M.)

163 Rope-dancers and stage in tent: watercolour by Peeter Bout, dated 1683. (V. & A.2.: no. 9280.7.)

164 Tennis-court theatre at the fair in The Hague: engraving in Venne, A. van de, *Tafereel van de Belacchende Werelt*, The Hague, 1635, p. 69. (A.C.)

For similar entertainments in tents, see **32**, Fig. 83 and **34**, 80; for English prints suggesting that female rope-dancers were a Dutch speciality, **217**, VIII, 4, Pls 6–7; and for a tennis-court in its unadapted form, **154**, Fig. 17.

165–7 Stage, auditorium and ground-plan of the Schouwburg built by Nikolaes van Kampen in 1637 (first performance Jan. 8, 1637/38): etchings of stage and auditorium by Jacob Lescaille, and of ground-plan by W. van de Laegh. (Archief Bibliotheek, Amsterdam.)
There are in the Archief Bibliotheek several different 17th-c. prints showing this view of the stage, all clearly deriving from the same source; and the source is probably Salomon Savry who, according to Thieme-Becker, did some views of the theatre in the very year in which it was built, 1637. Jacob Lescaille's two etchings therefore probably relate directly to 1637, but the ground-plan was both drawn and etched by W. van de Laegh in 1658.
There is also an oil painting by H. J. van Baden of the interior of this Schouwburg (**218**, III, 1, Pl. IIIb), which gives a good side view of the stage and shows spectators in the side galleries above the stage.

168 Ground-plan of the 1665 Schouwburg, when burnt in 1772: detail of etching from *Atlas; van de Stad Amsterdam*, Vyfde Verzameling, Amsterdam, 1774. (T.M.A.)
Very similar ground-plans, with oblique wings downstage and parallel wings behind them, survive for the Teatro di Tor di Nona in Rome, which was built in the 1660s, the same decade as this Schouwburg (reprod. **175**, p. 105 & 111).
However the Tor di Nona diagrams show that the back-scenes there were still of the old 'shutter' variety, extended wings joining in the middle. This Schouwburg diagram is, as far as I know, the first to show incontrovertible drop-cloths (marked Y): the accompanying text explains that 'YYY are the three drop-cloths, which, like the borders, could be raised and lowered by counterweights' (**226**, 12). If the Schouwburg had had this system since it was built in 1665, it must certainly have been one of the first theatres to use flown cloths.

169 Forest setting on the Schouwburg stage: etching dated 1749 by S. Fokke. (Archief Bibliotheek, Amsterdam.)
The only possible glimpse of a groove earlier than this is in a painting of Hogarth's in 1731 (**135**, Figs 30–1), which has been argued on rather slight evidence to show an improvised upper groove, fitted up for a children's performance (**135**, 189–93). The chandeliers seen in Fokke's print below the proscenium could be lowered to the stage to be lit, and some can be seen lowered in a French print of 1726 (**11**, IV, 1).

170–1 The Schouwburg setting known as *De Aloude Hofgalerij* (the ancient court gallery), and the same adapted to a general's tent: etchings published by J. Smit, *c*. 1765. (170, T.M.A.: 171, Koninklijke Bibliotheek, The Hague.)

172–3 The same Schouwburg setting adapted to a throne room and a vista of tents: etchings after W. Writs from *Atlas; van de Stad Amsterdam*, Zesde Verzameling, Amsterdam, 1775. (172, T.M.A.: 173, H.T.C.)

For photographs of similar tent settings on the stage at Drottningholm, see **187**, 230–1.

174 Farmhouse wings: etching in Lambranzi, G., *Deliciae Theatrales* (also entitled *Nuova e Curiosa Scuola dei Balli Theatrali*), Nuremberg, 1716, Part I, p. 7. (B.M.1.)

175 A setting in the new Schouwburg known as *Armoedige Wooning* (miserable dwelling): etching, *c*. 1780. (T.M.A.)
A sketchbook of late 18th-c. settings by Pietro Travaglia contains many interesting examples of furniture painted on wings and backcloth; a selection is reproduced **208**, Figs 37–47.

176 Farmhouse setting on the stage at Drottningholm. (T.M.D.)

177 Design for etched frontispiece to *The Knight of the Burning Pestle* in the collected plays of Beaumont and Fletcher, London, 1778: watercolour by M. A. Rooker. (B.M.2.: folder 198.a.22.)

178 Prison setting by Marcantonio Chiarini, 1694: etching by Buffagnotti in David, D., *La Forza della Virtu*, Bologna, 1694. (T.M.M.)

179 Prison setting by Ferdinando Bibiena, 1703: etching by Buffagnotti in Bibiena, F., *Varie opere di Prospettiva*, Bologna, n.d. (V. & A.2.)

180 Setting by Giuseppe Bibiena for performance at Dresden in 1719: etching by Pfeffel in Bibiena, G., *Architetture e Prospettive*, n.p., 1740. (V. & A.2.)

181 Diagram of how to paint a setting on the wings: etching from Bibiena, F., *Direzione della Prospettiva Teorica*, Vol. II, Bologna, 1732, Pl. 51, Fig. 6. (V. & A.1.)
The line A–C is a taut string along the eye-line; the other string slides along it on a ring and can be placed against the wings to draw lines in precise perspective.

182 Ground-plan of prison setting by Ferdinando and Antonio Bibiena, Fano, 1718–19: drawing. (Biblioteca Federiciana, Fano, ms. Amiani 19, fol. 139 v.–146 v.; A.F.C.)

183 *Scena per angolo*: etching in Lambranzi, G., *Deliciae Theatrales*, Nuremberg, 1716, Part I, p. 16. (B.M.1.)

184 Setting and stage diagram for Teatro Ottoboni, *c*. 1710: drawing by Filippo Juvarra. (V. & A.2.: Juvarra sketchbook, fol. 43.)
It is possible that the Teatro Ottoboni was a puppet theatre using almost lifesize puppets; for the arguments, see **218**, I, 2, p. 5 ff.

185 Cross-section of the Comédie Française with a *scena per angolo* on the stage: etching in Diderot, D., *Recueil de Planches*, Tom. X, Paris, 1772. (B.M.1.)
The two castle theatres of the late 18th c. in Czechoslovakia, at Krumlov and Leitomischl, both include *scene per angolo*

among their surviving settings, though for the most part only painted on drop-cloths; e.g. **22**, V, Figs 49–50.

186 Lighting stand, *c.* 1700: wash drawing. (N.M.S., on loan to T.M.D.)

A more restricting alternative was to attach the lights to the backs of the wings; they can be seen there in a German print of the late 18th c., **31**, Fig. 208.

187 Machinery for lowering footlights, Ipswich, early 19th c.: drawing in ms. compiled by H. R. Eyre, entitled *Interesting Matter Relating to the Scenery, Decoration etc. of the Theatre Royal Tacket Street Ipswich*, p. 36. (Public Library, Ipswich.)

Footlights can be seen in a great many illustrations of the 17th, 18th and 19th centuries. One of the most ostensibly interesting is the drawing of the first night of *Jeppe paa Bjerget* in Copenhagen in 1723 (**12**, IV, Tav. X and **22**, V, 474), since it shows a uniformed candle-snuffer actually tending the footlights during a performance. Unfortunately it has no validity, being a modern reconstruction in a cleverly pastiche style. The artist, Rasmus Christiansen, was born in 1863.

188 A dragon's head with transparencies, *c.* 1700: drawing. (N.M.S.: Tessin coll., vol. S7, fol. 218.)

189 Stage-hand working moving sky panorama, *c.* 1750: watercolour. (N.M.S., on loan to T.M.D.)

For a discussion of Inigo Jones's use in the early 17th c. of similar ground-rows for scenes 'in relieve' upstage, see **135**, 57–81.

190 Setting by Dominico Mauro, 1685: etching in Terzago, V., *Servio Tullio*, Munich, n.d. (Staatsbibliothek, Munich.)

For other structural pieces set between or behind wings, see **12**, I, Tav. CXIII (steps) and **12**, III, Tav. 6 (stairs).

191 Method of producing lightning: woodcut in Sabbattini, N., *Pratica di Fabricar Scene*, Ravenna, 1638, p. 157. (A.C.)

192 Method of producing thunder: etching in Diderot, D., *Recueil de Planches*, Tom. X, Paris, 1772. (B.M.1.)

193 Emblematic costume for the Watery Phlegmatic Humour, Turin, 1641: watercolour in ms. of *Il Carnevale Languente*, fol. 19. (Private Collection, Attilio Bigo.)

The most extreme of all emblematic costumes are the prints reproduced **15**, Port. XI, Pls XII–XVI. And **15**, Port. I, Pl. VI reproduces a charming pair of flower-covered gardeners by Lodovico Burnacini.

194 Costumes of the Hocricanes and the Hofnaques in *Ballet des Quatre Parties du Monde*, Paris, 1629: watercolour. (B.N.1.: ms. Qb. 3. rés., drawing no. 17 for this ballet.)

A more famous and earlier use of the same idea is the pair of English woodcuts, *c.* 1606, for *Nobody and Somebody* (**11**, III, 27), repeated in Germany in 1608 for *Niemand und Jemand* (**22**, III, 358). For more purely grotesque costumes, see those by Lodovico Burnacini, **15**, Port. VIII, Pl. XV and **22**, III, 505.

195 Garrick in his costume as Sir John Brute in *The Provoked Wife*: etching dated 1776 from Bell's *British Theatre*. (A.C.)

196 Actress in Roman male costume, *c.* 1750: wash drawing. (B.N.1.: vol. Tb.20.a, fol. 43.)

There are innumerable illustrations of the Roman theatrical costume of the 17th and 18th centuries in all its ludicrous extravagance; among the best are **11**, III, 181 (Molière as Caesar); **12**, III, Tav. CCI; **15**, Port. I, Pl. I (by Burnacini); **22**, III, Fig. 40 and IV, Fig. 44 & p. 489; **31**, Fig. 216. The earliest drawing connected with Shakespeare, the Longleat sketch of *Titus Andronicus*, shows the Roman costume of 1595 (**31**, Fig. 152). At the other extreme the Delacroix portrait of Talma as Nero shows Roman costume after the late 18th-c. movement towards historical accuracy (**248**, frontispiece).

197–8 Humorous costumes: etchings in Lambranzi, G., *Deliciae Theatrales*, Nuremberg, 1716, Part I, pp. 18 & 45. (B.M.1.)

199 Costume for two men as a centaur: drawings by or after Jean Bérain, late 17th c. (N.M.S.: Tessin Coll., vol. K1, fol. 49.)

For similar drawings showing a costume for two men as a camel, see **13**, Pls 95–6; a machine allowing a single man to play a centaur with the help of attached mechanical rear legs, **70**, 277; and a magnificent pantomime horse by Picasso, **12**, III, Tav. CXXXIV.

200 Strolling actresses dressing in a barn: engraving by Hogarth, dated 1738. (B.M.2.)

Hogarth's original painting, from which he engraved this print, was unfortunately destroyed by fire in 1874. An interesting variety of scenic pieces belonging to a travelling company can be seen in the yard outside a country theatre in a print of about 1820, reproduced **310**, opp. p. 262.

201 A theatrical auction: coloured aquatint by Theodore Lane in Egan, P., *Life of an Actor*, London, 1825, facing p. 249. (B.M.1.)

202 The green room of the Kongelige Teater, Copenhagen, *c.* 1830: etching. (T.M.C.)

203 Elderly spectator and actress: lithograph after C. Philipon, dated 1830, in the series called *Compensations*. (V. & A.2.)

For a particularly lecherous green room visitor in Regency times, complete with eye-glass, see **287**, opp. p. 128.

204 A box at the Schouwburg in Amsterdam, *c.* 1820: etching. (T.M.A.)

The theatre is recognisable as the Schouwburg by the proscenium arch with its two pillars and a statue between them, a feature of the earlier Schouwburg which was retained in the rebuilding after 1772 (cf. Pl. XXIV, pp. 194–5).

205 A box at the Opéra in Paris: etching by J. B. Patas after J. M. Moreau the younger, in Restif de la Bretonne *Monument du Costume Physique et Moral de la Fin du XVIIIe Siècle*, Neuwied sur le Rhin, 1789, opp. p. 32. (V. & A.1.)

206 *Les Petits Comédiens*: etching, early 18th c. (M.M.)

Views of spectators on the French stage are fairly common, e.g. **11**, III, 135 & 257 (top); **12**, VII, Tav. CLXIX; **22**, IV, 83. The *banquettes* at the Comédie Française can be clearly seen both in views of the stage (**11**, III, 244 and **22**, IV, 417) and in a diagram (**218**, IV, 1, Pl. Ia). It has been argued (**145**, 142) that the earliest illustration of spectators on the French stage is for Rotrou's *Hypochondriaque* in 1628 (reprod. **11**, III, 257 bottom); from the costume and attitudes of these figures it appears more likely that they are characters in the play, though there is in fact nothing in the scene (Act V, sc. 2) to suggest that other characters should be watching this fight between two thieves.

The best illustration of spectators on the English stage is Hogarth's of *The Beggar's Opera* in 1728, which survives both as an oil painting (**126**, centre spread, in colour but printed the wrong way round), and as a print (**12**, I, Tav. CCIX). For the very intriguing but unauthentic spectators in the wings for *Jeppe paa Bjerget* in 1723 (**12**, IV, Tav.X), see note 187 above.

207 A Danish prompter, 1796: although a satirical drawing, this represents the orchestra and the prompter with very literal accuracy. (T.M.C.)

One of the best illustrations of such a prompter is a German oil painting of *c*. 1780, reproduced in colour **167**, Taf. IV.

208 O.P. Riot at Covent Garden in 1809: etching. (V. & A.4.)

For various other riotous audiences, see **22**, VIII, Fig. 14; **126**, 134; **282**, 148.

209 The *chef de claque* in action: lithograph, *c*. 1840, after Bourdet by Caboche. (Dubech, L., *Histoire Générale Illustrée du Théâtre*, Paris (Librairie de France), 1934, Tom. V, p. 28.) For a satirical view of a *claqueur* at the Théâtre Odéon in Paris, see **12**, III, 931.

210 Tournament theatre built by Alfonso Chenda in 1639 in the Sala del Podestà in Bologna: painting in *Insignia degli Anziani del Commune*, Vol. VII, fol. 15 r. (Archivio di Stato, Bologna.)

A drawing of Aleotti's (**20**, after p. 158, Fig. 7) shows that he considered having tiers of boxes in the Teatro Farnese but then rejected the idea. The earliest diagram of the modern type of auditorium antedates both Amsterdam in 1637 and Bologna in 1639, being Guitti's design for the theatre at Ferrara in 1627 (**20**, after p. 158, Fig. 5). For other early views of this type of auditorium, all mid 17th c., see **12**, V, Tav. XXIII & XL and **31**, Fig. 311. A most interesting little theatre on the island of Hvar in Yugoslavia has an auditorium remarkably similar to that of the 1637 Schouwburg, with a double curved row of arched boxes around a standing area in the pit (photos of it from two angles, **6**, Fig. 254 and **22**, III, 608). It was built in 1612, and therefore the structure itself antedates all these other examples; but the interior was reconstructed in 1803 (**6**, 285), and it is not clear how much its basic shape was altered.

211 Ballet for Paisiello's opera *Pyrrhus* on the stage of the Warsaw court theatre, 1790: oil. (Warsaw, National Museum, on loan to Theatre Museum.)

There are other views of pleasantly small 18th-c. theatres in **10**, 384; **12**, VI, Tav. 15 & VII, Tav. 21; **83**, Fig. 170. A tiny 18th-c. theatre survives unaltered at Grein in Austria; watercolour, **22**, V, 131. For excellent photographs of Europe's best surviving 18th-c. auditoria, see **6**, Figs 253–336.

212 The interior of the Teatro Argentina in Rome in 1747: painting by Paolo Pannini. (Louvre, Paris.)

Some views of the new vast auditoria: **12**, VII, Tav. CLXXIII; **22**, V, 577; **31**, Fig. 243; **126**, 108.

213 The interior of the Teatro Regio in Turin, *c*. 1740: oil by D. Olivero. (Museo Civico, Turin.)

For sentries in the auditorium or on the stage, see **12**, V, Tav. 15; **17**, Pl. 108; **126**, 134; **282**, 230 & 236.

214 Goethe in *Adolar und Hilaria* in the park at Ettersburg in 1780: oil by G. M. Kraus. (G.M.W.)

For a painting of Goethe's *Die Fischerin*, performed in the open air at Tiefurt, see **12**, V, Tav. CLXV.

215 Adaptable structural setting for the Weimar stage: sketch by Goethe, early 19th c. (G.M.W.: drawing no. 1360.)

Other stage drawings by Goethe, **12**, V, 1403 & Tav. CLXVI.

216 The opening night of *Hernani*, 1830: caricature, etching by J. J. Granville. (Maison de Victor Hugo, Paris.) Another view of the same occasion, **11**, V, 19.

217 Caricature on Weimar theatre: watercolour by S. Trifft, *c*. 1800. (G.M.W.)

218 Setting by Friedrich Beuther for *Die Jungfrau von Orleans*, Weimar, 1815: coloured aquatint, published 1816. (T.M.M.) **22**, V, 230 reproduces an interesting print of 1806 which, he maintains, represents Iffland's production of the procession scene in *Die Jungfrau von Orleans*, but he gives no details. The same print is reproduced with a date of 1801 in **1**, Fig. 186 and **17**, Pl. 78, in both cases wrongly attributed to Schinkel who designed no sets until 1815.

219 Setting by Karl Friedrich Schinkel for *Die Jungfrau von Orleans*, Berlin, 1817: lithograph in Schinkel, K. F., *Decorationen auf den beiden königlichen Theatern in Berlin*, Erstes Heft, Berlin, 1819, Bl. 5. (V. & A.1.)

220 Setting by W. Gordon for *A Midsummer Night's Dream*, London, 1856: watercolour (V. & A.2.: no. D.1567–1901.)

221–3 Settings by Cuthbert and Jones for *Hamlet*, London, 1858: watercolours. (V. & A.2.: nos D.1658–1901, D.1659–1901 and D.1663–1901.)

224 Setting for a Zoroastrian Temple by Antonio Basoli, 1847: pen and sepia drawing. (T.M.S.)

225 Maquette by Gaspare Galliari, *c.* 1820. (T.M.S.)
V. & A.2. has a good collection of similar but considerably earlier maquettes by Philippe de Loutherbourg; one in particular, for *The Wonders of Derbyshire*, Drury Lane, 1779 (**12**, VIII, Tav. CLXXXIX) uses a technique of huge cut-out cloths very similar to Galliari's. **1**, Fig. 491 prints a Munich setting of 1881 which consists exclusively of a series of cut drop-cloths: they are a little more practical in that the hole cut in each reaches right down to stage level, but the principle is the same. And for a single drop-cloth of this type, see Fig. 3 above.

226 Scenery and machinery for *La Tour Enchantée*: print in Moynet, G., *Trucs et Décors*, Paris, n.d. (1895), Pl. 18. (A.C.)
The prints commissioned for Moynet's book provide the most complete and varied illustration of 19th-c. stage effects.

227 Ground-plan of stage-setting, Stockholm, *c.* 1820. (T.M.D.: *Maskinmästarejournalen*, Vol. I, p. 265.)
For a very clear ground-plan of the same combination of flat wings with a structure of steps etc. upstage, as used by Tieck at Potsdam in 1843, see **1**, Fig. 274. And for an interesting print, giving both the ground-plan and the appearance on the stage of a setting which, as early as 1802, combines flat wings in some areas and large set pieces in others, see **7**, Bild 49.

228 A setting for *Die Höhle Soncha*, Vienna: hand-coloured etching, dated 1828, in Bäuerle, A., *Gallerie drolliger und interessanter Scenen der Wiener Bühnen*, 2. Jahrgang, no. 19. (H.M.W.)
For a two-level setting rather similar to this in England in 1833, see **217**, IX, 1, Pl. 3. A wide selection of Bäuerle's excellent prints is published in **166**.

229 Setting for *La Ronde du Commissaire*, Paris, 1884: print in *Il Teatro Illustrato*, 1884.

230 Setting the stage at Booth's theatre, New York: print in *Appleton's Journal*, May 28, 1870. (V. & A.1.)
A view of Booth's theatre from the auditorium, on the opening night in 1869, **202**, opp. p. 194.

231 The first act of *L'Africaine* on the stage of the Opéra in Paris, *c.* 1892: etching by Paul Renouard, in Renouard, P., *L'Opéra*, Paris, n.d., no. 17. (B.M.2.)

232 A Danish pantomime, *c.* 1900: watercolour by Poul Fischer. (Kongelige Bibliotek, Copenhagen.)
For other late views of the old system of wings surviving, see **135**, Pls 34, 56 & 58.

233 'A Glance Behind the Curtain': etching in *The Illustrated Sporting and Dramatic News*, Oct. 2, 1886, p. 76. (V. & A.1.)

234–5 Two settings for *Der Apfelkönig und der Menschenfeind*, Vienna: coloured etchings, dated 1829, in Bäuerle, A., *Gallerie drolliger und interessanter Scenen der Wiener Bühnen*, 3. Jahrgang, nos 4 and 19. (H.M.W.)

236 A turbulent sea: lithograph by Honoré Daumier from *Croquis Parisiens*, 1856. (A.C.)
For another view of boys under the sea tarpaulin, and for the same effect being achieved more recently by mechanical arms, see **12**, VII, Tav. CLXI. Sixty-four of Daumier's theatrical lithographs are published in Rothe, H., *Daumier und das Theater*, Leipzig, 1925.

237–8 The effect and technique of Pepper's Ghost: prints from Moynet, G., *Trucs et Décors*, Paris, n.d. (1895), pp. 277 & 279. (A.C.)
For an excellent account of Pepper's Ghost, and the uses to which it was put, see *Le Merveilleux et les Arts du Spectacle* (Société d'Histoire du Théâtre), 1961, pp. 48–56. The very same technique is still used in a modern television studio, where the performer's or newscaster's script is reflected on a sheet of glass in front of the camera lens.

239 American miniature poster cut for *Mazeppa*, *c.* 1860: print in the volume called *Specimens of Show Printing*. (H.T.C.)
The reason why Mazeppa, a male hero, has such feminine features in this cut is that the most famous performer of the role was a woman, Adah Isaacs Menken. The entire volume of miniature poster cuts was recently published in facsimile by Cherokee Books under the title *Early American Theatrical Posters*, Hollywood, n.d.

240 View of *Mazeppa* from the wings: cartoon by Tenniel in *Punch*, vol. XXI (1851), p. 201. (B.M.1.)
Admittedly the point of Tenniel's cartoon was that this successful show was about to be produced simultaneously in a second London theatre and that a new horse would therefore have to be coaxed into a 'wild career' – but any more frantic dash across the stage was hardly possible with such a speech to deliver.

241 Detail from a satirical design for a drop scene for Drury Lane: etching by 'Thaumaso Scrutiny' in *The Satirist*, May 1, 1808. (V. & A.2.)

242 Animal act in Venice with lion and dogs, 1762: oil painting by Pietro Longhi. (Pinacoteca Querini, Venice.)
For 18th-c. prints of dogs and monkeys performing in contemporary costume, see **12**, III, Tav. CX and **126**, 118.

243 A performance of *Timour the Tartar* at the Theatre Royal, Crow Street in Dublin, *c.* 1820: etching. (Beard Collection, Cambridge.)
Other examples of horsemanship and drama combined, **3**, Pl. 148; **256**, opp. p. 128; **327**, II, Fig. 27.

244 Moving tracks for a horse race: print in Moynet, G., *Trucs et Décors*, Paris, n.d. (1895), Pl. 42. (A.C.)
For a simpler pony race through the auditorium of Sadler's Wells in 1822, see **12**, IV, Tav. CLXX. But it is Dublin which offers by far the earliest illustration of this type – a print in *Walker's Hibernian Magazine* for 1795 shows ponies racing on

a track built round the entire auditorium, with the pit patrons completely enclosed by it, at the Theatre Royal, Crow Street (**211**, opp. p. 174).

245 Interior of the Dagmar Teater in Copenhagen, 1887: print showing Act II of *Landsoldaten* on the stage. (T.M.C.)

246 During the interval in one of the upper galleries of the Kongelige Teater, Copenhagen: drawing by Erik Henningsen, dated 1900. (T.M.C.)

247 Dick Wildfire at the *Café de la Paix* in Paris: coloured aquatint by George Cruikshank from Carey, D., *Life in Paris*, London, 1822, opp. p. 305. (Beard Collection, Cambridge.) For the best selection of interior views of British music halls in their early days, see **131**, Figs 1–54.

248 Lamb's Exhibition Rooms, New Road: anonymous etching, *c.* 1850, pasted into a volume called *Norman's Scrap Book*. (Boston Public Library, Rare Books Dept: no. **T.13.2.) I have been unable to find the origin of this print. An interior view of a small theatre, published **256**, opp. p. 128, is wrongly described as a penny theatre, being very much too lavish and respectable. The two original illustrations by Phiz for Grant's *Penny Theatres* are reproduced **268**, pp. 11 & 23.

249 The interior of the New Theatre on Chestnut Street in Philadelphia, built 1791: print in *The New York Magazine*, April, 1794. (H.T.C.) The print showing the interior of the John Street Theatre in New York *c.* 1767, which has often been published as the oldest view of an American theatre (e.g. **199**, 25 or **3**, Pl. 246) has been proved to be a forgery done in 1872, deriving at two removes from the view of the Westminster school play in Fig. 91 above. For the proof see **217**, IV, 4, 85–8 and Pls 1–2.

250 The interior of the Park Theatre, New York, 1821: wood engraving by Lansing, frontispiece to *The Rejected Addresses* for the opening of the new theatre in 1821. (New York Historical Society.) There was a long tradition in the 19th c. of drawing theatre interiors from far back in the dress circle so that the curves of the galleries make a surprising frame to the view. Early examples are some of the Pugin-Rowlandson views for their *Microcosm* (e.g. **217**, III, 4, Figs 5–6). The style continues in a lithograph by H. A. Thomas of the Chatham Garden Theatre in New York in 1825 (**199**, 85). And it reaches its most intriguing peak in the mysterious series of watercolours of London theatres in the 1860s, signed A.B. but so far unattributed, which are now in the H.T.C. (**217**, IV, 3, Pls 1–16).

251 The interior of the Park Theatre, New York, during a performance by Charles Matthews: watercolour by John Searle, dated 1822. (New York Historical Society.) For the vast American theatres of the mid 19th c., see **10**, 441 (top) and **199**, 236.

252 A variety show at Cheyenne, Wyoming: print in *Frank Leslie's Illustrated Newspaper*, Oct. 13, 1877. (H.T.C.)

253 Performance of the Hasty Pudding Club at Harvard in 1856: wash drawing, signed Dunster. (Hasty Pudding Club, Harvard.)

254 Sketch by the Duke of Meiningen for *Julius Caesar*, 1867: ink and wash drawing. (T.M.M.)

255 The abandoned camp of the Greeks, a setting for Berlioz's opera *La Prise de Troie*, Paris, 1899: photograph in *Le Théâtre*, 1900, Vol. I, no. 25, p. 6. (B.M.1.)

256 The *assommoir* or bar, a setting for Zola's *L'Assommoir*, Paris, 1900: photograph in *Le Théâtre*, 1900, Vol. II, no. 47, p. 15. (B.M.1.)

257 The school room, a setting in Antoine's production of *La Clairière*, Paris, 1901: photograph in *Le Théâtre*, 1901, Vol. II, no. 65, p. 26. (B.M.1.) It would be wrong to suggest that this element of distinctive design was always present in Antoine's productions; see, for example, **68**, Fig. 32. A good selection of photographs from Naturalistic productions of the period is provided by Denis Bablet in his *Décor de Théâtre* (**68**, Figs 30–47). Dr Bablet's book is by far the best account of the crucial years in the development of the modern theatre, from 1870 to 1914, and I am much indebted to him in my choice of illustrations for this period.

258 A farm yard in a storm, a setting for Antoine's production of *La Terre*, adapted from Zola, Paris, 1902: photograph in *Le Théâtre*, 1902, no. 90, p. 10. (B.M.1.)

259 Design by Adolphe Appia for Klingsor's castle in *Parsifal*, 1896: original sketch. (Fondation Adolphe Appia, Collection Suisse du Théâtre, Berne.) For a good selection of designs by Appia and Craig and their followers, see **68**, Figs 85–150.

260 Design by Adolphe Appia for a 'rhythmic space' in *Götterdämmerung*, 1909: original sketch. (T.M.M.)

261 Design by Edward Gordon Craig in the series entitled *Scene*: etching, 1907. (V. & A.2.) For Craig's first sketch and notes for this series, showing the details and measurements of the screens and cubes, see **68**, Fig. 138.

262 Setting by Isaac Grünewald for *Samson and Delilah*, Stockholm, 1922: sketch by Robert Edmond Jones reproduced in Macgowan, K. and Jones, R. E., *Continental Stagecraft*, London (Ernest Benn), 1923, opp. p. 122. (A.C.)

263 Setting by Jo Mielziner for Maxwell Anderson's *Winterset*, New York, 1935: original sketch. (Artist's collection.)

264 Setting by Mikulas Kravjansky for Lorca's *La Casa de Bernarda Alba*, Bratislava, 1957: original sketch. (Artist's collection.)

265 Setting by Edward Carrick for *Macbeth*, Stratford-upon-Avon, 1949: original sketch. (Artist's collection; photo, John Vickers.)

266 Setting by Maxime Dethomas for *Le Carnaval des Enfants*, Paris, 1910: original sketch. (Musée des Arts Décoratifs, Paris.)

267 Setting by Leslie Hurry for *Hamlet*, London, 1942: production photograph.
The ballet was revived in 1958 when new settings were painted, but to the original designs. This photograph is of the new settings when the company was on tour during 1965.

268 Setting by Leon Bakst for *Schéhérazade*, Ballets Russes, Paris, 1910: original sketch. (Musée des Arts Décoratifs, Paris.)

269–71 Designs by Oscar Schlemmer in Bauhausbücher, no. 4, *Die Bühne im Bauhaus*, Munich, 1924, pp. 8, 17 & 32. (B.M.1.)

272–3 Settings by Alexandra Exter for *La Dama Duende*, Moscow, 1919, and *Don Juan*, Cologne, 1929: original sketches. (V. & A.2.: nos E.1595.1953 and E.1594.1953.)
For an excellent selection of constructivist settings by Exter, together with her very machine-age costume designs for *La Dama Duende*, see *Russian Stage and Costume Designs*, International Exhibitions Foundation, 1967, Figs 50–68.

274 The laundry, a setting for Zola's *L'Assommoir*, Paris, 1900: photograph in *Le Théâtre*, 1900, Vol. II, no. 47, p. 4. (B.M.1.)

275–6 Original sketch and production photo of setting by Luciano Damiani for *El Nost Milan*, Milan, 1955. (Photos from I.T.I., Rome; and Piccolo Teatro, Milan.)

277 Setting by Karl von Appen for Brecht's *Pauken und Trompeten*, Berlin, 1955: original sketch. (Artist's collection.)

278 Setting by Vladimir Egorov for Andreev's *The Life of Man*, Moscow, 1907: original sketch. (State Central Theatre Library, Moscow.)
The production was by Stanislavski, a year before his more famous production of *Blue Bird*, and this sketch shows how far he had already moved from Naturalism.

279 Open-air setting by Georges Annenkov in the Winter Palace Square for *The Storming of the Winter Palace*, Leningrad, 1920: original sketch. (Private collection, Nikita D. Lobanov-Rostovsky.)

280 Setting by Donald Oenslager for Monteverdi's *Orfeo*, New York, 1960: original sketch. (Artist's collection.)

281 Setting by Lodovico Burnacini, 1668: etching by Küsel from Sbarra, F., *Il Pomo d'Oro*, Vienna, 1668. (M.M.)
This was the most lavish of all the many 17th-c. opera libretti which were published with etchings of the scenes; the plates number twenty-four (one view of the interior of the theatre, and twenty-three different settings). For a selection of them, see **182**, Pls XXVIII–XXXVII and **235**, Abb. 18 ff.

282 Detail of setting by Peter Rice for *Ariadne in Naxos*, London, 1961: detail from original sketch. (Artist's collection.)

283 A ship on wheels for passing through the sea upstage: woodcut in Furttenbach, J., *Mannhafter Kunst-Spiegel*, Augsburg, 1663, Pl. 13, detail. (B.M.1.)
Peter Rice's only deviation from perfect academic accuracy is in the scale of the ship; the original was designed to carry Jonah and several sailors.

284 Interior of the Casino Teater in Copenhagen, 1933: oil painting by Christian Bogø. (T.M.C.)

285 Production by J. Savits of *King Lear* on the 'Shakespeare-Bühne' designed by Karl Lautenschläger, Munich, 1889: print after H. Riffarth. (T.M.M.)
The earliest attempt to reconstruct an Elizabethan stage was for Karl Immermann's production of *Twelfth Night* in Düsseldorf in 1840 (**68**, Fig. 151). For an excellent selection of illustrations showing the developing experiments with different types of stage, see **68**, Figs 151–79.

286 Stage designed by J. Hista for the production by Lugné-Poe of *Measure for Measure* in the Cirque d'Eté, Paris, 1898: from *Le Petit Bleu*, Dec. 12, 1898. (Bablet, D., *Le Décor de Théâtre*, Paris (Centre National de la Recherche Scientifique), 1965, Fig. 175.) (A.C.)

287 Production by Max Reinhardt of *The Miracle*, London, Olympia, 1911: print from drawing by J. Duncan. (V. & A.4.)

288–9 Plastic stage by Walter Neuzil, Franz Lowitsch and Rudolph Scherer, Vienna, *c.*1925, and theatre project by Wilhelm Treichlinger and Fritz Rosenbaum, Vienna, *c.*1925: from Fuerst, W. R. and Hume, S. J., *XXth Century Stage Decoration*, London (Alfred Knopf), 1928, Vol. II, Figs 380 and 385. (A.C.)
For other similar stages and projects of the period, see this same volume by Fuerst and Hume, Figs 376 ff.

290 Artist's impression of the interior of the theatre designed by John Bury, to be built at the Barbican as the London home of the Royal Shakespeare Company: specially drawn by Elizabeth Bury for this book. (A.C.)

BIBLIOGRAPHY

This bibliography is in two parts. Part I is a select list of modern illustrated books on the theatre, arranged according to subject and country. Part II contains all the other works referred to in the footnotes or in the notes to the illustrations.

Part I, the select bibliography, is designed as a practical guide to other modern works reproducing the type of material with which I have been concerned in this book – authentic paintings, drawings and prints which reveal details of life within the theatre at various periods. It is compiled, therefore, within fairly precise limits. It includes theatre, opera and ballet, but not puppets, toy theatre, or works concerned exclusively with theatre architecture. I have excluded books in which the illustrations are mainly portraits or production photographs: and, in order to keep the list reasonably compact, I have also excluded monographs on single designers or actors or theatrical families, and even on individual famous theatres or companies, except where they happen to include iconographical material of more general interest. The list lays no claim, therefore, to be a complete survey of the subject, and even within its own limits there are several omissions since I have included only those works which were available to me while writing this book; several other likely titles, listed in bibliographies as containing plates, have had to be omitted because I have been unable to find a copy in order to check the nature of the illustrations. Nearly all the books in the list are profusely illustrated; those which contain only a few illustrations have been included on the grounds that their plates are particularly interesting and not reproduced elsewhere. Some of the books are grouped by subject and others by the country with which they deal, even though in several cases such classification is inevitably a little arbitrary. The editions listed are not necessarily either the first or the most recent; they are merely those that I have used, and to which my notes and references therefore refer.

Key to the footnotes
In both the footnotes and the notes to the illustrations I have referred to books by their number in this bibliography. Thus 1, 96 means ALTMAN, G. *Theater Pictorial*, page 96; and 2, III, Tav. 14 means AMICO, S. *Storia del Teatro Drammatico*, Vol. III, Tavola 14.

PART I
Modern Illustrated Books

GENERAL

1 ALTMAN, GEORGE (with R. Freud, K. Macgowan & W. Melnitz), *Theater Pictorial*, Berkeley & Los Angeles, 1953.

2 AMICO, SILVIO D', *Storia del Teatro Drammatico*, n.p., 1950, 4 vols.

3 ARPE, VERNER, *Bildgeschichte des Theaters*, Cologne, 1962.

4 BABLET, DENIS & JACQUOT, JEAN, *Le Lieu Théâtral dans la Société Moderne*, Paris, 1963.

5 BAPST, GERMAIN, *Essai sur l'Histoire du Théâtre*, Paris, 1893.

BIBLIOGRAPHY

6 BAUR-HEINHOLD, MARGARETE, *Theater des Barock*, Munich, 1966.

7 BERGMAN, GÖSTA M., *Regi och Spelstil*, Stockholm, 1946.

8 BORCHERDT, HANS H., *Das europäische Theater im Mittelalter und in der Renaissance*, Leipzig, 1935.

9 BROCKETT, OSCAR G., *The Theatre, an introduction*, New York, 1964.

10 CHENEY, SHELDON, *The Theatre*, New York, 1929.

11 DUBECH, LUCIEN, *Histoire générale illustrée du Théâtre*, Paris, 1931–4, 5 vols.

12 *Enciclopedia dello Spettacolo*, Rome, 1954–66, 9 vols and 2 supplements.

13 FREEDLEY, GEORGE & REEVES, JOHN A., *A History of the Theatre*, New York, 1941.

14 GHILARDI, FERNANDO, *Storia del Teatro*, Milan, 1961, 2 vols.

15 GREGOR, JOSEPH, *Monumenta Scenica: Denkmäler des Theaters*, Vienna, 1924–30, 12 portfolios (also New Series 1954, one portfolios).

16 GREGOR, J., *Weltgeschichte des Theaters*, Zürich, 1933.

17 HARTNOLL, PHYLLIS (ed), *The Oxford Companion to the Theatre*, London, 2nd ed., 1957 (1st ed., 1951).

18 HEWITT, BARNARD (ed.), *The Renaissance Stage*, Documents of Serlio, Sabbattini and Furttenbach, Florida, 1958.

19 HÜRLIMANN, MARTIN (ed.), *Das Atlantisbuch des Theaters*, Zürich, 1966.

20 JACQUOT, JEAN (ed.), *Le Lieu Théâtral à la Renaissance*, Paris, 1964.

21 KELCH, WERNER, *Theater im Spiegel der bildenden Kunst: Deutschland und Frankreich in der ersten Hälfte des 18ten Jahrhunderts*, Berlin, 1938.

22 KINDERMANN, HEINZ, *Theatergeschichte Europas*, Salzburg, 1957–65, 7 vols.

23 KRANICH, FRIEDRICH, *Bühnentechnik der Gegenwart*, Munich, 1929–33, 2 vols.

24 LECLERC, HÉLÈNE, *Les Origines Italiennes de l'Architecture Théâtrale Moderne*, Paris, 1946.

25 MACGOWAN, KENNETH & MELNITZ, WILLIAM, *The Living Stage*, New York, 1955.

26 MCMANAWAY, JAMES G. (ed.), *Shakespeare 400*, New York, 1964.

27 MANTZIUS, KARL, *A History of Theatrical Art*, London, 1903–21, 6 vols.

28 MERCHANT, W. MOELWYN, *Shakespeare and the Artist*, London, 1959.

29 MOUSSINAC, LÉON, *Le Théâtre des Origines à nos Jours*, Paris, 1957.

30 NAGLER, A. M., *A Source Book in Theatrical History*, New York, 1959 (1st ed., 1952).

31 NICOLL, ALLARDYCE, *The Development of the Theatre*, London, 3rd ed., 1948 (1st ed., 1927).

32 NICOLL, A., *Masks, Mimes and Miracles*, London, 1931.

33 NICOLL, A., *World Drama*, London, 1949.

34 POUGIN, ARTHUR, *Dictionnaire Historique et Pittoresque du Théâtre*, Paris, 1885.

35 SIMONSON, LEE, *The Stage is Set*, New York, 1963 (1st ed., 1932).

36 *Spectacles à travers les Ages, Les* (eds. Denys Amiel, *et al.*), Paris, 1931–2, 2 vols.

37 SPEMANN, W., *Das goldene Buch des Theaters*, Berlin, n.d. (1902).

38 Theatre Arts Prints, Series 4, *Stages of the World*, New York, 1941.

39 TINTELNOT, HANS, *Barocktheater und Barocke Kunst*, Berlin, 1939.

40 VARDAC, A. NICHOLAS, *Stage to Screen: Theatrical Method from Garrick to Griffith*, Cambridge, 1949.

PRIMITIVE

41 AVDEEV, A. D., *Proiskhojdenie Teatra*, Leningrad, 1959.

42 HUNNINGHER, BENJAMIN, *The Origin of the Theater*, New York, 1961 (1st ed., 1955).

PAGEANTRY

43 JACQUOT, JEAN (ed.), *Les Fêtes de la Renaissance*, Paris, 1956–60, 2 vols.

44 KERNODLE, GEORGE R., *From Art to Theatre*, Chicago, 1944.

45 MAGNE, EMILE, *Les Fêtes en Europe au XVIIe Siècle*, Paris, 1930.

46 MOUREY, GABRIEL, *Le livre des Fêtes Françaises*, Paris, 1930.

47 PILON, EDMOND & SAISSET, FRÉDÉRIC, *Les Fêtes en Europe au XVIIIe Siècle*, Saint-Gratien, n.d.

48 ROEDER-BAUMBACH, I. VON, *Versieringen bij blijde Inkomsten*, Antwerp, 1943.

POPULAR AND COMMEDIA DELL'ARTE

49 DISHER, M. W., *Clowns and Pantomimes*, London, 1925.

50 DUCHARTRE, PIERRE L., *La Comédie Italienne*, Paris, 1924.

51 ENGBERG, HARALD, *Pantomimeteatret*, Boghallen, 1959.

52 MCKECHNIE, SAMUEL, *Popular Entertainments through the Ages*, London, n.d.

53 MIC, CONSTANT, *La Commedia dell'Arte*, Paris, 1927.

54 NICOLINI, FAUSTO, *Vita di Arlecchino*, Milan, 1958.

55 NICOLL, ALLARDYCE, *The World of Harlequin*, 1963.

56 PANDOLFI, VITA (ed.), *La Commedia dell'Arte*, Florence, 1957–61, 6 vols.

57 SIMON, KARL G., *Pantomime*, Munich, 1960.

58 WELSFORD, ENID, *The Fool*, London, 1935.

MASQUES

59 (NICOLL, ALLARDYCE), *A Book of Masques, in honour of Allardyce Nicoll*, Cambridge, 1967.

60 NICOLL, A., *Stuart Masques and the Renaissance Stage*, London, 1938.

61 ORGEL, STEPHEN, *The Jonsonian Masque*, Cambridge, 1965.

62 WELSFORD, ENID, *The Court Masque*, Cambridge, 1927.

BALLET

63 BEAUMONT, CYRIL W., *Ballet Design, Past and Present*, London, 1946.

64 BEAUMONT, C. W., *Complete Book of Ballets*, London, 1949 (1st ed., 1937).

65 GREGOR, JOSEPH, *Kulturgeschichte des Balletts*, Vienna, 1944.

66 READE, BRIAN, *Ballet Designs and Illustrations, 1581–1940*, London, 1967.

SCENERY AND COSTUME

67 ADAMI, GIUSEPPE, *Un Secolo di Scenografia alla Scala*, Milan, 1945.

68 BABLET, DENIS, *Le Décor de Théâtre de 1870 à 1914*, Paris, 1965.

69 BJURSTRÖM, PER, *Giacomo Torelli and Baroque Stage Design*, Stockholm, 1962.

70 BOEHN, MAX VON, *Das Bühnenkostüm*, Berlin, 1921.

71 CHENEY, SHELDON, *Stage Decoration*, London, 1928.

72 COGNIAT, RAYMOND, *Décors de Théâtre*, Paris, 1930.

73 FERRERO, MERCEDES VIALE, *La Scenografia del '700 e i fratelli Galliari*, Turin, 1963.

74 FISCHEL, OSKAR, *Das Moderne Bühnenbild*, Berlin, 1923.

75 FISCHER, CARLOS, *Les Costumes de l'Opéra*, Paris, 1931.

76 FRETTE, GUIDO, *Stage Design*, Milan, n.d. (*c*. 1955).

77 FUERST, WALTER R. & HUME, SAMUEL J., *XXth Century Stage Decoration*, London, 1928, 2 vols.

78 HAINAUX, RENÈ (ed.), *Stage Design Throughout the World since 1935*, London, 1956.

79 HAINAUX, R. (ed.), *Stage Design Throughout the World since 1950*, London, 1964.

80 KOMISARJEVSKY, THEODORE, *The Costume of the Theatre*, London, 1931.

81 KOMISARJEVSKY, T. & SIMONSON, L., *Settings and Costumes of the Modern Stage*, London, 1933.

82 LAVER, JAMES, *Costume in the Theatre*, London, 1964.

83 LAVER, J., *Drama, Its Costume and Décor*, London, 1951.

84 MACGOWAN, KENNETH, *The Theatre of Tomorrow*, London, 1923.

85 MAYOR, A. H. (with V. Mercedes, A. della Corte & A. G. Bragaglia), *Tempi e Aspetti della Scenografia*, Turin, 1954.

86 MOUSSINAC, LÉON, *La Décoration Théâtrale*, Paris, 1922.

87 MOUSSINAC, L., *The New Movement in the Theatre*, London, 1931.

88 *Orientamenti della Scenografia*, Milan, 1960–1, 2 vols. (Extracts from the periodical *Prospettive*, published in volume form.)

89 PARMELIN, HÉLÈNE, *Cinq Peintres et le Théâtre*, Paris, 1956.

90 RAVA, CARLO E., *Nuovi Orientamenti della Scenografia*, Milan, 1965.

91 SCHÖNE, GUNTER, *Die Entwicklung der Perspektivbühne*, Leipzig, 1933.

92 SCHOLZ, JÁNOS, *Baroque and Romantic Stage Design*, New York, 1950.

93 SCHUBERTH, OTTMAR, *Das Bühnenbild*, Munich, 1955.

94 SHERINGHAM, GEORGE & LAVER, JAMES, *Design in the Theatre*, London, 1927.

95 SHERINGHAM, G. & BOYD MORRISON, R., *Robes of Thespis: Costume Designs by Modern Artists*, London, 1928.

96 SONREL, PIERRE, *Traité de Scénographie*, Paris, 1956 (1st ed., 1944).

97 ZUCKER, PAUL, *Die Theaterdekoration des Barock*, Berlin, 1925.

98 ZUCKER, P., *Die Theaterdekoration des Klassizismus*, Berlin, 1925.

ACTORS AND ACTING

99 CALENDOLI, GIOVANNI, *L'Attore*, Rome, 1959.

100 GILDER, ROSAMOND, *Enter the Actress: The First Women in the Theatre*, London, 1931.

101 JOSEPH, BERTRAM L., *Elizabethan Acting*, London, 1951.

102 JOSEPH, B. L., *The Tragic Actor*, London, 1959.

103 MAWER, IRENE, *The Art of Mime*, London, 1932.

GREECE AND ROME

104 BEARE, W., *The Roman Stage*, London, 2nd ed., 1955 (1st ed., 1950).

105 BIEBER, MARGARETE, *The History of the Greek and Roman Theater*, Princeton, 2nd ed., 1961 (1st ed., 1939).

106 DUCKWORTH, GEORGE E., *The Nature of Roman Comedy*, Princeton, 1952.

107 FLICKINGER, ROY C., *The Greek Theater and its Drama*, Chicago, 4th ed., 1936 (1st ed., 1918).

108 PICKARD-CAMBRIDGE, A. W., *The Theatre of Dionysus in Athens*, Oxford, 1946.

109 WEBSTER, T. B. L., *Greek Theatre Production*, London, 1956.

THE EAST

110 ARLINGTON, L. C., *The Chinese Drama*, Shanghai, 1930.

111 BENAZET, ALEXANDRE, *Le Théâtre au Japon*, Paris, 1901.

112 EDWARDS, OSMAN, *Japanese Plays and Playfellows*, London, 1901.

113 ERNST, EARLE, *The Kabuki Theatre*, London, 1956.

114 KINCAID, ZOË, *Kabuki*, London, 1925.

115 MAYBON, ALBERT, *Le Théâtre Japonais*, Paris, 1925.

116 NIPPON GAKUJUTSU SHINKŌKAI, *The Noh Drama*, Tokyo, 1960 (1st ed., 1955).

117 RIDGEWAY, WILLIAM, *The Dramas and Dramatic Dances of non-European Races*, Cambridge, 1915.

118 SCOTT, A. C., *The Classical Theatre of China*, London, 1957.

119 STOPES, MARIE, *Plays of Old Japan: The 'Nō'*, London, 1913.

120 ZUNG, CECILIA, *Secrets of Chinese Drama*, Shanghai, 1937.

ENGLAND

121 BEVAN, IAN, *Royal Performance*, London, 1954.

122 BOOTH, MICHAEL R., *English Melodrama*, London, 1965.

123 CAMPBELL, LILY B., *Scenes and Machines on the English Stage during the Renaissance*, Cambridge, 1923.

124 CLINTON-BADDELEY, V. C., *All Right on the Night*, London, 1954.

125 CLINTON-BADDELEY, V. C., *The Burlesque Tradition in the English Theatre after 1660*, London, 1952.

126 CLUNES, ALEC, *The British Theatre*, London, 1964.

127 DISHER, M. W., *Greatest Show on Earth*, London, 1937.

128 DORBE, RÉGIS, *Matériaux pour une Iconographie de la Scène Elisabethaine*, Toulouse, 1962.

129 HODGES, C. W., *The Globe Restored*, London, 1953.

130 *London Stage, 1660–1800, The*, Carbondale, 1960 ff. (many volumes and various editors).

131 MANDER, RAYMOND & MITCHENSON, JOE, *British Music Hall*, London, 1965.

132 MANDER, R. & MITCHENSON, J., *The British Theatre*, London, 1957.

133 ODELL, GEORGE C. D., *Shakespeare from Betterton to Irving*, London, 1921, 2 vols.

134 ROWELL, GEORGE, *The Victorian Theatre*, London, 1956.

135 SOUTHERN, RICHARD, *Changeable Scenery*, London, 1952.

136 SOUTHERN, R., *The Georgian Playhouse*, London, 1948.

137 WICKHAM, GLYNNE, *Early English Stages*, London, 1959–63, 2 vols.

FRANCE

138 AGHION, MAX, *Le Théâtre à Paris au XVIIIe siècle*, Paris, 1926.

139 ALLÉVY, MARIE-ANTOINETTE, *La Mise en Scène en France dans la première moitié du XIXe Siècle*, Paris, 1938.

140 CAIN, GEORGES, *Anciens Théâtres de Paris*, Paris, 1920.

141 CHRISTOUT, MARIE-FRANÇOISE, *Le Ballet de Cour de Louis XIV*, Paris, 1967.

142 COHEN, GUSTAVE, *Le Théâtre en France au Moyen Age*, Paris, 1928–31, 2 vols.

143 DACIER, E., *Le Musée de la Comédie-Française*, Paris, 1905.

144 DECUGIS, NICOLE & REYMOND, SUZANNE, *Le Décor de Théâtre en France du Moyen Age à 1925*, Paris, 1953.

145 DEIERKAUF-HOLSBOER, S. W., *L'Histoire de la Mise en Scène dans le Théâtre Français à Paris de 1600 à 1673*, Paris, 1960.

146 DEIERKAUF-HOLSBOER, S. W., *Le Théâtre du Marais*, Paris, 1954–8, 2 vols.

147 GAIFFE, F., *Le Drame en France au XVIIIe siècle*, Paris, 1910.

148 JACQUOT, JEAN, *Shakespeare en France, mises en scène d'hier et d'aujourdhui*, Paris, 1964.

149 KOCHNO, BORIS, *Le Ballet en France du XVe siècle à nos jours*, n.p., 1954.

150 LAWRENSON, T. E., *The French Stage in the XVIIth century*, Manchester, 1957.

151 MACGOWAN, MARGARET, *L'art du ballet de cour en France (1581–1643)*, Paris, 1963.

152 MÉLÈSE, PIERRE, *Le Théâtre en France au XVIIe siècle*, Paris, 1957.

153 VALMY-BAYSSE, JEAN, *Naissance et Vie de la Comédie-Française*, Paris, 1945.

154 WILEY, W. L., *The early Public Theatre in France*, Cambridge, 1960.

GERMANY AND AUSTRIA

155 BAUER, ANTON, *Das Theater in der Josefstadt zu Wien*, Vienna, 1957.

156 GREGOR, JOSEPH, *Das Theater des Volkes in der Ostmark*, Vienna, 1943.

157 GREGOR, J., *Wiener Szenische Kunst*, Vienna, 1924–5, 2 vols.

158 GRUBE, MAX, *Geschichte der Meininger*, Stuttgart, 1926.

159 HERRMANN, MAX, *Forschungen zur deutschen Theatergeschichte des Mittelalters und der Renaissance*, Berlin, 1914.

160 HOLL, KARL, *Geschichte des deutschen Lustspiels*, Leipzig, 1923.

161 KAISER, H., *Barocktheater in Darmstadt*, Darmstadt, 1951.

162 KAUT, JOSEF, *Festspiele in Salzburg*, Salzburg, 1965.

163 KINDERMANN, HEINZ, *Theatergeschichte der Goethezeit*, Vienna, 1948.

164 KNUDSEN, HANS, *Goethes Welt des Theaters*, Berlin, 1949.

165 Michael, W. F., *Frühformen der deutschen Bühne*, Berlin, 1963.

166 ROMMEL, OTTO, *Die Alt-Wiener Volkskomödie*, Vienna, 1952.

167 SCHÖNE, GUNTER, *Tausend Jahre deutsches Theater, 914–1914*, Munich, 1962.

168 SIEVERS, HEINRICH, *250 Jahre Braunschweiges Staatstheater*, Braunschweig, 1941.

169 TRIEBEL, L. A., *Rasser of Alsace*, Melbourne, 1954.

HOLLAND AND BELGIUM

170 ALBACH, BEN, *300 Jaar Stadschouwburg*, Amsterdam, 1938.

171 RENIEU, LIONEL, *Histoire des Théâtres de Bruxelles*, Paris, 1928, 2 vols.

321

BIBLIOGRAPHY

172 WORP, J. A., *Geschiedenis van den Amsterdamschen Schouwburg*, Amsterdam, 1920.

ITALY

173 AMICO, SILVIO D' (ed.), *Storia del Teatro Italiano*, Milan, 1936.

174 BACCHIELLI, RICCARDO, *Teatro e Immagini del Settecento Italiano*, Turin, 1953.

175 BJURSTRÖM, PER, *Feast and Theatre in Queen Christina's Rome*, Stockholm, 1966.

176 FERRERO, MERCEDÈS VIALE, *Feste delle Madame Reali di Savoia*, Turin, 1965.

177 KENNARD, J. S., *The Italian Theatre*, New York, 1932, 2 vols.

178 MAGAGNATO, L., *Teatri italiani del Cinquecento*, Venice, 1954.

179 MARIANI, VALERIO, *Storia della Scenografia Italiana*, Florence, 1930.

180 *Museo Teatrale alla Scala, Il*, Milan, 1963.

181 NAGLER, A. M., *Theatre Festivals of the Medici, 1539–1637*, New Haven, 1964.

182 PRUNIÈRES, H., *Cavalli et l'opéra vénitien au XVIIe siècle*, Paris, 1931.

183 RASI, LUIGI, *La Caricatura e i Comici Italiani*, Florence, 1907.

184 RICCI, CORRADO, *La Scenografia Italiana*, Milan, 1930.

185 WORSTHORNE, SIMON T., *Venetian Opera in the 17th Century*, Oxford, 1954.

SCANDINAVIA

186 BEIJER, AGNE, *Bilder Från Slottsteatern på Drottningholm*, Stockholm, 1950.

187 BEIJER, A., *Slottsteatrarna på Drottningholm och Gripsholm*, Stockholm, 1937.

188 BERGMAN, GOSTA M., *Regihistorika Studier*, Stockholm, 1952.

189 BJURSTRÖM, PER, *Teaterdekoration i Sverige*, Stockholm, 1964.

190 HILLESTRÖM, GUSTAF, *Drottningholmsteatern förr och nu*, Stockholm, 1956.

191 HILLESTRÖM, G., *The Royal Opera, Stockholm*, Stockholm, 1960.

192 HILLESTRÖM, PEHR, *Gustaviansk Teater*, Stockholm, 1947.

193 KROGH, TORBEN, *Aeldre Dansk Teater*, Copenhagen, 1940.

194 NEIIENDAM, ROBERT, *Teatermuseet ved Christiansborg*, Copenhagen, 1963.

SPAIN

195 PRAT, ÁNGEL VALBUENA, *Historia del Teatro Español*, Barcelona, 1956.

196 SHERGOLD, N. D., *A History of the Spanish Stage; from Medieval Times until the end of the XVIIth Century*, Oxford, 1967.

197 SHERGOLD, N. D. & VAREY, J. E., *Los autos sacramentales en Madrid en la época de Calderón, 1637–1681*, Madrid, 1961.

198 SUBIRÁ, JOSÉ, *La Opera en los Teatros de Barcelona*, Barcelona, 1946, 2 vols.

U.S.A.

199 COAD, O.S. & MIMS, E., *The American Stage*, New Haven, 1929.

200 GREGOR, JOSEPH, *Das amerikanische Theater*, Vienna, 1931.

201 HEWITT, BARNARD, *Theatre U.S.A., 1668–1957*, New York, 1959.

202 HUGHES, GLENN, *A History of the American Theatre, 1700–1950*, New York, 1951.

203 ODELL, GEORGE C. D., *Annals of the New York Stage*, New York, 1927–49, 15 vols.

OTHER COUNTRIES

204 ARROM, JOSÉ J., *El Teatro de Hispanoamérica en la Epoca Colonial*, Havana, 1956.

205 BATUŠIĆ, SLAVKO & NIKOLIĆ, MILENA, *The Theatre in Yugoslavia*, Belgrade, 1955.

206 BEAUMONT, CYRIL W., *A History of Ballet in Russia (1613–1881)*, London, 1930.

207 HEPNER, VÁCLAV, *Scénická Výprava na Jevišti Národního Divadla*, Prague, 1955.

208 HORÁNYI, MÁTYÁS, *Das Esterhazysche Feenreich*, Budapest, 1959.

209 PROPERT, W. A., *The Russian Ballet in Western Europe, 1909–1920*, London, 1921.

322

210 SIVERTA, TADEUSZA, *Teatr Warszawski Drugiej Polowy XIX Wieku*, Wroclaw, 1957.

211 STOCKWELL, LA TOURETTE, *Dublin Theatres and Theatre Customs*, Kingsport, Tenn., 1938.

PERIODICALS

212 *Maske und Kothurn*, Vienna (Institut für Theaterwissenschaft an der Universität Wien), 1955 ff.

213 *Revue d'Histoire du Théâtre*, Paris (Société d'Histoire du Théâtre), 1948 ff.

214 *Shakespeare Quarterly*, New York (Shakespeare Association of America), 1950 ff.

215 *Shakespeare Survey*, Cambridge (University Press), 1948 ff.

216 *Theatre Arts Monthly*, New York (Theatre Arts), 1917 ff.

217 *Theatre Notebook*, London (Ifan Kyrle Fletcher), 1946 ff.

218 *Theatre Research*, n.p. (International Federation for Theatre Research), 1958 ff.

219 *Theatre Survey*, Pittsburgh (American Society for Theatre Research), 1960 ff.

PART II
Other works referred to in the notes

220 ADAMS, JOHN C., *The Globe Playhouse*, London, 2nd ed., 1961 (1st ed., 1942).

221 ANDREWS, CYRIL B. & ORR-EWING, J. A. (eds), *Victorian Swansdown: Extracts from the Early Travel Diaries of John Orlando Parry*, London, 1935.

222 *Annual of the British School at Athens*, London, 1896 ff.

223 *Appleton's Journal*, Vol. III, no. 61, London, 1870.

224 ARMSTRONG, W. A., *The Elizabethan Private Theatres*, London (Society for Theatre Research, pamphlet no. 6), 1958.

225 ARNOTT, PETER, *An Introduction to the Greek Theatre*, London, 1961.

226 *Atlas; van de Stad Amsterdam*, Amsterdam, 1767–75, 6 issues.

227 AURELI, A., *Il Favore degli Dei*, Parma, 1690.

228 BÄUERLE, ADOLF, *Gallerie drolliger und interessanter Scenen der Wiener-Bühnen*, Vienna, 1827–32.

229 *Ballet du Roi des Festes de Bacchus*, Paris, 1651.

230 BARLAEUS, GASPAR, *Marie de Medici entrant dans Amsterdam*, Amsterdam, 1638.

231 Bauhausbücher, no. 4, *Die Bühne im Bauhaus* (Gropius, W. & Moholy-Nagy, L., eds), Munich, n.d. (*c.* 1925).

232 BEAUIOYEULX, BALTASAR DE, *Balet Comique de la Royne*, Paris, 1582.

233 BEIJER, AGNE (ed.), *Le Recueil de Fossard*, Paris, 1928.

234 BERVE, HELMUT & GRUBEN, GOTTFRIED, *Greek Temples, Theatres and Shrines*, London, 1963 (1st ed., 1961).

235 BIACH-SCHIFFMANN, FLORA, *Giovanni und Lodovico Burnacini*, Vienna, 1931.

236 BOADEN, JAMES, *Memoirs of Mrs. Siddons*, London, 1827, 2 vols.

237 BOWERS, FAUBION, *Theatre in the East*, New York, 1956.

238 BREITHOLTZ, LENNART, *Die Dorische Farce im Griechischen Mutterland vor dem 5 Jahrhundert*, Stockholm, 1960.

239 BROSSES, CHARLES DE, *Le Président de Brosses en Italie*, Vol. II, Paris, 1858.

240 BRUFORD, W. H., *Theatre, Drama and Audience in Goethe's Germany*, London, 1950.

241 *Bulletin de L'Institut Français d'Archéologie Orientale*, Cairo.

242 CAREY, DAVID, *Life in Paris*, London, 1822.

243 CARTWRIGHT, JULIA (Mrs Ady), *Isabella d'Este*, London, 1903, 2 vols.

244 CHAMBERS, E. K., *The Elizabethan Stage*, Oxford, 1923, 4 vols.

245 CHAMBERS, E. K., *The Mediaeval Stage*, London, 1903, 2 vols.

246 COHEN, GUSTAVE, *Etudes d'histoire du Théâtre en France au Moyen Age et à la Renaissance*, Paris, 1956.

247 COHEN, G., *Histoire de la Mise en Scène dans le Théâtre Religieux Français du Moyen Age*, Paris, 1926.

248 COLLINS, HERBERT F., *Talma*, London, 1964.

249 CRAIG, EDWARD GORDON, *On the Art of the Theatre*, London, 1962 (1st ed., 1911).

250 CRAIG, E. G., *Scene*, London, 1923.

251 CRAIG, HARDIN, *English Religious Drama of the Middle Ages*, Oxford, 1955.

252 CUNNINGHAM, JOHN E., *The History of the Theatre Royal, Birmingham*, Oxford, 1950.

253 DELACHENAL, R., *Chronique des Règnes de Jean II et de Charles V*, Paris, 1910–20, 4 vols.

254 DESROCHES-NOBLECOURT, C., *Tutankhamen*, London, 1963.

255 DICKSON, ARTHUR, *Valentine and Orson*, New York, 1929.

256 DISHER, M. W., *Blood and Thunder*, London, 1949.

257 DOWNES, JOHN, *Roscius Anglicanus* (edited by F. G. Waldron, and with additions by Thomas Davies), London, 2nd ed., 1789 (1st ed., 1708).

258 DRIOTON, ETIENNE, *Le Texte Dramatique d'Edfou*, Cairo (Supplément aux Annales du Service des Antiquités de l'Egypte, cahier no. 11), 1948.

259 DRIOTON, E., *Le Théâtre Egyptien*, Cairo, 1942.

260 DURAND, ESTIENNE, *Discours au Vray du Ballet Dansé par le Roy*, Paris, 1617.

261 EGAN, PIERCE, *Life of an Actor*, London, 1825.

262 (ENTHOVEN, GABRIELLE), *Studies in English Theatre History, in Memory of Gabrielle Enthoven*, London, 1952.

263 FRANSEN, J., *Les Comédiens Français en Hollande au XVIIe et au XVIIIe siècles*, Paris, 1925.

264 GARRISON, LLOYD M., *An Illustrated History of the Hasty Pudding Club Theatricals*, Cambridge (Mass.), 1897.

265 GILLILAND, THOMAS, *The Dramatic Mirror*, London, 1808, 2 vols.

266 GIRARDOT, BARON A. DE, *Mystère des Actes des Apôtres, représenté à Bourges en avril 1536*, Paris, 1854.

267 GORELIK, MORDECAI, *New Theatres for Old*, London, 1947 (1st ed., 1940).

268 GRANT, JAMES, *Penny Theatres*, London (Society for Theatre Research, pamphlet no. 1), 1952 (1st ed., 1838, in *Sketches in London*).

269 HAMPE, THEODOR, *Die Entwicklung des Theaterwesens in Nürnberg*, Nuremberg, 1897.

270 HARBAGE, ALFRED, *Shakespeare's Audience*, New York, 1941.

271 HAVEMEYER, LOUIS, *The Drama of Savage Peoples*, New Haven, 1916.

272 HONE, WILLIAM, *Ancient Mysteries Described*, London, 1823.

273 HUGHES, DOM ANSELM (ed.), *Early Medieval Music up to 1300*, London, 1954.

274 HUGO, VICTOR, *Hernani* (ed. Pierre Richard), Paris, n.d.

275 *Ioyeuse & Magnifique Entrée de Monseigneur François, La*, Antwerp, 1582.

276 JACQUOT, JEAN (ed.), *Les Théâtres d'Asie*, Paris, 1961.

277 KEAN, CHARLES (ed.), *Shakespeare's Play of A Midsummer Night's Dream*, London, 1856.

278 KEAN, C. (ed.), *Shakespeare's Play of The Winter's Tale*, London, 1856.

279 KIRKMAN, FRANCIS, *The Wits or Sport upon Sport*, London, 1673.

280 KYSEL, F. E., *Das Theater in Nürnberg von 1612 bis 1863*, Nuremberg, 1863.

281 LANCASTER, HENRY C., *A History of French Dramatic Literature in the XVIIth Century*, Baltimore, 1929–42, 9 vols.

282 LAWRENCE, W. J., *Old Theatre Days and Ways*, London, 1935.

283 LAWTON, H. W., *Térence en France au XVIe siècle*, Paris, 1926.

284 LOWE, ROBERT W., *Thomas Betterton*, London, 1891.

285 LUCIAN, *Part of Lucian made English from the Originall . . . by Iasper Mayne*, Oxford, 1664.

286 MACGOWAN, KENNETH & JONES, ROBERT E., *Continental Stagecraft*, London, 1923.

287 MACQUEEN-POPE, W. J., *Theatre Royal, Drury Lane*, London, 1945.

288 MAHELOT, L., *Le Mémoire* (ed. H. C. Lancaster), Paris, 1920.

289 MARKER, LISE-LONE, *Aspects of Medieval Theatre in Scandinavia, II*. Duplicated typescript of lectures to 2nd International Course on Theatre History, International Federation for Theatre Research, Venice, 1964.

290 MASSENA, V., *Les Livres à Figures Vénitiens*, Paris, 1907–14, 5 vols.

291 MEZGER, V., *Narro und Hansele*, Konstanz, 1956.

292 *Mistere par personnaiges . . . Valenciennes . . . 1547*. (Ms. in B.N., Paris, Salle des Manuscrits, Fonds Rothschild 3010, Côte I.7.3.)

293 MOTTER, T. H. VAIL, *The School Drama in England*, London, 1929.

294 NAOGEORGUS, THOMAS (Kirchmeyer, T.), *The Popish Kingdome, Englyshed by Barnabe Googe*, London, 1880 (1st ed., 1570).

295 NICOLL, ALLARDYCE, *A History of English Drama, 1660–1900*, Cambridge, 1923–59, 6 vols.

296 NOGAME, TOYOICHIRŌ, *Zeami and his Theories on Noh*, translated by R. Matsumoto, Tokyo, 1955.

297 *Nopces de Pélée et de Thetis*, Paris, 1654.

298 O'NEILL, P. G., *Early Nō Drama*, London, 1958.

299 PEPYS, SAMUEL, *The Diary* (ed. H. B. Wheatley), London, 1893–99, 10 vols.

300 PICKARD-CAMBRIDGE, A. W., *The Dramatic Festivals of Athens*, Oxford, 1953.

301 PLATTER, F. & T., *Felix et Thomas Platter à Montpellier*, Montpellier, 1892.

302 PRITCHARD, J. B., *Ancient Near Eastern Texts*, Princeton, 1950.

303 PRUNIÈRES, H., *Le Ballet de Cour en France avant Benserade et Lully*, Paris, 1914.

304 RACCA, CARLO, *Burattini e Marionette*, Turin, n.d. (*c.* 1910).

305 RAGHAVAN, M. D., *Folk Plays and Dances of Kerala*, Trichur, 1947.

306 RENNERT, HUGO A., *The Spanish Stage in the Time of Lope de Vega*, New York, 1963 (1st ed., 1909).

307 RESTIF DE LA BRETONNE, *Monument du Costume Physique et Moral de la Fin du XVIIIe Siècle*, Neuwied sur le Rhin, 1789.

308 REYNOLDS, GEORGE F., *The Staging of Elizabethan Plays at the Red Bull Theater, 1605–1625*, New York, 1940.

309 RICHTER, HORST, *Johann Oswald Harms*, Emsdetten, 1963.

310 ROSENFELD, SYBIL, *Strolling Players and Drama in the Provinces, 1660–1765*, Cambridge, 1939.

311 ROSENFELD, S., *The Theatre of the London Fairs in the 18th century*, Cambridge, 1960.

312 ROSSI, BASTIANO DE', *Descrizione dell'Apparato, e degl' Intermedi*, Florence, 1589.

313 SABBATTINI, NICOLA, *Pratica di Fabricar Scene, e Machine ne' Teatri*, Ravenna, 1638.

314 SALTER, F. M., *Medieval Drama in Chester*, Toronto, 1955.

315 SAXON, ARTHUR H., *Enter Foot and Horse*, Yale, 1967 (t.s. of dissertation).

316 SCHINKEL, K. F., *Decorationen auf den beiden Königlichen Theatern in Berlin*, Berlin, 1819.

317 SERLIO, SEBASTIANO, *Architetûra*, Venice, 1551.

318 SETHE, K., *Dramatische Texte zu Altaegyptischen Mysterienspiele*, Leipzig, 1928.

319 SHATTUCK, C. H., *A Victorian Stage Manager*, article in *Theatre Notebook*, London, 1968.

320 SHERSON, ERROLL, *London's Lost Theatres of the XIXth Century*, London, 1925.

321 SOUTHERN, RICHARD, *The Medieval Theatre in the Round*, London, 1957.

322 SOUTHERN, R., *The Seven Ages of the Theatre*, London, 1962.

323 SPEAIGHT, GEORGE, *The History of the English Puppet Theatre*, London, 1955.

324 SPECK, FRANK G. & BROOM, LEONARD, *Cherokee Dance and Drama*, Berkeley, 1951.

325 STAHL, E. L., *Shakespeare und das deutsche Theater*, Stuttgart, 1947.

326 STANISLAVSKI, CONSTANTIN, *My Life in Art*, London, 1962.

327 STOTT, R. TOOLE, *Circus and Allied Arts: A World Bibliography, 1500–1957*, Derby, 1958–62, 3 vols.

328 STOW, G. W., *Rock Paintings in South Africa*, London, 1930.

329 STUART, D. C., *Stage Decoration in France in the Middle Ages*, New York, 1910.

330 STRUTT, JOSEPH, *Sports and Pastimes of the People of England*, London, 1810.

BIBLIOGRAPHY

331 SUMBERG, SAMUEL L., *The Nuremberg Schembart Carnival*, New York, 1941.

332 *Tabs*, London (Strand Electric and Engineering Co.), 1937 ff.

333 *Tatler, The*, London, April 12 1709 to January 2 1710/11.

334 TERZAGO, V., *Servio Tullio*, Munich, 1685.

335 TILLIOT, M. DU, *Mémoires pour servir à l'Histoire de la Fête des Foux*, Lausanne & Geneva, 1741.

336 TOSCHI, PAOLO, *Le Origini del teatro italiano*, Turin, 1955.

337 VALLADIER, ANDRÉ, *Labyrinthe Royal de l'Hercule Gaulois Triomphant*, Avignon, 1601.

338 WAGENAAR, JAN, *Amsterdam, in zyne opkomst, aanwas, geschiedenissen, voovregten, koophandel, gebouwen . . . en regeringe*, Amsterdam, 1760–8, 13 vols.

339 WALEY, ARTHUR, *The No Plays of Japan*, London, 1921.

340 WEBSTER, T. B. L., *Monuments Illustrating New Comedy*, London (University of London, Institute of Classical Studies, Bulletin: Suppl. no. 11), 1961.

341 YATES, FRANCES A., *The Art of Memory*, London, 1966.

342 YOUNG, KARL, *The Drama of the Medieval Church*, Oxford, 1933, 2 vols.

343 FINDLATER, RICHARD, *The Unholy Trade*, London, 1952.

344 MANDER, RAYMOND & MITCHENSON, JOE, *The Theatres of London*, London, 1961.

345 WITKOWSKI, G. J. & NASS, L., *Le Nu au Théâtre*, Paris, 1901.

INDEX

The index contains three categories of reference. The first group of figures, in roman numerals, give page references; the second group, in italics, refer to the illustrations; and the last group, preceded by a small 'n.', refer to the *Notes on the illustrations*. Thus 'Plinge, Walter 168–9, 201; *XXIII*, *151*; n.182, 195, 201' would mean that Mr Plinge is referred to on pages 168–9 and 201, that he either appears in or is closely connected with Plate XXIII and Fig. 151, and that more information about him (usually about other illustrations of him) is given in the notes to Figs 182, 195 and 201.

The majority of the subject references in the index are grouped under ten main headings: Audiences, Auditoria, Costume, Effects, Lighting, Machinery, Masks, Props, Stages and Scenery, Theatres and Theatre Companies. All references to individual theatres are grouped under this last heading, without cross-references in other parts of the index.

330

332